WOLF ROCK

Recent Titles from Peter Tonkin

The Master of Defence Series

THE POINT OF DEATH *
ONE HEAD TOO MANY *
THE HOUND OF THE BORDERS *
THE SILENT WOMAN *

The Mariners Series

THE FIRE SHIP
THE COFFIN SHIP
POWERDOWN
THUNDER BAY *
TITAN 10 *
WOLF ROCK *

ACTION *
THE ZERO OPTION *

* *available from Severn House*

WOLF ROCK

Peter Tonkin

This first world edition published in Great Britain 2005 by
SEVERN HOUSE PUBLISHERS LTD of
9–15 High Street, Sutton, Surrey SM1 1DF.
This first world edition published in the USA 2005 by
SEVERN HOUSE PUBLISHERS INC of
595 Madison Avenue, New York, N.Y. 10022.

British Library Cataloguing in Publication Data

Tonkin, Peter
Wolf Rock. - (Mariners series)
1. Mariner, Richard (Fictitious character) - Fiction
2. Marine accidents - Investigation - Fiction
3. Sea stories
I. Title
823.9'14 [F]

ISBN 0-7278-6188-3

Typeset by Palimpsest Book Production Ltd.,
Polmont, Stirlingshire, Scotland.
Printed and bound in Great Britain by
MPG Books Ltd., Bodmin, Cornwall.

For Cham, Guy and Mark,
as always

THE WRECK

1: The Bishop

The distress call came in at the same instant as the dangerous weather alarm sounded. Richard Mariner lowered his binoculars and turned, striding in from the starboard reach of the brand-new SuperCat *Lionheart*'s bridge. For the last few moments, he had been looking back along his great vessel's stormy wake, keeping watch on the distant, dancing arc of the Bishop's Rock Light through the driving murk of the worsening weather and calculating the odds.

He had felt no stirrings of premonition beyond a line or two of misquoted poetry ill-remembered from his school days which kept running through his mind with the persistence of a melody:

> . . . the vessel struck with shivering shock.
> Oh God! It is the Bishop's Rock . . .

But he thrust such childish things aside now as he moved, still calculating grimly what best to do with *Lionheart* in the gathering gale. The experimental vessel's proving-run down to Spain had been too widely publicized to be called off lightly. But the weather was getting fouler by the instant and even a massive SuperCat could founder under a westerly storm in the vicious Bay of Biscay. Only the huge supertankers and container vessels that passed them in steady and unvarying series, coming in and out of the Channel like coaches behind some unimaginable locomotive, could ride out Biscay's spite with relative ease.

It was time to run for safe haven by the sound of things unless the distress call was anything they could help with.

Robin, Richard's wife and partner, moved at his side, crossing to the radio to lean over the officer seated there, conducting a whispered conversation while Richard paused at the weather display. Only the years they had both spent at sea allowed them to move so swiftly and surely across the heaving deck.

'What is it?' Richard asked Doc Weary, his friend and associate, who was seated easily in the nearest of the twin command chairs; seated easily, noted Richard as he steadied himself on the console, but strapped in tight.

'This.' Doc's great leonine head turned as his strong finger swooped down towards the weather monitor, killed the sound-alarm and dulled the flashing red warning signal. Then touched the button marked PREDICT. The weather-pattern displayed on the screen was projected forward in time by the advanced program in the computer that controlled the thing.

The vicious swirl of the approaching Atlantic storm currently battering *Lionheart* with its leading outskirts, as observed from far on high by a series of weather satellites, tightened and intensified in computer graphic. The winds whirling around it gathered power and speed. Storm force became near-hurricane in an instant. And it all pounced eastward past the Fastnet Rock with most unnerving speed, coming in across the Western Approaches as though set on destroying them all at once.

'When and where?' grated Richard.

'Two hours' time. It'll bottom out somewhere north-east of our current position back beyond the Scillies. Say just about over Wolf Rock,' answered Doc, his Australian drawl becoming obvious in the longer sentence.

'Wolf Rock,' echoed Robin at once, her voice high, clear and strong against the howling batter of the head-on wind. 'That's where this distress call is coming from.'

'From the lighthouse?' Richard's voice was incredulous. Not least because Wolf Rock, like the Bishop beside them, like all Cornish lighthouses, was automatic and unmanned.

'No,' Robin answered tersely. 'From a vessel drifting down on to the shoals there.' She looked up at Richard, her eyes apparently luminous in the dimness of the crowded bridge, the gold curls of her hair a-gleam in what little light there was, intensifying the pallor of her worried face. 'Darling, I'm afraid it's the *Goodman Richard*.'

'Who's going out to her?' Typically, Richard thrust aside all non-essentials for the moment. And there were quite a few, for he knew the *Goodman Richard* and almost everyone likely to be aboard her.

A new voice entered the conversation – that of Sparks, the Radio Officer who, like the SuperCat's Captain, had been silent so far. 'No one,' he said. 'All the RNLI lifeboats from Start Point to the Scilly Isles seem to be out already. There's the chance of a Sea King getting over from the Royal Naval Air Station at Culdrose, but that's about it and I don't know what help they could be. There's forty crew and—'

'Sixty youngsters,' grated Richard. 'I know. She's an adventure training ship. Four-master, square-rigged. Never goes out with less than one hundred souls aboard.'

'If you say so,' said Sparks dully. 'The Sea King will be useless, then. Even the lifeboats'll be hard-put to get that many safely off. Their main mast is gone by the board and the power's down except for emergency back-up to the radio. They're helpless by the sound of things.'

'And even the St Mary's boat is out?' Richard's voice was full of shock – but that only seemed to make it more decisive and energetic.

'Penlee, Lizard, Falmouth,' confirmed Sparks. 'They're even out at Sennen Cove, St Ives and Padstow.'

'Vessels nearby?'

'Mostly in trouble themselves – and being seen to by the lifeboats. Except for those, of course.' Sparks nodded through the rain-swept clearview at the black bulk of yet another huge bulk transporter, sailing through the gathering darkness like a ship-shaped black hole, edged with glitters of navigating lights and gleams of tumbling foam. It had no real character except the faintest glimpse of a name – the something *Maru*, ill-lit on the cliff of the departing stern.

They all looked at the mysterious giant. And they all knew there was no real hope of help or rescue there, for the great ships moved by almost planetary laws of motion. Even could one slow its massive progress or turn aside from its preprogrammed course, it was likely to do more harm than good, upsetting the rigid series of its fellows' closely prescribed speeds and courses; unleashing the potential for collision and disaster of almost incalculable proportions. No. Though they owned some of the passing supertankers and had sailed upon others, Richard and Robin knew all too well that they could never expect help from those quarters.

'Looks like it's got to be us, then.' Captain Tom Bartlett's voice was quiet but commanding. Slim, slight and young, he was nevertheless a steely character, by no means overwhelmed by all the power and expertise of the men and women around him. Unconsciously echoing sentiments often expressed by Richard himself in moments such as this, he continued, 'Someone needs to do something, and it looks as though we can do more than most. So let's get on with it, eh?'

Richard glanced around the bridge, calling to mind in an instant – and for an instant only – the specifications of the vessel whose skeleton crew they were. *Lionheart* was nearly three hundred feet in length. One hundred in the beam. She was hulled in aluminium – designed by the same team that fashioned Ferrari cars. Her twin keels sat ten feet below the restless surface for she was running in ballast now. Her four huge diesels produced over 5,000 kilowatts of energy and could thrust her forward at 100kph. And, best of all, she could accommodate several hundred passengers. So a hundred soaking kids and crew from *Goodman Richard* would be neither here nor there. If they could reach the drifting hulk in time. And if they could somehow get everybody off, in the teeth of the weather predicted by *Lionheart*'s red-flashing weather monitor. Get them off *Goodman Richard* and on to *Lionheart*. It would be a close-run, immensely dangerous undertaking.

And there was one more – vital – consideration. 'Just a moment, Tom,' said Richard. 'I'd like to draw a line here. This is your vessel and you're the Captain. So it's your decision and I agree with it. But I am the Owner and as such I am responsible at law for the hull and the safety of everyone aboard. I want you to know that. The order is yours. The responsibility is mine. Are you comfortable with that?'

'Fine,' said Tom Bartlett with no further thought or hesitation. He reached forward until his own seatbelt creaked and reached for the microphone of the hailer. 'This is the Captain,' he announced, his voice booming eerily through the empty, cavernous vessel. 'We are answering a distress call from near the Wolf Rock Light. Engine room, I will need bow thrusters in a moment and full power soon after. Everyone else, batten down as tightly as you can. Now, *prepare to come about*.'

'That was a bit pompous,' whispered Robin a moment or two later. They were wedged on the opposite tilting bridge wing, beyond Sparks but close enough to hear his contact with the *Goodman Richard*; watching the Bishop's Rock Light wheel towards them through the night like a meteor predicting the death of kings as *Lionheart* obeyed the first of her Captain's orders.

'Pompous,' he admitted. 'But necessary. With the new law on Corporate Killing as it is, we need to be clear where the buck stops if anyone might get hurt or – heaven forfend – killed. And you only have to look outside to see how likely that is.' As if to emphasize his words, a wilderness of hail swept out of the screaming murk to shatter across the glass beside them like shrapnel, seeming to splinter even the passing beam of the lighthouse light.

'And the buck stops with you?'

'As CEO of Heritage Mariner, yes it does. You know it does. That's what Corporate Killing means. If any negligence of commission or omission can be proved. Any failure of health and safety. And anyone dies. Criminal prosecution of the Chief Executive Officer. You were at the Full Board's briefing. You read the Legal Department's report.'

'I thought there was something called Consent – like when you play rugby or enter a boxing ring; you agree to a certain amount of risk. I didn't think the new law was supposed to slow up rescues and so forth.'

'It probably isn't. But it is designed to make us think – if not *stop* and think; to ensure we avoid foolhardy risks. And you can never be too careful. Anyway, Consent has its limits. What about that rugby player who was arrested for fouling the opposing winger and crippling him? Consent or no Consent, he ended up in prison for Grievous Bodily Harm or some such thing. He won't be out for another year and more.'

Robin paused, her eyes narrow, then she decided, 'Perhaps we'd better make sure everyone aboard has a clear idea of what they're getting into here . . .'

'We have plenty of time,' said Richard gently. 'It's forty

miles back to Wolf Rock. That'll take at least an hour in this. Even with the wind astern.' The SuperCat gave a strange lurch and shuddered as though she had been booted up the behind. Robin staggered into Richard's arms. He grinned wryly down at her. 'Especially with the wind astern,' he said, 'the wind and a following sea . . .'

The searchlight beam of the lighthouse found them out as he spoke, suddenly surprisingly close at hand, almost like a spotlight. The smile in his eyes faded and his face gathered into a frown.

'. . . the vessel struck with shivering shock. Oh God! It is the Bishop's Rock,' he whispered.

'You've got your Southey all mixed up,' she answered bracingly. 'It's Bishop *Hatto* – and he gets eaten by rats. It's the *Inchcape* Rock and that's away up in the Firth of Forth off the east coast of Scotland. And, in any case, my darling, it's the *Wolf Rock* you want to watch out for . . .'

2: The Run

As *Lionheart* powered north-eastwards, running at full speed across the forty storm-tossed sea miles separating her from the Wolf Rock Light and the ship-killing shoal sweeping south-west from its foot, Richard was seemingly everywhere aboard at once.

Following his conversation with Robin, he ensured that he visited everyone, individually and in groups, to talk over their responsibilities – and the dangers that those might lead them into during the rescue. To be fair, he had orchestrated an enormous number of rescues in the past – had survived as many hair's-breadth escapes on land and at sea – and he had always been careful to brief his teams. It was one of the marks of his leadership. And one of the reasons he had survived as long as he had. He did little in these meetings that he would not have done in any case – but he was extra-sensitive, perhaps, to the crossing of some corporate *t*'s and the dotting of some legalistic *i*'s. Though, as it turned out, he was largely wasting his time.

He appeared like a tall dark genie everywhere from the throbbing chamber of the engine room, where he held an intense conference with the Chief, to the echoing caverns of the untenanted car deck, where he stood alone and narrow-eyed, calculating. He even called in to the Chief Steward's office and went on through into the shadowy and sketchily supplied galley to hold a hurried conversation with the men liable to find themselves supplying tea and sympathy – at the very least – to one hundred seasick survivors.

But it was the bridge that remained the hub of his activity. Here he ran over with Tom Bartlett the plans he was constructing and constantly updating for the rescue. Plans that Robin and Doc became increasingly involved with – for they were effectively First and Second Officer here – sitting between the Captain and Sparks the Radio Officer in command responsibility as well as in physical fact. It was a testing run, after all, in spite of the iffy weather checks; something of a jaunt with a skeleton crew and a couple of friends out on a bit of a lark.

But as it happened, that, too, was no bad thing, for between them Richard, Robin and Doc Weary had more experience than whole crews could normally command. Robin and Richard had both commanded supertankers, and knew the Western Approaches better than anyone else alive. Furthermore, they had both been highly trained in handling SuperCats as soon as Heritage Mariner had bought them in and set them to working on routes as near at hand as Dover to Calais across the Channel and as far afield as Thunder Bay to Chicago across the Great Lakes.

Doc was the designer, architect – and the prize-winning captain – of the *Katapult* series of multihulls, whose popularity was part of the foundation of the fortune of Heritage Mariner, who produced them for the commercial market. Whose largest and greatest offspring, *Katapult VI*, all eighty feet of her – sixty-foot beam from one outrigger to the other – was being prepared in Southampton even now to win the next Fastnet Ocean Race hands down in little more than fourteen months' time. There was nothing Doc did not know about the sea, its moods, and getting multihulled vessels effectively and efficiently through them. He had survived both the Fastnet of 1979 and the Sydney–Hobart of 1998 and done more – he had come near to winning both. Though that, against the cost, counted for little enough in his eyes.

'It's her speed that's your best bet,' Doc observed again, turning to Tom for support, as if he needed it.

'Doc's right,' agreed the Captain. 'Fast in and fast away. Safe in harbour before the worst hits. Penzance is only ten miles or so beyond the Wolf Rock Light. We could do that in fifteen minutes, everything being equal.'

'Timing will be tight, though,' warned Robin, able to join in the conversations because *Goodman Richard*'s radio was all but dead; the last of its power being preserved for the vital moments of rescue. 'It's taking the better part of an hour to get back. That'll leave another hour before the worst of it hits. Fifteen minutes into Mount's Bay at full speed maybe – but not from a standing start. We'll have to stop to pick up survivors. Then we'll have to go round the reef, of course. That will add a good few minutes. Even with everyone safe and sound aboard, there'll still be half an hour and more to safe haven . . .'

'And therefore only half an hour to get one hundred people off a sinking wreck,' said Richard, nodding. He had seen this coming long ago. Hence his meticulous planning. Meticulous perhaps – but planning for the unknown, even so. 'But we have an edge of sorts.'

'What is that?' demanded Robin.

'Wind and tide. Even if it isn't a particularly high tide, it's on the ebb and flowing out westwards. The laws of physics . . .'

'Oh, come on, Richard . . .'

'Think it through. *Goodman Richard* is dismasted and drifting down on to the shoals at Wolf Rock. Agreed?'

'Agreed,' said Robin, frowning with concentration as the others nodded in agreement too.

'Then she is up-wind of the reef.'

'Yes . . .' More nods.

'A reef that juts out south-west of the light itself. Therefore . . .'

'Therefore what, Richard? Jesus, it's like talking to Hercule Poirot!'

'Therefore she's on *our* side of the reef! Upwind; to the west of the danger. A good deal closer to us!'

'No shit, Sherlock!' said Doc with a laugh. He leaned across to the collision alarm radio and stabbed a finger down at a target dead ahead that had just flashed from amber to red for 'Dangerously Close'. 'Then that'll be her now. You think?'

He flicked a switch with his thumb and the edges of the radar scan jumped back to wider view. The Wolf Rock Light shone dead ahead as well, perhaps twice as far again as the bright-red target. And there was nothing in between, except for the eerie scimitar of cloudy green denoting the reefs and shallows all too close at hand.

'How far away?' demanded Richard, crossing to the bridge wing and pressing his night-vision binoculars to his eyes.

'Maybe five miles.'

'We'll be down on her in ten minutes at this speed,' called Tom Bartlett. 'Even if I begin to throttle back.'

'Can't see her as yet,' said Richard. 'Sparks, can you update them please?'

'Done!' sang out Robin.

And even as she spoke a distress flare soared up into the scudding overcast dead ahead. It looked for all the world like a rocket launched six months early for Guy Fawkes Night. Except that it was red. It was a red ball of brightness – cherry at its heart – and it trailed red fire behind it as it rose above the roiling wilderness of white water that the Channel had become. As it mounted, so it began immediately to flicker, its urgent trail pulled to pieces by the black-clawed wind; its bright heart guttering in the low skirts of scudding overcast, snuffed abruptly by the huge maw of the storm clouds above.

And, as if in mocking answer, a shaft of lightning pounced down, seemingly exactly along its trail; apparently directly on to the helpless, crippled ship. 'Ach!' Sparks gave half a snarl and half a shout as he ripped his headphones from his ears.

'God!' said Robin, starting back. 'What on earth was that?'

'The sound of a radio dying,' answered Sparks.

'Well, it certainly didn't die quietly!' she observed, shaking her head.

'As long as it died alone,' he observed darkly. And that observation was enough to reduce them all to slightly sickened silence.

The silence lasted another minute, maybe more, until Richard sang out, 'There she is!'

Robin, no longer needed at the useless radio, was on the opposite bridge wing and at Richard's call she pressed her own binoculars back to her eyes. 'Yes!' she confirmed. 'Dead ahead.'

'Her mainmast is down and so is her foremast by the looks of things. Her mizzen and jigger are bare, thank God, or I think she'd have blown right over. Lord! Did you see that, Robin? That wave nearly broached her. But at least it showed us a little more. The wreckage of her masts and sails is this side, Tom. You'll have to watch out for it as you close with her. Her hull's the main thing for the wind to take, I expect, so that'll be moving fastest and dragging everything on behind; all of it caught in the counter-pull of the ebbing tide. And it's all over her starboard side, dragging like a sea-anchor. Keeping her beam-on to the weather and the water. Gracious! That was another big one. Though perhaps it looks worse than it is. What do you think, Robin? It looks to me as though all that mess in the water is taking some of the sting out of that storm swell . . .'

'Yes. Maybe . . .'

'Can't see anyone on deck, though. Robin? Your eyes are better than mine . . .'

'Nothing. But there's someone aboard all right. The flare. The radio. They haven't abandoned.'

'They'd be mad to do so. What's the rule? Step up into your lifeboat . . .'

'As the water closes over your command. She's still well afloat. They must be still aboard.'

'Afloat until she hits the reef at any rate. And look! That wreckage over her starboard side has taken half her lifeboats. Do you see what's left of them tangled in the rigging there?'

'Oh Lord, yes. You're right. Tom, how much longer?'

'You'll need to speed up again, Captain,' called Doc over Robin's question. 'I've a tanker coming up on our beam and he's not going to slow for the likes of us.'

'Right, Doc. Thanks. A couple of minutes, Robin. Richard. Now is the time to start telling me what you want me to do!'

Lionheart surged forward again, helped by the heave of a following sea. 'How close is she to the reef, Doc?' Richard demanded.

'Couple of miles.'

'Can we estimate the speed of her drift?'

'Couple of knots. Wind's gone over fifty and will pick up pretty quickly.'

'An hour until she strikes then.'

'An hour tops.'

'But a good deal less than that before she starts to break up. There's a wilderness of white water around the reef and the outwash must reach back nearly half a mile. That alone will tear her to pieces.'

As Richard spoke, bellowing to overcome the rage of the storm outside, the brunt wind faltered. Richard swung through 180 degrees, looking back at the massive tanker that was crossing their wake, cutting off the wind with her high sides.

'Tom. Can you take *Lionheart* round the back into the lee of her hull? Put her at the clean side, between the sip and the shoals?'

'I can get there but I wouldn't be happy to wait there for any length of time.'

'Get in there and drop me off aboard. Me and a radio and maybe a volunteer or two. See us safely on to the deck, then back off until I call you in again. Her hull will give you a bit of protection. She's leaning down that side – but she won't roll over with all that mess in the water upwind. She should be pretty steady, all things considered and with any luck at all. And you'll still have the power to blast your way out even if things go wrong and we run out of room or time.'

'Yes, I can do all that,' said Tom.

'Then let's get on with it.'

'But just let me get one thing clear in my mind, would you?' asked Tom, a little shakily.

'What?' demanded Richard, suddenly impatient.

'You did say you were going aboard her yourself?'

'Of course he did,' answered Robin, her voice also shaking with ill-suppressed emotion. It might have been pride or it might have been fury. She couldn't really decide which one it was herself. 'Whatever made you think he could possibly miss out on a hare-brained adventure like that?'

'Well,' said Richard shortly. 'I'll be happy to stay where I am if anyone else has a better idea . . . Come on. Anyone at all . . . Don't be shy. Speak up . . .'

3: The Howl

As Tom Bartlett carried out Richard's instructions and began to position his sleek command between the wreck and the reef, Richard himself went below and completed the preparations he had been planning for the last half hour or so.

No sooner had Richard left than Doc too rose and drifted off. Robin sat in the warmth of the big man's seat and strapped herself in tight, at Tom's shoulder. She rested her hands lightly on the familiar levers and handles as she divided her acute attention between the instruments and the view. The *Goodman Richard* seemed almost shapeless as they swung down around her, for the leaning curve of her starboard side was all but concealed in the great mess of shattered masts and spars, woven into a huge cloak of rigging and sailcloth. There was no sense of deck or deck-furniture – merely the helpless swell of her heaving under the dictates of the great combers that crashed relentlessly and regularly over her.

And, beyond, terrifyingly close at hand, the scene was repeated on an infinitely larger scale. But instead of four hundred feet of hull there was a couple of miles of reef stretching away on either hand, swelling in two great foam-washed heaves with the narrowest of channels in between. In place of pathetic masts nodding under the dictates of the thick, wet wind, the great solid thrust of the lighthouse standing sure against the worst the Atlantic could throw at it, casting the golden arm of its light-beam relentlessly through the murky air. And even as Robin focused on the huge solidity of the thing, on the steady turning of that apparently solid beam of light, her ears were assaulted by the deafening power of the Wolf's howl. It took a moment for her to realize that the air was, in fact, thick enough to have started the fog-horn.

Richard too looked up, alerted by the piercing howl and pulled out of a brown study by its urgent summons. He was standing alone in the Chief Steward's cabin, mindlessly sorting through the pile of clothing and equipment he needed to pull on before he ventured out into the night. As he did so, his mind skipped once again over the simple plans he had made – and then, for the most part, discarded. The orders he had given and whether, like this one, they had been faithfully and efficiently obeyed.

At first he had considered wedging *Lionheart*'s stern against *Goodman Richard*'s side, holding the SuperCat in place with her bow thrusters while he opened the rear upward-sliding doors into the great caverns designed to hold her passengers' cars. That way there was a fighting chance of getting one hundred people off one vessel and on to the other in double-quick time. He could even get Tom to raise the hinged bow-section and open the front of the car-deck. But that seemed more dangerous still. Either way, there were simply too many risks. Both bow and stern access to the car decks were designed for safe havens, calm waters and vessels securely lashed to specially designed docking facilities. It would be sheer madness to attempt anything on that scale in these circumstances. And the spectre of the *Herald of Free Enterprise* had risen unbidden to warn him of the danger he was running.

It would have to be the slower but safer route across the fore deck, therefore. But that too would require great care – and detailed preparations aboard the wrecked vessel herself. It was at this point in his planning that he had ordered the wet-weather gear to be brought in here. And other, more vital work to be done on the fore deck. Even so, once *Lionheart* came close-in to *Goodman Richard*, pushing the slim point of her needle-bow against the wreck's sloping side, the real danger would begin – in spite of all his careful preparations. For then the slightest vagary of storm or swell could lift the dismasted hulk with sufficient force to tear the whole front of the SuperCat wide, and send her down like a stone. Then there really would be grounds for a Corporate Killing case; but nobody left alive to answer it.

These grim thoughts were enough to see Richard through the donning of his wet-weather gear, his life jacket and his safety harness. They filled his head, but not to the exclusion of everything. As his mind raced and his fingers dealt decisively with familiar straps, buckles and zips, his seafarer's senses told him of his SuperCat turning across the wind – briefly taking the tumbling sea on her beam – and settling back into her preferred position with the weather on her slim, strong bow. He tightened the wrists and ankles of the suit, suspecting that this would be little more than a waste of time. He picked up the gloves and looked down at them. Looked at his huge, powerful, sensitive hands. Put down the gloves again. Listened to the Wolf's howl. Uncharacteristically, hesitated.

But at last there was nothing to do but to place his shoes neatly beside the neatly folded suit that lay on the Chief Steward's desk and sit in his creaking chair to pull on the massive orange boots – then pick himself up and get on with it.

As he turned to climb back up to the bridge on his way out on to the deck, he sensed a movement in the shadows. At once he thought it must be Robin come to wish him well and give him a kiss for luck. But no. At once disappointed and relieved, he recognized Doc. The big Australian fell in beside him. Waterproof sleeve whispered against waterproof sleeve. As they came into the light Richard saw that Doc was dressed exactly as he was himself – except that, in his gloved right hand, he held a waterproof walkie-talkie and in place of a sou'wester he had a hard hat on his head.

Doc had been shot in the head as a young soldier during his one tour in Vietnam. Only a miracle had saved his life – and only a fortune in surgery had rebuilt his brain so that his memory began to work properly again. Clearly he was not going to put any of this at risk. No matter what other risks he was willing to take at Richard's side.

'Robin has the second chair,' he said conversationally, his tone light and cheerful at the prospect of action and danger. 'She'll be a better back-up to Tom. She's had the training.

She's got the touch. They don't really want a horny-handed old matelot like me in among all their high-tech super-spec stuff. So I thought you might like a hand aboard *Goodman Richard*. I'm the only actual sailor you've got. The only man who has sailed with sails, after all.'

'Certainly the only man who's actually captained a four-masted, square-rigged, sailing ship like *Goodman Richard*,' acknowledged Richard. 'Probably the only man aboard apart from me that knows the significance of her name.'

'Oh, come on. Someone else aboard this tub must have heard of John Paul Jones and the *Bonhomme Richard*. Even if they've just been to Annapolis and seen his tomb there. Mind, that's the way I'd want to go. Entombed in marble; preserved in alcohol.'

'That's as may be,' acknowledged Richard lightly. 'But I'd just rather be rescuing a ship that has *not* been named after a vessel famous for sinking English shipping.'

'Built in New England, named in New England. Though the original was French and a rotten tub by all accounts. Nothing sinister in that.'

'That's what Charles Lee told me when he talked me into going on to the committee of the charity that runs her.'

'Well there you are then. No one knows more about the Luck Dragon than Hong Kong Chinese businessmen. Even if their offices are in the Heritage Mariner building on Leadenhall in London. And Charles is another proper sailor too. You know he's the only bloke at H.M. who's crewed all of the *Katapult* series? Didn't he buy his own *Katapult IV* and race her himself?'

'Yes,' said Richard feelingly. 'He named her *Robin* after my Robin and then pitchpoled her at nearly forty knots off Cowes. He was lucky to survive. He's stayed with yachts since as far as I know, even if he's worked *Katapult V* and *VI* with you in his spare time. Still, all in all I really do wish he was here.'

'Who?' asked Robin as they finished their conversation by stepping into the bridge.

'Charles Lee.'

'Ah.' Robin did not entirely approve of Charles, his extravagant bachelor lifestyle, his girlfriends and his gambling, his very secret spying in Hong Kong and China itself – and his ruinously expensive sailing. But he was an outstanding businessman and Heritage Mariner owed more than a little of its fortune to him. And his place beside Richard on the board of the charity that ran the *Goodman Richard* as a character-building adventure for disadvantaged and anti-social youngsters had seemed like the first step of his reclamation to her.

But in the end it had only been the first step on the long road to this situation. This danger. Here and now.

She might have said more, but the Wolf howled again. Long and loud – and so she held her peace. She looked out through the clearview ahead of her with dry and icy eyes. From side to side her entire vision was taken up by the tilting cliff of the wrecked sailing ship. And from this side, with the reef still well astern, she actually looked like a ship. She must have been four hundred feet long and would have sat too high in the water for *Lionheart*'s bow to come anywhere near her weather deck – even with her four masts standing and her full suit of sails aloft. But she was all but awash now, her two remaining masts waving like the minute hands on a clock-face uncertain whether the time was ten past the hour or a quarter past. Her mainmast and her foremast shattered stumps, thrusting through the sprung boards of her decking like the stumps of rotten teeth.

Another big sea reared up behind her and broke over her as though she were already part of the reef she was sluggishly drifting towards. Her deck sloped further as her masts nodded, looking more like a wooden hillside than the flat plain it should have been. A hillside behind a waterfall. At least there was no more debris to be washed off her, thought Robin grimly.

Nor anything much for Richard to hold on to when he climbed aboard either. The empty davits of a smashed or long-gone lifeboat. A few lines. The rope ladder of some rigging still belayed to the side and attached to a spar in the mess on the far side.

The trough of the next wave approached as *Lionheart* sat up on the foam of the broken crest. Robin looked down on the deck from on high, and the running boards seemed to be levelling off. The masts once again were pointing at the overcast rather than the wave-tops.

'We'd better be going,' said Richard after the briefest of pauses. 'Time and tide . . .'

Richard led Doc down the forward companionways that were normally the preserve of the crew and out through the weather-deck doorway. Up until the moment that he opened the strong metal door it had been possible for Richard to think, to plan, to work out ways in which he would overcome the monster that held them all in its fearsome grip. He paused, holding the icy handle in his gloveless hands, smiling slightly foolishly down at the puddle of water on the floor beside his feet. A puddle which told of yet more orders carefully obeyed. With a surge of confidence, he opened the door.

But the instant he stepped out on to the deck, all reasoned thought had to stop. He could concentrate only on the here and now. Focus like a warrior only on what lay immediately within his arm's reach. He had to fight with all his strength and will simply to stay upright, to breathe, to step forward.

The power of the wind came at him like a wrestler, wrapping its icy, foam-strengthened arms around him. It battered his senses with a totality that made the Wolf's howl die to a whisper. That drove all warmth from him with an unforgiving immediacy. That penetrated his wet-weather gear with the ease of abyssal deeps. That choked him with the casual ease of great waters. That sneaked like cunning ice beneath his feet so that the instant he began to move through the disorientating – dizzying – blast of it like a drunkard in the cold night air, he slipped and slithered helplessly towards the side.

As he had known he would.

Knowing his enemy of old and all her terrible wiles, he knew the best defences he could draw against her. And therefore that first, fatal, drunken, slithering lurch was brought up sharp by a safety wire and the shaking, almost palsied, fists clutched on the steady line and clipped his harness home. Then, held safe, he turned to see his companion echo his every move – from slither and slide to safety.

Then, looking – and feeling – like the weakest of geriatrics, the pair of them hunched themselves unsteadily down the shrieking, shuddering, spindrift infinity of the fifty-foot walk to the bow.

4: The Wreck

Richard only realized he had reached the point of *Lionheart*'s bow when the white metal safety-railing stopped his progress. He closed his fists upon its icy solidity and raised his head. As he looked forward, a flaw in the storm allowed him an instant's clear vision of *Goodman Richard*'s deck. He was still staring up at it, awe-struck, when Doc collided with his shoulder. Then they stood there, side by side, clinging like limpets.

Like the storm itself, the four-master had been distanced, reduced, somehow contained by the view from *Lionheart*'s bridge. Close to, she was huge and, in her wrecked state, immensely threatening. The streaming black cliff of her deck stretched beyond the edges of Richard's vision on either hand. He had to turn his head to encompass the enormity of her. The shrouded crest of her starboard side rose almost to the seething overcast. He had to look up to distinguish it from the clouds. The movements of his head, robot-like, from side to side then up and down seemed only to make her larger. And the larger she was, the more threatening. She seemed on the point of rolling over entirely, of stamping them out like flies.

The boards of her decking, sprung, splintered and simply torn open by the destruction of her masts, seemed to ripple as though they too were liquid, become part of the element that was bent upon consuming her. Wind battered round her, moaning and howling in every line, strut and stay. Water thundered over her, streamed down her, roared through her. And she herself was screaming.

The relentless pounding of the cataclysm which wrenched her first one way and then another was simply beginning to break her apart. Even before the black rock jaws of the reef got to chew on her, the boiling saliva of the foam was beginning the ocean's strange, slow digestion of this pretty morsel. Her keel was writhing; her structural frames were twisting deep within her. Her stout sides, designed to flex with the roughest seas, were simply being wrenched apart. The decks between them, like her weather deck, were losing their strength, their integrity. Nails, pins, nuts and rivets were tearing loose. Planks were rubbing together like the ends of broken bones. And all of this unnatural movement made a thousand individual squeals and shrieks that built together into the great ship's overwhelming death-scream.

The two men on the point of the forecastle may have been standing, overawed, but the team who backed them were more alert. As Richard and Doc remained, stricken by the scene before them, Robin and Tom were easing *Lionheart* forward as they had planned. Luck favoured their simple bravery. The wild ocean relented. Or perhaps it was the passage of yet another slow and solid tanker close enough at hand to break the power of wind and water for a vital moment or two. As *Lionheart* eased in, *Goodman Richard* rolled back into a trough followed by short sharp chop – not more great rhythmic rollers. Richard found himself given those moments' grace to look down on to a nearly steady, almost horizontal deck fortuitously webbed with the rope ladder Robin had noticed earlier. He unclipped his safety harness and laboriously climbed over the safety rail. Doc's strong hands held him – and, although he did not know it, his safety line as well.

At the first instant of stasis he leaped. It was a fall of perhaps a yard. Doc didn't even need to release his hold on the line until Richard's strong hands closed on the rope ladder stretched so tautly across the deck. And there, beside the ladder, another line stretched, just as taut, but with no rungs knotted across it. A convenient jackstay for his safety line if nothing else.

But to be fair, thought Richard as he pulled the end aboard and clipped on, he should not be too surprised to find lines and ladders here. Up until a few hours ago, this had been a fully-rigged four-masted sailing ship. There were miles and miles of lines, sheets, stays, braces, tacks and God knew what else aboard. The miracle was that these ones were not lost in some mare's nest of a tangle like the ropework over the far side. His prayer was that they would hold safely for another half an hour or so. And, aptly enough for the thought, he remained on his knees.

Doc's harness clip thumped into his chest then and there was enough slack in it for him to secure it beside his own before the Australian leaped forward and down on to the deck beside him.

The instant Doc leaped, *Lionheart* engaged her bow thruster and was edging safely back before the next swell came in. Up went the mare's nest to seaward. The deck began to tilt. The arrival of tons and tons of water became very imminent indeed. And considering what it had done to a well-found vessel, neither of the would-be rescuers wanted to guess what it could do to flesh and bone. The pair of them clung on to the ladder for dear life, scrambling upwards like bright-yellow tree frogs in some storm-bound Amazonian rain-forest. The rope ladder heaved and tautened beneath their almost prehensile fingers, seeming to Richard at least to attain the consistency of steel cable – cable spiked with needle-splinters. Only the fact that the cross-rungs were of thinner rope than the main lines allowed them to grip them at all, for the thick cords gouged their knots into the shrieking, splintering wood beneath their unbelieving eyes.

Now the deck was not quite as flat and featureless as Robin had believed. Further up the majestically steepening slope ahead of Richard and Doc there was a raised hatch cover. Unlike a tanker or a liner, the sailing ship had been designed with almost nothing on the deck in any case – no cabins, shelters, scarcely even a cockpit bridge house to get in the way of the sail-handling. But Richard had been aboard, shown round by Charles Lee as part of the plan to get him on the charity board. And Richard knew that these raised hatch covers, secured with weather-boards and sealed with strong, sliding hatches, gave directly on to the ship's main accommodation areas in a series of small, low-roofed interlinking rooms. The hatch immediately up-slope from them was one of the largest, standing almost knee high and presenting a solid wall a good six feet in length that would, with any luck, break the power of the deluge that was all too imminent. Or it would do so if they could get close enough to it in time.

And then, thought Richard grimly, they might just have a

chance to open up, scramble in and close it again before the next inevitable hammer-blow of water. If there was anyone below ready, willing or able to loosen the hatch locks. The upward heave of the deck stopped. The change from movement to stasis was quite sudden – there was no slowing or faltering. An immense thundering appeared from the heart of the raving cacophony around them. '*Here it comes!*' bellowed Richard. But only the tearing of his throat told him he had spoken – he didn't even hear the words. He sucked in a great gasp and wrapped himself, spider-like, in the rigging. The water exploded all around them. For a strange, unearthly moment it was as though they were behind a waterfall looking out as the first wash of the water soared over the hatch cover as Richard had prayed it would. That and that alone saved them. For when it collapsed into a bruising welter – more like brick than liquid – some at least of its vicious power was gone. But still it pounded them, tore at them, exercised almost unimaginable force on them. Richard felt his shoulders crack, felt the steel-hard rope he was clinging to gouge into his flesh as it gouged the teak deck earlier. He felt it crush his head like a nut in a cracker. He knew with soul-deep certainty that his legs would tear free at any instant and when they did so, his spine would break and – likely as not – the bottom half of his body would be torn away leaving only his tattered torso wedged immovably in the rigging.

But no.

The deck began to swoop vertiginously, like a lift-car whose ropes have snapped. And as suddenly as the upward heave had stopped, the wash of the water was gone. Richard's arms tore his body upwards and – for a miracle – his legs were still attached and able to thrust as well. He knew he had reached the hatch cover when the top of his head crashed into it with enough force to make him see stars. An instant later Doc's yellow helmet struck with equal force – but hopefully less damage.

Richard was already pounding with his fist, shredding skin from his almost senseless knuckles. The downward swoop was beginning to slow. The wind was howling closer. They were coming into the trough. Now was the moment.

And the hatch slid back.

Richard went in head-first immediately like a great fish slithering into the hold. He found himself sliding on his belly past the slim form of the person who had opened the hatch and away down a wooden companionway. No doubt he would have slithered on to the deck at its foot and away down the slope had his safety line not jerked him to a halt. Doc was thinking more clearly, however, and after a moment, the tight line slackened and Richard crawled on down on all-fours on to the deck.

Doc swung in more conventionally and stood, helping the man on the companionway get the hatch cover closed again. And not a moment too soon. What had been a downward slope began to rise. The angle of the companionway became almost horizontal, leaning sideways like something out of Escher's artwork. Doc found the man who had stood at his shoulder lying full-length on top of him and only the hatch-sides held him safe from falling down through the banisters. The thunder of the next wave was like an avalanche scant inches above their heads.

Richard crawled back to the foot of the companionway and hauled himself erect. He was breathless with cold and winded into the bargain. He was gulping in great bites of air. So, next after the sound, it was the stench that hit him. There was an unexpectedly dry, dusty element to it – all the microscopic debris trapped in numberless wooden seams and joints had been released by the destructive working of the frames. But there was the wet smell too – the rotting slimy aroma of bilges let loose and toilets overflowing because of the unnatural angle of the hull. The dangerous dampness of brine invading areas designed to be dry. Of sickness, compounded by the sickly-sweet aroma of everything aboard which had once been contained in a breakable vessel long since smashed and leaking. Of burning. Of terror.

The deck began to right again. Richard looked around. He was in the mouth of a corridor leading between closed doors into oddly angled darkness. He realized that all the illumination available was coming from a few naked bulbs on a string suspended from the ceiling. For every bulb still burning there were three or four shattered and dark.

The man in charge of the hatchway slid off Doc and came clattering down the stair. Richard caught him and they leaned together, gasping. Introductions were unnecessary. Richard had met First Officer Paul Ho along with Captain Jones and all the rest of the crew when Charles Lee had shown him round.

'Did the Captain get to you, then?' gasped Ho.

'No. We got your distress call. We've brought *Lionheart*. Did you get any of our radio messages at all?'

'Nothing much. I don't think our radio was working very well at all. Sparks is pretty badly hurt as well. The Captain took our best radio into his lifeboat. Said he'd be able to get help one way or the other.'

'The Captain?' demanded Richard. 'The Captain abandoned?'

'The Captain and several officers. Over an hour ago just before the really bad blow started. The masts had gone by then, though. The wind came up too suddenly and caught us with far too much canvas up. Mainmast went and took the foremast just like that. They took all the starboard lifeboats with them and smashed them to pieces. The Captain took the biggest portside boat and went for help. The Scillies, he said. We were expecting him back with the St Mary's lifeboat . . .'

'Well we're what you've got instead. We two and my SuperCat *Lionheart*.'

'A SuperCat? We need a lifeboat. And a big one at that. We could really use a tow if we could get one rigged.'

'That's not very likely, mate. And we're all there is,' said Doc, arriving beside them, having double-checked the hatch locks. 'And we're in a hurry.'

Paul Ho looked around ruefully. 'Yes. She hasn't got a lot more in her. Two or three hours I'd say before she starts leaking really badly. Power won't last much longer either.'

'It's worse than that,' Richard explained as Paul began to lead them down the corridor. They walked with their arms out as though miming crucifixion. The rolling tilt of the corridor kept their hands in constant contact with one wall or the other. 'You'll be on the reef at Wolf Rock in thirty minutes.'

'Christ! Are we that close?' Paul looked over his shoulder, his face horrified. Behind the doors literally on either hand, things shifted, slid and crashed about. The first door Richard touched seemed to be bulging slightly with the strain of containing whatever wreckage was behind it.

'And getting closer,' grated Richard. 'We need to move. How many have you got aboard?'

'Forty crew. Sixty cadets.'

'What sort of state are they in?'

'See for yourself.' As he spoke, Paul opened the door at the end of the corridor and the three men stepped into what must have been the one fairly sizeable area aboard. It looked as though it had been the dining room – the mess. And it really was a mess now. Everything that could be stripped out had been stripped out. There was little left other than benches secured to the walls and holes in the floor where tables had been screwed tight. The shaft of the mizzen mast thrust through the middle of it with a festoon of lights tacked to it, the bulbs jumping and shimmering strangely as the wooden column flexed and vibrated in the storm immediately above.

The considerable area of bare flooring was covered with bodies. For a fleeting, horrific moment, Richard thought they were all dead – they lay there limply enough; they were pale enough. And the place smelt badly enough. But no. There were figures on the benches too, holding themselves carefully against the ship's motion. And, as the list became more pronounced with the arrival of the next big wave, so the apparent corpses on the floor all tensed themselves to keep from slipping, sliding and rolling into a heap.

Richard looked around the place. It seemed to him that the people on the benches were mostly crew and the bodies on the floor belonged to the kids. And, he thought as his eyes cleared further still, to the wounded. He hoped most fervently that there was no one too completely exhausted or too badly hurt to walk. The deck came level. The mast stopped juddering. The light steadied and the raving of the storm died for an instant.

Richard stepped into the room and began to speak, using his quarterdeck bellow and starting as slowly as he dared, hoping to get their attention focused squarely on him for the really important part.

'My name is Captain Richard Mariner,' he began. 'I've crossed aboard here with my colleague Captain Weary from our vessel *Lionheart* which is just beside us now. And we've come to rescue you . . .'

5: The Rescue

Richard had been in this kind of situation before, but never in such dire straits as these. From the sight of the ship, the experience of coming aboard her – and the sensation of being below decks within her – he was half-expecting to find only the helpless, the halt and the lame. Such was the destruction and danger so obviously all around – the sense of the fabric of the vessel and everything aboard being so relentlessly reduced to splinters and atoms by the sea even before the inevitable crushing crash upon the rocks – that he supposed he would be talking only to the terrified and the refractory.

He had forgotten that these people, men and women, crew and youngsters, had been sailing *Goodman Richard* for several weeks already. Even the least adventurous city-street kids – more used to PlayStations than to watch stations – had been up and down the rigging like rats. They might not be using them at the moment, but they all had found their sea-legs long since. And, as this was designed to be a character-building exercise, there were characters here that had been built in strength and abundance.

They were not defeated, they were dormant. They were not helpless or hopeless. Even in the face of the enormity of what was going on around them – even in face of the inevitability of what seemed likely to be facing them – they were waiting; conserving their energy and heat, and waiting for help.

The instant that he entered he had their attention. The presence of a stranger alone would have meant hope. But the fact that it was Richard himself – known to all of the crew in person and most of the youngsters by sight and reputation – meant more still. He had their undivided attention long before he even mentioned 'Rescue'.

While Richard spoke, wedged in the restless doorway to

stop himself from staggering about, his audience began to stir. As they pushed back the coats, blankets and duvets with which they had covered themselves, so his heart leaped. Every one of them was wearing wet-weather gear. Not a breast but had a deflated life preserver tied in place across it; not a torso that was not safety-harnessed. Had he had the leisure or the opportunity to count, he would have found in one hundred right hands one hundred lifelines coiled neatly, ready to be snapped on to a jackline at a moment's notice.

His speech completed – and much of it, though vital, blessedly unnecessary – he turned to Paul Ho. 'This is extraordinary,' he said. 'How have you managed it?'

'Practice over the last few weeks,' said Paul Ho shortly. 'And we've had lots of time this afternoon since the masts came down and Captain Jones and the others went for help. We planned for help to arrive, prepared for rescue – and waited. They're an extraordinary bunch of cadets, too. That helped.'

Richard nodded decisively. 'How have you got them organized?'

'In watches. Red and green. Eight kids in each, ten including the officers. Red Upper Watches One and Two, Red Lower Watches One and Two; Green the same.'

'And you've agreed the order for abandonment?'

'The order I just said. That was the easy bit. But you have one vital decision, I'm afraid. Injured first or last?'

'How many? How bad?'

'Four. Two walking – but with broken arms. Two stretcher cases. One broken leg when the masts came down. One radio operator caught by lightning less than an hour ago. Shocked and burned.'

Richard was used to the brutal decisions of leadership. He was well aware that he would have to answer for any he made now – to his own conscience if to nothing else. To his conscience armed with hindsight, with all risks run for better or worse and all bets settled with life or death. But the worst thing to do in situations like these was to waste time trying to second-guess Fate. 'The injured go last. If we take them first, we'll be fresher and they'll get help quicker – but they'll make the first crossings riskier and more time-consuming – and they'll slow up all the rest.

'I'll go out and wait at the rail to help the kids up on to *Lionheart.* Doc, you wait at the hatch to help them out and clip the safety lines on. I tested mine coming in – they should be fine and dandy going out. You have the radio, too, Doc, you keep Robin and Tom up to speed. You'll need to count them all out – they'll count them all over and in. I've got the foredeck crew and the Chef Steward briefed for that. Paul, you get your eight watches up and out in order, officers with their kids. Then your non-assigned officers. The last four work in pairs with one walking wounded each. When everyone else is safe, you and your best officer, Doc and I will take care of the stretcher cases. But I'll want you to do one more thing. It'll be tough, so you'll need someone quick-thinking and sprightly. I noticed that the rope-ladder we came up goes on up to the high side. Before you send out the first of the injured you'll have to send a keen pair of eyes up there with night glasses and some way of signalling. They'll give the all-clear when things look as though they'll be calm enough to get the stretchers out. You see? We can't run the risk of getting caught on deck with them. Get that set up and then call me back when you need me.'

'If you have the strength,' warned Doc. 'You'll have been on the deck for half an hour by then. Half an hour at least.'

'I know. But that's the way we'll do it. OK?'

'Aye aye,' said Paul Ho, formally.

'Right. Oh. One more thing.'

'Yes, sir?'

'I'd feel safer if I had a knife. Preferably a sharp one on a lanyard. You never know when I might need to cut someone free . . .'

'Aye aye, Captain,' echoed Doc, missing Richard's hesitation. He put the radio to his lips and turned, supporting himself with an out-thrust arm as he walked down the angled slope of the corridor. 'You hear this, Robin? Richard says we're coming out now. Over . . .'

Paul and Doc eased the hatch-cover open and Richard slid out. He went out as he had come in, flat on his stomach, offering the lowest possible profile to the storm and the swell as Doc clipped his safety line in place at his hip. The black, shrieking power of it closed down on him at once with the same disorientating force as before. But as before, he was as well-prepared as possible. And he was given what help was possible. No sooner was the cover closed behind him than all of *Lionheart*'s lights came on. From the isolated hesitancy of blindness, he went at a stroke to the sure-footed confidence of clear sight. Every strand of the ladder he was easing down sprang into crystal-clear relief. Even under the stretching heave of the steepening angle of the deck he could see the gaps beneath the cross-pieces which would allow safe purchase for fingers and toes. If 'safe' was a word that could ever be used in the circumstances. And when he glanced up as the upward motion seemed to hesitate, the brightness revealed to him the crest of the incoming sea and gave him those extra vital moments he needed to prepare for the waterfall of foam it poured down upon him.

By the time this happened, he was in fact right down at the ship's side, standing as securely as possible on the angle between the deck and the solid safety rail which edged it. The slightly sloping design of the deck – with a low watershed ridge running down the middle between the masts – meant that there was no real need for scuppers at the outer edges. And the purpose of the vessel – to serve as a training ship for the inexperienced – meant that the safely rail was higher and very much more substantial than it might have been. Richard was able to find a firm foothold, therefore, and remain secure – with the restless aluminium ridge of *Lionheart*'s needle bow between three and six feet away from him, depending on the relative movements of the hulls. He paused there for the briefest moment, slipping Paul Ho's knife safely into the square chart-pocket over his breast, easing the lanyard round his neck, wanting to be neither stabbed nor strangled. Even looking up as he did this, it did not occur to him that the SuperCat might slip out of control and crush him. Not at this stage, anyway.

But then he had no real notion of how terribly close and threatened he seemed to be from the bridge, where he regularly vanished from Robin's anxious view beneath the flare of the forecastle itself.

That was as good as it got, however; and as there were positive things Richard had not relied on but was happy to make use of, so there were dangers he had not thought through. And that first cascade of water made him alive to the first of these at once. Hunched and tensed against the bruising force of it as it roared down the deck towards him like a breaker on a beach, he was caught utterly unprepared for the backwash as several hundred pounds of it splashed back off *Lionheart* just at the very instant that he thought the worst was over.

But he had no time to do anything but shake himself like a terrier. For the instant that the wave was past, the hatch on high slammed open and the first cadet came scrambling down the ladder like a monkey escaping from the zoo. All he had to do was leave hold of the ladder with one hand, grab a fistful of harness and heave, steadying the youngster in their scramble up on to the SuperCat. Then he had an instant to unclip the safety and see it whip up like a tail behind them as the foredeck crew above him took over and snapped on for the run up to shelter.

The first few were inexpressibly vivid to Richard. He would feel the power of the water wash away from him, its simple – massive – weight begin to ease. He would break his death-grasp on the ladder and raise himself, brutally disregarding the complaints of battered bones, torn and chilled muscles. He would unclench that one fist as his foam-filled boots fought to give the frozen clubs of his feet the solid purchase they would need. He would blink the burning brine out of his eyes and strain to see up through the dazzling brightness. The next vivid shape would come slithering down towards him like a salmon or a seal wrapped in orange peel. As often as not, boots would strike him somewhere – and he soon learned to lean back at the crucial moment so his chest and not his face got the worst of it.

They always tried to say something. 'Thanks' was most likely. But there was no hope of hearing them and no time for repetitions. Each young face, black, white, oriental, masculine and feminine, seemed to sear itself into his memory in that moment. All of them apparently preserved under glass, all of them covered with a bright varnish of water. He would give a reassuring grin – with no idea how terrible his amicable expression actually looked – and grab tight hold of their harness. Knuckles complained arthritically. Wrists ached as though strained. Shoulders, neck and back were just one big cloak of agony. But he heaved with all his might and the agile bodies vanished upwards, one after another, times without number, dragging the tails of their lifelines behind them.

And so it fell into a kind of rhythm. The seas were long and high, terribly powerful and destructive, but they were fairly regular. They signalled their coming and going with familiar, apparently unvarying signals that the dying ship transmitted as faithfully as an ancient sheepdog. They were able to get three people out between inundations. So, by the time Richard had been battered thirty times or so – though he was long past counting – the back of the work was broken.

The easy part, at least, was done. And the worst was yet to come.

Richard had not thought through the mechanics of dealing with three people at once beyond the necessity of setting extra watch. It was something likely to be incalculable in any case. The only way to work out what he needed to do was to do it. A classic 'suck it and see' situation. It was presented to him quite unexpectedly. He had lost count of the individuals he had heaved aboard *Lionheart* and had no idea he had already saved so many. So he was simply shocked to see a bunch of three suddenly slithering down towards him, and a fourth figure vertiginously above them hanging on to ropework like Tarzan and gesturing wildly.

He had to cudgel his mind, frozen into almost robotic simplicity by the repetitive nature of his work so far. But he managed to kick it into reluctant gear as he watched them coming towards him. In this situation, the injured crewman must go first. There was a team waiting to receive him above, and three pairs of hands to help from below would make the transfer as safe as it could possibly be.

Which was not one whole hell of a lot, thought Richard, prophetically.

The three figures arrived – the middle one clearly hurt, the other two too young to be full officers, thought Richard. Officer cadets in all probability. But nonetheless, able and quick-thinking officer cadets – as he was just about to discover.

Richard pushed the leading helper gently aside and caught the patient's harness. He gripped and heaved. The injured cadet reached up automatically – obviously forgetting that he had a broken arm just for that fractional, fatal instant – and screamed. It must have been quite a scream because Richard heard it over the storm. With his writhing burden halfway to safety, Richard hesitated, stricken. The cadet reached up again with his good arm, but the momentum of the transfer was gone. His full weight fell back on Richard's arm, tearing all the muscles from his fingertip to his spine. The quicker-thinking of the officers grabbed the falling body and heaved. Boots battered Richard's ribs and chest with bruising force not even the icy numbness of his nerves could hide. A massive voice bellowed through the night – Robin had seen the danger and used the external tannoys combined with her quarterdeck yell. A member of the foredeck crew leaned forward and snatched the screaming boy upwards. The second officer providentially thought to snap his safety clear while Richard hung there almost helpless, fighting to regain his breath.

But he knew he had no time. The stricken ship was lifting already up the front of the next big sea. Mouth wide, lips back from tombstone teeth, unaware that he was shouting as well as gasping, Richard heaved the upright officer upwards – not by the harness but by the seat of her pants.

Incongruously, in the midst of everything else that was happening, Richard's fist had no doubt at all of the gender of the seat he was elevating, as the second officer unclipped the lifeline again. Richard turned, working with feverish speed. The clip came free. He heaved the officer up and was just turning to cling on again when something slammed across his cheek. He looked up to see the last man teetering on the brink, his lifeline reaching back in a straight, solid black line, more like a javelin than a tail. Then it struck him: the line was still secured. Screaming with frustration, Richard turned back to see that, in the confusion, the officer had not loosened his own lifeline at all. He had loosened Richard's. The mechanics of the situation turned unstoppably around that clip. The clip was a steel climbing clip with hook and safety. There was neither time nor chance to loosen it properly for the ropes were holding it rigidly. The man above was gripped by strong and anxious hands. The hulls were straining to pull apart, but the SuperCat, trapped, was grinding across towards Richard and he had nowhere to go. He just had presence of mind enough to reattach his own clip as he tore at the waterproof seal of the chart pocket. He ripped the knife out with such force that the lanyard burned his neck but it served its purpose. The blade whispered through the straining line and Richard was thrown down by the reaction as the hulls leaped apart even before the deluge came.

It was as well that Doc had not treated Richard's offer to help with the stretchers very seriously. He arrived now with the first stretcher and two helpers to find Richard very nearly at the end of his strength. He actually had to slap him twice before the ice-blue eyes gained their usual focus. 'Watch man says there's a bit of peace and quiet upwind,' bellowed the Australian. 'We're moving the stretchers now and the last broken arm when they're over. OK?'

Richard nodded.

'You just take a breather while we get on with things then,' bellowed Doc. 'You look all tuckered out in any case.'

'I'm fine. I'll wait.'

'You're the nearest thing the old girl's got to a captain, I reckon. Maybe it's right and proper . . .' And he was gone.

Time played tricks then. The stretchers came and went with astonishing speed. The last of the officers appeared and swung themselves upwards – Richard content simply to snap their lifelines loose as they went, forcing the last of his strength back, for there was still one more walking wounded left.

And at last he appeared, supported on one side by Paul Ho and on the other by Doc. 'This is it,' Doc yelled. 'There's no one else left. All absent but accounted for . . .'

As with the first – nearly fatal – attempt, Richard knew what to do, and, with the concentration of a man with no strength left save for his strength of will, he pushed up the injured man first. He was gentle this time, remembering the screams. At least he didn't need to keep an eye on Doc to be certain which clip was undone, he thought. He released his grip on the injured man and he was gone. As he did so, he felt the deck beginning to rise and he knew that the storm's brief respite was over.

He helped Paul next, concentrating so utterly, that time itself seemed to slow and the deck just seemed to rise and rise and rise beneath him only a little less slowly than the departing Lieutenant's heels.

Then he turned to Doc. And Doc just looked up at him, apparently awestruck, as he hooked his fist into the safety harness and hurled the Australian over on to *Lionheart*.

Only then did it strike him. He threw his old friend over – not upwards. He was standing almost upright on the safety-rail which ought to be vertical but was now almost horizontal. He looked directly into the stricken faces of the foredeck detail. And, beyond, into the ivory oval of Robin's face as well.

And Robin was still on the bridge beside Tom Bartlett.

It was as though he was in an elevator going upwards. The whole of the hull he was standing on slammed up into the air, taking *Lionheart*'s forecastle head with it. The SuperCat seemed to leap up out of the water as she felt the massive upper-cut under her slim jaw. The safety-rail snapped off like matchwood and the top of it tore away. With the same vivid instant of revelation which had told his fingers about the girlish bottom he helped over some uncounted time ago, the soles of his feet itched almost unbearably. And so he learned that they still rested on the stump of the upright, which was all that remained of the safety-rail.

Richard looked up then and saw the crest of the wave arrive at last. The crest of the wave so big that it had sucked in the last few waves before it creating those sinister moments of calm.

Goodman Richard was the better part of four hundred feet long. Slim-hipped, she was nevertheless seventy-five feet wide where Richard was standing, at her widest point. And he saw twenty feet more of water coming over the top of her. Twenty feet of cold green water before the breaking crest began.

He didn't see it clearly because it was shrouded in the sail, wrapped in rigging and spiked with spars. He had a mad, fleeting impression that the quaking ship was being attacked by the great white whale, Moby Dick.

Somewhere in his reeling mind he remembered that salt water weighs sixty-four pounds per cubic foot. The top of the wave was a hundred feet long, twenty feet high and say fifty feet thick. With typical seaman's acuity and the shock sharpened sense of irrelevance granted to men staring death in the face, he realized that this would be about a hundred thousand cubic feet.

That was 6,400,000 pounds of water.

And all of it was coming down on him.

6: The Reef

Richard jumped. Holding his body stiff, with his arms crossed over his chest and his legs straight, he plunged directly into the shrinking space between the ship's side and the SuperCat's heaving bow. It was a gamble based on several factors, the first of which was his knowledge of Robin's seamanship. She, like he, would have seen the oncoming monster; would have made some assessment such as his – and come to the same conclusion. Six and a half million pounds of wave would be enough to turn the ship right over. Robin would have called for full thrust from the bow thrusters. That fact alone made the overturning of the *Goodman Richard* more likely, for the weight of the wave pushing forward on top of her would be supplemented by the force of the waterjets pushing away beneath her.

And he was right on the first count at least. His lifeline was six feet long and his body longer still. By the time all twelve feet of their combined length had reached the end of the tether, the lower four feet were being thrust back forcefully by the power of the water jets as *Lionheart* backed away. Richard felt his body being blasted westwards, the pendulum motion of still being anchored by the clip beginning to swing him upwards. He was thinking of nothing much, too overwhelmed by action and experience even to send up a prayer. The only thing in his mind was the heading. He was being pushed exactly along the line *Lionheart* was holding at his order: 262 degrees. At right angles to the drift of *Goodman*

Richard along 82 degrees due east on to the Wolf Rocks behind. Had he been able to pray or calculate he would have been trying to work out whether the power and weight of the wave would be sufficient to turn the boat right over – and to pray that it would.

For it was the energy of the wave that was most dangerous to him now. The weight of it would dissipate rapidly in the water above his head – but as it did, so it would release massive amounts of energy, which would be expressed in currents, cross currents, downdraughts of water that would suck him down to where his lungs would burst and throw him up so fast his blood would boil and tear him limb from limb. But the good ship *Goodman Richard* would soak up all that energy – or most of it at least – if she allowed the wave to turn her right over.

And, were he able to think at all, let alone calculate, he would have seen that there was a fair chance that the greatest part of all that weight and energy would be thrown forward towards Wolf Rock – and *Lionheart.* That it might well simply roll over the top of the rolling hull of the dismasted sailing ship leaving a little area of quiet water immediately beneath – like the calm at the eye of the storm.

When the lifeline tightened behind him and hauled him backwards through the water with bruising force, he thought, *Christ, I hope Robin's well clear of this*, and that was all.

For once in her life Robin was not thinking about Richard even though her last sight of him jumping straight under the flare of *Lionheart*'s forecastle would likely be her final view of him alive. She and Tom were reaching forward side by side, with the controls of the bow thrusters set at maximum and the reverse thrust on the main engines right up there with it, tearing *Lionheart* in full reverse along 82 degrees, though the automatic compass still read her heading as 262 – the way she had been facing since Richard gave the command. Paul Ho and Doc were standing, breathless and dripping, looking back out of the aft sections of the bridge wings with their night glasses, ready to bellow warning if it looked as though they were reversing the SuperCat up on to either section of the channel-split reef.

But all of Robin's concentration was taken up with the wreck that was falling down upon them. Millions of pounds of water were tearing through the sails as though the strengthened canvas had been tissue paper, turning the last of what the lesser waves had left into shreds. Spars were sticking up out of the mess like the fangs of a palisade. But underneath that deadly, foaming crest, the rest of the square-rigger's deck was coming at her like a collapsing wall.

Then the first of the foam hit and washed away the terrifying view. It hit so hard it cracked the windows and ripped away the wipers of the clearview system. It came close to ripping the whole bridge off its footing in the deck and chucking it over the Cat's square stern, throwing everyone aboard flat on the floor except for Robin, Tom and Sparks, who were all strapped in tight. But it still hit hard enough for Sparks to flatten his nose and Tom to bite the tip of his tongue right off and for Robin to crack her jaw on the console in front of her as *Lionheart* leaped back a good twenty feet through the water.

So that the next thing Robin saw – other than stars – was the wall of foam thrown up by the foundering of the spinning hull as it came roaring out towards them. She just had time to reverse the positions of her hands – so that when the wall of raging foam arrived, the power of the thrusters was dying and that of the great waterjets behind was just beginning to grip. Robin felt the SuperCat's head fight to turn as she was forced up that avalanche of foam. She saw Tom's knuckles whiten as he held her straight and true, knowing as well as she did that if they turned they would be overwhelmed more easily even than *Goodman Richard* had been. And they would not right themselves or stay afloat at all, because they were made of heavy metal not of buoyant wood. For an instant it hung in the balance, but the great motors just had enough green water to bite on and their power gathered as Robin's fists – as white as Tom's – remained relentlessly holding the handles of the throttles at Full Ahead and the heading still held at 262 – though the weight of the wave continued to push her back along the reverse heading.

The moment passed. Her head stayed up and did not waver. The wave passed under her and she began to overcome it. And immediately, she began to leap ahead. The instant Robin felt the sturdy hull settle and set to work, her hands slammed back with sufficient force to tear her shoulder-muscles, into the original positions. The game vessel faltered, almost wallowing, and even Tom looked across at her in some confusion. But the grey eyes glared with steely certainty while the shaking, sweating fists stayed exactly where they were and the bow thrusters began to push once more, while the great engines fought with the last of the departing foam to suck her back towards the reef again.

And not a moment too soon. The heaving water immediately in front of them parted as the *Goodman Richard*'s copper keel thrust up into the storm, astonishingly clean and colourful. Like the back of Nemo's *Nautilus* surfacing. Robin continued to back away as fast as she could all too well aware that, with the hull's position in the water now reversed, all the mess of sail, spar and cordage would be on this side now, washing towards them in the grip of the current. And it wouldn't take much of it to foul them, render them powerless and link them with fatal inevitability to the whole wreck drifting helplessly down on to the Wolf Rock.

Completely unbidden, there rose in her mind the nightmare possibility that it might be Richard, lost under the heaving hulk, and secured there by his lifeline, who fouled them and dragged them down to death with him. The thought was doom-laden madness, but it had force enough to wind her. Especially as it was her first conscious thought about him since he jumped off the ship in the instant she turned turtle.

But in fact both of Robin's nightmare visions were unfounded. The steepness of the incoming seas – as she would have realized had she been allowed an instant's clarity of thought – bore testimony to the strength of the outgoing tide, still stripping bare the fangs of the Wolf so close behind her. And that tide, ebbing at full force westward into Biscay, was taking the mess of rigging with it. And, away before the first of the grasping serpentine coils of it, coils which writhed like the arms of an army of octopi embracing the wreckage of wooden stockade, went Richard, pulled by his lifeline towards the west-facing port side, and pushed by the westering tide.

At the instant he felt the lifeline snap taut again, jerking him upright just beneath the reach of the turbulence on the surface,

Richard pulled the toggle of his life-preserver and heard the hiss of the CO_2 canister beside his ear as it inflated. He had waited until now because he – like Robin – had entertained lively but instantaneous nightmare visions. Of getting caught by *Lionheart*'s motors and sucked into her. Of becoming entangled in the octopus coils of submerged rigging. Of inflating his life jacket too soon and getting trapped under the hull itself.

But he was out of air, beyond thought and acting on impulse now. Up he came towards the surface, and into the rolling restlessness of the waves. Upwards with surprising force and speed, heading for the life-giving air. The stygian element around him lightened abruptly by the brightness of the emergency beacon at his shoulder and the promise of moonlight at the surface as the eye of the storm approached – just as Doc had predicted that it would.

When he jerked to a halt three feet short he came dangerously near to giving up. Only the shock of it, actually, jolted him awake. The line stretched beneath him to the submerged deck of the upturned hulk and there was no way there was enough length in it to see him to the surface. A lesser man might have panicked then. He had come so far and achieved so much. And he was only a yard or so short. It was so unexpected. So unfair. He floated on his back, looking up at the silver string of bubbles that were the last of his breath and he thought of the black shaft of the lifeline leading, straight as a spear, to the upturned deck below him. The top of his head slammed into the side of the ship. Pain lanced through him. And frustration. And simple, white-hot rage.

And revelation.

His shaking fingers slipped beneath the fat bulk of the inflated life preserver to the ruin of the chart-pocket at his breast. Along the lanyard there to the handle of the knife still trapped in his wet-weather gear. It needed all his nerve to draw it out, for it was wedged tightly in place by the all too fragile bulge of the gas-filled material. He was tempted to turn the sharpness down, trusting the feeling of it slicing through his chest rather than risk a puncture. If the lifebelt failed now, the weight of his clothing would take him down like a stone. The risk did not bear thinking about. But he was thinking, dreamily, floating with his hand on the handle, slipping away into death, when *Goodman Richard* smacked him on the head again. The rage rekindled. He pulled the knife out and reached behind him for the line. A moment later he was free. He exploded through the surface into both storm-swell and moonlight and began being thrown against the great hull with a vengeance. But in the thick air and the thin moonlight, the arresting brightness of his emergency beacon was joined at once by the insistent pulse of the emergency radio locator signal.

Only then did he begin to surrender, so that it seemed to him a mere instant later that there was someone in the water beside him. It was Doc and he had a long line ready to clip on to Richard's harness. A heartbeat or two after that Richard was aboard *Lionheart*.

There was no doctor aboard. There was a sickbay but it was over-filled already. Robin hid her massive relief at finding him so swiftly and getting him aboard so easily by a robust refusal to mollycoddle him. Wrapped in dry towels and clutching a warm drink, therefore, he found himself almost dreamily strapped in the seat beside Tom's shoulder as the SuperCat eased herself round the end of the wreck and began to head for the south-west end of the shoal on her way in to the safety of the Cornish coast.

But the awful grandeur of what the pale full moon revealed slowed them, almost made them turn aside. For no sooner were they clear of *Goodman Richard* than the outwash of the reef took hold of her. Tom took them south of the spreading turbulence, but just as the Bishop's Rock Light had stood at the point of their turn at the beginning of this, so the Wolf Rock Light remained a fixed point now. And on the reef at its feet, like some kind of ritual sacrifice, the sea offered up the ship.

The outwash disturbed the brief equilibrium that had held her upside down, buoyant deck-boards lowest and ballasted, copper bottom uppermost. No sooner did the boiling water touch her than she heaved herself over again. But the reefs were not an even-sided sea-wall. They were uneven, inconsistent, the spine of a little underwater mountain range with that gully Richard had noted running through the midst of them. The outwash, carried down the falling tideway, took hold of some parts of her but not some others. Her rigging remained a potent drogue. And the last two masts, which had stood by her so well so far, let her down in the end, catching on the black-rock bottom as she turned.

So that she not only heaved herself upright, she swung herself around to meet the foaming destruction bow first. There wasn't much left of her bowsprit any more. And there had never been much of a figurehead beneath. But it was with these she faced the inevitable end. The waves did not abate. Even under the falling wind, the brief calm at the heart of the storm, they marched eastwards in terrible series, their white fangs gleaming in the moonlight seemingly away as far as Finisterre.

And each set beat against her high square poop, thrusting her onward and upward through the foam, seemingly on to the Lighthouse itself. The foghorn had stopped its howling now, but the swinging of the light-beam seemed to count the lingering seconds of her death with the steady inevitability of a hangman's clock.

They were pulling away when she struck. And even though the wind had fallen there was still so much noise from the surf and the engines that none of them actually heard anything else. But they saw it clearly enough. A sight that none had seen in their millennium and few enough had witnessed in the century before its turn. The sight of a full sized, four-masted sailing vessel being driven on to the rocks. The shock of her first strike stopped her in the water and brought down what little was left of her rearmost masts. She backed off, shaking her head, like a stag brought to bay by a bigger stag. Then she lunged in again, tossing her head up this time, lifted by some vagary of the foam beneath her, to smash down on to the black and unforgiving rock.

Robin cried out and Richard was shocked out of his lethargy by the lively horror of it. She rolled on to one side a little and seemed to be trying to slide back again. But the rocks had her now and there was nothing else for her to do. The next sea lifted her again and swung her as it pushed her higher still. It swung her right across the narrow channel Richard had noticed. They all saw it now. Little more than a tenth of her length, it came almost perfectly halfway along her, and when the next wave slammed her down like a wrestler performing some terrible blow, it simply broke her back. The middle of her deck, right along the line where Richard and the others had centred their rescues, simply folded downwards like a closing hinge. The pale side of her, even to the very point where his safety clip still hung, burst. Bow and stern sections lifted and she simply exploded open.

As though it too had seen enough, the moon pulled a black veil across its white face then. The wind backed viciously as the next storm front swept over them and what had been an even sea full of parallel combers coming up behind them was suddenly full of sharp, triangular sharks' fins thirty and more feet high.

'Time to go,' said Tom, easing the throttle wider still, and seeking for that safe, easterly 82 degrees. But instead of rising, gull-like, above the nasty-looking waters, the SuperCat stuck her nose into the back of the nearest wave like a porpoise, and green water swept up towards them.

'Oh shit,' said Doc. 'That's not supposed to happen is it?'

7: The Time

'No it's bloody not,' answered Richard, shortly. 'Better ease back on the throttles, Tom, while we go and take a look.'

'No,' said Tom with unexpected authority. Then, incongruously, he eased back on the throttles after all and the SuperCat's head came up, shouldering aside water like a breaching whale. But he continued speaking as he acted. 'Robin, you hold her on the heading we agreed and just where she is at half power, please. I'll go with Richard. She's my command after all.'

Richard, Doc and he left the bridge together. Richard glanced back from the doorway to see Paul Ho ease himself into the left hand seat. He hesitated fractionally as the young man introduced himself. 'This is all a bit of a shock after sailing a vessel that's a century or so out of date,' he said dryly. 'But just tell me if there's anything an old fashioned foursquare man can do to help . . .'

Yet another sailor happy to flirt with the other Captain Mariner, thought Richard wryly and he closed the door and left them to it.

Richard, Doc and Tom came side by side on to the pulpit that looked down into the main accommodation area and were stopped by a wave of applause. It was weak but it was heartfelt. The better part of half of the seats were occupied now, by pale, seasick, but very grateful survivors from *Goodman Richard*, all of whom had seen her terrible end from the port-side windows and knew exactly what they had been rescued from. The Chief Steward and a couple of sailors were moving amongst them with warm drinks. Nobody there, apparently, had noticed *Lionheart*'s strange behaviour just now. Or, if they had, they were confident that these three could sort it out.

Side by side, after the briefest modest acknowledgement, they hurried down the forward companionway to the door marked CAR DECKS. Then they ran on, this time with Tom in the lead, for as he had said, it was his command. The topmost of the three car decks seemed fine. Tom opened the door into the huge cavern, stepped over the metal sill into the dim-lit echoing cavern and looked around. Richard caught up almost instantly, stepped through on the slighter man's heels and stood at his shoulder, all his senses on the alert.

Beyond the bellow of the storm and the thudding of the cross sea, beneath the rumble of the half-power motors, there was the drip, hiss and tinkle of running water, but no evidence of it close at hand. No evidence of any quantity large enough to have pulled down the head of a vessel designed to fly with this and two more decks jam-packed with a hundred vehicles.

So, out they came and down they went. To the same scenario as the one above. Nothing obvious at all.

And out they came again. And down they went. It was not that they became careless or even blasé. It was simply that they were in a hurry. And there was nothing at all to arouse their suspicions. Tom simply opened the third metal bulkhead door and stepped over the sill, exactly as he had done with the two above.

And vanished.

There was no warning, nor at first glance was there any explanation. Richard ran forward to the empty doorway where the captain had been standing an instant earlier. He looked through into the car-deck, bellowing, 'Tom? Tom!'

The lights burned dully. The calls echoed briefly and without reply. The sounds and sensations were all the same as they had been one deck and two decks higher but Richard stood frozen, eyes busy, refusing to move until he understood.

And then he saw. It was the floor. Up to the very level of the raised metal sill – the better part of eighteen inches above the main deck – the floor was under water. And the water, smooth and silent as ice, black and almost invisible against the metal of the deck itself, was rushing back along the length of the Cat with sufficient force to have snatched the unsuspecting Tom away in a twinkling.

That was very bad, thought Richard. For, below these decks there were at least three others, full of equipment, ballast and bilge. All of them full of water now too, by the looks of things. Logic dictated that he should close the door and go back up to discover where the water was coming from. But, remembering the terrible blows that the slim bow had taken as the great waves slammed *Goodman Richard* up and down – and also the fact that the bow was designed to open to allow cars to come and go – there seemed little enough doubt. Doc could pass his thoughts along via the radio transceiver he still held. There were others better qualified to sound out his suspicions. And in any case, he was unwilling to leave Tom.

But even as Richard stood, calculating the full danger of what was going on here, the first quicksilver rush of it gushed over the sill and out into the stairwell at his feet. Jerked back from the realms of speculation, he looked around for yet another lifeline, talking to Doc as he did so. 'There's a bad leak for'ard, Doc. Get on the radio to engineering and tell the Chief, if he doesn't already know. He needs to send a team to look at the seals on the bow doors. Start at car deck two.'

There, beside the door was a fire-point. It had an axe, an extinguisher and – blessedly – a hose.

An instant later, as Doc finished talking to the Chief, Richard was securing the hose around his waist, slowed only by the weight of the metal nozzle. Then, taking careful grip of the doorframe and glancing back at Doc, who was ready to take the strain, he stepped over the little Niagara at his feet.

Even though he was expecting it, the vicious tugging of the millrace at his ankle and shin nearly tripped Richard up immediately, as it had obviously tripped Tom. But he found that if he angled himself forward against the pull of Doc's safe hands on the hose, he was able to slop forward from handhold to handhold along the wall.

He knew the layout of the decks well enough. There were two central columns, each seemingly square and solid from the outside, but each containing a stairwell. He had come down the forward one of these, and the water was rushing past that and the second one aft of it, towards the stern. Both had hand rails and doorways to port and starboard, but nothing much to hold on to fore and aft. Beyond these the deck was as open as a football field and not a lot different in size. Say one hundred yards long and fifty wide.

The lights in the deck-head above were burning brightly enough for Richard to see the swirl of the water, which, as he took his third or fourth step, attained sufficient depth to flood over his boots. By the time he had reached the after end of the stairwell, the water was foaming up towards his knees and he had to be careful not to lose his boots altogether with every step he took. And he still could not see Tom.

But then, as Richard hung on to the aft-most handhold, looking back down the heaving deck, he saw Tom at last. The Captain had been swept on to the forward end of the next stairwell – either by good luck or by quick thinking. He was sitting there now, with his back against the upright and the water foaming against his chest, holding him upright with its simple force.

'TOM!' bellowed Richard, and the Captain's eyes flickered. Widened.

Spreading his feet as wide as they would go, Richard released his handhold and began to surge forward against the steadying pressure of the hose around his waist. He had taken ten more steps when the line behind him tightened. He was at the end of the tether – and not for the first time that night.

He stood like a colossus in the speeding flood, feeling the water snapping at the tender flesh behind his knees. 'Come to me!' he bellowed again, opening his arms.

Like a lizard with prehensile hands, Tom oozed up the wall, helped by the unrelenting pressure of the water pushing him against the white metal cliff. Little by little, spreading the wetness like a contagion all around him, Tom writhed upwards until he was standing erect. Twenty steps separated the men. Richard could go no further, so no matter what his condition, Tom must come to him. But the gap seemed huge and the Captain was white – obviously hurt. Richard strained until his ribs felt as though they would break. Another step. A second. He leaned right forward, reaching out with his long, strong arms.

And Tom plunged, frog-like towards him. Water exploded against the leaping body, seeming to reach upwards as the desperate man jumped out of its grasp as best he could. He landed on all fours, halfway home. The surface smashed him backwards, seething up over his face, but the intrepid – desperate – man would not give in. He gathered himself and leaped again. But he only managed half as far, as though he was re-enacting the Pythagorean conundrum of the frog that could only leap half as far with each succeeding attempt – and was doomed to hop for eternity.

'Well done! That's the ticket,' yelled Richard, as Tom settled back on his haunches once again. If his body gave way against the overpowering thrust of deepening water, his feet at least stayed firmly anchored now. But his face was bone-white and his eyes were closed. He had one more attempt, perhaps, within him. 'One more,' called Richard, wondering if Tom could even hear him any more. 'Come on, Tom. Go for it!'

At Richard's final cry Tom leaped. His legs heaved his body up above the grasping surface. His back straightened and his arms reached.

And his wrists slapped into Richard's palms, as though they were high on the flying trapeze. Even before the exhausted body could collapse back into the wild rush beneath, Richard jerked backwards, hurling the pair of them up towards safety. The steadying strength of the hose slackened at once, then jerked tight again as Doc began to reel them in.

It was a brief but brutal struggle, but the three of them fought it together grimly. Until, battered and bruised, Richard could pull the fainting Captain over the gushing sill and into the stairwell. It really was a well now. From knee-depth down to the bottom of the vessel, the square box of the companionway was full of the same black water as the lower car deck.

Richard turned anxiously to Tom. 'Can you walk?' he began. But his answer was a hacking cough which ended with a gurgle and a thin dribble of blood.

'That's a broken rib,' Doc told him helpfully.

'And it's damaged his lung,' said Richard. 'He needs to lie down until we can get him proper medical attention. Or sit up, more likely. But not on the bridge.'

'Thank God we've got Robin on the throttle then,' said Doc more soberly.

'Thank God on bended knee,' agreed Richard quietly. 'But she needs to know about this as soon as possible.'

Doc took Tom back to the Chief Steward while Richard ran up to the bridge. In a few brief, grim, words, he warned Robin what was going on. Had he himself been sitting with one hand on the helm and the other on the throttle levers of the engine room telegraph, he would have entered into at least a brief discussion with her. An exchange of ideas at least, a shared weighing of alternatives. But she just nodded her golden curls once, decisively, and got on with the job in hand.

Richard glanced out through the cracked and foam-smeared clearview. On the far horizon, under the swirl of the lowering storm, it was just possible to see a band of brightness which promised land just below the black heave of the water ahead, as though there were a city beneath the sea down there. 'I'll go down to the second car deck. See if I can assess how much time we've got.'

She nodded again. 'Time to the Lizard?' she demanded.

'Still thirty minutes,' answered Paul Ho.

'That's how much time we've got,' she said.

8: The Loss

Richard crossed the second car deck to the group of engineers gathered around the Chief. The Chief was crouching at the junction of the hinged forward section and the deck itself. In a dark line above his head stood the seam that stretched up through one more deck to the weather deck itself. Away to one side of him an inspection hatch stood open like a square man-hole cover opening down to the deck below. The conversation as Richard crossed the echoing chamber was hushed. When he came right up to them they fell silent and looked up at him like doctors waiting to deliver a fatal diagnosis.

Which, in a way, he thought, they were.

The seam above the Chief's head was not perfectly vertical. It was, in fact, angled through two planes. It led at an angle of perhaps eighty degrees from aft to forward along the line where the bows would open. It angled slightly but appreciably inwards from the outer flare of the bow towards the narrower 'V' of the keel. For these reasons it was not at first possible to see the stream of water cascading along its length, for the little river was contained in a decided valley and held by the Coander Effect which guides water drops in curved tracks along the outsides of bell-shaped glasses. It disappeared through the deck at the line where the bow detached from the horizontal when the front was open. Through the man-hole it was possible to see it cascading with redoubled force down the wall of the area below into the rapidly filling lake where Car Deck 3 had been.

'The same the other side?' asked Richard. Nodding across to another despondent little group.

'Worse,' answered the Chief. 'The damage was worse over there and that's the weather side.'

'How long?'

'Trying to calculate now. The faster we go the more rapidly it comes in. But the slower we go the longer it's got to flood us out. How long do we need?'

'At this speed, half an hour.'

The Chief sucked his teeth, looking very worried indeed. 'And of course,' he said, simply thinking aloud, 'the quicker we go, the higher her bow sits – and the faster my engineering areas get flooded out at the stern. Once the motors get wet we all get wet.'

'Any way you could barricade the vital areas – seal off the bulkheads and let the water drain away? It's only for twenty minutes or so.

'Look,' he continued, thinking feverishly. 'The forward car-deck door got us into this. Could we maybe open the rear ones a foot or two and let this just shoot on through while we power on home? If we could get her head up and ease up towards full ahead, we'd be at Land's End in fifteen minutes.'

Typically, this appealed to Richard. It was neat, clear and decisive. And it allowed the maximum of action.

'I can't say yea or nay,' said the Chief. 'It has a certain wild appeal, particularly as the third car deck's flooded anyway so it'd be straight in the front and straight out the back if you got it right. But you'd have to ask the Captain. If it can be done it would need to be done with a great deal of delicacy, mind. And it'd take me maybe ten minutes to prepare.'

'Go and get started,' said Richard. 'I'll talk to the Captain now.'

'Are you mad?' said Robin. 'Open the rear doors on a moving SuperCat in the middle of a storm? One big sea would poop us and we'd go down like a brick.'

'We're on our way down anyway. You need half an hour. You simply haven't got it. *Lionheart* is lost. It's just a choice of where she's going to founder and who she's going to take down with her. If you maintain this course and speed where will you be in twenty minutes?'

'The Runnel Stone,' both she and Paul answered together.

'Then that's where you'll go down. I know you've been in constant touch with the coastguard but you must see that they can't help us anyway. They haven't got a lifeboat. They certainly don't have anything big enough to get us all off. And even if they had a tug or two up their sleeves, they'd never be able to tow us home. Once the water gets up past the second car deck then we're going down. Like a brick, as you so rightly say. And there's nothing anyone can do about it. Except for us. Where will you get to if you come up to three-quarter speed?'

'If we *can* come to speed; if we can keep the engines dry; if we can open the rear car-deck door just so far and hold it; if we don't get swamped by a big wave from behind before we can start running faster than the seas and if she doesn't start porpoising again . . .' began Paul.

'Penzance,' snapped Robin. 'We could maybe make Penzance.'

'That's it then,' said Richard. 'The Runnel Stone Light with fifty metres of cold green water beneath you and a mile and a half swim up to Hellas Point. Or Penzance Harbour with maybe six feet to a safe, sandy bottom and a short stroll up to the prom. The Chief says it's the Captain's choice.'

'And I'm in the Captain's chair.' Robin hit the engine room hailer without further thought. As she waited for the Chief to answer she said to Paul, 'You'd better fasten your seatbelt. We're in for a bumpy ride. Paul, update the logs. We want this all clear when we hand them over to the inquiry . . .'

'Chief here!'

'Captain here. We go with Richard's plan. I'm easing towards Three-Quarters Ahead now. Tell me when the engines are secure and we'll open the rear doors as I come towards Full Ahead. But gently.'

'It's your decision, Captain.'

'Yes, Chief. I know.' She switched off and immediately started easing the levers forward. 'Sparks, tell the Coastguard of our change of plan. I know there's nothing they can do but keep their own log of our movements and decisions but we'll keep them up to date. Richard. Make yourself useful. I want Doc up here and both of you on watch. Tell him to bring Tom if there's any way at all he can be moved.

'Paul, I didn't really mean it about the belt. It was a line from a movie. I'll probably need that chair for Tom if he's strong enough . . .'

'Sharing the responsibility?' asked Paul, self-consciously loosening his seatbelt again as Richard turned to go.

'Looking for a bit more expertise,' she answered easily. 'And it is his ship I'm getting ready to rip apart.'

In fact Tom was nowhere near well enough to be up on the bridge but the instant he felt the change in the speed and disposition of his command, wild horses would not have held him back.

'How's she answering?' he gasped as Richard eased him into the seat Paul had just vacated.

'Well enough,' answered Robin. 'You think she's strong enough for this?'

'Built like a jumbo jet,' he answered, bracingly.

'Then we only need to get the physics right.'

'I'd say so. And the luck, of course.'

Richard stood on the port bridge wing looking ahead through the night glasses, swinging easily out to port and back to full ahead. Ahead, there were lights along the horizon now, shining from the cliffs between Land's End and Hellas Point. Nearer and brighter, but away out to port, was the bobbing flash of the Runnel Stone Light. As *Lionheart* gathered way and began to lift her head fraction by fraction, so the light got brighter but began to swing away further still from port beam to three-quarters aft.

Richard watched it and scanned the stormy sea around it with the automatic method of a practised watch-keeper, missing nothing at all with his eyes even though his mind was far away. For, at the same time as he was keeping watch, he was so utterly involved with what was going on at his right shoulder that he could sense, see, feel it all as clearly as he could hear it.

'Looks like an area of relative calm ahead,' said Robin.

'Flaw in the wind down to Force Seven, I'd say,' he answered instantly. 'Sea running low and regular as far to port as the Runnel Stone.'

'Just what we need,' wheezed Tom.

'How're things coming, Chief?' asked Robin into the mic. 'I have a window of opportunity now. Coming up to Three-Quarters.'

'Engine room secure and dry,' answered the Chief's tinny voice. 'I don't know where the water's going but it's not coming in here.'

'OK. As we come past Three-Quarters I want you to open the rear doors. One foot. On my mark. Mark!'

At Three-Quarter speed *Lionheart*'s bow should be lifting, thought Richard. But she was being terribly, terribly slow. Thank God for the low seas ahead.

But then, as the rear door lifted out of its footing and began to slide up, the whole frame seemed to leap. Richard staggered back, as though a hand had been placed in his chest to push him down a slight slope. He banged the back of his head against the edge of the hard hat Doc had not yet taken off. 'That seemed promising,' someone said.

'On my mark, another foot, Chief,' ordered Robin. 'Mark!'

Somewhere at the rearmost section of the great box-like car

deck area, the door slid up another foot, like a portcullis being raised in an ancient castle. Out from under it there gushed the maelstrom of water that had snatched Tom along the lower car deck. The head at the forward end of the SuperCat lifted further. More of the damaged seam came up out of the water. But the pressure against the larger, lower, section that was still cutting through the waves intensified almost geometrically. What had been a trickle into the equalized pressure of the bilge and forward engineering areas became a flood, spraying inwards as though through a cracked high dam. And all of it surged backwards, moved by inertia and gravity against the vessel's gathering momentum and slope. This was not good. But it felt good, for *Lionheart* seemed faster, more responsive. Or she did until they tried to make her turn.

At Robin's order, the rear door was raised another foot. The foaming gush of water no longer touched its lower edge, simply flowing out of the SuperCat, seemingly as fast as it was flowing in through the damage at the front. So the vessel surged towards Full Ahead with the Runnel Stone Light rapidly falling behind her port beam and Penzance only twelve minutes distant, round the corner marked by Mousehole. But that was still hidden behind Boscawen Point.

'Boscawen Point dead ahead,' called Richard.

'Full Ahead,' called Robin. They both said the word 'ahead' at once.

Lionheart was skimming over the relatively quiet area at more than sixty miles an hour now. Her head was up; and if her petticoats were trailing, then that seemed to be no great problem. For the moment at least.

The quiet section of sea sat before them, pushed forward by the new storm-front at almost their own fierce speed. And it remained under their flying bows all the way to Boscawen Point.

Level with the Point but still some miles out, they edged gingerly on to a new heading almost due north. This leg was designed to bring them up past Mousehole so that they could swing into the broad bay which housed the safe havens of Penzance and Newlyn, both protected from the worst of the south-westerly weather by the cliffs of the headland above Mousehole.

The adjustment to speed and heading was slight, less than ten degrees to port, but to Robin's super-sensitive hands it registered a problem. She didn't even hear Richard sing out, 'Mousehole dead ahead!' She was completely absorbed in feeling how *Lionheart* was responding.

The SuperCat's back end was heavy and even with the slight adjustment it nearly slewed out of control. They had certainly swung too far. Mousehole should be safely off the port quarter, like the Runnel Stone had been. It should not be dead ahead. More gingerly still, she eased over until everything settled back on Due North.

Richard's pride and joy – still, more than twenty years after he bought it – was an E-Type Jaguar. It was massively overpowered, in Robin's opinion, with a huge V12 engine. She had driven it once or twice, but never for pleasure. And never anywhere near its full potential. She thought rather queasily that this was like driving it at full speed with one of the rear tyres flat.

Just that little turn made the whole aft section of the Cat swing dangerously one way and then the other; and that made the hairs on the back of her neck stand up. When they got into the right position, five minutes north of Mousehole, they were going to have to swing 90 degrees to port. Nearly ten times further round than the turn that had nearly taken her out of control just now.

Her hands burned to ease back on the power but she simply didn't dare. They couldn't founder now. Not here. The coast was a grim buttress of cliffs, plunging to twenty or thirty metres below sea level. There was no safe haven – hardly even a landing spot this side of Mousehole – for anything as big and powerful as *Lionheart*. No matter what damage it did to the SuperCat she had to bring her round that tight turn north of Mousehole and into the protected shallows of the bay.

But then, as *Lionheart* settled on to her new course, she steadied and seemed content to plunge forward across the quartering sea. It would take them little more than five minutes at this speed to get to St Clement's Isle, which guarded the harbour of Mousehole. Dare she change course again here, but this time through 45 degrees to take her north-west and again 45 degrees when the hull had steadied – to settle them safely on course towards Penzance.

At least, thought Richard grimly, feeling the hull's gathering certainty after the dangerous little swing and unconsciously in tune with his wife's darkest fears, the change of course north of Mousehole, dangerous though it might be, would bring them swiftly in behind the headland and out of these ruinous seas. The bay would shelve swiftly but the only big combers would be those that swung round in their wake. And with any luck *Lionheart* would almost surf home on them.

'Coming past St Clement's Isle and Mousehole,' he sang out, only vaguely aware of how completely the swiftly passing moments were putting Robin on the horns of a dilemma. Should she risk two 45 degree turns – with the first still likely to sink them in the teeth of the storm if anything went wrong? Or should she wait for the wind shadow of the cliffs and try the full 90 degrees – hoping that if things went wrong then at least they might be able to swim across to Penzance as Richard had said.

Robin's right hand tightened on the throttle levers. She came within a whisker of pulling them back but she forced herself to release them. She transferred her right fist to join her left, both of them trembling slightly, on the neat little steering wheel of the helm. She had been thinking of Richard's E-type. This wheel was smaller than the Jaguar's; almost unsettlingly so. She looked at the course monitor – what was left of the ancient compass binnacle which Paul, no doubt, had used on his square-rigger. She tensed herself to turn through 45 degrees.

'Still water dead ahead,' said Richard gently, as though this were their sitting room at home in Ashenden, and they were discussing the doings of the day. 'If you let her run on for three or four more minutes you'll be able to make the full turn there and then out of the storm. With only a three-minute run up into the bay.' In some distant part of her mind she realized how effectively the measured calm of his tone was keeping the rising panic at bay within her.

Robin hesitated, calculating. He, and the thought he generated, was a distraction. There was no sense in which she deferred to him – nor that he expected her to. In command situations he discussed things, shared responsibility – team-built. She didn't. She made up her mind and got on with it. But his apparently unthinking collegiality distracted her. And at sixty miles an hour – with a following storm pushing her ever faster down into a valley of relative calm – she didn't have to be distracted long for the moment to have slipped past.

She looked up, frowning. She looked down. The calm closed around them in a twinkling. It all seemed to happen that quickly. The course monitor showed her that this was the optimum moment for a 90 degree turn into Penzance. And she acted. Still with the throttles at Full Ahead, she spun the wheel to port through 90 degrees.

The massive motors behind the skimming SuperCat reacted perfectly and she span through the degrees of the turn as she surged across the area of calm and into the throat of the bay. But beneath the engines, was three decks – and more – of cold green water, weighing 64 pounds per cubic foot. It weighed less than the 100 vehicles she was designed to carry, perhaps; but it was not secured. It had motion and momentum of its own. Crucially, unlike the cargo she was used to, this was not a part of the vessel. It was a free-moving, dangerously destructive entity. A loose cannon weighing hundreds of thousands of pounds.

And all of its destructive power was focused with almost fiendish ruthlessness upon the SuperCat's weakest, least stable point. As *Lionheart*'s bow swung round through 90 degrees, so the unstable mass of water deep within her took motion and continued to spin her long after the motors had settled on to the new heading dictated by the helm. Had *Lionheart* actually been the E-Type, she would be skidding wildly out of control now. And Robin reacted accordingly. As soon as she felt the rear section swing away she turned on to a counter-course, steering into the skid. Her foot automatically stamped down for a brake – but there was none there. And then it released the pressure anyway, some long-forgotten driving lesson reminding her that it was bad to brake in a skid. The vessel's square body angled, digging one hull deeper into the water. The spin intensified. Then began to ease. She glanced over at Tom but he was comatose. Somewhere along the way he had slipped into a shallow sleep.

And the SuperCat continued hurling forward at a steady

sixty miles per hour. While Robin fought to keep control of her, she leaped across Mount's Bay towards the enfolding arm of the land. Land, which protected them from the storm because it was high, rugged and solid. Land, which would destroy them if they hit it at this speed because it was high, rugged and solid. And, while the arm of the bay cut off the power of the storm, it also cut off an increasing number of alternatives as *Lionheart* surged across the bay still at full speed.

'Penzance dead ahead,' said Richard calmly.

With disorientating rapidity Robin's view through the cracked and foam-washed windscreen went from open water to a wall of land. And the wall was coming towards them incredibly swiftly, seeming to widen out to port and starboard, cutting off all hope of manoeuvring. Now at last she was forced to cut the power. But the wildly swinging vessel continued to surf forward, with the out-wash of the storm-seas behind her. 'Where are you planning to put her?' asked Tom, conversationally, jerked awake, seemingly, by Robin's simple tension.

'Newlyn dead ahead,' said Richard. And his hand closed for a moment on her shoulder. His touch steadied her and allowed him to repeat, gently, 'Newlyn.'

Robin swung the wheel over again. 'Where Richard said,' she gasped in reply to Tom. Suddenly settled and full of confidence. 'On the prom. Near as dammit. Or, more precisely, on the beach below it.' She released the throttles in their Full Reverse position. Reached forward and pushed the button on the loud hailer. 'Please fasten your seatbelts and prepare for collision,' she said. She did not need to repeat herself. 'Richard, Doc, the rest of you. If you can't strap in, then get down on the deck with your backs against something solid.'

And her order came not a moment too soon. For the shoreline was pouncing towards them more rapidly than any movement she had ever seen afloat. The coastal slopes that reached up to Penzance and Newlyn seemed as threatening as any of the great waves they had encountered so far. For all they were bright with lights – even the occasional set of headlamps desperate enough to be out on a night like this. The brightly spangled darkness reared up the sky as though the end of Cornwall were taking flight, sweeping in low over her head.

But Robin was not looking up; she was looking down. Richard and she had enjoyed a blissful week down here early in their marriage and she remembered as well as he the long sandy beach that joined Newlyn to Penzance at the water's edge. She remembered how it had been a part of the secret, almost coded language that they had shared before the twins arrived. Newlyn. Sea, sun, sand – and safety. And, because it was low tide now, the beach was long and flat. Because it was the middle of a stormy night the long, flat beach was deserted.

That was clearly the plan that Richard had shared with her – and that was as far as the conscious part of it ever got.

Lionheart's still-low rear end touched bottom. Her high-riding bows slammed down into the surf. Three keels, water-jets, the lot, tore through the bottom of the sandy bay – until the sand and the friction started some tearing of their own. The simple power of her momentum drove her on and on, as though she were a crashing aeroplane and not a sinking ship. Up out of the surf she slammed, screaming and shaking as she began to tear to pieces. The great bow waves of water became slightly lesser bow waves of wet sand.

But even when she slid out of the water altogether, she still behaved like the yare lady she was, slipping over the beach as she had sliced through the waves, beginning to swing from side to side, but never enough to pitch or roll. Only friction could slow her now, and so it did as she broke through into a softer, dryer layer and settled. But beneath the softer layer there was a shelf of rock and this gripped her at last, ripping away the broken bottom of the SuperCat, and bringing her to a shuddering stand at last.

There was a moment of utter silence as the fact that they were safe and sound ashore sank in.

And then the cheering really began in earnest.

THE INQUIRY

9: The Last Calm Day

It was the last summery day of that autumn, nearly six months after the loss of *Goodman Richard*, and there was nothing in the still, calm dawn to hint at the fury to come. Certainly, Richard had no intimation of looming disaster when he first awoke into it. He rolled out of bed a little before sunrise as he habitually did, smiled as Robin rolled automatically into the warm indentation left by his large frame and slept on oblivious. He silently shrugged on a dressing gown and padded out through the French window. If anything, at that moment, he was luxuriating in the freedom which came immediately after the teenage twins Mary and William went back to their boarding school, as they had done yesterday, Sunday, at the end of half term. The freedom, the space and the simple silence.

The master bedroom at Ashenden, like the big sitting room beneath it, opened on to marble flooring railed and colonnaded as though this were a wealthy residence in the Deep South of the United States rather than a traditional English one. The balconies looked over the blue-green slope of the achingly fragrant camomile lawn, over the formal and kitchen gardens – flower, vegetable and herb – and over the fence erected to contain the twins in childhood. Beyond the fence there was no more land. For the garden, like the house above it, stood teetering on the topmost cliff top on the southernmost reach of East Sussex's white chalk coastline.

As he leaned thoughtfully on the railing, therefore, Richard was presented with a vista of calm sea and utter peacefulness. It seemed to stretch from the Dover Strait in the eastern distance, over the western part of the Channel itself, all the way down to the French coast – a smudge of French blue on the southern horizon today – and west to the Western

Approaches. The Atlantic beyond lay, like Robin, still asleep beneath the softest blanket of departing darkness.

But there, away on Richard's left the sun was just beginning to rise. Such was the situation of Richard and Robin's beloved home that on certain mornings – like this one – when the position of the earth and the state of sky and sea were all just right, the sun came up out of the North Sea. Such mornings brought fleeting instants of green-gold glory to that dull grey sea. Just for a moment, as dawn swept over Antwerp, there was nothing but water on the curve of the earth between Richard's dazzled eyes and the slowly rising sun. For a lingering instant as the great star came up from behind the curve of solid earth the whole eastern end of the Channel lit up. At its heart there was a jewel of burning emerald, framed with darkest sapphire. Then it was as though Richard could see the long beams of gold come pouncing over the surface of the world towards him, flooding everything that he could sense with light and warmth and the bustle of a new day.

The gulls high on the cliffs beneath his feet launched themselves into the air screaming their first feeding call. A tanker heaved out of the mist south-west of him, bustling in towards Europoort, its night lights still burning. The 06.00 SuperCat scythed south towards Calais. A slower ferry steamed peacefully out of Dover. How old-fashioned the labouring vessel seemed to Richard, when put alongside the sleek SuperCat. Slow and bulky and well past its sell-by. As out of date as the *Goodman Richard*, which lay now in the chilly deeps beside Wolf Rock, as lost and drowned and dead as her Captain James Jones.

'Penny for your thoughts,' whispered Robin, so close behind him that he jumped.

He turned to find her wrapped in the duvet, eyes sleepy and hair tousled, frowning slightly in the brightness and the hour. She was not a morning person.

'I was looking at the six a.m. SuperCat and thinking about *Lionheart*,' he answered, less than accurately. 'We were lucky there was less damage than there seemed to be, both to the hull and the promenade – and that the insurers came round so quickly.'

'Good publicity,' she said. 'All those grateful kids and heroic headlines. No wonder people are fighting to ride on the things – independently of the comfort, speed and convenience.'

'Wasn't it Oscar Wilde who said there's no such thing as bad publicity?' he joked.

'Sounds more like Robert Maxwell. But I'm not sure he was right. Look at *Goodman Richard.* Captain and several senior officers presumed drowned. Hull declared a complete loss. Everyone from here to the Receiver of Wreck cutting up nasty. Poor old Charles Lee says they'll have to wind up that charitable board that ran her. He may even have to cover some losses himself. Sell one of his ocean-going racers. Perhaps even pull out of next year's Fastnet Race.'

'Really? I didn't realize,' said Richard, thinking for a wicked moment how good that would be for Doc and *Katapult.*

'Oh Richard! You're on the board of the charity yourself. It was his last letter to you that gave me the information. You must keep up with these things!' Richard was a man of action, not of letters. He could be notoriously slapdash with his paperwork.

'I've been busy,' he declared, aggrieved.

'Yes,' she relented, snuggling up beside him. 'So you have. And "busy" is putting it mildly. I don't think anyone could have done as much as you have in the time. Leaving *Goodman Richard* aside, you've put everything back just the way it was – from *Lionheart*'s bows to Newlyn's prom. Our stock is riding high again in every way.'

'Always a good thing for a publicly quoted company,' he rumbled in cheerful agreement.

There was a distant crunching of wheels on gravel, audible from the front of the house only because of the utter silence of the day.

'Papers and post,' said Richard, eager as always to get his hands on both. As he spoke, a motor revved and the wheels crunched over the gravel again, departing.

Richard was gone as soon as the sounds were, leaving Robin standing high and dry – and suddenly chilly. She lingered, frowning, some vague premonition darkening the dazzle of the day, some fey, fairy-given ability passed down from her Scottish Border grandmothers. She looked westwards, away over the Western Approaches. The blue of the Atlantic sky was marked with patterns of cloud; speckles and swirls of hazy whiteness – as though God had begun an Impressionist painting there.

'I don't like the look of that at all,' she said. And she shivered.

Richard was waiting for her at the kitchen table when she got downstairs. He hadn't brought her up her usual cup of tea, so she knew something was distracting him and had rushed through her morning routine with unusual – unsettling – speed. Something about the deceptively summery day made her fear the worst but to begin with there was nothing to sharpen her fears. Richard was sitting at the table reading. There was a big teapot steaming fragrantly from beneath its cosy, apparently forgotten. The table was laid and the makings of a continental breakfast supplemented by the aroma of simmering porridge.

'Look at this!' he said as soon as she appeared, holding out the paper. It was pink in colour – the *Financial Times*, therefore. As always he had folded it so that the article which interested him was uppermost and the headline would have drawn her eye in any case:

HERITAGE MARINER STOCK RIDES HIGH

'Just exactly what you said!' Richard continued. 'Word for word. You know you amaze me sometimes.'

'Did they interview you?' she asked, frowning over the article.

'Nope. I'd have mentioned it.'

'Hmm. I'm not convinced; we haven't actually completed a sentence since the twins came home ten days ago.'

'True enough. But I'd have told you somehow. They haven't been near me.'

'Nor me. Well they can't have talked to Daddy or Helen; they'd have mentioned it. They at least seem able to get words wedged in edgeways – even when the twins are home.' Robin's father, Sir William Heritage, and his second wife, Helen DuFour (French, Republican and most militantly *not* Lady Heritage), were senior executives of the company, with Richard and Robin. And Charles Lee, their Hong Kong Chinese finance director. Together, with some stock held in trust for the twins, the family held the controlling 51% of the buoyant Heritage Mariner stock.

'They'll have got it from Charles, then. He's the darling of the City at the moment in any case.'

'Of the chattering classes at any rate,' agreed Robin thoughtfully, still reading. 'He's such a colourful character you never know whether you'll find him in the financial sections or the social sections. Or the gossip columns. With his mistresses, his yachts, his charities. And his gambling.'

'He says he spends more in a month of sailing than he loses in a year of gambling,' said Richard. 'And he's been a great supporter of the *Katapult* series. How many of them have we sold on his say-so? To his expensive friends and contacts?'

'Hmmm.' Robin didn't sound all that convinced.

'Who was it said that sailing is like standing under a cold shower tearing up fifty-pound notes?' asked Richard.

'I don't know. But I sometimes think Charles has progressed to one-hundred-pound notes. Thank God it's his family fortune and not our salary that he's pissing away.' Robin could get quite animated on the subject of Charles Lee – and not always in a ladylike way.

Richard poured her a cup of tea as she continued to read and fulminate, 'Yes, this is Charles's doing all right. His is the only Heritage Mariner name in the whole article – and he has managed to slip in references to the Fastnet Race, his latest brainless blonde bimbo, and what on earth is *this*?'

Richard, uneasily, knew exactly what *this* was. 'The new limited edition Lamborghini Murcielago with the removable roof and . . .'

'And how much did it cost him?'

'Nearly half a million dollars. Including shipping and import costs. He bought it in New York. You can't get them here yet but he couldn't wait. Or she couldn't . . .'

'Ye Gods! Boy and toys! There ought to be a law!' She threw the paper down in some disgust and sucked fiercely on her tea, scalding her lips and adding to the darkness of her mood. 'What are those letters?' she demanded.

'Would you like some breakfast? Porridge perhaps.'

'No. I've just burned my bloody mouth on that bloody tea. Bloody porridge is not an option today. What are those letters?'

'One for you and one for me. I haven't opened them yet,' he answered evasively. And she came down on the slight uneasiness in his tone like a hawk on a hare.

'You know what they are, though, don't you?'

'Yours is from the Marine Accident Investigation Branch of the Department of Trade . . .'

'That'll be something to do with the inquiry, I suppose. Yours?'

'Mine's from London . . .'

'London? It looks like the sort of envelope that you get wedding invitations in. Or summonses to tea with the Queen. Very high-quality. Who's it from?'

'It's from Bentley Motors Limited. From Andrew Assay, their marketing director, I suppose. I've been expecting it.'

Robin sat for a moment, her face so cold it should have cured her scalded lips.

The Bentley was a sore point. A very sore point indeed.

Some time ago, when Richard had taken full control of Heritage Mariner on Sir William's retirement, the board had agreed that, as CEO, he really needed a car that reflected his importance. And the importance of the newly floated company as quoted on the stock exchanges in London, New York, Hong Kong . . .

Neither the E-Type nor the Range Rover Freelander that he and Robin currently owned would do. Richard must follow in his father-in-law's footsteps and get a Bentley.

With a certain amount of reluctance, Richard agreed. Robin, unwisely, left him to it, busy with her own concerns and thinking nostalgically of Sir William's Turbo Mulsanne and the Queen's specially adapted Red Label Arnage. This had been a ghastly mistake. She saw that all too clearly and she never ceased regretting it. It was particularly regrettable that he saw it as a huge coup, and was filled with unredeemedly boyish enthusiasm whenever they talked of it.

He had been up to Crewe to be fitted for it – as though he were going to Lobb's for his hand-made shoes or Gieves for his bespoke suits. He had agreed colour, trim and all the rest, endlessly popping across from Heritage House to the salesrooms in Conduit Street over this detail or that.

The promise of the super car seemed to ignite something in him that Robin had never quite seen before. Boyhood fantasies filled with the 1929 4.5 litre that John Steed had driven in *The*

Avengers on TV, with its racing-green paintwork, Vanden Plas coachwork and its massive gill-slitted bonnet held closed with leather straps seemed to emerge from nowhere – Robin had supposed him a fan of Westerns, not spy stories.

But no. For, perhaps more influentially still, he talked dreamily of the three battleship-grey Bentleys that James Bond had driven in Ian Fleming's original books. The 1930 4.5 litre Blower he had used until Hugo Drax's henchmen had destroyed it in *Moonraker*; the open-topped Mark VI tourer he replaced it with, until he was seduced by Aston Martin before *Goldfinger*. And the Mulliner-made, Capron-bodied dangerously supercharged Mark II Continental with which he had swept his soon-to-be wife off her feet in *On Her Majesty's Secret Service*.

In short, sent out to buy a sedate saloon, he had instead bought himself a Bentley Continental GT sports car, in silvered steel, with battleship-grey interior – or as close as the people at Bentley would let him come to it. Or, more accurately, he had added his name to the long list of prospective buyers. It had a huge 6-litre, W12, turbocharged engine and could go from 0 to 60 in a good deal less than five seconds; and (downhill and with a following wind) it might be expected to top 200mph. But never, of course, in England. Even with a full range of mouth-watering extras, the Bentley cost much less than half as much as Charles Lee's Lamborghini, which it could, at a push, outperform. But that did not appease Robin at all.

Nor did the fact that it was a breathtakingly beautiful, if immensely powerful and toweringly impractical car – broad-shouldered and slim-hipped; long-nosed and a little brutal. Two-doored – if four seated; seeming to close out the twins altogether, and invite aboard ladies like Charles Lee's – John Steed's and James Bond's – lissom fantasy escorts, rather than the practical, down-to-earth mistress of Ashenden.

All of which got on Robin's nerves as absolutely as it had got under Richard's skin. Which was some going for a vehicle that neither of them had actually seen yet – let alone driven.

In not very companionable silence they each slit their envelope open. Robin spoke first. 'Yup. That's it. The inquiry into the wreck of the *Lionheart* will be held at the magistrates' court in the Guildhall, Penzance, one week from today. I must attend, according to this. My travelling expenses and loss of earnings may be defrayed on application but not the cost of any legal representation I might elect to bring. Lucky I wasn't proposing to take any then.'

'Why haven't I got one of those?' demanded Richard, who had been more closely involved than Robin in the legal – and financial – results of the adventure so far.

'You weren't in the driving seat, my love. You weren't even in a fit state to drive, as I recall.'

The acid comment caused the blue dazzle of his gaze to fall, prompting her to ask at once, 'Yours?'

'You were right. It is an invitation – though not quite to tea with the Queen. The Bentley's due in next Monday. Can I go up for final fitting, test drive and such?' Even though he fought to keep his tone matter-of-fact, she caught the tremor of excitement in the gravelly rumble of his voice.

'I'll drop you at the station on my way down to Penzance,' she offered. 'Unless you want to take the E-Type up and garage her at Heritage House while you get to know the new love of your life.'

'Don't be silly, darling. I'm coming down with you. I daresay I can pick up the Bentley anytime.'

'No, love,' she persisted with gentle, honeyed malice. 'You've been looking forward to this for simply ages. I dare say picking up the Bentley will be much more complicated than giving evidence to an inquiry. It'll be the simplest formality I'm sure. You pick up the Bentley and drive on down to join me. It's a bit extravagant taking two cars all that way, but I love driving the Freelander and it'll give you a great opportunity to test your new toy. You can introduce me to her personally by taking us both around Cornwall for a day or two after we've finished. I expect I can garage the Freelander at my hotel down there. You never know; it might be good fun!'

'Well,' he temporized, wracked between guilt and desire. 'We'll see.'

And so, unknowingly, they sowed the seeds of disaster before they had even had breakfast.

It was that kind of day.

10: The Falling Glass

In fact, after a week of distractingly hectic effort on both the social and professional fronts, Robin left for the inquiry in Penzance on the next Sunday. One or two questions soon revealed that *Lionheart*'s Captain Tom Bartlett had been summonsed, as had Sparks and the Chief. Doc had gone back to Australia in the interim and by all accounts it wasn't held to be an important enough hearing to summon him back. There had been damage to the hull – since fixed; damage to a beach – since repaired. There had been no loss of life. And the facts of the matter had been presented by the media in a manner unquestioned by any of the bodies involved and seemed to be clear and undisputed. The inquiry was just dotting a few *i*'s and crossing a few *t*'s for the sake of legal form.

Robin's attendance might be the merest formality, but she wished to prepare for it by settling in to her hotel and getting a good night's sleep. It was a six hour drive to Penzance in any case. Leaving at 3 a.m. to be certain of arriving for 10, seemed to Robin neither advisable nor practical. Especially as she and Richard had capped the week off with a charity ball at the Grosvenor House in London, arranged by Charles Lee, on the Friday night.

Richard had still received no summons – but they thought little of it, for his involvement in the actual damage to *Lionheart*, by chance, had been less immediate than hers. When the inquiry into the loss of *Goodman Richard* was set up, he expected to be summonsed to that. But to the *Lionheart* inquiry? Perhaps not. They tried to contact Andrew Atherton Balfour, their solicitor and friend, but the best they could do was to catch a distant glimpse of him and his dazzling wife, the barrister Margherita DaSilva, at the ball on Friday night. Charles, expansive, ebullient and surrounded by glitteringly expensive women as always, had shown neither knowledge of nor interest in the *Lionheart* inquiry and so they pursued the matter no further.

Richard in particular had also been so frantically busy during the daytime overseeing the deployment of the last of the new SuperCats on their cross-Channel routes – with all the resultant publicity, glad-handing and meetings with everyone from Heritage Mariner part-board to insurers and the Department of Transport – that he was hardly at home in any case.

Their return home from the ball in the wee small hours of Saturday morning was the first time that Robin and he shared a bed since he had rolled out of it and wandered on to the balcony last Monday morning. Had he not been asked especially by the vicar to perform his duties as churchwarden at matins, he would probably have stayed up in London for the whole weekend. Certainly it would have made much more sense to pop across from Grosvenor House to the Heritage Mariner company flat on Leadenhall Street rather than driving back to Ashenden through the night. But Richard, tee-total for more than twenty years and full of restless energy despite the strain and the work, didn't mind a midnight spin – even through driving rain.

So, as things were, they spent a tense and snappish day together at home with Robin packing and Richard fussing, then they rose late, broke their fast coldly and went to church. They returned in silence, ate cold cuts again, locked up Ashenden and left.

It was a grey and gusty day, a fitting representative of the whole week, which had seen the unobserved glass in Richard's untenanted study falling steadily and the needle swing relentlessly from WET to *STORMY*. As Robin drove south-westwards towards the nearest en route town where Richard could catch the London train without adding too many more miles to her Penzance drive, the clouds thickened threateningly, the day darkened relentlessly and the wind thumped increasingly powerfully against the high sides of the Freelander.

'Looks like it'll be a nasty journey,' said Richard glumly as the first squall of rain dashed across the square windscreen like a handful of gravel.

'For you but not for me,' she answered. 'This lot is staying in the east. It's warm and sunny west of Worthing. I may sunbathe on Newlyn prom before dinner. I shall certainly be taking a long walk to think things over.'

The opening phrase of Robin's dark and vaguely threatening answer rang a distant bell deep beneath his conscious mind which distracted him from any other messages it might have contained. Apparently inconsequentially, as he stood alone on the windswept, streaming platform, waiting for the London train, an hour or so later, he found himself singing the old First World War song so beloved of Lord Peter Wimsey in Dorothy L. Sayers' famous detective novels:

> *'The bells of Hell go ting-a-ling-a-ling*
> *For you but not for me*
> *And the little Devils all have a sing-a-ling-a-ling*
> *For you but not for me . . .'*

On a more conscious level as he sang, Richard found himself reaching into the capacious store of useless knowledge that he – in common with many sea-farers – carried around with him. The fruits of long night watches enlivened by books, newspapers and magazines without number. Hadn't 'Mrs Merdle', Lord Peter Wimsey's car, been a Bentley?

No other thought could have seduced him away from worrying about Robin's long drive – and the inquiry to which it was leading – but this one did. Which was why, one might suppose, Robin mistrusted the whole idea of the Continental GT in the first place.

Hardly surprisingly, Richard had the first-class compartment to himself as the train sped Londonwards. It was Sunday lunchtime – others like him who habitually came up from the country in such luxury as the train companies offered would all be at table at home now; recently returned from post-sermon, pre-prandial pubs, awash with best bitter, gin and good-humour. Their prospects would be of roast meat followed by brisk walks through woods with dogs or across golf-courses with friends; thoughts of travelling to town far distant from their minds.

There was a feeling of illicit adventure to the experience, therefore. One which was compounded almost deliciously as he opened his weekend case and brought out from beneath his neatly folded clothes the bright stack of brochures and booklets that Bentley had supplied him with in preparation for tomorrow. The shiver of anticipation – foreign and poignantly novel to the cheerfully monogamous family man – was something he supposed equivalent to re-reading passionate, secret correspondence from a glamorous mistress awaiting his arrival in some secluded little love-nest.

He had just finished when the train pulled into Charing Cross and he hopped out into the stormy afternoon. He loved walking around London and would normally have marched up the Strand and along Fleet Street towards Leadenhall and Heritage House. But such a move on such an afternoon would have been simply stupid, so he stood in the shelter of the great terminus's awning and hailed a cab.

'Where to, guv?' asked the driver in an interesting mixture of Cantonese and Cockney intonations.

'Leadenhall, please. No. Wait. Let's go to Conduit Street first.'

'Lighty-ho. But it's in the opposite direction.'

'I know. I just want to look in at a showroom there.'

'Lighty-ho.'

'Are you local?'

The cabby laughed. 'Not what you call "local", guv. Even you not count grandparent and parent born Canton, I work Hong Kong till ten year ago.'

'I thought I recognized the accent.'

He stood outside the closed Bentley showroom like a child outside a sweet shop, oblivious after all of the pouring rain and the squally wind whipping round the corner out of Regent Street.

'You thinking of buying one of those, chief?' asked the cabby as he climbed back in.

'Captain,' corrected Richard thoughtlessly.

'You buying one then, Captain?' repeated the cabby cheerfully.

'Continental GT. Had it on order for a while. Picking it up tomorrow.'

'Not sure as I approve, mind.'

'What do you mean?'

'Well, it's nor really British any more your Bentley, is it? I mean it's all bits and pieces from Audis and Volkswagens. Even if they is all screwed together at Crewe.'

'I know what you mean,' answered Richard thoughtfully. He too had entertained some doubts for he had always driven cars that were designed, manufactured and built in Britain. From the E-Type to the Freelander. And had been happy to do so. But there was something about what the new management had done with the post-Arnage generation of Bentleys that he found impossible to resist.

The conversation that unwound between the captain and the cabby as the cab rolled back along Regent Street and Haymarket into Trafalgar Square and then away east towards the City, became very technical indeed. And so intense that even when they reached the corner of Leadenhall and St Mary Axe, the cabby simply switched off the meter and stayed parked until they had finished it. Though whether either of them convinced the other of his own point of view remained a thoroughly moot point.

Richard ran over to the unremarkable little door at the side of Heritage House that opened into the lift lobby beneath the flat. He opened it and walked through into the lift. A few moments later he was shrugging off his wet coat in the all too familiar environs of the company flat. Even though he had spent much of the week here, the place seemed cold and unwelcoming. It was still and silent – as though no one had entered for years rather than days. He looked around the sterile opulence, lost in thought; suddenly a little lonely. The list of contacts in the book beside the phone did not tempt him however. Lonely, he nevertheless did not feel like company. All he felt, apart from Robin's absence, was a stirring of hunger. He knew the contents of the fridge and fancied none of it. Nor did he particularly fancy exploring the locality in search of a supermarket. Though as it was after four on a Sunday they would most likely be closed in any case. Uncharacteristically hesitant, he stood, wavering, until the quietest of sounds distracted him.

With the bustle of the City stilled as well, it was so quiet that Richard could even hear distant voices from the H.M. communications rooms that sat atop the huge building just a soundproofed wall away. He resisted the immediate, almost overwhelming temptation to go through and chat to the staff who manned the place 24/7, overseeing the movements of the fleets of tankers, ferries, container ships and specialist waste transporters that his company owned. Even in the Crewfinders office he would prove a disruptive distraction. Here the branch of the company he had founded himself supplied crews of any sort and any size for any purpose to any ship in any legal situation anywhere in the world at twenty-four hours' notice. This required masterly organization, split-second timing, constant updates on the whereabouts of officers and crew on call as well as almost limitless minute-by-minute awareness of which seats were available on what flights going where; so any interruption could be fatal.

He stood for a moment longer, therefore, looking around indecisively, then he glanced at his watch and reached for his coat again. It was well after five. And high time for Chinese.

It was surprisingly easy to get another cab. This one also was driven by a Hong Kong Cockney, but Richard was more struck by the coincidence that a Chinese driver should be driving him to a Chinese meal than by the fact that this was the second such cabby. He stepped out of the cab at Gerrard Street and went into his favourite restaurant in the heart of Chinatown.

Suddenly almost ascetic, he eschewed the full-flavoured, the battered and the deep-fried, in favour of a dinner that was largely steamed. The rice was plain and fragrant, served in porcelain bowls as light and fragile as the lotus blossoms on which they were modelled. Eaten slowly with the finest of chopsticks, though even their needle-ends seemed too clumsy for the little bowls. Chicken and fish served only with the lightest sauces of lemon and garlic, ginger and chilli. Noodles with the faintest deepening of sesame and soy. Tea that only the most discriminating of palates could distinguish from boiling water.

The food was so simple but so exquisite, it transported Richard back to the years that he and Robin had spent in Hong Kong themselves. Years when he had mostly been stressed and exhausted; irate and almost impossible to live with. Not that he was all that much better now, allowing her to go down and face the inquiry alone while he ran off like some kid in a toy-shop after his boy's-toy Bentley. He was suddenly overwhelmed with a disorientating combination of guilt and tenderness so powerful it verged on self-pity. Chewing on a strand of ginger, he found himself wondering how on earth Robin had ever put up with him over all these years. And whether she would bother to keep up her indulgence in the future.

He pulled himself to his feet, paid and left. He hesitated at the door, pulling on his coat and looking out into the drizzling murk. He would walk back to Heritage House, he decided. The weather would suit his mood. He pulled up his collar, thrust his hands deep into his pockets and strode out towards Cambridge Circus. He was lost so deeply in his thoughts that he never really registered how quiet things around him had become. It was after six on a wet Sunday evening. The rabbit warren of streets that form the border between Chinatown and Theatreland were empty and shadowed. He knew them as well as he knew any of his past commands, however, and he wove his way decisively homeward, like a well-programmed robot. He had no idea at all that he was being followed.

The three muggers hit him all at once. He was big and they were teenagers so they used as much impact as they were capable of. One swept his legs from under him while a second hit him over the head with a makeshift club – a mercifully skimming blow that glanced off without doing much harm. And the third, following up with a kick to the temple, fortunately forgot that he was wearing trainers. Then they all fell to rifling his pockets as swiftly as they could.

Richard himself was only faintly aware of most of this of course. For a moment he was certain he had slipped and hit his head. By the time the stunning reality of the situation hit him fully, he was really too late to do anything other than to roll over and try to pick himself up. But even as he did so, he found himself at the eye of a different kind of storm. Three figures became six. Hissing of rain on the pavement was lost in the gasping of breath mingled with squeaking of footsteps on slick slabs. The rumble of the gusty wind was lost in the grunting of fighters and the soft thunder of blows. Then there were only three figures once again, the steady, strong shapes gathering around him as the other three ran off.

He was too disorientated even to think of defensive action as they reached down towards him. But these hands had come to help him not to hurt him. They helped him to his feet and held him there as he regained his breath and faculties. As his vision cleared he saw three tough-looking Chinese teenagers, none of whom was even faintly familiar to him. They were holding his wallet and his cellphone.

'You all right, Captain?' one of them asked quietly. For a disorientating moment it was as though he were talking to the first cabby.

'Yes, thanks. Fine.'

'Good. You want we call a cab? Cab be safer now.'

'I'd rather call the police!'

'Police not such good idea, Captain. Those three will be punish; we see to that. You call cab. Go back Heritage House now. Get your rest.'

It struck him then. These youngsters knew him. Really. Personally. He recognized not one of them but they all knew exactly who he was.

'Who are you?' he asked.

The leader of the trio smiled and he saw that she was a girl. 'My name is May Chung,' she introduced herself, handing back his wallet and taking his phone from her colleague. 'I was an officer cadet on *Goodman Richard*. I detailed to help the wounded but you help me *bettah*. You heave me on to *Lionheart* by the seat of my pants, Captain. You really save my ass.' She gave a throaty chuckle and he found himself smiling in return. He remembered her very clearly indeed.

The cellphone began to ring and she held it out to him. 'It's for you,' she said, and stepped back into the shadows.

It was Robin, gruffly reporting her safe arrival. By the time he finished talking to her – a brief and monosyllabic conversation which mentioned nothing of attempted muggings – a cab had pulled up at the end of the street. Its driver's window wound down to reveal a cheerful Chinese face which was calling, 'You go Heritage House now, Captain?' in Hong Kong Cockney tones.

11: The Gathering Storm

Richard stood naked in the bathroom of the company flat and surveyed the damage, thinking of May Chung's words and deciding whether or not to call the police after all. His knees were bruised – but no more badly than at the end of the last game of football he had played with the twins. His torso and ribs were OK. Arms and elbows likewise. Better, in fact, than they had been at the end of that brutally energetic game. The twins' version of football was by no means a non-contact sport.

He approached the glass. There was a welt across his cranium he could feel – in both senses of the word: as a lump and as a sore patch – but which he couldn't see. His temple seemed muddy – grimed, like his raincoat, rather than bruised – but nothing that a little cleaning wouldn't put right. No more wounds seemed apparent. No more aches and pains. Nothing, in short, that a good soak in a hot bath wouldn't fix. And a visit to the dry-cleaner's for his coat.

His cellphone was undamaged – as Robin's call had proved. There was nothing missing from his wallet and nothing else missing from his pockets.

Very well then. Nothing to worry Her Majesty's Finest over. He turned away and ran the bath.

An hour later he was stretched sleepily on the sofa wrapped in snowy terry-towelling, steaming contentedly as the video player sprang to life. It was a video he had been dying to watch – but one that he had hardly dared put on when Robin was anywhere nearby. The picture cleared. The enjoyable prickle of guilt returned. The voice-over began:

'No sooner had the First World War ended than British motoring exploded into life. Scores of ambitious individuals decided to start making cars. Motor companies sprang up in

sheds and garages all over the country – most of them one-man enterprises. But very few would even survive the 1920s.

'One of those who did survive was Bentley Motors, guided by its founder, W. O. Bentley himself.

'Walter Owen Bentley, seen here at the wheel of the very first 3 litre prototype which took to the road at the end of 1919, was born in London in 1888 . . .'

Richard was up well before eight and found himself to be surprisingly hale and supple, given his adventures of the previous evening. He bathed, shaved and dressed, then he did go through into Heritage House proper. He was starving and by no means inclined to forage for himself. But years of experience had taught him that Bridget, the cook whose genius enlivened the directors' dining room every lunchtime (and, indeed, the staff canteen come to that), arrived a little after nine, always well-supplied and usually happy to indulge him in the matter of bacon, eggs and coffee. And so it proved today.

At 9.40, replete and restless, he called down to James the doorman for a cab and left the raincoat with Sam the lobby porter – who agreed to get it cleaned a.s.a.p. – on the way out at 9.45. This time he did not talk to the cabby, preferring to let the man concentrate on getting out of the City and into Mayfair by 10.

At 10 a.m. precisely, he strolled off Conduit Street and into the gleaming reception area of the Bentley showroom, his heart pumping like that of a schoolboy out on his first hot date. At 10.01 he was seated in the office of Sales Director Andrew Assay and the final formalities were getting under way over two sizeable cups of Blue Mountain coffee and cream.

The car itself was waiting for him just behind the showroom and he talked inconsequentially to Andrew Assay, trying to contain his impatience as one of Andrew's acolytes ran a soft cloth over its gleaming, slightly silvery, steel-grey paint work for one last time. 'We have set the seats for yourself and Mrs Mariner,' Andrew was saying. 'Though we could have been just that bit more accurate if she could have come and sat in it. And we have programmed that information into the keys of course. This is yours and when you use it everything in the cockpit will be set for you. It's easy enough to readjust if there's a mix-up and you use Mrs Mariner's key of course. Or one of the spares that haven't been pre-programmed.'

Andrew handed over a bunch of electronically enhanced keys and cards. Continuing to explain the security and safety systems, he crossed to the car at last and opened the driver's door. The interior light glistened off walnut veneer as dark as tortoise-shell, and battleship leather with that same parade-ground gleam as his shoes. The aroma of the cockpit filled the showroom as though this were Chanel, not Bentley.

Richard slid into the seat, easing his long legs out and finding the practical patterned steel of the pedals perfectly at his feet. As was the steering wheel to his fists. The winged B gleamed in the lozenge of battleship leather almost level with his heart. He glanced up. The rear-view mirror was precisely set.

The door clicked shut. Automatically, moving with almost dream-like intensity, he reached for the safety harness, his eyes flicking to the door-mounted rear-view, each as perfectly positioned as all the rest. His left hand settled on the gear lever. Andrew slipped into the passenger seat beside him. 'Now, Captain, just before you start her up, there are one or two more things here to remind you about. Then we'll try one final little test drive, shall we? The tank is full of course and, as you see, the tax disc is current. We've paid today's congestion charge too. You updated your insurance as we discussed . . . ?'

Oddly, considering the way he felt about the Bentley, Richard was never nervous about driving it. Even the first time he eased the sleek, steely body out of the narrow gates and swung left down Conduit Street, he seemed to know the size of the car as though he had been driving it for years already. The immediate surge of power under his right foot was always under perfect control. The power-steering was so firm and precise. The combination of drive-controls on the steering wheel and the solid gear lever under his left hand was so unfussy that he was soon happy to experiment with the automatic system before settling on to the manual gearing he preferred – and upon which he had insisted from the outset.

'Those test drives at Crewe seem to have been an excellent

investment,' observed Andrew, as the Bentley swung out of Bond Street into Brook Lane, heading for Grosvenor Square. The satellite navigation system tracked them round the street-map of London, observing rather than directing, because no destination had been keyed in as yet.

'It's fine,' agreed Richard made terse by excitement. 'Once round the square, if they'll let us past the American Embassy, then back to Conduit Street if that's OK.'

'Fine.'

On Andrew's word, Richard's phone began to ring.

'Can I get that for you?'

'Thanks. It's in my jacket pocket.'

Andrew slid the phone out and opened it. Then he placed it in the cradle of the hands-free system and pressed a button.

'Richard? Hello, Richard? Are you there?' Robin's voice came out through the hands-free speakers. They were sensitive enough to register every nuance of her tone – and she sounded very worried indeed.

'Yes, Robin?'

'Richard. Thank God. Look, darling, something's not right here. You should have received a summons, apparently, and they're talking about contempt of court or some such. But that's not all. It's all turning into a witch—' The signal began to break up outside the American Embassy. Richard guided the Bentley round the square, licking his lips and waiting for her to come back on. '. . . Andrew Balfour. When can you get here?'

Andrew Assay whispered, 'Where is she?'

'Penzance. Robin, I didn't catch that last bit. Shall I get Andrew?'

'Talk to him. I'll text him. Bring him if you can. But get here.'

'Six hours to Penzance . . .' whispered Andrew.

'I can be there in six hours . . .'

'Four if you disregard the speed limit.'

'I'll try to get Andrew and bring him with me. See you in six or so. Don't worry, darling.' He broke contact but carried on speaking. 'No point in getting speeding fines, Andrew. Court'll be closed at four.'

'Sounds nasty.'

'It does. But I don't know why. Can I drop you on the corner of Conduit Street? I need to get to Heritage House then on down.'

'Certainly. And remember, if things get tense, she'll do 198 mph or so.'

'Nothing,' said Richard, slowing, 'will ever get that tense.'

Richard drove from Conduit Street to Heritage House and risked the single yellow line outside the side door as he ran up to the flat. Because he was still on the Crewfinders list himself, he always had a case there packed and ready to go at a moment's notice. He grabbed this, looked around, decided nothing else would be needed that he could not get hold of down there and returned to the car. A traffic warden in her late teens was standing beside the gleaming wing, pen poised but immobile. Her eyes were wide and almost worshipful. Inconsequentially, Richard thought, *And I thought traffic wardens hated cars!* 'I'm just moving now,' he said, keying the central locking and popping the boot. He slipped the case inside and closed it. She still hadn't moved. He opened the driver's door and climbed in. 'It was an emergency,' he said to her. 'Thanks for being so understanding.'

'No, sir,' she said. 'Thank *you.*'

Glad of the congestion charging that kept the once-choked streets clear, Richard guided the Bentley into Threadneedle Street, then down to Bank with Mansion House and Ludgate Hill beyond. Careful not to be distracted by the suggestions of the satellite navigation system, he negotiated his way down Fleet Street into the Strand and up through Trafalgar Square to Piccadilly, then back towards Mayfair, heading for Knightsbridge, Hyde Park Corner and the A4. The Bentley had its own ideas about the best route and to begin with these did not sit well with his own preferred pathways.

But Richard needed to be driving almost on automatic pilot as he tried to work out what on earth had spooked Robin so badly. Clearly there was some kind of witch-hunt in progress. And by the sound of it he was the witch being hunted. Beyond that he could see nothing but groundless speculation. But within that there was one clear course of action. He must contact Andrew Atherton Balfour. Andrew would be able to advise – might even be able to come and represent him. And in any case, by now Andrew should have received Robin's text and have a better idea of what exactly was going on. But the complex lane-system round Hyde Park Corner was by no means the best place to start calling one's solicitor.

The phone began to ring, just as Richard was swinging into the left-hand lane that would ease him round into Knightsbridge. A black cab cut him up, the cabby gesturing through the window.

Richard did not gesture in return but he did tap the button on the hands-free. 'Mariner?'

'Richard? Andrew Balfour. I have Robin's text. Where are you?'

'Hyde Park Corner. How about you?'

'Harrods. Shopping for Maggie.'

'That's handy. I'll be coming past in about five minutes. Can I give you a lift anywhere while we talk?'

'To Penzance by the sound of things. Maggie'll be grumpy but I'll placate her. It's only another Bar dinner. And I'll get my partners to cover my bread-and-butter in the meantime.'

'Good of you. I'll be outside in about three minutes.'

'I'll be there. It's quite exciting really. A bit like *ER*: doctor on call. What'll I look for?'

'Bentley Continental GT. Steel grey.'

'Bloody hell,' said Andrew.

Then, 'Bloody hell,' said Andrew again as he settled into the passenger seat and looked around as Richard accelerated away towards the Brompton Oratory. 'I'll bet Robin just *loves* this. Have you gone off your trolley? Talk about second childhood!'

'Cheaper than your old Aston Martin, I'd say.'

'Really? But probably no cheaper than the new DB.' Andrew sounded speculative suddenly. 'Still, what are the specs?'

Richard smiled. 'Later. We have six hours. Four, if I disregard the speed limit, I understand. But first of all, what did Robin's text say?'

'Well, it didn't actually use the words excrement and fan, but it left me in no doubt that one has hit the other.'

'How? Why?'

'Well, she's not a lawyer of course, so she's a bit out of her depth, but there seem to be several things going rapidly from bad to worse. First, the inquiry seems to be much more formal than she supposed. Lawyers all over the shop and one or two pretty high flyers. She mentioned Quentin Carver Carpenter. Never liked him. Something genuinely sinister about him in my opinion. Still, Maggie'll give us the lowdown on him if she ever speaks to me again because he's a member of her chambers. And that's very worrying of course.'

'Why?'

'They're the leading specialists in shipping law.'

'I see.' Richard thought through the implications of that for a moment, then proceeded. 'OK. What next?'

'Extremely formal court. Very High-Church if you see what I mean. Everything by the book and stuffy. Chairman, Mr Justice Somebody-Important, took it very badly that some of the summonses had not been served. Particularly upset that you aren't there. Silly old dinosaur. And an aptly timed observation if I might say so – isn't that the Natural History Museum?'

'It is. Anything else?'

'Something she can't quite put her finger on.'

'This sounds like a hell of a text.'

'I'm reading between the lines for most of it. But it does mention the vile Carver Carpenter. And it does mention *Richard*.'

'Well, I know it mentions me, Andrew. That's part of the problem surely.'

'No!' said Andrew as Richard negotiated them into the right-hand lane on to the Hammersmith Flyover and began to accelerate away towards the M4 motorway. 'Not you. The other Richard. *Goodman Richard*. The square-rigger that was wrecked with her captain and senior officers lost. Still no sign of them, is there? And a coroner's court is sitting on them currently, I understand. Well, not *on them*. On their disappearance. It'll be ruling Death by Misadventure, "Lost, presumed drowned", soon, I should think.'

12: The Road to Lookout

Richard and the Bentley's satellite navigation system fell into perfect harmony after the Hammersmith flyover – largely because he did what it told him to do. And the car did exactly what he told it to do, so that, while the potent thrill of the drive was never far beneath the surface, he was able to speculate with Andrew as to what was really going on.

'Have you upset the police or Crown Prosecution Service lately?' asked the solicitor as they sped past Heston Services at the start of the M4. 'Because this seems almost like some kind of a trap. It certainly looks as though someone orchestrated something.'

'But who? What? *Why?*'

Andrew's answer was forestalled by the ringing of his own phone. He spent the next few minutes in animated conversation with his wife and they had roared past the M25 interchange before he could talk to Richard again.

Richard, too, made good use of the interim. He caught enough of the gist of the conversation – one which turned around such practicalities as clean underwear and fresh linen – that he was struck by the obvious himself. And so he took the opportunity to leave a message with Robin's answering service asking her to make sure there were rooms – beds at least – for the pair of them at her hotel. The distractions were enough to put Richard's final, comprehensive three-part question firmly on the back-burner – for the moment at least.

There was silence for a little while after the phone conversations before Andrew roused himself from a brown study to observe, weightily, 'Women! Eh?'

'Indeed. But what about them in particular?'

'Unpredictable. Maggie doesn't seem to give a toss about

the bar dinner – she's already lined up half a dozen alternative escorts I bet – but she is outraged that I've come away without packing an overnight bag. How can I go into a court without a clean shirt? Will I have cleaned my teeth? Brushed my hair? That sort of thing. God it was like talking to my mother there for an instant.'

'There'll be shops in Penzance. Marks and Spencer if nothing else. And I dare say someone at the hotel will press your suit if need be.'

'That's what I said. Fuss about nothing if you ask me.'

'That's all she's worried about, is it?'

'Yes! Well, actually, no.'

'What?'

'Two things. Carver Carpenter and Justice Cross. She doesn't want me appearing in front of Carver Carpenter looking as though I've come through a hedge backwards. You know they're at the same chambers? Of course you do.'

'I can understand that she might want you to look your best in front of a professional rival.'

'Stands to reason, I suppose. He'd use whatever he could to undermine her. They're chalk and cheese. She's very social. Politically as well. Very trendy. He's the opposite. Conservative to the nth degree – probably conservative with a small *c* but you never can tell. Very cliquey. Trouser-roller of course.'

'Well, if it's important that he's a Freemason then he's scored one over on her she can never get back. They don't generally let women in the Masons.'

'One of the things she's touchy about. One of several, in fact. Of course he's a member of the M.C.C.'

So was Richard but it had never occurred to him that the admittedly male-dominated Marylebone Cricket Club could be used as a weapon against women. And he thought he remembered seeing Andrew in the distinctive egg-and-bacon striped tie that members wore.

'Not to mention White's . . .' continued Andrew mournfully.

'OK. I give up,' said Richard. 'I can see why she's touchy.' White's Club, the oldest in St James's, had an exclusively 'No Women' rule. Had maintained it since the late 1600s, if he remembered correctly.

'And Carver Carpenter is as nothing compared with your

Inquiry Chair. Mr Justice Cross,' concluded Andrew. 'She certainly doesn't want me showing her up in front of that picky old buzzard!'

'Lucky you'll just be sitting in the public gallery, then,' said Richard cheerily. 'We haven't actually retained you formally for the inquiry, so you don't have to get all gowned up or anything.'

'That's the thing. That's where Carver Carpenter is. In the public gallery. He's not there in any official capacity to do with the *Lionheart* inquiry, either, according to Maggie. But he's there for some reason.'

'Some reason to do with Shipping Law.'

'Has to be. And something to do with the powers that be. He's got all sorts of ambitions. All sorts of contacts. If he had a soul, he'd have sold it by now. If he can find a safe seat he's off to the Commons by all accounts. He'd like to be Attorney General, they say. He just can't make up his mind which party he belongs to. Can't decide who'll win the next election, I suppose. But he never does anything without an ulterior motive. And he sure as hell doesn't come cheap.'

'So he's there because there are financial or political pickings?'

'In the area of Shipping Law,' said Andrew once more, thoughtfully.

'Hmmm,' said Richard uneasily.

They stopped for a snack in the services at Taunton, something of an education for Andrew, who, childless and therefore protected from modernity, had never tasted a flame-grilled bacon double cheeseburger and fries. Perhaps fortunately, the experience left him speechless. Richard turned on BBC Radio 3 with the Travel Alert as they pulled away and they listened, uninterrupted, to selections from *The Flying Dutchman* as they drove south-west through the gloom. They had just left the M5 to join the A30 across Bodmin Moor when Robin rang again. It was just coming up to 4 p.m. and Mr Justice Cross had risen early, in the continued absence, as he bitterly observed, of several vital witnesses. She was just about to confirm their rooms and would talk further when they arrived. Both account and battery needed topping up on her phone, so the conversation was brief.

'We'll be there before six,' called Richard before she broke contact. 'What's the name of the hotel again?'

'The Lookout on Britons Hill.'

In the silence after contact was broken, the pair of them looked gloomily ahead across the moor. The hilly flanks heaved up towards the misty skirts of cloud that hung, drizzling just in front of them.

'I thought it was supposed to be hot and sunny down here,' said Richard, as the rain-sensitive wipers began to stir.

A huge red buzzard skimmed across the bleak landscape in front of them, its wingspan fully six feet wide, seemingly the size of a golden eagle. It banked and overflew the car, unimpressed with the Bentley's power and beauty, deciding, as lord of all it surveyed, whether or not to kill and eat it.

Robin brought the pair of them back to Richard's three-part question over dinner at The Lookout Hotel three hours later. They had already been talking for half an hour over a very reasonable selection of starters, largely of fresh local seafood, more of which was in prospect for the entrée. She had described the proceedings in as much detail as she – as a lay person – could remember. The first thing that had struck her was that Mr Justice Cross was obviously not the Chair the inquiry had been expecting. This had become clear at once for he had introduced himself gruffly to all and explained that Justice Fiona Goodbody was regrettably indisposed. But as he had been available, qualified and happy to replace her, it had been felt by the Ministry, the Marine Accident Investigation Branch and the Lord Chancellor's Department that the inquiry should proceed as planned.

'But he seemed to have been fully briefed?' asked Andrew.

'He was on top of everything that was going on, if that's what you mean,' answered Robin.

'They were very lucky to get another marine specialist to replace Fiona Goodbody at such short notice,' mused Andrew. 'But, as I was saying to you, Richard, with Quentin Carver Carpenter there into the bargain, luck may not have had all that much to do with it.'

'I don't know about that,' said Robin. 'And I don't know what the rest of the people involved were expecting. But they sure as hell weren't expecting Mr Justice Cross. He gave them all a rough ride from the first instant until the last.'

'Did they ask you any questions?'

'Other than where you were? No. They took testimony from the coastguards and the local lifeboat people, establishing state of weather and sea; the general situation for shipping that night. Particularly shipping in trouble. And around Wolf Rock. Then they asked Sparks some questions. Then they took lunch. This afternoon it was Tom Bartlett and the Chief.'

'They seem to be going pretty slowly,' said Richard.

'They're not. It's because there's quite a complex situation. The Marine Accident Investigation Branch of the Health and Safety Executive have a team there of course. But then so do our insurers. Did they tell you they'd be doing that, Richard?'

'They said they'd send someone down. Routine oversight. Nothing to worry about.'

'Well, it doesn't look routine. That's all I can say. There's a team from the local authority, of course – it was their prom after all. There's a sharp-looking oriental QC from London too. He's there apparently to represent the interests of some of the *survivors*. That's what he called them anyway. And Carver Carpenter keeps scurrying off to talk to this little collection of suits, but they're just watching from the sidelines. So far.'

'So what you're saying,' said Andrew, thoughtfully, 'is that an apparently low-key inquiry into a well-documented largely resolved incident, has been hijacked by a high-profile hatchetman in the shape of Judge Cross and we suddenly have four top-flight legal teams cross-questioning everyone who gives evidence?'

'That's about the size of it. Yes.'

'In fact the only people who are not represented – who didn't even get their summons served correctly – are the people who were in command of the vessel in question during the incident in question. Who own the vessel in question. Who actually effected the rescue of some one hundred officers and cadets from the other vessel, whose inquiry date has yet to be announced. And, indeed, who buggered up the promenade in question, come to that.'

'Yup,' said Robin. 'That seems to be about the size of it.'

'It's like the Ides of March all over again! And Heritage Mariner is playing Julius Caesar. Or, at least you two are. You've been set up.'

'But how?' asked Robin desperately. 'By whom? And *why*?'

'I'm damned if I know,' said Andrew. 'But I'd keep a damn good lookout at the inquiry tomorrow if I were you.'

13: Inquiry

'All rise,' called a voice Richard obeyed but could not identify. Robin stood at his side. Her hand crept into his and he squeezed it with gentle reassurance. He looked up into the public gallery, seeking in his turn the reassurance of Andrew's cheery face. No sign. He was probably still at Marks and Spencer trying to find a shirt. He had no trouble in identifying the little group of 'suits' that Robin had described, seated in the middle of the front row of the gallery. And, in their midst, the sharp-faced faintly familiar-looking individual who could only be Quentin Carver Carpenter QC. And as Richard was looking up, so Carver Carpenter was looking down. Their eyes met for a disturbing instant. Richard turned to face front.

Mr Justice Cross entered as he did so. There was no problem in identifying him for he took the ornate central seat on the highest level of the stepped dais which most of the court-room faced. He was not wearing wig or robes but was dressed in a charcoal three-piece suit with just the faintest of pin-stripes. It was exquisitely tailored to his spare and lanky frame. The dazzling white of his shirt – starched at collar and cuffs – was set off by the richness of a damasked silk tie asserted by a tasteful gleam of gold at pin and links. A ring gleamed by a bony knuckle as he laid his bundle of notes and papers on the bench, then bowed – half nod, half shrug – to the assembled Court of Inquiry and sat. His face was long, lined, ascetic and surprisingly dark of hue; his hooded eyes gleamed like the points of gold at cuff and tie-front. His hair was thin, black and shiny as a patent-leather skull-cap.

Cross nodded again and some official – was it the Clerk to the Court? Clerk to the Inquiry perhaps? – rose and read out the nature of the proceedings. As this worthy droned on, Richard continued to look around. The Penzance Guildhall court-room was a large, theatrical space. Like their church at home, it was two full stories high, rising in the middle straight to a vaulted ceiling but with a galleried balcony on three sides. On the third wall, facing the body of the room, hung a portrait of the Queen and the arms of the local authority.

Under these sat Cross, alone behind a long desk with an empty chair at each shoulder. Before him, at a lower desk, sat other officers of the court: the one that was speaking, someone keeping a record and another Richard could not identify. In fact, he only recognized one other face down there – that of the usher to whom he had identified himself at the door – along with Robin and everyone else who occupied the witness seats down here. The court officers were all in business suits, not robes, but they all had an unmistakable air of belonging there. At one end of the largely vacant lower level of this stepped dais stood what seemed to be a witness box.

Crowded on to two tables right at the front of the room, facing Chairman Cross and his acolytes, were the four teams of barristers Robin had described. Each little group wedged against the table was backed up by a larger cohort on the chairs immediately behind. There were quite a few of these and they stretched right across the room, in some places three rows deep. Then came the chairs filled by Richard and the others summoned to give evidence. Behind him a smattering of teenage faces – many of them oriental – some of the cadets rescued from *Goodman Richard*. With a shock that genuinely shook him, he recognized the face of the girl who had rescued him from the muggers. What was her name? May Chung. Almost guiltily he turned and continued examining the layout of the court-room in front of him, wondering why there were so few of them actually here.

There was what he supposed to be a press gallery back against a far wall, sideways-on between Cross and the four sets of barristers. And, opposite, the dock; vacant now because there was no one here accused of any crime.

Well, that was the theory at least.

And, when Cross started to speak, the theory seemed to be standing safely in practice. Or rather it did so to begin with. His voice was deep and mellifluous, his tone mild. 'We established yesterday that *Lionheart* was a well found, properly maintained, fully insured vessel. She was duly and legally at sea with the full knowledge of the relevant authorities, in the possession of well-known and well-respected owners – to wit Heritage Mariner, a public company quoted on all the major stock exchanges. And under the command not only of an experienced, senior company captain but also of not one, but two owners' representatives with a visiting expert in the handling of multi-hull vessels of all sorts.

'She was properly crewed for the type of voyage she was undertaking upon the day in question. What the Captain referred to as a "testing run" or the Chief Engineer called a "shakedown".

'We established that a dangerous storm arrived in the Western Approaches with unexpected dispatch, catching many vessels large and small by surprise and over-stretching the resources of the coastguards and the Royal National Lifeboat Institution. And we established that under these circumstances *Lionheart*, very reasonably, abandoned her testing run and ran for safe haven.

'We saw, however, that it was at this point that a distress call from the sail-training vessel *Goodman Richard* was received – whose circumstances we know, and the inquiry into whose loss has yet to be called.

'Under the circumstances appertaining on the afternoon in question, however, it does not seem unreasonable that the commander of such a vessel as *Lionheart* should attempt some kind of rescue. (The traditions of the sea, in fact, require it even if the law does not, in so many words.) Nor that, given the damage occasioned to *Lionheart* in the completion of that rescue, her commander should take all reasonable steps to ensure the safety of his own command, her crew and those he had successfully rescued.

'What we must seek to establish today, therefore, is whether there is any obvious failure of commission or of omission by the men and women in command of this vessel at the time. Whether the steps that were taken were in fact reasonable, given the damage occasioned to the hull of the *Lionheart* and the municipal works upon which it came to rest – to wit, the beach between Penzance and Newlyn. Whether the actions thus taken were reasonable under the circumstances or whether they might in fact have occasioned further and unnecessary danger or injury to the individuals so recently taken aboard. Many more of whom, I observe, are in the room as summonsed today. Whether, in fact, the actions of those in command of *Lionheart* at the time in question contravened any current legislation under the Health and Safety at Work Act and more recent ancillary legislation. Whether the damage to the hull occasioned in that very rescue was reasonable and inevitable – or whether it too could have been foreseen and avoided with no significant further danger to life. Who, in fact, was actually in command of *Lionheart* at these crucial points in the incident. And where any criminal responsibility might lie, should criminal responsibility be found and proven.

'But, before we proceed to that, may I satisfy myself that *all* the witnesses summonsed have arrived today? Even those so notably absent yesterday? Mr Clerk? Your list of those present before us?'

The Clerk to the Inquiry stood up and said, 'All present according to my list, My Lord.'

'Very well.' There was a moment's silence as Cross looked almost lazily around the chamber. 'Mr Snipe. I believe you will wish to open today's proceedings for the Department.'

The representative of the Marine Accident Investigation Branch of the Department of the Environment, responsible for the oversight of health and safety matters under such circumstances, rose weightily. 'I do indeed, My Lord,' he said, automatically reaching for the folds of his gown before remembering he was not wearing one. 'I would like to call, as first witness to these events, Michael O'Malley Weary.'

A stir ran round that section of the room who knew who – and where – Doc Weary was. But on Snipe's call, the door through which Cross himself had entered opened again and a computer monitor was wheeled out into the room. Its screen flared into life and Doc's face stared out of the machine. 'We have been fortunate in arranging this live video-link through the good offices of our colleagues in Sydney, Australia,' said Snipe. 'Mr Weary, as you are, I believe, fully aware, this is a Court of Inquiry. It is not a criminal proceeding but it is governed by the rules of perjury. You have taken the oath, have you not?'

'Yup,' said Doc, after an instant. The instant it took the light-beam of communication to get there and back. It made him seem a little hesitant. Almost calculating.

'Very well. We have also taken the opportunity, as you know, My Lord, of formally establishing identity and domicile so that we may proceed with examination with all dispatch, though under your control, of course. Now, Mr Weary, my name is Snipe and I have some questions for you. Then others of my colleagues may have further questions. As may My Lord himself. They will introduce themselves as My Lord switches from one Webcam to another. Do you understand?'

'Seems simple enough.'

'Quite so. Now. You were on the command bridge of the *Lionheart* at the moment she ran on to the beach at Newlyn?'

'That's right.'

'Were you in a position to see what speed *Lionheart* was doing?'

'Yes. She was going at about twenty knots when we struck.'

'In your seafaring experience, and as an accepted expert on multi-hulled vessels and their behaviour, is this a considerable speed for such an incident?'

'It's a fair speed to be doing anything at. But Captain Mariner had brought the speed down from nearly three times that as she completed the final turn and approached the beach.'

'Captain Mariner. Not Captain Bartlett?'

'No. Tom was injured. He was there but he wasn't in control.'

'Let me get this quite clear, please, for it confirms a point raised in evidence yesterday. Captain Bartlett was on the bridge but Captain Robin Mariner was in command because Captain Bartlett was hurt?'

'That's about the size of it.' Doc's great gold-maned head nodded.

'And Captain Richard Mariner?'

'He was there but he was hurt as well . . .'

Step by step, first Snipe and then the others led Doc back through the events of the afternoon and evening. Everything that could be checked was examined relentlessly through the withering clarity of 20/20 hindsight wielded by men whose experience of the realities of such danger came from the reports of precedent cases.

Was Captain Mariner competent to control such a vessel – particularly under such circumstances? Couldn't a truly competent captain have brought *Lionheart* to a perfect standstill resting on the sand – allowing disembarkation with no damage? Was the damage to the beach – in his expert opinion – strictly necessary? The damage to the hulls?

Wouldn't it have been feasible, in fact, to choose some other port of destination? Could he, as expert witness and Fastnet Race skipper, suggest anywhere? Some less dramatic mode of arrival? Was he aware of the potential for whiplash injuries in such a peculiar method of coming ashore? Had he himself seen any crew or recently rescued passengers hurt in any way? Had he been below at any time during the voyage in from Wolf Rock? Was he aware that several people had slipped over and sustained some injuries during the wild – some might say reckless – changes of course during the run in?

In his opinion was the speed with which that section of the voyage had been taken *wise*, under the circumstances? Was this speed something that Captain Bartlett had ordered? Captain Richard Mariner? Had he advised it himself, as the expert, under the circumstances?

What part had he played in the removal of the cadets and crew on to *Lionheart*? In his opinion, could a multi-hulled vessel such as *Lionheart* have been better positioned in relation to the wrecked vessel to effect the rescue? No? Then could such a uniquely configured vessel have been better positioned to limit damage to her own hull? No?

And what exactly was his relationship with the Captains Mariner and Heritage Mariner itself? For how long had he been their friend? For how long had he been their employee? Did he wish to reconsider any of his answers – bearing in mind that relationship and balancing it against the fact that he was on oath?

Five minutes after Justice Cross had ended the video link and Doc's computer image had been wheeled out of the room, Robin was in the witness stand. Identified, recognized by the inquiry and duly sworn in. Snipe, once again, went first.

'Captain Mariner, can you explain what experience you have had in actually . . . ah . . . *driving*, for lack of a better word, SuperCats?'

Robin explained how she and Richard had both been trained and retrained as the vessels became more modern. Would the court like to see her current certification?

'No, thank you, Captain. I believe the inquiry can accept that both yourself and Captain Mariner are fully qualified. Let us pass then on to why you took over the . . . ah . . . *driving seat* . . .'

'The helm, Mr Snipe,' she corrected gently.

'Indeed, Captain. Why you took over the *helm* when you did.'

'During the early part of the voyage Doc had been in the First Officer's seat on the Captain's right. When we went in to attempt the actual rescue, Doc went with Richard and left that seat vacant. I sat in it because I could strap in more securely and see what was going on. But Tom – Captain Bartlett – remained in control of the helm. He took *Lionheart* in for the rescue itself and held her there on heading 262, if memory serves, during the transfer. He remained in control until everything had been done and we left *Goodman Richard* to come round 108 degrees and head due east to run on back to land. It was not until *Lionheart* began to behave unusually that he took Doc and Richard to see what was up. I took control then, but as far as I was concerned Tom was still in command and I was following his orders.'

'And when did that situation change?'

'When Doc returned with the news that we were flooding below, and that Tom and Richard had both been injured. I then saw it as my responsibility to get *Lionheart* back to safety as swiftly as possible.'

'But there was a problem with that, Captain Bartlett has explained. Can you fill us in on what that was?'

Robin, tersely, did so.

'I see. So you sought to balance the speed of your progress

towards safety with the rapidity with which such speed would make the flooding in the decks below worse?'

'Those were the horns of my dilemma, yes.'

'And Captain Richard Mariner and Mr Weary were soon both well enough recovered to support and advise?'

'Yes. Just about. Though they were both utterly exhausted and in my opinion suffering from exposure. I would not have relied upon them over my own thoughts and experience, under the circumstances. In fact I needed neither support nor advice. Even from an expert such as Mr Weary.'

'And Captain Bartlett?'

'Again, returned to the bridge – at my request – but by no means fit enough to take full control. We discussed matters but the command decisions had passed to me. I recorded the time precisely when we made up the logs later.'

'*Made up* the logs?'

'The machine records, black box and computer files are contemporaneous. Like the record being made of this inquiry. The human bit has to be written up as soon as practically possible. Like the notebooks of a police officer after an arrest. The time lapse does not call their authenticity or accuracy into question.'

'Indeed. And your command decision was . . .?'

'To head for Newlyn Bay as fast as we could.'

'Why?'

'If we weren't careful we would sink in deep water and on a night like that we would all die. Speed was of the essence therefore, though it brought with it the problems of flooding and handling to which you have referred.'

'I see. Why Newlyn?'

'All the nearest land was cliff-bound. The bays on the western coasts are narrow, steep sided, rocky, lacking in beaches and open to westerly weather. Newlyn and Penzance are sheltered, with a gently shelving beach. I calculated that if I could get into Mount's Bay I could run *Lionheart* safely aground with a minimum of damage to all concerned.'

'I see. Well I believe that satisfies the Department for the moment. Perhaps my colleagues . . .'

And so Robin stood for another half an hour answering and re-answering questions. No, she could not have put *Lionheart* in any other bay. No, nor on any other beach. No indeed; nor on any other part of the beach. No, she could not have risked approaching the beach more slowly. No, she had no idea there was a rock shelf beneath the sand. No, she had neither the time nor the inclination to calculate the rock damage to the hulls – she had been too preoccupied with ensuring that the hulls stayed above the water. No, she had not personally assured herself that everyone was strapped in safely before she had come back to speed. No, she had not broadcast a warning before making a sharp turn off Mousehole. Yes, she had likewise failed to signal to those below that she proposed to make a sharp turn in the midst of Mount's Bay. But finally, yes, she had of course warned everyone aboard of the impending impact with the beach at Newlyn and advised them what action they should take to keep themselves from further harm. Like her husband and co-Director of Heritage Mariner, she had been fully briefed on the new health and safety rules as well as on all the recent Corporate Murder legislation.

This final answer seemed to take the wind even from the sharp young London silk's sails. And into the silence, the mellifluous tones of His Lordship proposed, 'Let us rise for the short adjournment there. And this afternoon we shall hear the evidence of Captain Richard Mariner . . .'

14: Arrest

'That seemed to go pretty well. You were fantastic, darling.' Richard passed Robin her keys to the Bentley as though they were a prize. 'What did you think, Andrew? Pass the vinegar, would you?'

They were in a fish restaurant down by the sea-front and Richard had a sizeable plate of cod and chips in front of him. Robin and Andrew seemed less hungry. They were contenting themselves with tea and toast, both a great deal less ebulliently confident than Richard.

'No,' temporized Andrew in reply to his main question. 'There was nothing obviously amiss. Nothing you could put your finger on. But even so . . .' He frowned and shrugged. Vinegar slopped over his hand.

'No sign of a trap at least.' Richard sprinkled the condiment as he talked, then filled his fork and tucked in heartily.

'That's the point of a trap, darling,' said Robin, slipping the keys into her handbag, but speaking as though explaining something to a wilfully obtuse child. 'You're not supposed to see it. Until you're caught in it.'

'But what have they proved?' asked Richard. He put down his knife and began to count off his answers by holding up his fingers, continuing to demolish the fish and chips left-handed. 'That *Lionheart* was in the right place, under the right circumstances, doing the right thing. That the storm was unexpectedly powerful and swift-moving, so that there were many vessels large and small at risk. That the coastguards and the RNLI needed a hand and *Lionheart* gave them one. That she was under appropriate command and control at all times. And even when things got hairier and hairier step by step between Wolf Rock and Newlyn prom, we all – and especially you, darling – took exactly the correct action. Even under the new H and S rules and the Corporate Killing legislation. Though why that should be relevant God alone knows: you kept everyone perfectly well alive.'

'No one could have died since, could they?' demanded Robin suddenly, her cup halfway to her mouth. 'Some cadet with a weak heart or crewmember with an unsuspected ailment? So that they're turning round now and saying it was our fault we didn't take better care of them once Richard had pulled them safely off *Goodman Richard* herself?'

'No,' said Andrew, shaking his red head decisively. 'We'd have heard. At the very least it would have been in all the papers. And in any case, they can't just spring a charge like that out of the blue. There's such a thing as Full and Proper Disclosure, for God's sake.'

'There you are then,' said Richard, who had reclaimed his knife during the exchange. 'I'll fill in any blanks they ask about this afternoon and we'll have a celebration dinner in the Lookout tonight. Then you and I will take the Bentley round the county for the rest of the week, Robin. I want you two to get to know each other. Can you reach the salt, Andrew? You know, this is the best fish I've tasted in years! You really should have tried some . . .'

'Now, Captain Mariner, we have it in your wife's evidence that she assumed command when Captain Bartlett was injured. And the logs were made up to that effect as soon as was reasonably practical.' Snipe was fiddling with his invisible robes again. 'And indeed, we have the logs themselves.'

'That is correct, Mr Snipe.' Richard took the front of the witness box, rising and falling slightly on the balls of his feet as he talked.

'*Correct*, Captain, but, I would submit, not quite *accurate*.' Snipe had hold of his lapels now and his hands were still.

'I'm afraid I don't quite follow . . .' Richard settled on to the flats of his feet. The blue dazzle of his eyes narrowed as his mind raced.

'In fact, Captain, as owner of both vessel and company, you were, in effect, the controlling mind, no matter who sat in the Captain's seat; no matter who controlled the helm. No matter what the logs seem to record. Is that not so?'

'No. I don't think that is right.' Richard shook his head decisively. 'I agree that I am Chief Executive Officer of Heritage Mariner and I also agree that Heritage Mariner owns *Lionheart*. But I would submit most strongly that I would never overrule a captain whose appointment I had approved, on his own bridge.'

'Even under circumstances as extreme as these?'

'There is no point, surely, in appointing an expert to a command post and then trying to second-guess him when he faces the circumstances one appointed him to face.'

'A good theory, Captain. But is it one you could adhere to? Especially when that commander becomes injured and has to be replaced – by your wife, let us say?'

Richard leaned forward a little, his face folding into a frown. 'Again, I disagree with your contention, Mr Snipe. My wife is the best qualified officer I know and I would trust her with my vessels and my life.'

'Very noble,' said Snipe, almost insultingly dismissive. 'So, it was Captain Bartlett, was it, who first suggested that he should take his command to the rescue of the *Goodman Richard*?'

'Yes,' answered Richard roundly. Then he thought, rummaging through his memory before repeating, 'Yes it was.'

'And the Captain would have made that decision absolutely without influence from you? Without the slightest knowledge, let us say, that you were yourself closely associated with the stricken vessel?'

'I couldn't say, Mr Snipe,' Richard replied formally – frostily. 'You would have to ask him that.'

'I have, Captain. And he assured the inquiry that you made no secret of the fact that you knew the vessel, and many of the people aboard her.'

'Then those will be the facts of the matter, Mr Snipe. Though I do not remember making a great point of the relationship with *Goodman Richard* or the charity board responsible for her.'

'Well, well. I'm sure that is the case, then,' said Snipe in turn. He released his right lapel to move some papers on the desk in front of him before he proceeded, silkily: 'But furthermore, Captain, is it not also the case that, once the decision had been made and *Lionheart* was proceeding towards Wolf Rock, you personally talked to every member of the crew about their responsibilities with regard to health and safety and even about the new Corporate Killing legislation?'

'That is correct. As I understand the legislation, my position on the board of Heritage Mariner might make me liable to arrest for Corporate Killing should my company be the cause of death through any action or omission. I wished everyone aboard to be duly aware of that.'

'Indeed. So, whether under your *effective* command or not, *Lionheart* proceeded to Wolf Rock.'

'That is correct,' answered Richard a little huffily.

Snipe smiled coldly. More of a grimace than an actual expression. 'And can you describe what you found there?'

'The *Goodman Richard*?' Richard asked, as though slightly confused.

'Indeed.' Snipe was dismissive of Richard's hesitation; suddenly impatient. 'Please tell us what you found of the *Goodman Richard*.'

'I can certainly do so but I don't quite understand, Mr Snipe. This inquiry is into the wreck of the *Lionheart*, surely?'

'It is, Captain. But in order to understand the damage the *Lionheart* sustained, we must be able to envisage the condition of the vessel you took her alongside. You can see that, surely?'

'Very well.' Richard cleared his throat and frowned with thought, rummaging in his memory again for the facts that would master this sudden change of tack. '*Goodman Richard* was effectively dismasted. She had lost her mainmast and her fore. They had taken her boats along one side, and those along the other were also damaged. No doubt because the spars and rigging were still attached and had smashed the boats that had not been destroyed in the first disastrous dismasting.

'We were further informed that her captain, James Jones, had taken his senior officers – except for First Officer Ho – in the last seaworthy lifeboat to seek help. There was no way for those remaining on board to abandon. And they needed to abandon somehow as a matter of urgency because the hull was flat on its side and in danger of rolling right over because it was beam-on to the seas . . .'

'Technical jargon if you must, Captain, but please explain it as you go . . .' Chairman Cross spoke for the first – and last – time during Richard's evidence.

'Certainly, My Lord.' Richard paused, cleared his throat again, rephrased his vivid description. 'The seas were extremely steep and fast-moving and they were coming in along the ship's side, causing her to roll further and further over while at the same time driving her rapidly down on to the reefs below the Wolf Rock Lighthouse. The situation could hardly have been more dangerous.'

'I see, Captain.' Snipe paused, almost as if he had lost the thread of his examination. Then he looked up in open enquiry, asking simply, 'And what did you do then?'

'I discussed with Captain Bartlett the possibility of taking *Lionheart* on to the lee side . . . The down-wind side of the ship. *Goodman Richard* was very large – four hundred feet in length – and she was sitting high while being held firm by the rigging lost overboard with her masts. I estimated . . . Captain Bartlett and I estimated that the hull would form an effective shield against the power of the storm while a couple of us might therefore have a chance to go aboard her and see if we could help.'

'And, in short, Captain, you and Mr Weary did just that?'

'We did.'

Over the ripple of sound that went round the court on the simple, modest admission, Snipe continued, 'That was very brave of you, Captain.'

'I thought it my duty to help, Mr Snipe.'

'The newspapers have been speculating that you might be expecting some award for your bravery.'

Richard's eyebrows rose in genuine surprise. 'That's the first I've heard of it. I believe I did nothing but my duty.'

'Just so,' said Snipe, once again almost dismissively. 'Your personal duty, Captain? Or your corporate duty?'

Richard's eyebrows came down again and gathered into a frown. It was a frown of real confusion. He had no idea how expertly he was being manipulated. 'I'm afraid I don't understand you, Mr Snipe.'

'Ah. Well. Perhaps we'll return to the point later. In the meantime, you and Mr Weary went aboard, while Captain Bartlett, with your wife now at his side, held *Lionheart* in the position you had ordered?'

'In the position we had discussed, yes.'

'And it was in this position that an unfortunate change to *Goodman Richard*'s situation led to the damage that sprang such a near-fatal leak?'

'I assume so, yes. But it is speculation. An extremely large wave caused *Goodman Richard* to rear catastrophically. Her side hit *Lionheart* with what might be described in boxing terms as "an uppercut". I should imagine that it was this that broke the seals on the moveable bow sections.'

'But, nevertheless, you managed to get all of the crew and cadets off the stricken vessel – in spite of its disastrously dangerous condition. And *Lionheart* suffered no further damage until your wife ran it up on to the beach at Newlyn.'

'Thus saving not only the *Lionheart*'s hull, but the lives of all of those aboard her; yes.'

'So you say. But, Captain, I would be glad if you could just clear up one last point for me, could you?'

'If I can.'

'At what point did you give your Corporate Killing speech to the crew and cadets of *Goodman Richard*?'

'I beg your pardon?'

'I believe you heard the question, Captain. I can't believe you are suddenly bereft of hearing or of understanding at this stage.'

'But I never gave any such speech to the people aboard *Goodman Richard*. Why on earth should I? We were there to rescue them! I didn't think I . . .'

'Didn't think what, Captain? Didn't think that you owed them the same responsibility as you owed the men and women aboard *Lionheart*?'

'Well, of course not . . . No. I didn't!'

'But we have established, surely, that it was your association with *Goodman Richard* that took *Lionheart* to Wolf Rock in the first place . . .'

Snipe grasped both his lapels very determinedly indeed and sat back down again.

The door into Chairman Cross's room opened as though this had been some kind of a signal, and one of the suits who had sat clustered around Quentin Carver Carpenter came out. He mounted the third level of the raised platform and whispered something into the Chairman's ear. Cross nodded once, looking across at Richard.

'Captain Mariner,' he said. 'Could you please step into the office?'

The man in the suit came down again and came forward towards Richard. Richard was struck simply – and solely – by how young his face looked. 'Could you step this way, Captain?' he murmured, like a doctor leading a son to his father's deathbed.

Richard suddenly went cold, deep inside, just as though he had been impaled with an icicle. 'It's the twins,' he thought. 'The twins have had an accident.' He glanced across towards Robin. She was seated, frowning. Her face as white as marble beneath her golden curls. Her eyes huge.

The young man took him by the arm and led him up the three levels – two steps up each – to the door. Behind it there was quite a mundane-looking office. Richard stepped into this, struck, if anything, by the ordinariness of the place which had housed His Lordship, the Chairman of the Inquiry. And by the ranks of vivid, beautifully tooled law books on the shelves around the walls.

'Captain Mariner,' said the well-suited young man, calling Richard to himself.

'Is it the twins?' asked Richard, still terrified.

'No, sir. It's not the twins. It's something else.'

Relief flooded through him. At once his mind cleared and his faculties returned to their normal height.

The young man in the suit was getting something out of his pocket and Richard recognized it at once. It was an ID card. The young man was a police officer.

Richard suddenly became very focused indeed.

'Captain Richard Mariner,' the young man said formally, 'I am arresting you for the Corporate Killing of James Jones, Captain of the *Goodman Richard*. I must caution you that you do not need to say anything. But it may harm your defence if you do not mention when questioned something which you later rely on in court. Anything you do say may be given in evidence.'

Richard opened his mouth, then closed it again, too wise to utter the first words that sprang into his mind: *For God's sake make sure that the Bentley's safe and sound.*

THE TRIAL

15: Snow Job

Richard was in shock. He was also in a situation far beyond his experience. He had been arrested once, in Hong Kong, but that was long ago and in circumstances utterly different to these. He experienced the succeeding hours, therefore, as a series of intensely vivid, almost dream-like experiences which came individually, without apparent pattern or any meaning beyond themselves.

The young police officer who had arrested and cautioned him took him gently by the arm and began to lead him towards the street door. 'Wait,' said Richard, slowing.

'We can't do that, Captain. There is a car waiting.' The arresting officer gently pulled him into motion once again.

'But my wife is in the court.'

'She will be kept fully informed, sir.'

'My solicitor . . .'

'You may contact your solicitor in due course, Captain Mariner, but we must hurry now.'

'My solicitor is in the court.'

'Then I'm sure your wife will talk to him as soon as she has been informed, sir.'

At the door stood several uniformed constables. As Richard and the arresting officer reached them, so they moved to form a blue-walled passage from the court-house door to the door of the waiting police car. Both doors were open. Behind the constables' square and solid shoulders, the contents of the press gallery, almost magically enhanced, jostled and shouted questions. Lights for videocams blazed like spotlights, flashes for cameras exploded.

Richard had no alternative but to get into the rear of the police car and the arresting officer sat beside him, pulling the door firmly closed. 'Where are you taking me?' he asked. The car began to move.

'To Snow Hill police station. That is where I am based.'
'Snow Hill?' asked Richard. 'Is that near here?'
'No, sir. Snow Hill is in London.'
'Oh for God's sake! All my stuff is down here. My car—'
'It will all be taken care of, sir, you must not worry about that. But we must get on. This is a very serious situation.'
Richard was silent for a moment. Then he said, 'Yes, of course. I see now . . .'
And those were the last words he spoke until he was seated in the interview room at Snow Hill Police Station, Snow Hill, London EC1. But in his mind, he began to go through everything he could remember from his briefing on the Corporate Killing law. He had been briefed on the new requirements and responsibilities as the CEO of Heritage Mariner, of course. That was what he had applied to the situation aboard *Lionheart* in the incident which caused the inquiry he had just left. But now he began to apply it to his actions as a member of the *Goodman Richard* charity board.

Robin stood in the pandemonium of the inquiry room, almost as shocked and disorientated as Richard in the room next door. His Lordship had announced that the proceedings were suspended and left the bench. The court officials and the teams of lawyers were all bustling away, as though they were completely au fait with what was going on. But nobody else around Robin seemed to know any more than she did. 'What on earth's going on?' asked Tom Bartlett.
'Damned if I know,' said the *Lionheart*'s Chief. 'Sparks?'
The young Radio Officer shook his head.
'Where have they taken Richard?' Robin asked.
They shrugged. 'Into that room . . .'
'But *why*?'
Andrew arrived, having fought his way through the confusion, looking, thought Robin, as though he had been through a hedge backwards after all. 'I know why,' he puffed. 'I think we'd better go somewhere we can talk.'
His tone chilled Robin – but not as much as the sight of the uniformed female PC who followed hard on his heels. 'Please come with me, Mrs Mariner,' she said formally. 'I have news for you.'

'Is it my children? Oh God, it's not the twins, is it?'

'No, Mrs Mariner . . .' The PC took her by the arm.

'It's Richard. They've arrested him,' said Andrew, taking her other arm.

'This is my solicitor,' said Robin to the PC. 'He goes with me.'

'Very well, Mrs Mariner.'

She led them to a small ante-room and sat Robin on a spectacularly uncomfortable bent-wood chair. 'I have some bad news for you, Mrs Mariner. Your husband has just been arrested. He is being taken to a police station now. He may be formally charged there in due course.'

'Arrested? What in heaven's name for?'

'I understand he may be formally charged with Corporate Killing, Mrs Mariner.'

'That's ridiculous. Richard hasn't killed anyone. For God's sake, we've just got through proving that he saved more than one hundred lives!'

'I'm afraid that's all I can tell you, Mrs Mariner. I suggest you return home and await events. You'll be contacted there.'

'I'm not going to go back to East Sussex and leave him alone down here, woman! I'll stay here with him. See what's going on. Arrange bail—'

'But he isn't here, Mrs Mariner. They've taken him to London. I most strongly suggest that you go home and wait there for news. We have a team of specially trained officers waiting if you or your family needs any further support . . .'

The seemingly innocent and supportive words hit Robin like a slap in the face. This had all been carefully planned. They had been preparing this for sufficient time to have organized a support team for her in East Sussex. She recalled her conversation with Richard over the fish and chips only a couple of hours ago. There had indeed been a trap. And now it was sprung. And Richard, it seemed, was firmly caught within it.

She began to get angry then. 'Right,' she snapped. 'Thank you, constable. Tell your superiors that they'll be hearing from me.'

The PC rose and left.

'How bad is it?' Robin asked Andrew.

'Hard to say. Looks bad. They've arrested him for Corporate

Killing, according to the people I talked to. They're taking him to Snow Hill in London to lay charges, apparently. You were right about a trap. Jesus, this looks like a snow job to me.'

'A snow job in Snow Hill.' Robin laughed, a little hysterically.

Andrew frowned. 'You don't seem to realize quite how serious this is, Robin. I thought you'd been briefed on the new legislation. It's been long enough coming, after the *Herald of Free Enterprise*, the Ladbroke Grove crash, Paddington, Potters Bar, Southall and Hatfield. Rail disasters and so forth. But it's here now, and with all the teeth they promised, designed to hold corporate executives personally and criminally liable for failures in their companies that lead to death. Beyond even the old Gross Negligence Manslaughter laws that most of these matters have been dealt with so far. Corporate Killing is equivalent to Murder in the eyes of the law.'

'Murder!'

'Yes, Robin. Murder.'

'Richard has just been accused of *murdering* James Jones?'

'Effectively, yes. That is what the new Corporate Killing law means. He was the controlling mind behind the failures that led to the Captain's death. But this is the first time a case has ever come to court, of course. That's why they've taken him to Snow Hill. And it explains Carver Carpenter too, I should suppose.'

'What do you mean?'

'This looks like the first major trial of a high-profile piece of flagship legislation. It's a trial in all senses of the word, Robin. The legislation is as much on trial as the accused – the thinking behind it, the interpretation of it – the words that were used to phrase it. It's all going to be tried by the judge, almost as much as Richard is. That's why everything is being done so carefully by the book.'

Andrew took a deep breath and then continued, his open, boyish face unnaturally earnest. 'This is front-page stuff, Robin. Six O'Clock News all over the world. Snow Hill is the nearest police station to the Old Bailey in London. If that's where they're charging him then that's where they'll be trying him. The Old

Bailey; Court Number One, if I'm any judge of the matter.'

'This isn't *bad*, Andrew, it's terrifying! What on earth are we going to do?'

'Well, fight, of course. But step by step. The first thing we need to do is go back to the hotel, pay the tab and pick up our stuff. Then we need to get back to town and start putting a team together.'

Suiting the words to the action, he took her gently by the arm again and pulled her to her feet. Then, as they walked increasingly purposefully out of the Guildhall and up towards the hotel – blessedly unmolested by reporters for the moment – Andrew continued to talk.

'They'll hold Richard at Snow Hill until they charge him, which they have to do within the day unless they get special extension. Which isn't too hard these days to be honest: *Habeas Corpus* isn't as strong as it once was. But they won't have got this far without something fairly solid to hand. So they'll charge him. We'll see him, of course, probably after the fact now, but we'll be able to arrange bail I'm sure.'

'Bail for murder?'

'You'd be surprised. It's his position as a leading international businessman that'll exercise them most, I expect. They'll ask for a surety and a substantial security as well. They'll take his passport and set up a fairly rigorous routine for reporting in. May even tag him, I suppose. They won't want him disappearing to somewhere far afield they can't extradite him from like old Ronnie Biggs in the sixties.'

'But I'll be able to take him home?'

'Within thirty-six hours. I'm certain.'

That assurance was enough to get them to the Lookout and they grabbed their stuff, settled their bills and prepared to leave.

'I say,' said Andrew ingratiatingly as Robin hesitated on the hotel's steps looking down into the car park. 'Was that your new Bentley keys Richard slipped you over luncheon?'

'Yes.'

'Well, look. You have your Freelander down there. And I don't have transport. So, I was just wondering . . .'

'What? Oh! Yes of course. Take it!'

'Wow! Gladly! So the day's not a total loss after all eh?'

'For heaven's sake, Andrew! Where's your sensitivity?'

'Ah! Sorry. Never my strong point, sensitivity. But still and all, you must admit . . .'

'Is that it? That steel-coloured car over there? Oh yes I see the winged B. My God! Yes, Andrew. It is a very beautiful car and I understand. Boy's toys. I am not immune myself. In fact if you don't hurry, you'll be driving the Freelander back to town.'

Andrew took Robin at her word, grabbed the proffered keys and started down the steps. But she called him to a halt. 'Andrew! It also looks like a very fast car. So drive it carefully, please. The last thing Richard needs is for his lawyer to get him a series of speeding fines from every speed camera between here and Heritage House.'

16: In Charge

The arresting officer's name was Harry Nolan and he was a detective chief inspector. Richard only really registered his rank and surname when the policeman identified himself for the interview tape. He had discovered that he had been christened Harry during a brief exchange with the custody officer in charge of Snow Hill police station on their arrival, when Richard had gone through the induction process and Nolan had gone off to prepare for the interview.

'Now, Captain,' said the Custody Officer after the initial proceedings were complete, 'I have noted the name of your solicitor and we have tried to contact him. His wife, a leading barrister, I understand, has taken a personal message and assures me that Mr Balfour himself will be here as soon as possible. Would you like to consult the duty solicitor in the meantime?'

Richard, frowning, shook his head.

'Very well, then, sir. Are you willing, sir, to talk to the Detective Chief Inspector? He just has one or two questions. Little points he wants to clarify. They may well sort out the whole of this mess and make your further detention unnecessary. If you wouldn't mind, sir. Or you can wait for your own solicitor if you would prefer. . .'

Again, Richard shook his head. He was thinking, *the quicker I talk to this man, the sooner it'll all be cleared up.*

The interview room at Snow Hill was neat and tidy, well presented and almost restful. Richard felt none of these things. A brief stop-over at a nameless service station had allowed him to relieve himself but he felt dirty, rumpled and increasingly outraged. Precisely where his rage should be aimed was something of which he remained uncertain at the moment, so he aimed the bulk of it at Inspector Nolan and, after a few more moments, Nolan's associate, Sergeant Ragalski. And finally – sometime later – his anger was aimed at himself for being stupid enough to accede to the Custody Officer's apparently innocent request and answer Inspector Nolan's questions.

'Captain Mariner, can you first tell me when you became associated with the board of governors of the *Goodman Richard* charity?'

'I can't remember precisely. Eighteen months ago, I suppose.'

'I have here the minutes of a meeting held two years ago almost to the day. Can you please read out the Chairman's opening remarks as highlighted?'

'Where did you get those?'

'From the charity's main offices in Brewer Street. We have all of the charity's minutes, correspondence and so forth from its foundation right up to date. It is the time of your arrival on the board we are trying to establish. Would you read the marked section, please?'

'"First of all I would like to welcome Richard Mariner to the board. Unfortunately he can't be here in person today, but I'm sure we'll soon be a regular part of his busy schedule . . ." Yes. I see.'

'And that welcome is countersigned in the margin?'

'By Charles Lee as chairman, yes.'

'How often did the board meet, Captain?'

'Every couple of months, I suppose . . .'

'And how often did you attend yourself?'

'Every other meeting perhaps.'

'Four times since you joined, in fact; though there were

actually regular monthly meetings with a couple of special meetings called. Would it surprise you to learn that you attended four meetings out of twenty-six in all?'

'Yes. Well, I was far more busy than I had supposed I would be during the last couple of years . . .' The admission sounded weak and self-serving to Richard. He frowned with mounting anger at himself.

'I see. Of course,' said Nolan, calming the situation. 'Now, how many regular board members were there, Captain? Can you remember?'

'Half a dozen or so. Mr Lee. Mr Smithers, a friend of his – a retired corporate accountant. They oversaw the funding by and large. Together with Dr Walton they made up the backbone of the project. Dr Walton had the contacts that allowed us to select the disadvantaged youngsters who went aboard the ship herself. But he resigned. Then there was a retired QC who kept us all legal and decent . . .'

'Who unfortunately died some months ago . . .'

'Really? I had no idea.'

'You sent flowers, Captain.'

'Did I really? The same way as I never forget my wife's birthday, I'm afraid: I have a very good secretary.'

'I see. Well, who else was on the board?'

'Helen Levin to begin with. She's the actress; quite a fine one by all accounts. She was there largely because she could get on that Sunday morning slot on the radio, I'd guess. I remember hearing her broadcasting for charitable donations. Very effective . . .'

'That's as may be. But she left the board last year.'

'She got a big part in an American soap-opera if I remember. I've never seen it . . . Then there was Captain Jones, of course. He got an automatic seat as Captain of the *Goodman Richard* herself. I can't think of anyone else.'

'No, Captain. That really only leaves yourself.'

'That's it then.'

'And you divided the corporate responsibilities between the board members . . . *How*, precisely?'

'As I've said, very generally. Charles and Smithers looked after fundraising and accounts. Smithers also acted as secretary. The QC looked after the legal matters. Miss Levin kept an eye on publicity. Dr Walton kept us in contact with deserving cases and Captain Jones kept us in contact with the ship herself.'

'I see. And who had responsibility for health and safety matters?'

'Captain Jones.'

'Aboard the ship, of course. But who was it on the board?'

'Well, I—'

'Captain, would you look at these minutes – again drawn in your absence, but countersigned in the margin by Mr Lee?'

'I . . . What? I have never seen these before in all my life.'

'Your perfect secretary again, perhaps. I dare say she has them filed somewhere. Alongside a list of your wife's most recent birthday gifts, perhaps. They are duly dated and we have no reason to doubt them. They are the minutes of the meeting nearly three months ago. You sent your apologies to them and to all subsequent meetings. But could you read the highlighted section, please?'

'No. I will not read them. Where is Charles? Where is Charles Lee?'

'Mr Lee and Mr Smithers appear to have disappeared, Captain Mariner. We have no knowledge of their current whereabouts, although we are of course actively seeking both of them. Other than the recently retired Dr Walton and Miss Levin, in fact – who also resigned as you say a year ago and moved to Los Angeles – we have no knowledge of where any of the board members are. None of the *current* board members, in fact. Except for yourself, of course. Would you read the minutes as marked, please?'

'No. I wish to consult my lawyer. I will not answer any more questions until I see him.'

'I have cautioned you, Captain Mariner, so you are aware of the damage that silence could do to your defence. And I must further tell you, sir, that I propose to charge you formally with the Corporate Killing of Captain James Jones under Section One of the Corporate Killing Act 2007. Which states that any executive of any enterprise, holding senior office or responsibility for health and safety, who causes the death of an associate or employee through commission, omission or negligence shall be deemed personally liable for the said death.'

* * *

'Damn!' said Andrew Balfour, waving a newspaper under Robin's nose the moment she entered Heritage House. 'Just look at that, would you? Look what the sneaky sods have done here!'

But even when she saw what he was pointing at, she didn't understand its importance. Not at first.

Andrew had arrived at Heritage House before she did but he did not have the key for the flat. He was tempted to go straight to Snow Hill in case Richard was somehow getting himself into more trouble – a feeling compounded after he talked to Margharita on his cellphone. But he had agreed to meet Robin here and so he thought he should wait for a little while at least. He had parked in the main car park and taken up residence in the main lobby. Soon bored, he picked up a current newspaper and started leafing through it. The report was on page 5. He read and reread it avidly but the headline and subhead told him all he really needed to know:

INQUEST FINDS JONES OF THE *GOODMAN RICHARD* DEAD BY MISADVENTURE

> Yesterday's Coroner's inquest declares Captain Jones and his missing officers lost, presumed dead, through failures of health and safety

'Don't you see?' Andrew said intensely to Robin as she was still trying to catch her breath. 'That's where the majority of people from *Goodman Richard* were yesterday. Why they were so obviously not at our inquiry. And the people who arrested Richard at the inquiry were simply waiting for this verdict before they moved. There was perhaps not a trap *per se* but there was certainly some pretty tricky timing. And it's going to be a field-day for conspiracy theorists.'

'It's too much, Andrew, I can't get my head round it . . .'

'Look. It must go something like this. The government passed their Corporate Killing legislation. It's long-awaited, high-profile, flagship legislation. The Department for the Environment – with the police – have responsibility for applying the new law, and must have come under increasing pressure to do so as time went by. The loss of the *Goodman Richard* comes along. It looks like an excellent test case. In all the papers. Full of heroics. But with a ship at the heart of it that might not have been perfectly maintained and run. A ship whose captain and senior people are missing presumed dead.

'So. The three elements of it are prepared as quickly as possible – the *Lionheart* inquiry, the coroner's inquest into Jones and co, the *Goodman Richard* case. Quickly but carefully – we can tell that by the way the inquiry was hijacked . . .'

'Hijacked, perhaps, when it became a racing certainty how the inquest was going to come out . . .' said Robin, thoughtfully.

'There you are! Conspiracy theory! I knew you'd get the hang of it.'

'What do they say? *A paranoid is only somebody who* really *knows what's going on.*'

'That's about it. Yes. And, if you follow that line of thinking you can see how fully they have prepared for this contingency. Their whole game-plan was in place, wasn't it? Straight back to Snow Hill for the charges so they can use the Old Bailey for the trial. I wouldn't be surprised if they haven't got a judge in mind. The judiciary are of course completely independent of the political process – like the police. But some are more independent than others – stands to reason if you think about it.' He made a gesture as though rolling up his trouser leg. 'Now, back to Richard. He's on the charity board that runs the *Goodman Richard*, so he's in the frame for the Corporate Killing charge . . .'

'But so are all the other members of the board.'

'And they could all be sitting in police stations up and down the country. Or, given where Richard is – and why – they could all be sitting in various interview rooms or holding cells in Snow Hill.'

'Is that likely?'

'Who knows? In a case of conspiracy where there are several people involved in the same crime they don't usually charge everyone in the same police station. But they've been known to. And of course there's a *point* to laying the charges at Snow Hill, isn't there?'

'Plus, of course, there's never been a case quite like this one anyway. So they'll be testing things out as they go along.'

'Precisely.'

'Right. So what do we do? Stroll up to the police station and demand to see Richard?'

'We could try. Why the hell not? At the very least we could find out who else they have in custody. And we'd better get on with it too. I don't want him persuaded into any little chats with the investigating officers unless I'm there to hold his hand.'

17: Bail

'Conditions of bail are set in the warrant,' the Custody Officer explained. 'They include a security in the sum £100,000. Surrender of passport. Regular reporting to a specified police station or stations.' He noted the way Robin was reaching into her bag. 'A personal cheque will not suffice for the security,' he warned.

Robin shot him a withering look and produced Richard's passport. Seeing his eyebrows heading for his hairline she explained, 'We guessed this would be part of it. We keep them at Heritage House. I am also aware that a personal cheque will not do. I assume, however, that a banker's draft will.'

'You – or whoever set bail – will be aware that Captain Mariner's business calls him all over the world at a moment's notice,' amplified Andrew. 'They are kept in a safe at the office as a matter of routine.'

'Well,' said the Custody Officer quietly, 'I'm afraid the Captain will be answering no such calls until this matter is resolved, sir.'

Robin was reaching into her bag again and this time she pulled out a personal phone. She keyed in a number from the memory and turned away as the phone was answered on the second ring. 'Harry? Yes, it's me. I'll explain later, but what's the quickest way to get a banker's draft for £100,000? I see. That quickly? OK. Could I ask you to do that? Bring it to me yourself. No.

Not Heritage House. Snow Hill police station; it's not far.'

She turned back. 'Mr Black, my accountant, will bring the banker's draft himself within the hour. What else was there?'

'I have to see Richard himself of course,' said Andrew.

'Captain Mariner has to agree to report to the police every forty-eight hours . . .' continued the Custody Officer, reading from a set of notes – supposed Robin – or perhaps from the warrant itself. Who knew?

'How in God's name can he be expected to run a business if he has to do that?' she exploded irritably.

Andrew was still hovering, for the Custody Officer was focusing all his attention on the dynamic, almost overpowering Robin. 'We agree which station – or stations – are most appropriate,' the Custody Officer began. 'They all have electronic access. We fax or email each other—'

'And besides,' interjected Andrew prophetically. 'Running the business is likely to go on the back-burner a bit for both of you until this thing is sorted out. You remember how it was in Hong Kong, Robin. This isn't quite the same of course, but it'll still take your life over, even if things go swiftly and smoothly. Now I really must insist on seeing my client . . .'

'Of course, Mr Balfour. And as the charge has been laid, I believe you may take Captain Mariner out of custody as soon as the conditions of police bail have been met.'

It was as well Harry Black, their friend and accountant, senior partner with B. W. G. Accountants, stayed with Robin after he brought the banker's draft. For when at last Andrew brought Richard out she nearly fainted dead away, and Harry's arm, strengthened by many years of crewing yachts and counting money, held her steady as Richard came shambling out of the shadows towards them.

To Robin, Richard looked dreadful, as though he had been in custody for weeks rather than hours. He needed a shave – he was a man who shaved twice on formal days – and his grey-jawed face seemed terribly pale and lined. He shuffled towards them with Andrew fussing at his side like a big bear with its keeper. He looked used-up, utterly exhausted from the way he was walking – but Harry said, 'Shoes.' And a downward glance reassured Robin that his strange gait came from the fact that his handmade footwear kept falling off whenever he tried his customary energetic swagger.

He held his tie, braces and shoelaces in his left hand and kept his right hand in his pocket. It came as a second shock to Robin to realize that this was not a casual pose – it was the best way to keep his trousers up. His shirt was open at the neck and looked strangely casual with the formality of his dark court suit. He straightened up when he saw her and his face lit up with an overwhelming grin of relief.

He said nothing other than, 'Hullo, darling. Good to see you, Harry . . .' until they had completed all the formalities with the Custody Officer. Fortunately, Robin, in mother mode, almost as if she were picking up one of the twins after a clothes-wrecking scrape, insisted on a pit stop before they proceeded. The group of them gathered around Richard, rethreading laces, reattaching braces and retying tie before they moved on. She even pulled a comb out of her capacious bag and tidied the black waves of his hair.

So that when the press pack hit them on the threshold of the station, at least the accused looked presentable, confident, thoroughly in charge of events. And fortunately, looking good was all that Richard had to do at that point, for it was Andrew who did all of the talking – though he could never remember afterwards exactly what he said.

Andrew was simply outraged that Richard had been naive enough to agree the interview with Detective Chief Inspector Nolan. 'But you did agree to it, I suppose, so we won't be able to make much out of it in court. We'll send an official complaint of course, but . . . Well, let's hope there wasn't too much damage done. I'll be able to assess that immediately, and anything else when we get the disclosure pack in due course . . .'

'He told me as much as I told him, I think. Maybe more,' said Richard, bracingly; very much his old self, back on form.

It was half an hour later and they were gathered in the flat at Heritage House. They were assessing what had happened so far – the facts and their implications. They hadn't begun to plan their campaign as yet. Richard was holding the strongest drink he allowed himself these days – pure High Mountain arabica coffee, straight from the filter; as black and thick as oil. The others were making free with the drinks cabinet. 'He had all the minutes and so forth of the various meetings since Charles Lee set up the charity. He was simply confirming with me that I had been designated as health and safety officer.'

'But you weren't . . .' Robin turned, almost as pale as the white-wine spritzer she was holding.

'That's as may be, darling. But it seems to be a part of their case. Anyway, I was a board member and as such may be liable if they can prove their case. And that's the important thing to recognize at the outset, it seems to me. I am the only board member left.'

'What do you mean?' She paused, the palely fizzing glass halfway to her lips.

'One resigned, one gone to America, one dead and two disappeared without trace. I'm the only one they've got. So – and correct me if I'm wrong on this, Andrew . . .' as he talked he ticked the points off by touching his fingers with his coffee cup, '*if* they are going to prove Corporate Killing against the charity because of a failure of health and safety aboard *Goodman Richard* – a failure of the "Controlling Mind" as they call it – and *if* they are able to establish that such a failure led to the death of Captain Jones and his officers, then *I'm* the man they'll seek to prove guilty of the killing in question.'

'That's about the size of it,' said Andrew.

'Unless they can find these two who are missing,' added Harry Black thoughtfully.

'The Chairman and the Company Secretary, who also ran the accounts . . .' nodded Richard.

'This man Smithers,' said Robin stormily. 'And Charles bloody Lee.'

'Is he one of the Hampshire Bloody-Lees?' quipped Andrew.

'Related to the Essex Sodding-Lees?' Harry matched him without thinking. They chuckled and Richard – whose humour tended to match their own, began to laugh as well.

Their attempt to lighten the atmosphere was well-meant, but it didn't work. 'You two can just . . .' snapped Robin stormily. Richard put down his coffee cup and rose, catching Andrew's eye. He jerked his head towards the door and held his hand out. *Keys*, he mouthed. Andrew threw them and turned. Harry would give him a lift to the office, he hoped.

'You three . . .' hiccoughed Robin, her eyes suddenly overflowing. She put her glass down without looking and it toppled off the edge of the table, spilling all over the carpet. 'Oh now,' she flared. 'Look what you *bloody* men have made me do!'

As Andrew hurried towards the lift he heard Richard soothing, 'Oh come on, darling. White-wine spritzer. It's self-cleaning. It's probably a perfect stain *remover*.'

And her muffled, tearful reply. 'And who's going to clean the stain off *you*, Richard?' she demanded, and then continued on a rising note of anger and near hysteria, 'Who's going to clean it off you and your reputation? Off the family? The company? Off all of us?'

The lift doors hissed open and Andrew stepped in beside Harry. They looked at each other, and Andrew answered the question just as though they had all been in the same room.

'We are,' he said. 'Especially when we get Maggie on board with us.'

Which oddly enough, was exactly what Richard was saying.

But Robin's mind had gone off at a tangent. 'The family,' she said. 'Oh God, the family. We have to tell Dad and Helen about this. And your parents.'

'I'll call them at once . . .'

'And the children. We'll have to call the school, Richard and then go down ourselves. We can't possibly let the children find out about this on the TV or the radio. Or on the phone – that'll be a big enough shock for the parents as things are. But we have to tell the children face to face.'

Her gaze grew so intense it seemed to be bordering on madness. But Richard knew better. He had seen her in this mood before. It was how she dealt with crises – and she had handled quite a few in her time, he thought.

'All right,' said Richard. 'We'll do it all this evening on the way home to Ashenden. But just do me one favour, darling, please.'

'What?'

'Let me drive.'

'Of course,' she said, before she saw the implication of the words.

* * *

Robin called the school first and spoke to the headmistress. No, the twins were at early prep. They had seen and heard nothing of the outside world since lunchtime. Yes, their ignorance would remain in place until the Captains Mariner arrived.

Then Robin called her father at home in his big old house Cold Fell on the Scottish borders. Sir William was shocked and upset and, man of action as he once had been, he would have fired up the Mulsanne Turbo and been on his way down the M6 by darkfall if she had let him. But she knew the instant they broke contact, phones would start ringing in the unlikeliest of places as 'Wild' Bill Heritage started waking up old contacts and calling in old favours.

She talked to Richard's mother and broke contact again – all too well aware that she would simply have started a trickle that would soon become a river, flowing in their support.

No sooner had she fallen silent than the radio, which had been playing quietly in the background, abruptly broke in with the local traffic update. Hold-ups on the A23 and areas south of Gatwick. A report half listened to – irrelevant to them. Then 'And now the local news headlines on Radio Sussex. A local resident and international businessman is the first in the country to be charged under the recent Corporate Killing legislation. Captain Richard Mariner, Chief Executive Officer of Heritage Mariner, was arrested in Penzance today . . .'

Half an hour later, Richard pulled on to the drive outside his children's boarding school. Robin had called in from fifteen minutes out and the youngsters were there to meet them.

Suddenly wary and apprehensive, Richard pulled himself out of the car and stood as they ran down the school steps towards him. 'What's up?' called William, his pale face frowning under the shock of blue-black hair he had inherited from his father – having been blond, seemingly until a year ago.

'Is it the grandparents?' asked Mary, just as tall, just as slim and pale. Just as worried under her golden mop.

'No,' he said quietly, enfolding them to his breast and giving them a bone-crushing hug. 'It's nothing life and death, but it's something I have to talk over with you so you don't hear it from anybody else. You remember the briefings Mum and I went to last year? I told you about them for your General

Studies course? About Corporate Killing? The new law that's just been passed? You remember? Well, my darlings, I'm sorry to tell you that I've been arrested and accused of Corporate Killing.'

'Did Heritage Mariner kill someone, Daddy?' asked Mary, her eyes square on his, as still as deep blue pools.

'No, darling. It's more complicated than that.'

'Are you guilty, Daddy? Has someone died because of you?'

'No, darling, I'm not. I haven't killed anyone and we're going to fight this case. Aren't we, darling?'

'Of course, darling,' answered Robin. 'We'll all stand together. Just like we always have. Won't we? Won't we, William? William?'

But William, every inch his father's son, wasn't paying any attention at all. 'Wow, Dad! So this is it eh? God . . . gosh it's fantastic! Even better than Grandad's Mulsanne Turbo. The new Bentley Continental GT. Now that's what I call a cool car!'

18: Bank

'This hearing falls under Section 51 of the Crime and Disorder Act of 1998,' said the Crown Prosecution Service barrister quietly.

His voice carried easily across the hush of the City of London Magistrates' Court, which stands opposite Mansion House at Bank. It carried to the elevated dais of the Bench where the three magistrates sat in series under the bright arms of the Mayor and City of London. It carried also to Richard, who stood silently in his allotted place, wondering at the slow majesty of a system which, even six weeks after his arrest and charging, had not yet got around to asking him whether he was guilty or not.

One of the junior barristers at Maggie's chambers – whose

weight and experience were thought to be more than equal to the task of this hearing – rose. 'My client is accused of an indictable offence under Section One of the Corporate Killing Act 2007, sirs. This hearing is simply a transfer hearing at your discretion to the most suitable court for a Plea and Direction hearing. Bail conditions were set by the original warrant and— '

'We are aware of that, sir,' answered the Chairman of the Bench, looking up from the bundle of papers piled tidily in front of him on the desk. 'And even were we not, we can read. And even could we not read, the Clerk to the Court would so advise us. And, in the unlikely event of *his* incapacity, we have the Crown Prosecution Service simply falling over themselves to help.'

'I stand corrected, sir,' said the eager young barrister and sat, crestfallen and blushing.

There might have been the faintest whisper of derisory mirth from the CPS team.

Richard looked across at Robin and gave a tight grin.

They had been preparing for this moment – the first step in a long process – for more than a month now as November darkened Christmaswards. They had returned from the twins' school and spent and exhausted evening and night pondering the terrifying vastness of the unknown that lay before them – far more unsettlingly than even the stormiest ocean. But then the phone calls started to come in. All their friends and associates gathered round them, offering support and advice; repaying in some small measure the good that Richard and Robin had done for so many of them over the years.

Doc's was the first one in; waiting on their answer service called through the instant he got up from the Web-link; supplemented some time later by a second after he had seen the news of Richard's arrest, which seemed to have reached Australia before it reached the Home Counties. But then the rest had come in a warm deluge of good wishes and promises of help. Everything from luncheon to lawyers might be theirs on a whim.

It had taken the better part of a day – again with Andrew's attendance – to sort out the details of the final bail condition.

Richard had reported (within twenty-four hours, as stipulated) to the police station nearest his home in East Sussex. Here he had to agree also a practical system of reporting which would allow him some freedom of movement in order to pursue his business. And, Richard being Richard, to investigate more details about what was currently happening to him. He was, after all – as Andrew pointed out – innocent until proved guilty. Of a crime he had been arrested for and charged with – but about which he hadn't even been formally asked to plead guilt or innocence as yet.

In fact, it wasn't too hard to manage in the end. He was expected to report every two to three days either to his local station or to Snow Hill – which was quite convenient to Heritage House.

More difficult was the situation that Andrew had warned Richard about. The case increasingly ate into his time. And even when he was not engaged in some aspect of it, the thing was still a potent distraction. Being the man he was, Richard oversaw the putting together of the team that would oversee his defence. Then he insisted on being kept up to date with every aspect of their work. He attended every hearing and legal briefing in person – even those where he was not strictly required. And, within the limits of his bail conditions, he became active in a range of the investigations – particularly those that looked dirty or dangerous.

On the other hand, his normal workload was so extensive that his increasing distraction from the workings of his company required some radical changes. Particularly as Robin worked there as well – and his involvement in the case pulled her away at his side. And, to cap it all, the mysteriously vanished Charles Lee had extensive responsibilities that had to be picked up somehow, while calling favours from here to Hong Kong in the continuing search for him made everything simply worse.

Fortunately, to begin with, Sir William and Helen were able to shoulder a lot of the workload, simply by moving into Richard and Robin's offices and restarting many of their own old jobs. Although well into their retirement, both of them remained strong enough to handle the workload and – for sentimental reasons, perhaps – had luckily retained the necessary legal powers to do the day-to-day work.

But their near-total involvement – though vital – was not an enormously lengthy one. Immediately junior to Richard were a small number of executives ready, willing and able to take on his workload while delegating elements of their own. Heritage Mariner had always been a model of open management and lateral responsibility, even though its financial base – 51% of the shares that controlled the power in the company – remained within the keeping of the family and senior board who had been in place when it was floated.

Richard had almost completely handed responsibility of running Crewfinders over to John Higgins, a senior captain and long-time employee. And the only aspect that really gave them pause in the early days was the fact of Charles Lee's continued disappearance. But, like Richard himself, Charles had put competent, reliable teams in place beneath him, and so the bread-and-butter of his financial management could carry on without him – for the time being at least.

'What did Oscar Wilde say?' asked Richard wryly at one of the early meetings, when his office at Heritage House had been transformed into a legal war-camp, 'I advise anyone who thinks he is indispensable to take six months' vacation at once . . .'

'Something like that,' said Margherita DaSilva, Andrew's wife and – for the second time, after the debacle in Hong Kong – Richard's defence barrister. 'But I'm afraid I know more about Widgery than Wilde, more about Diplock and Donaldson than Dante and more about Scarman than Shaw or Shakespeare.'

The basis of the accusation against Richard seemed clear, as he had in fact stated it to Andrew in their discussion after his interview at Snow Hill. It turned around the answers to half a dozen or so deceptively simple-seeming questions. Was he the nominated party on the charity board responsible for health and safety? Or was the fact that he was the only board member currently available enough to make the accusation stand? Had there actually been a failure of health and safety in the corporate mind of the enterprise and aboard *Goodman Richard*? And had that failure led directly to the disappearance of Captain Jones and the three other officers missing presumed dead?

Where were Captain Jones and his officers? And, finally, where were Charles Lee and his friend Mr Smithers?

Even before Maggie was let loose on the legal interpretations of the 2007 Act and the application of its legalistic wording, assumptions and theory in the real, practical, workaday world, there were a good number of facts to be established.

To do this – or as much of it as Richard would allow someone other than himself to do – Maggie and Andrew came with a pre-prepared team – like a freezer-meal from Sainsbury's, as Robin observed. Andrew had a range of expertise areas matched by a wide range of contacts and Maggie had much the same – but in a far different field. Their combined experience was vast, legally, socially, ethnically, nationally and internationally. But it was only the beginning.

Andrew and Maggie came with full P.I. back-up. Not just one specialist investigator – but a whole agency. Almost a whole detective force. The back-up called themselves Bacon, Constable and had offices on Fleet Street; they specialized in the discovery of missing persons, the tracing of vanished assets, the investigation of genealogical associations – in the matter of wills and so forth. Jim Constable was a big, reliable-looking ex-copper and Frances Bacon his partner was a slight, intense woman who had spent many years as a computer specialist at a London-based American security firm. They both seemed enormously competent and capable of doing a lot more things than were mentioned in the literature they brought with them to that first meeting.

Just as the case against Richard split into seemingly simple sections, so did the preparation of his defence. To begin with, Richard himself was certain that he had copies of all the relevant paperwork from the charity board – going back over the two years of his association. His secretary surrendered the file and Maggie's acolytes got to work. 'Don't often get a sight of so much of the evidence before Preliminary Disclosure,' she exulted – though obscurely enough to Richard and Robin who were not yet *au fait* with the whole process.

Other people at her office began to go through the Act. Normally a team would be going through Archbold and associated texts looking for judicial rulings that set precedents for precise interpretations of the minutiae of the Acts and their extrapolation in the courts.

But there was no precedent, simply because this was the first case ever to come before a court. So every phrase of the Corporate Killing Act, as penned by the parliamentary draftsmen who had drafted it at the Government's behest was scrutinized, disembowelled and scrutinized again. Imaginary applications of the Literal Rule and the Golden Rule and the Mischief Rule were tried. The only thing likely to help them further was the ruling as to actual court and the subsequent, resultant, naming of the judge who would sit on the case – for each of the likely contenders had his own reputation, character, track-record to be factored in.

In less rarefied and much more practical levels, there were the other members of the charity board to be contacted – those whose whereabouts were known and those who had vanished without trace. There were the full details of the board's dealings – all of which should be somewhere in the public domain – to check; particularly the financial position of the charity in the face of the loss of its major – perhaps single – asset. There were the crew and cadets of *Goodman Richard*, whose evidence about health and safety aspects aboard would be crucial. Maintenance of hull, masts, rigging; of lifeboats, rafts and ancillary equipment; safety requirements and procedures aboard; the schedules for emergency drills and how fully they were implemented. Corporate policies and whether they were fully adhered to aboard. If they were, were they adequate? If they were not, then who broke the rules and why?

And, as with the charity board itself, just because some people were missing was no justification for assuming they were dead – even if a post-mortem had declared them to be so.

This final point was the most crucial of all, and the fact was apparent to all of them right from the outset. For, even were Richard guilty of a range of failures of responsibility, commission and omission in the matter of health and safety on *Goodman Richard* – either individually or as the last remaining member of the board still in post – he was only guilty of Corporate Killing if someone was, in fact, dead.

* * *

The chief magistrate of the City of London Magistrates' Court looked up from his pile of papers and glanced around the quiet court-room. 'Very well,' he said, as quietly as both the sniggering CPS barrister and Richard's still-blushing defence brief. 'This is, as you gentlemen have pointed out, a hearing under Section 51 of the Crime and Disorder Act 1998. Subsection one of that Section is quite clear, and I quote: "Where an adult appears or is brought before a magistrates' court charged with an offence triable only on indictment, the court shall send him forthwith to the Crown Court for trial – for that offence." That covers almost all of it, I think. I so order, therefore.

'Captain Richard Mariner, you will present yourself to the Central Criminal Court at the Old Bailey at a time and date of which you will be duly notified. In the meantime I note that the terms of your bail are detailed in the warrant for your arrest. I see no reason to vary them. Bail as before, therefore, and continuous to trial.

'Thank you, ladies and gentlemen. That is all, except that, as I note this is our final session before Christmas, may I wish everyone the compliments of the season.'

19: Pleas

'Captain Richard Mariner. You are charged with Corporate Killing under Section One of the Corporate Killing Act 2007 in that, through omission or commission, as a member of the board of governors of the enterprise known as the Goodman Richard Charity, you did cause the death of Captain James Jones of the vessel *Goodman Richard*. How do you plead to count one?'

Richard looked away from the Clerk of the Court with his list of charges, across the well of the steep-sided Court Number One of the Central Criminal Court at the Old Bailey up to the stony, faintly vulpine, face of the judge in the gilded, galleried chair.

Then, over his shoulder to where Robin was seated, bright and pale as a candle flame, in the crowded public gallery high up behind him.

'Not guilty,' he answered, as he turned back to face the charge. He spoke loudly and firmly, just as Maggie had told him to. He felt disorientated and slightly foolish – and that was apt enough, for this was April Fools' Day.

'Very well,' said His Lordship the judge after a moment of silence. He folded his rising grey eyebrows into a judicious frown between his yellowing wig and his pallid eyes and wrinkled his nose in something of a snarl. And the Pleas and Directions hearing got properly under way. 'Mr Carver Carpenter?'

'My Lord,' began Quentin Carver Carpenter, rising to his feet with the smoothly oiled motion of a piston, 'it is the contention of the Crown that the accused was a member of the charity board of the Goodman Richard Charity, whose sole asset was the vessel of the same name. Whose business was to fill her with teenage cadets drawn from youngsters many of whom had already been through the juvenile justice system.

'Further, it is the Crown's contention that such a charity falls within the definition of the term "enterprise" as used in Section One of the Corporate Killing Act, though of course we await your direction upon that matter. As a member of such a board, the Crown contends that the defendant would have had responsibilities under the legislation in any case. But it is the further contention of the Crown that Captain Mariner as an experienced seafaring man, holding equivalent responsibilities within his own organization Heritage Mariner Limited, was given specific health and safety responsibilities by the Goodman Richard board, specifically to meet the requirements of the legislation. The Crown contends that Captain Mariner never took these responsibilities seriously, and was at the least derelict in his exercise of them. Indeed, My Lord, that the whole controlling mind of the enterprise was one of dereliction amounting to gross negligence. The Crown holds extensive documentation demonstrating regular non-attendance by Captain Mariner at vital meetings of the board. The Crown contends that, although he visited the ship and met the crew he did so only socially. Captain Mariner never at any time gave any direction for – or indeed made any mention of – health and safety.

'It is the contention of the Crown that, as a direct result of this omission, when the *Goodman Richard* went to sea on that final, fatal voyage, her hull and her equipment, her practices and procedures, left much to be desired. So much to be desired, indeed, as to amount to a gross negligence within the definition of the phrase as given in the Act. Which is, in turn, given with reference to which your Lordship will be well aware, to earlier gross negligence legislation and precedent. I refer particularly to the House of Lords' ruling upon R. v. Adomako 1995.

'And it is the Crown's contention, My Lord, that these shortcomings, in hull and equipment, lay at the root of the disastrous dismasting that befell the unfortunate *Goodman Richard* close by Wolf Rock on the day in question. While these further shortcomings in the matters of practice and procedure led Captain Jones and the senior officers of his crew to the desperate expedient of taking the last sound lifeboat and seeking help.

'And the Crown contends that this final, desperate, act led to their disappearance – a disappearance which a duly constituted coroner's inquest has adjudged to be presumed as death by misadventure.

'Finally I must note a matter of which I am certain your Lordship stands well aware – to wit that this death of a British subject occurred upon a British registered vessel within British territorial waters. It therefore falls well within the remit of this court. I would not normally refer to precedents in this place or at this time, My Lord. But as this is the first time this legislation is to be brought to trial, I will with your permission refer to the precedents of R. v. O'Connor 1997 in the matter of the loss of *Pescado*, a fishing vessel. And in the case of R. v. Litchfield 1998 on the loss of crew aboard a square-rigged vessel off the coast of Cornwall. A case, I must say, with strikingly similar circumstances to this one which lies before your Lordship now.'

Carver Carpenter sat with dramatic control, apparently unaware of the whisper of comment that echoed round the confined spaces of the court-room.

His Lordship the judge pulled his thin, dark lips into the brief 'V' that passed for a smile with him. 'As you point out, Mr Carver Carpenter, it is the first time the legislation will have come to open court. I approve entirely of your approach in the matter therefore. In order that we all may be clear about the central issues in this case, therefore, I will take the unusual step of outlining my own preliminary view of the Act. Firstly, and most crucially, it seems to me that the Act is clear in its intention that the term "enterprise" should cover the widest possible range of businesses, public enterprises, local authority activities, schools, hospitals, charities and so forth. I believe this fact is made clear in the explanatory notes ancillary to the Act. The Goodman Richard Charity falls well within the definition, therefore.

'As to whether all members of the board should be co-equally guilty I am not as certain, but I will rule it to be so, in the hope that the missing Chairman and Secretary might in time be discovered and brought before the courts.

'Finally, I do have precedent on my side when I rule that the case can proceed even though Captain Jones and his officers were lost at sea. Even without your very helpful reference to R. v. O'Connor – where several of the deceased crewmen of the sunken vessel, I believe, remain lost at sea – your case can proceed, even in the absence of a body. As is established I believe by the precedent laid down for murder in R. v. Onufrejczyk, 1955.'

'My Lord,' Carver Carpenter pistoned to his feet again as though his movement drove the great turbine of the Law itself. 'May I express my gratitude? It is always a pleasure to have Law from such a distinguished line of lawyers as the Burgo-Blackstones . . .'

'Oh my good Lord,' said Maggie, three weeks earlier, when Richard handed the envelope franked *OHMS: Central Criminal Court* into her uncharacteristically trembling hand, 'Lord, *let it not be Burgo-Blackstone* . . .'

'What's the matter with Burgo-Blackstone?' asked Richard, watching Maggie narrow-eyed across the littered occasional table on the 'entertainment' side of his office.

'Look at it like this,' said Andrew. 'If Ann Widdecombe

or whoever, was right about Michael Howard and there is "something of the night" about him, then there's more than a touch of Halloween Night about Burgo-Blackstone.'

'He makes Count Dracula look like Father Christmas,' amplified Maggie, pulling out the letter and unfolding it. 'Oh let's not beat about the bush, he is the Lord of the Undead, the Devil Incarnate. And – oh *shit*! – we have him. Look at this, Andrew. Burgo-bleeding-Blackstone. Christ, it's just as well the motto of the DaSilvas is "Strength Through Adversity".'

'Lucky the motto of the Balfours is "Balls Through Bad Luck",' rejoined her husband, not to be outdone.

'What's yours, Richard?' demanded Maggie, who was tearing the name of the presiding judge out of the letter very carefully and glancing pointedly down at her cigarette lighter.

'"*Noli Illegitimi Carborundum*",' he answered manfully. 'Don't let the bastards grind you down.'

'Oooh, it's *Latin*!' carolled Maggie, grimly girlish. 'Burgo-Blackstone will just *love* that!' She held the cursed name above the ashtray and set fire to it; held it still until the flame threatened the perfection of her nail-varnish, then dropped it. Then she had an even better thought, picked it up and used its last flicker of flame to light one of her colourful Sobranie Cocktail cigarettes. The smell of the rich Russian tobacco filled the office and Richard was glad Robin was out. The moment was bad enough without her disapproval.

Robin had become increasingly tetchy and short-tempered – almost bitter – at the weeks and weeks of work which seemed to be leading nowhere at all. Even the apparently solid, tangible things they had done as the late-running spring approached – like interviewing Paul Ho and the surviving crew of *Goodman Richard* – and indeed May Chung and the cadets – had pinned down nothing securely. Even their most positive and supportive testimony – and there was plenty of it – might just prove to be fool's gold in the face of the definitions the judge presiding pulled out of the wording of the new law. Paul Ho's deposition was as representative as any.

'Yes,' he'd said, going through things with Maggie in preparation for the actual case, 'Captain Mariner had been aboard. Yes, he had looked around. He had talked to them all – to Captain Jones and everyone within his command. Yes, he had mentioned the hull, the masts and rigging; he had commented upon the general appearance of good order . . .'

'Did he mention health and safety?' Maggie had asked, impersonating Carver Carpenter.

'No. There was no reason for him to do so . . .'

'None you knew of. Who did you think was responsible for health and safety?'

'The Captain. And I was myself.'

'Good. So you were intimately acquainted with the standard of the rigging, the strength of the masts and so forth . . .'

'No. My duties were to oversee matters below decks. The lading, the cadets . . .'

'Who was Captain Jones's sailing master, then?'

'The Second Lieutenant . . .'

'So the Captain and the Second Lieutenant would have been able to tell us whether the masts and rigging were shipshape. Or whether, through management failure and penny pinching they merely *looked* ship-shape . . .'

'Well, yes. I guess so.'

'And where is the Second Lieutenant now?'

'He went overboard into the lifeboat with the Captain . . .'

'You see how it'll be, Paul? When Carver Carpenter starts on you?'

'Yes, Ms DaSilva. Are you sure it will be Mr Carver Carpenter?'

'Certain. We share chambers, remember. He's making no secret of it, though I haven't challenged him face to face. We're avoiding each other as a matter of fact. But he's the best man for the job, not a doubt about that. If cost is no object. Right, OK. Let's have the rest of your statement now, Paul. Take us through the actual afternoon in question. Pay particular attention to the incident when you lost the masts, please . . .'

Richard's filing system was no greater help. He had promised his own copies of the minutes he had been shown by Inspector Nolan at Snow Hill, but they were simply not there – with or without counter-signature by Charles Lee. And the pile of papers his secretary surrendered earlier had proved useless – her log book showed no record that the actual minutes in question had ever actually arrived at his office at all. As Maggie observed, this might make them more suspicious of what game Charles had been playing – but it would also make the prosecution very suspicious of what game Richard had been playing. Better wait to see if they had anything more to disclose.

But that, in fact, only brought them back to the central, most bitterly frustrating element of the whole matter. The one question whose answer would shed the brightest of lights on to the darkest corners of the whole affair. Where in God's name were Charles Lee and his friend the accountant Smithers? Right from the word 'go' Frances Bacon and Jim Constable had been searching high and low for them. Maggie was certain Carver Carpenter was doing so as well – though he used a different agency for preference. So were the authorities, of course. The Crown Prosecution Service – and the police with whom they were working – would no doubt think either man as important an element in their case as Richard thought they would be to his. For precisely the opposite reasons, of course. And then, in the second month of the case, the authorities' interest in the missing men became wider still, for the Goodman Richard Charity was insolvent now that *Goodman Richard* herself was lost. Because the ship was the charity's only asset. And it had carried no insurance of any kind at all. There were certificates – for insurance of the hull, of the crew and cadets against accident and all the rest. Papers duly signed and counter-signed – and some of them copied in Richard's files as well as the police's. But the syndicate at Lloyds of London who supposedly insured everyone against everything had ceased trading some time earlier and the policies weren't worth the paper they were written on.

'What I don't understand,' mused Frances Bacon at one of their meetings soon after the Section 51 hearing at the Mayor and City of London Magistrates' Court, 'is why there's no money missing with them. I mean it looks like a classic scenario for embezzlement and fraud, doesn't it? It'd all make sense if there were millions missing from Heritage Mariner and hundreds of thousands from the charity. But there just don't seem to be. Unless I'm missing something here, these men have vanished leaving behind them perfectly well-balanced accounts with every penny where it should be, properly accounted, safe and sound. Even with the insurance mess the charity seems to be in, there's nothing actually *missing* if you see what I mean.'

'Except for one lost ship, and a hell of a lot of missing people,' said Robin, who had taken to the intense young private eye and accompanied her whenever the opportunity arose.

'It's not one of those cases where the whole point of the thing is that there's nothing missing is it?' wondered Richard thoughtfully. He had been reading a lot of law lately. And attending everything to do with his case, even down to the Initial Papers meeting a couple of weeks ago. 'Like that case where a student took a draft exam paper, long before it was due to be sat, read it and then returned it so that it would appear not to be missing. And that he could pass it all with flying colours sometime in the future – or sell it on to those who might? What was important was not the paper but knowledge of what was written on it. Not what was done at the time but its potential for fraud and profit in the future?'

'Oxford v. Moss,' called Maggie helpfully, in a cloud of fragrant Russian tobacco smoke, and for some reason the case name stayed in Richard's memory.

'It's an inspired thought, though, isn't it?' asked Jim Constable thoughtfully. 'What if the whole point of this situation is nothing to do with what is happening now. What if it's just as Richard says and this is all to do with something that's due to happen in the future?'

20: Directions

Burgo-Blackstone's grey-hued, slightly pointed chin rose from the bundle of notes in front of him as the Pleas and Directions hearing continued. His lips folded into the 'V'. His cheeks wrinkled into that unconscious snarl. 'Mizz DaSilva? Your outline of the case for the defence?'

Maggie rose, gathering her robes about her as she did so.

'The case for the defence shares the broad outline of the Crown's case, my lord, but is of course designed to question or refute it in all its major points.'

'Of course it is,' murmured Burgo-Blackstone derisively. 'Or it would *be* the prosecution case.'

'Quite so, my lord. And very wittily observed.' Unlike Carver Carpenter's, her voice dripped with gall, not honey, on the flattering words. 'Our case will proceed as follows. We agree that Captain Mariner served on the committee of the Goodman Richard Charity, but first of all we contend that his appointment was a social gesture suggested by a man he saw as a close friend and long-time colleague. Captain Mariner received no remuneration for such work as he did, unlike the other, more committed committee members. We further contend that he had no assigned responsibilities. That he was never formally warned of the committee's intention to assign him such duties. Especially in the crucial area of health and safety, where he has been so active – as my learned friend for the prosecution noted – in his own company, where he does have such responsibilities. We contend that the corporate mind of the enterprise, to the extent that it can be clearly established, was in fact active in the areas of health and safety aboard the *Goodman Richard*.

'We were preparing to question whether the Act does in fact assign general responsibility to all board members co-equally when your lordship helpfully clarified the situation by outlining your thoughts as you did. We would point out, however, echoing your Lordship's very welcome comment, that if this is held to be the case then there are at least two board members whose responsibility is considerably greater than Captain Mariner's. And although they are missing they have not, like the officers of the *Goodman Richard* herself, been declared dead. We have a lively expectation that their whereabouts will soon be discovered and it will be they – not Captain Mariner – who will be brought to justice, as your Lordship observed.'

'I am flattered that you have hung upon my every word, Mizz DaSilva,' interrupted Burgo-Blackstone, 'but I feel bound to correct you on at least one point. I did not mean that Lee and Smithers should face justice instead of Captain Mariner, but as well as Captain Mariner. I had in mind Conspiracy or Corporate Responsibility rather than alternative culpability. And I must observe – though I know it is a traditional refuge amongst those with weak defences – that I sincerely hope you are not going to hang everything on blaming the dead or the missing.'

'Thank you for your thoughts and your further clarification, my lord,' answered Maggie. 'They are most helpful as always. Next, we will be seeking to prove that *Goodman Richard* was not, in fact, badly maintained. That her hull, masts and rigging were sound and that she had well established, regularly followed health and safety procedures well known to both officers and cadets aboard. That the catastrophic dismasting to which my learned colleague referred was a result of overwhelming circumstance or perhaps faulty seamanship rather than of ill-maintained equipment. That Captain Jones's decision to go for help might have been a brave one but was nevertheless against stated policy. That such loss of life as occurred – and I have to say that Captain Jones and his men are still the subjects of the most active search – occurred in spite of the good practice dictated by the charity board, not because of any bad practice allowed by their negligence.'

'I am sure that when Mr Lee and Mr Smithers turn up, they will be relieved to hear that,' said Burgo-Blackstone thoughtfully. 'Though I assume your inquiry agents seeking Captain Jones and his officers must be Randall and Hopkirk (Deceased).'

There was a short silence as Maggie folded her black robes across the figured white silk of her court blouse and sat.

'Very well,' decided Burgo-Blackstone after a moment longer, his voice filling with energy and decisiveness. 'I think we will be able to proceed . . .'

'I think we will be able to proceed . . .' said Justice Burgo-Blackstone in the distance.

'Robin!' whispered a voice much closer at hand.

Robin turned to see Frances Bacon gesturing to her from the back of the gallery. Robin rose and began to make her way towards the intense young woman. It was perhaps fortunate that Burgo-Blackstone was consulting his timetable at that moment or the disruption to his court would have attracted some less than welcome comment.

'What is it?' asked Robin by the door. 'Have you found something?' Any kind of progress after such an achingly long time was not just welcome, it was almost like a charm. A totem. A sign that things were about to change for the better. Frances knew this and that is why she had come to tell Robin about it. To do more than that, indeed.

'It's the doctor,' she said. 'He's agreed to see us.'

'The doctor?' Robin had brief paranoid visions of some new medical disaster about to overtake them. The previous months were really beginning to take their toll now.

'Dr Walton. The board member who had supplied worthy cases to become cadets aboard *Goodman Richard*. The one that resigned just before the shit hit the fan.'

'I thought he didn't want to talk to us. Is this some kind of April Fool's joke?''

'Of course not. He didn't want to at first. He does now. That's all.'

'Should we wait for Richard?' They were hesitating in the doorway to the gallery of the court.

'You can if you like, but I'd better not. There's a risk if we wait too long. Dr Walton's booked on a flight to Rome for an early holiday. I think he's only willing to have a quick chat now because he's off. I suspect the police warned him off us when they interviewed him. But that's a long time ago now. He's obviously had second thoughts.' As Frances talked, so they crossed the balcony outside the upper storey of the court and came to the head of a flight of stairs leading down into the lobby.

'Can the police do that?' asked Robin, shocked and breathless as they rushed on downwards. 'Warn witnesses off like that?'

'No.' Frances paused at the foot of the stairs to look back over her shoulder, her face twisted in a strange smile. 'Of course they can't do that.'

Dr Walton lived in a flat in Gerrard Street. It didn't need the bric-a-brac and eastern furniture to tell Robin that he was an old Far East hand. He had the complexion, the accent, the touch. And he seemed ill-contained in the little residence, as though he was used to verandas, punkahs and dawns that came up like thunder. India perhaps, Malaya possibly – but most likely Hong Kong. The fact that he had settled here in the heart of Chinatown was one fact that made that most likely on its own.

But he wasn't a 'pink gins at noonday' merchant. He was plainer, blunter, more down to earth than that. 'Sit ye down,' he said, in tones more reminiscent of Yorkshire than Wan Chai, after Frances introduced the pair of them. 'Will ye take a cuppa tea?'

'That would be lovely,' said Robin.

'It's green, mind. Can't stand anything else these days.'

'That would be lovely.'

'Ye'll have to excuse the mess. I could say it's because I'm just packing up for the off, but I'd be lying. It's been like this since the missus died. I keep meaning to get in a cleaner but I've neither the brass nor the will, really. You're the first western women to come in here in over a year. May Chung and her friends come up sometimes – they say they're here to help and their hearts are in the right place but they haven't a clue. Modern teenagers, eh?'

Dr Walton was able to continue his rumbling monologue as he made the tea because his tiny kitchen was little more than a cupboard separated from the cluttered living area by a curtain of gaudy glass beads.

'But still,' Frances wedged the words in with a salesman's expertise, like a foot into a door, 'you were happy to recommend them to the charity for sail training aboard *Goodman Richard*?'

'Aye. I was. And it did most of them a world of good, too. Even though the Chinese parent is much firmer than your western parent in my view, still discipline has gone to pot amongst these youngsters. And the authorities don't do anywhere near enough, for all they try to help.' He reappeared with a tray laden with the makings of proper Chinese green tea.

'Is that why you joined the board of directors?' asked Frances quietly as he slowly, carefully, sat with the tray. He placed it on a rickety little brass-topped table between them and went through the ritual as he answered. 'Yes. It seemed like such a good idea at the time. And it still does if anyone wants to set up another scheme like it. But I couldn't be doing with the two that ran it after a while. I liked the old lawyer, he was a dry old stick but he made me laugh and he seemed to have his feet planted firmly on the ground. And I could have stayed the course if that actress girl had stayed or if Captain Mariner had showed up on a more regular basis. The Captain was a man's man if you see what I mean. I'd have relied on him under any circumstances. And it was him that saved the kids in the end. He's quite a man, your husband, and I'm right sorry for his trouble now. But the long and the short of it was that he was hardly ever there and being alone with that Charles Lee and his sycophantic little friend Smithers just got on my tits in the end. Oh. Begging your pardon, ladies.' He covered his confusion by handing out the tiny cups of foaming tea.

'So you resigned because of a clash of personalities?' persisted Frances. 'You had no concern about the way the charity or the vessel were actually being run?'

'Well, as to that, let's see. What did I tell the police? I didn't like either of them. I didn't like their plans. I didn't trust their judgement, so I packed my bags and left.'

'What was it you didn't trust them on? Can you be more specific?'

'Aye. Course I can. They made plans without minuting them. They told me about them because they wanted me to help but they swore me to silence like this was one of them spy novels. Or the Famous Five more like.'

'Plans?'

'Oh aye, they had great plans did those two. They were all set to use Captain Mariner's name and standing – with *Goodman Richard* herself as collateral, mind – to buy another ship.'

'They were expanding the sail-training programme?' Frances was surprised – as was Robin – but not shocked at the revelation.

'No. That's the point, d'ye see? The ships weren't going to be used for sail training no more. They were going to be commercial pleasure boats. Filled with paying passengers going cruising under sail, d'ye see? They was set to get it all set up under the cover of the charity, to split the officers between the vessels – then use the best of the cadets to do the rest! I saw at once how the charity was just a platform for their larger plan. Had been from the start, I'd say. Though it was a good idea for what it was at the outset. But then it all went wrong on them, what, nearly a year ago.'

'How?'

'Nay, I've no idea. The first whiff of disaster and I'd packed my bags. I've some standing amongst these people here, d'ye see. I can still do some good, in the face of the triads and the gangs, the gangmasters and the slaveworkers, people smugglers and drug pushers. But I'd lose any standing I have if I got mixed up in anything dirty myself. No. The minute I saw the writing on the wall I left. And what did the writing say? Ye'd have to ask Laurel or Hardy that.'

It took Robin an instant to realize that he was talking about Lee and Smithers. 'We can't find them let alone question them,' she said, leaning forward earnestly. 'Isn't there anything further that you can tell us?'

'Nobbut what I've told the police.'

'What's that?'

'They worked together but they didn't like each other particularly. Chalk and cheese like. Wherever they are they're not likely in the same place. Lee, now he could be anywhere from here to Hong Kong, and going first class all the way. But Smithers? I'd have bet good money that he'd be on that old boat of his down on the river. And if he's disappeared on purpose, like, I'd have laid an equal sum to say he'd have taken her with him. She was wife and daughter to him that boat. Him being a man as had neither. And here's what I gave the police. No more, no less.' He passed a piece of paper over to them with the address of a boat-dock on it.

There was a ring at the bell and the doctor crossed to the window. 'Right,' he said, turning. 'That's May Chung telling me her uncle's here with my taxi. I've no more time, ladies, and you'll have to go, I'm afraid. Leave everything there, just. I'll do the washing-up when I get back from Rome. And, from the look of things, Mrs Mariner, the next time I'll see you will be in court. As they say.' But Robin wasn't listening to the bit about the washing-up. She was wondering about that name. May Chung. Could it have been May Chung who finally made the old man talk to them?

* * *

The address was between Richmond, Kingston and Hampton, close beside Stevens Eyot. It was at the end of a battered, sad little street that looked to have been derelict before the Blitz. The narrow, pitted roadway led out on to a mud track across some sad grey grass between the buildings and the water. The track led down to a crazy little wooden pier with a long battered looking wooden-hulled boat at its end. Its name was *Argo* and it was just possible to distinguish the faded gold lettering and the pallid blue eye on the bow beneath the mud and verdigris. Unless Dr Walton was correct and Smithers was hiding aboard, it certainly looked as though no one had been near her for five months or so.

Frances and Robin stepped silently aboard. No doubt when the police came they arrived in a Day-Glo car with flashing lights and sirens. If Smithers wanted to remain invisible he would have found it easy to avoid such a visit. But if Dr Walton was correct, this was still the most likely hiding-place for the accountant and stealth might catch him unawares.

But the boat was empty. A modest, mouldering *Mary Celeste*. It wasn't the size of a proper houseboat but it would house one man with extremely limited wants. They searched it from the damp, water-marked stem to the sprung and leaky stern. The decks were empty apart from the lines attaching the vessel to the pier; lines long enough to accommodate the limited tidal range so far up the river and the other changes in water level that resulted from flood or drought upstream. The cabin was perhaps ten feet long and no more than four feet wide. Like most ships' cabins it was a three-dimensional jigsaw where everything fitted inside something or folded out from somewhere. And it was empty. The newspaper on the table with the half-full whisky bottle on it and the supplement beside the tiny toilet with a pencil close at hand were both dated the day of Charles Lee's last charity ball. To which Smithers, seemingly, had been invited, for the invitation was still there. But Robin could not remember having been introduced to him there, and Richard hadn't mentioned seeing him.

The only things there that were of more recent date were the letters piled untidily on the table. The vessel had an address and therefore could be written to. And the local postman clearly a tee-totaller who took his duties seriously. Unable to resist,

Robin looked through them, judging the contents from the envelopes. They were clearly mostly service and utility bills and circulars. And, oddly, there was a series from Moss Brothers, the tailors and hire specialists.

Frances crouched and opened the hatch in the floor. The smell of oil and bilges filled the little room. 'There's a hatch down to the motor on the aft deck,' said Robin.

'If you can call it a deck,' said Frances. 'It's about the size of a pocket handkerchief.'

But they checked it out nevertheless. And, except for a venerable diesel motor, it too was empty.

As they stood, hesitating, on the after deck, so a boat swept by going downstream. It was by no means a big boat and it was travelling well within the speed limit. But it set up a wake and, in the narrow confines of the river, the wake washed rapidly over to *Argo*. The little vessel stirred, rising and falling unhandily, her ropes groaning as she moved. The water rumbled under her stern but, noted Robin's sea-wise eyes, it washed through the hawse-hole and on to the port quarter of the foredeck. Frowning, she edged past the raised section that was the roof of the accommodation and walked forward. 'There's something here,' she called, 'a bit odd . . .'

Frances followed, calling, 'What?'

'Look,' said Robin when they were both on the little foredeck. 'The river has left watermarks all across the deck there. You see why?'

'Well . . .'

'Because the anchor is down.'

'Ah. So?'

'Don't you see? No, I don't suppose you do. Any more than the people the police sent down to look for him last year. It's a sailor thing. He has land lines out. And they're loose enough to let the vessel rise and fall. But the anchor's down as well. And that is working against the land lines, pulling her head down under the water. No sailor in his right mind would do that.'

'So. What? We pull the anchor up?'

'We do. This is a hand winch here. We turn this handle here.'

And so they did. The ratchet clanked and the rope groaned. The sounds of a medieval rack echoed across to Stevens Eyot and back. The vessel shuddered and the women puffed. And little by little the rope came in. Surprisingly few turns sat dripping on the winch's drum before the foot came through the surface, tangled in the rest.

A foot, and then a leg, dressed in the rotting remains of evening trousers.

'That explains a lot,' said Frances, grimly.

'It explains all those letters from Moss Bros. at least,' agreed Robin dryly.

Burgo-Blackstone looked up from his timetable as the pleas and directions hearing came to a close at last. 'Very well,' he said. 'I believe, if I clear a case or two of the Hilary Session, I can make this court available by the early summer.' He beamed at Carver Carpenter and glanced at Maggie DaSilva. 'Ladies and gentlemen, please have your cases prepared to present to me in three months' time, shall we say, on the first Monday of July?'

Oh, wonderful, thought Richard. *The twins are always complaining that they have nothing to do over the summer. Now they can come to the Old Bailey and watch Daddy go to trial.*

He turned right round and looked up into the gallery for Robin. But there was no sign of her at all.

21: Disclosure

'July!' cried Robin. She had recently returned from a lengthy interview with the police about the discovery of the late Edgar Smithers and she meant *three more months of this – 'til the summer.*

'Yes,' said Maggie. 'July! Precious little time to get the final elements in place. And just look at what that bastard Carver Carpenter has added to the secondary disclosure list. I thought the disclosure list he gave us in the first place was bad enough, but just look at this! I mean I don't know whether he's playing head games with us and using this stuff to send us off on wild-goose chase after wild-goose chase – or whether he's serious and expense really is no object.'

'What do you mean?' asked Richard, who was sitting with his arm round Robin's shoulder. He didn't know whether he was more upset about her ordeal – or by the fact that the procedure after the court hearing had prevented him rushing to her aid.

'Look at this witness list. We'll likely have to check them all out! The time, the effort. The man-hours!' She looked across at Jim Constable, who was looming protectively beside Frances Bacon. Frances was a computer expert. She was not supposed to deal with decomposing corpses, waterlogged or not, and the experience had left her, too, shaken.

'Right, let's start at the beginning. He's got an open summons for Charles Lee, of course. And I assume he'll have crossed off the summons for Edgar Smithers. But he'll still have men out looking for Lee – especially as they have another potentially suspicious death on their hands.' She paused, consulting the list given by the defence at the second time of asking. Then she continued, 'He's called Helen Levin back from Hollywood . . .'

'But I hardly knew her!' said Richard. 'What on earth's the point of that?'

'Publicity. She'll help it go world-wide.'

'Oh wonderful!'

'And Dr Walton of course. That just about does it for the board.'

'Unless he's sending a ghost-hunter after the late QC,' said Robin. 'Like Burgo-Blackstone suggested.'

'Do not name that creature in front of me.' Maggie made a cross out of her index fingers and nearly dropped her turquoise-coloured cigarette. 'Even his jokes are cryptic. Get that? *Crypt* – ic. Oh please yourselves. Anyhow. The next few witnesses are the remaining officers from *Goodman Richard* and a selection of the cadets. A little more conservative and down to earth, thank God.'

'Their testimony will be going towards state of hull, masts and cordage; safety procedures and such, I would guess,' said Richard.

'Indeed. But they haven't got Paul Ho, he's with us. And so is a posse of the brighter cadets, led by the considerable May Chung. And so is *Goodman Richard*'s radio operator.

'Interestingly, as they don't have him, they've called the radio operator of Hong Kong registered superfreighter *Sanna Maru*, a Mr Elroy Kim. That was the ship nearest to the incident, according to the coastguards, anyway. Oh. That'll cost the CPS a tidy sum if he comes in. She's docked in Brisbane as far as I can see. Or she was three days ago, according to this. She may be on her way to Perth by now. Fancy a trip to Perth to check him out, Jim? No? Thank God for that then.'

'He'll be someone Sparks got in contact with before he got through to us, I should say,' said Richard. 'One of those vessels like the supertankers that passed us that afternoon but didn't dare risk slowing. Though what this testimony is really worth is beyond a guess . . .'

'Nothing obvious. Nothing noted here at any rate, beyond the coastguard's list of nearby vessels. But there's been no response from anyone to do with her – not from Radio Officer Kim, his captain or the owners, as far as I can see. Though of course we'll have to go through all this lot again with a fine-tooth comb and a microscope.

'Then they've called the people you'd expect. Coastguards. RNLI people. Cox of the St Mary's lifeboat, that sort of thing. Chopper pilots.'

'What can they say? They couldn't get through to *Goodman Richard* on the day! Why pull them all into it now?' huffed Richard, mightily upset by the prospect of wasting the time of such vital people.

'If they were my witnesses, they'd say that things were hairy and they were a bit stretched but it wasn't that bad really,' answered Maggie, a little brutally. 'Certainly nothing to endanger a fully crewed, properly sailed, four-masted, iron-sided square-rigger nearly four hundred feet in length. Not if she was properly maintained, especially in terms of hull, masts and rigging . . .'

'Oh. Yes, I see . . .'

'That's more or less what all these people are being brought in to say, Richard,' Maggie continued more softly. 'It's not personal between them and you; it's just that Quentin Carver Carpenter finds that their opinions – as far as they've expressed them so far – help support the case that the Crown Prosecution Service are paying him to make. And that's the case that we are going to destroy. OK?

'Yes.' Richard's tone was more positive; almost square-jawed.

'Good. Finally, they have called several members of *Lionheart*'s crew – no doubt for the same reason; it was bad but not *that* bad. And because *Lionheart*'s crew will have witnessed the state of *Goodman Richard* as you found her. How she was when you boarded her. How long she survived when you got off her. And of course, how she appeared during the final break-up on Wolf Rock itself. Remember, they won't be asked about your heroics – not by the prosecution anyway. Carver Carpenter will simply be trying to establish what a suspiciously total wreck she was. How rapidly she went from bad to worse. How amazingly completely she was smashed to pieces on the rocks. He'll be trying to make a landlubber jury, without even a weekend sailor among them like as not, think that a sound ship should have held on longer. That she only came to pieces like she did because she was old, uncared-for, badly maintained and rotten to the core. And he'll be trying to blame that all on you. Which, if he does so, will make you guilty in the eyes of the Act – unless we can find a loophole in the wording somewhere. And, as you know, we are exploring that avenue too, even though it's simply insurance.'

'Remind me. Who are *we* calling?' asked Richard, after a moment more of silence and a steady hug from Robin.

'Well, we've had some pushing and shoving over their list to begin with,' said Maggie. 'Some of their witnesses are likely to give testimony that would sit better on our side. But if they open with them, I'll try and get our version out under cross examination if not before.' She stubbed out her cigarette and unconsciously rolled up the sleeves of her tiger-striped silk blouse at the thought.

'As to the people we've called, there will be you, Richard, of course,' she continued. 'Calling the defendant as a defence witness is *de rigueur* – a simple necessity in a case like this. Then we have an embarrassingly full list of character witnesses to fall back on if we have to. Starting with an ex-Secretary General to the United Nations, who seems to owe you a favour . . .

'More directly, we have Doc Weary. He'll be flying in soon anyway because the Fastnet Race is being sailed this year and he has every intention of going through all the qualifiers –

and then winning it, I understand. Hardly surprising, after all the preparation he put in last summer when all of this really began. But he'll take time out to come to the Old Bailey. Next, although the Lloyds' syndicate that insured *Goodman Richard* has folded, they do seem to have been largely legitimate – to begin with at any rate. We have Mr Cornwall, the marine surveyor they employed to give *Goodman Richard* her last certificate of seaworthiness – and that was less than a year before she was lost. We have, as I said, Paul Ho, the cadets led by the considerable Miss Chung, Sparks. And of course we have the Radio Officer, the Captain and the Chief Engineer of the good ship *Lionheart*.'

'Any lines of enquiry beyond that?' asked Robin, stirring.

'I've a contact in Rome who'll keep an eye on Dr Walton,' rumbled Jim Constable. 'But other than that, it'll just be the same old same old. Priority One is still trying to find Charles Lee.'

'There might be something to help us here,' said Frances Bacon, suddenly, pulling out of her bag the pile of correspondence that had lain on Edgar Smithers's table aboard the apparently deserted *Argo*. 'I wasn't thinking quickly enough, though,' admitted the investigator. 'I should have taken the invitation too.'

'This invitation?' asked Robin, pulling the square of marbled pasteboard out of her own capacious bag. 'The whole newspaper was far too big to take and anyway it didn't seem even to have been opened. But I thought this might be useful too,' she added, pulling out the supplement that had been aboard as well. 'Given where it was, and the manner in which some people pass the time there and the fact that there was a pencil lying on top of it.'

'You've heard the one about the constipated mathematician?' asked Andrew irrepressibly. But his good lady beat him into silence with the witness list before he could proceed.

They opened each piece of mail, whether it was clearly junk mail or not, with perfectly forensic care. They put all the obviously unsolicited offers of loans, insurance, prize draws and so forth over in one gaudy pile, each flyer with its envelope carefully clipped to it. They opened the increasingly irate letters from Moss Formal Wear Hire of Teddington, who would clearly never get their dress suit back. Nor the shirt, nor the shoes. Not that they would want them if they could see the state of them in any case, Frances observed, shuddering. There were letters about arrears owed for the docking charges – and the riverine equivalent of an eviction notice. And yet his bank statement – from Barclays Bank in Hampton – showed his account healthily in the black – in spite of a range of payments out and in by cheque, and a range of standing orders, and by an active use of his debit card. 'Frances, if you take a copy of those, I dare say you could check up on quite a wide range of financial contacts, couldn't you?'

'I may even be able to trace the owners of whatever accounts these cheques came from,' she said. 'Though none of them seem large enough to make it worth my while. There's something funny here at once, though. Look at that pattern of withdrawals from a hole-in-the-wall in Kingston there. That's not his bank is it?'

'Could be anything,' said Jim almost dismissively.

'True, but it's a start.'

But that was all there was in the mail. 'A clean life,' observed Andrew as though intoning an obituary, 'unhampered with any relationships at all. None with people who could write, at any rate.'

'Well, there's the invitation to Charles Lee's last ball,' said Robin. 'Someone wrote to him with that. Charles Lee himself, in fact.' She held up the expensively printed invitation. On the top of it was written in florid script: 'Dear Edgar, I do hope you can come. The first of many. My people will come for you at 7. Be ready. Charles.'

'That's a bit sinister isn't it?' said Andrew. '"My people will come for you at seven?" Given what must have happened at about seven?'

'I agree, it could sound threatening in the context,' said Jim slowly. 'But surely, even if there was an unconscious threat there, only a fool would write it on an invitation like that and then send in a team of heavies to pitch him into the Thames?'

'Or a desperate man who knew he was going to vanish within a day or two and wanted to leave no loose ends behind?' persisted Andrew. 'Hence the tricky "First of many", suggesting a relationship continuing into the future . . .'

'I think you may have been reading too many detective stories, Mr Balfour,' said Jim stolidly.

'More importantly,' interrupted Robin, 'who are these *people* of Charles's? Richard, have you any idea?'

Richard shook his head. 'I must admit,' he rumbled, 'I'm surprised by how little I do know about Charles Lee, given how long he's worked with us. But he's always been all surface, all smoke and mirrors. A dark horse really.'

That only left the supplement that Robin had taken so speculatively from the floor of *Argo*'s tiny toilet. And as soon as they opened this they saw that, if Edgar Smithers had lived a small life, he seemed to have dreamed big dreams. The articles – food, fashion, home decorating – all seemed to be unread. There was a small society section – with some doodles in the margin showing that he had at least glanced through it. But between the regular features and the Readers' Offer section at the end there were half a dozen adverts for travel to exotic locations. The Antarctic seemed to have taken his fancy somewhat. At first glance, at any rate. 'I don't know though,' said Robin with ready insight, after a while. 'It's the stuff about the cruise liner he's underlined and annotated. I suspect it's the ship rather than the destination that's caught him. Its facilities – dancing girls and three casinos. Mind you, what he has in the bank would only get him that cabin he's marked for about two days.'

The same was true of the cruise around the eastern Mediterranean – though there were some sites in Egypt he had underlined. But the Far East seemed to have attracted him more than Egypt. 'Dr Walton's influence?' wondered Richard. 'I seem to remember them discussing Hong Kong, Macau and Singapore on at least two of the occasions I was there.'

'Perhaps,' temporized Jim. 'But look. What he's underlined most forcefully in all of the sections of the Far East tour is that stuff about the casinos.'

'The Chinese are notorious gamblers,' speculated Richard.

'Edgar Smithers isn't what you'd call a Chinese name,' observed Maggie.

'Even Englishmen have their weaknesses,' said Andrew, piously.

'Ha!' exploded Maggie. 'Birching and bug . . .'

'You speak for yourself, my love,' Andrew overrode her

cheerfully. 'And anyway that was just the Navy.' He caught Richard's eye. 'The *Royal* Navy, I should say. Never the Merchant Marine. But look, even if Smithers was a gambler he was modest about that too, wasn't he? I mean, his account was still in the black.'

And on that thoughtful note, Robin turned to the last of the travel ads. It was a double-page spread for Australia and it was covered in notes, circles, highlightings and underlinings. The only section untouched was a photo of a string of pelicans flying past the Sydney Opera House. There were casinos fully annotated. There were stick-figures added to white yachts cruising the Great Barrier Reef. There were others along the sky-line of Ayers Rock. There were skimpily clad dancing girls outrageously enhanced. And in the topmost, right-hand corner, there was a lengthy series of numbers.

'Now that,' said Richard thoughtfully, 'looks like a telephone number.'

Jim Constable nodded decisively. 'Personal cellphone,' he agreed. 'What we need to do with that is copy it out carefully and take it down to my office in Fleet Street, switch on the recording equipment and dial it. Just to see if Mr Charles Lee answers it.'

Twenty minutes later they were all ready, grouped around the big plastic and steel slab of equipment, all digital readouts and back-lit sound graphs. Not one recordable minidisc but two – and an old-fashioned but still sensitive tape section – both cassette and reel-to-reel. All of it hummed nearly silently and glowed with ill-contained power. It reminded Andrew and Richard irresistibly of the Bentley Continental GT. Frances pressed a series of RECORD buttons and Jim punched the number into the telephone keypad.

There was a moment or two of agonizing suspense for all those present as the whispers and crackles of connection seemed to stretch out interminably. But then there came a ring-tone.

The tone chirruped five times before connection was made.

At once the room was filled with a creaking, clanking industrial background. Seagulls screamed in the distance. Some other bird called nearer at hand. Someone shouted. Someone shouted back.

'Yes?' said a voice in reply to the call.

They looked at each other, wrong-footed by the speed with which their own little gamble seemed to be paying off.

'Yes?' repeated the voice.

Jim dived into the silence. 'Charles, is that you?' he asked.

'What?'

But the three words struck some chord deep in Richard's massive memory. He knew that voice. *He knew that voice.* 'Jones?' he called. 'Captain James Jones?'

There was a microsecond of further contact.

Then the line went dead.

'That was him!' said Richard. 'It was Jones, I'm certain of it!'

'Wait a moment!' said Maggie. 'Let's be clear about this. Richard, are you saying that's our Jones?'

'Yes!'

'Jones of the *Goodman Richard*?' asked Jim, frowning.

'Yes!'

'The man whose death is the basis of the charge of Corporate Killing laid against you? *That* Jones?' repeated Maggie slowly.

'I'm certain of it! And if he's alive after all, then I have no case to answer! We must get this all to the police. We must get it to the police at once!'

Five minutes after they had all left the office, the phone began to ring. It rang four times and then the call-minding cut in. Jim's voice went out on to the whispering infinity of the line, saying, 'This is Bacon, Constable Investigations, London. We cannot take your call at the moment, but if you leave your name and number after the tone, we'll get right back to you . . .'

22: Desperation

They took the information to Snow Hill. Logic – any pause for any thought at all, indeed – might have suggested that they should seek out the centre of the investigation into Edgar Smithers's death, but Richard was so excited by the information he had found about James Jones that Snow Hill seemed logical to him.

It really never occurred to Richard to wonder what sort of reception they might expect. Had he stopped to think he might have seen the inevitability of what happened. After all, he was proposing to present an investigating officer with the thinnest possible 'proof' that the case he had been working on for the better part of a year was without foundation. And such proof as there was depended on an extremely questionable conversation with someone in a remote and mysterious location who had actually given away nothing tangible at all.

Finally, the source of this proof was a bundle of potentially important evidence removed from a possible crime scene.

Had Richard allowed Jim or Frances to get a word in edgeways. Had he paused to listen to Andrew or Maggie. Had he even paid more attention to Robin's hesitancy, things might have proceeded differently. But he did none of these things and so they went from bad to worse.

Inspector Nolan was in, the desk officer told them. He rang through, then, after a short wait he said that the Inspector was available to see them. Richard and Robin went through alone. The others, suddenly reluctant, remained in the waiting area. Richard put the pile of letters and the supplement on Nolan's desk and topped them off with the tape of the phone call. He could hardly contain the excitement he felt. This was it. He was vindicated. At the end of the tunnel. Out of the woods.

'What is this?' asked Nolan quietly.

'All in all, it's proof of my innocence,' answered Richard. 'This is the tape of a phone call . . .'

'Where did these letters come from?' Nolan had seen the address on an envelope.

'Edgar Smithers's boat *Argo* . . .'

'Where did you get them?'

'That's not important. Listen. On the supplement here there's a phone number—'

'I think it is important, Captain Mariner. But we can discuss that when I understand exactly what it is you wish to show me. A phone number on a page of this supplement?'

'Yes. The advert for tours of Australia . . .'

Nolan riffled through the magazine. 'I see. This page? This phone number?'

'Yes. We thought it must be Charles Lee's . . .'

'But clearly it wasn't.'

'That's right. We phoned it and got through. Someone answered.'

'I see. Who answered?'

'Captain James Jones.'

There was a short silence. 'I find that hard to believe, Captain. Mrs Mariner, did you talk to Captain Jones too?'

'No. But we all heard him. It was on one of those answerphone machines that broadcast incoming calls.'

'And Captain Jones identified himself?'

'Not in so many words, no. But Richard recognized his voice.'

'It's all on the tape,' said Richard, unable to contain himself.

'I'm sure it is, Captain. I'm just trying to prepare myself. Clarify what exactly I'll be listening for.'

'I see,' said Richard, more hesitantly. Seeing, in fact, that things were beginning to slide off the rails here.

Nolan took the tape and, crossing to a tape deck on a side table, he snapped it in place. 'And you got all this stuff from *Argo*?' he continued conversationally as he fiddled with the mechanism.

'That's right . . .'

'I got it,' said Robin quite forcefully. 'I talked to Dr Walton before he left for Rome and he told me about Mr Smithers's boat. I went there and found this stuff. Then I found the body—'

'Yes. I'm aware of that. You and Frances Bacon, an investigator. Didn't Ms Bacon warn you that tampering with personal effects in a private residence like this was against the law?' He made it seem like a tiny misdemeanour mentioned in a friendly discussion. He continued to fiddle with the recorder, looking away from them.

'She didn't see me take any of it,' said Robin. 'I know it was silly but I was desperate. We're getting nowhere. And after so long—'

'But you've certainly got somewhere now, haven't you?' observed Nolan quietly, his tone beginning to betray just the suspicion of a barb.

He pressed PLAY as he spoke and the room suddenly filled with the whispers and crackles of connection.

Then, a ring-tone. Five rings.

Connection. A hissing, bubbling overlain with clanking and crashing. Seagulls' birdcalls closer. Shouting. An answer.

'Yes?'

The bubbling. The clanking. A whirr of motors, a scrape of something being dragged or lifted. Bird sounds. A clapping.

'Yes?'

Very loudly, '*Charles, is that you?*' Drowning everything at the far end of the connection out. So loud it echoed for an instant.

'What?'

Bird sounds. Clapping.

'*Jones?*' Again, very loud. Drowning out everything else.

'*Captain James Jones?*'

A micron of time, filled with hissing, bubbling, the rest.

CLICK.

The hiss of empty tape.

Nolan let it play. One second; two; three. He snapped the recorder off. 'That's it?' he asked. He sounded weary.

'Yes!' answered Richard. 'That was James Jones. I'd swear to it.'

'Of course you would. And I'm sure there are several other people who would swear to it as well. All right. This is the phone number?'

'That's it.'

Nolan punched it into his phone and flipped a little switch that broadcast the sounds of contact – just as Jim's had done. Richard wondered whether it was taping the contact too. Then he began to wonder what else of what was happening in the room was being taped.

The hiss of connection broke.

For a heart-stopping instant Richard really thought it would ring; that Jones would answer again. But no. Instead of a ring-tone there was a hissing, burbling scream as though the handset at the far end were being boiled in burning oil. The sound was so sudden, so loud, so painful that the three of them jumped. After three agonizing seconds, Nolan switched the speaker off. 'It seems that number is no longer available,' he observed quietly.

'But we have the tape . . .' Richard was at last beginning to feel just how far out of his depth he was here.

'Captain Mariner, let me explain some things to you. First of all, your wife and Ms Bacon committed a trespass in going aboard the *Argo*. This is a serious offence exacerbated by the fact that the owner of the boat was a witness for the prosecution in a case against you. Secondly, at some time during the trespass they stole various goods and correspondence belonging to Mr Smithers. If they did this before they knew he was dead then it is just plain theft. If they did it after they knew he was dead then it was perverting the course of justice. You certainly knew he was dead before you opened these things and went through them. That is certainly perverting the course of justice. You have by some collective madness talked not only the two private enquiry agents but a solicitor and a barrister into conspiracy to pervert the course of justice along with you. And for what? What have you gained from this? A tape of a conversation that means nothing. With someone who could never be properly identified beyond a reasonable doubt. On a tape which has effectively been created as the result of a series of criminal acts. A tape whose provenance would be questionable unless you could prove without a shadow of a doubt that you really were talking to Captain Jones where and when you say – and that this is a full, undoctored recording of the conversation.'

'Ah,' said Richard. 'I see my mistake.' The quiet tone of his voice warned Robin of his rage and she tried to stop him speaking with an elbow in his ribs – but it was already far too late.

'I should hope you do,' answered Nolan. 'A whole catalogue of mistakes, in fact.'

'My mistake was in assuming that you would be interested in the *truth* rather than in the *case*. In thinking that if I could bring you proof that Captain Jones was still alive, the provenance of the proof would not be important – because you would see that I had no case to answer!'

'That's not the way it works, Captain. Particularly as you have actually brought me no proof whatsoever. This situation will not go away in a puff of smoke. It is something you will have to face and deal with within the limits of the law. This isn't some water-borne derring-do where you can pretend you're James Bond and sort it all out with a Walther PPK and a dry martini. There will be no heroics, no "With one leap, Jack was free". It doesn't work that way at all!' He paused. Took a deep breath, and switched his gaze to the naked desperation on Robin's bone-white face. 'But on the other hand there is no reason for institutional inhumanity.'

Without raising his voice he called, 'Ragalski, get the others in here now please.

'You see,' he continued, 'I ought to be arresting Mrs Mariner and Ms Bacon for trespass and theft. I should be arresting all of you for perverting the course of justice. Arresting you. And I wouldn't even need to lean on the new arrest rules either. This would be a good old-fashioned "going down for five years and more" arrest. Prison terms served. Licenses revoked. Law Society and Bar Council hearings.' The door opened and Ragalski ushered the other four in. He repeated himself with them standing there, like a weary headmaster addressing a bunch of recalcitrant students, and he lingered over the last three sentences.

Then he continued, 'But what's the point? The prisons are full enough as it is. You've done yourselves and your case no good; but you've done no real harm either. I won't even insult you with the You Should All Have Known Better speech. Just count this as a word to the wise. Legitimate enquiries. Proper case-making. No more gumshoe stuff and mysterious phone calls, or I will haul you all over the coals, and it won't just be the Captain here who'll risk seeing the inside of Belmarsh or Holloway. Leave the stuff from the *Argo* on your way out. I have colleagues down at the Kingston nick who need to see it as well.'

As soon as the desk sergeant rang through to say they had all left, the inner door into Ragalski's office opened and Quentin Carver Carpenter came out. 'That was an unexpected addition to our little prosecution meeting,' the prosecuting counsel observed. 'But was it wise to be so lenient, Inspector?'

Nolan looked up at him coldly. 'One: I'll be watching them. Or Ragalski will with as much of a team as I can get the finance for. Two: consider the impact to your case if we throw the whole of the defence team in clink. I mean, do you want it done and dusted before you retire or do you not? Three: I thought you'd enjoy having Mizz DaSilva exactly where you want her. I mean, one of you's going to make their name, their career and their fortune from this case, aren't they? You have the whip hand now.'

'And you, Mr Nolan, what do you have?'

'Why, I have the satisfaction of knowing, sir, that I'm just an honest copper doing an honest copper's job.'

And the way he said it, without inflection or intonation, left Carver Carpenter genuinely uncertain whether he actually meant it or not.

23: Touch

'The hell of it,' said Richard, his voice trembling with sheer rage, 'is that I know that was James Jones. The bastard's alive out there somewhere. So it's a racing certainty that everyone else in the lifeboat is OK too.' The six of them were walking in a group back along Snow Hill in three close-bunched pairs.

'But how *are* we going to prove it?' asked Robin, soothingly, giving him a gentle, lingering hug. She hadn't really thought her words through – she was just quietening him as she quietened the twins when they were sick as babies, by the tone of her voice not by what she was saying.

But Jim Constable answered her question. 'We have the recording,' he said. 'We'll start with that. If anyone has any kind of a record of Captain Jones's voice we can do an audio match. They're almost as accurate as fingerprints, retinal scans and DNA. Then we can see if there's any way of beefing up the background. I know it's a bit James Bond, but it's doable. Places have sound signatures as individual as voices and if we can get a fix on where he was speaking from it'd be a good start.'

'It was on board a ship,' said Richard without thinking. 'That much was obvious.'

'Then maybe we can even work out where the ship is – or was when we spoke to Captain Jones,' said Jim thoughtfully.

'Cool,' said Maggie. 'Then I'd better get busy trying to support the provenance of our tape. Richard, what we need is some kind of recording of Captain Jones's voice. If we can get that, then I know this professor who specializes in the field. Professor German—'

'But what about Inspector Nolan?' Robin almost wailed. 'He told us to stay within the law! No more gumshoeing!'

'Three things,' said Jim. 'One, this is within the law. Two, if I did everything the police told me I'd be broke in a week. Three, I am a gumshoe – gumshoeing is what I do.'

'We,' corrected Frances. 'It's what *we* are – what *we* do . . .'

'Right,' said Richard, beginning to spark again at the prospect of action. 'What do we do first?'

'Back to Heritage House,' ordered Jim. 'I would say the Inspector wasn't just threatening us for fun. He said he'd be watching us, so I assume he is. We'll lie low for a bit and then I think the girls ought to sneak out and do a little anonymous shopping.'

'Wow!' said Maggie. 'It's a while since anyone called me a girl.'

'I wasn't thinking of you,' answered Jim. 'You couldn't do anything anonymously. And I'll bet you don't do the kind of shopping I have in mind. Not in Tesco's at any rate.'

'Tesco's?' asked Maggie, her voice dripping with innocent ignorance. 'What on earth is Tesco's?'

The evening was clement and dry. It was hardly out of place that two of the kitchen staff from Heritage Mariner should pop out – still in their cover-alls – to pick up some extra supplies from the local Tesco's. Almost immediately that they did so, Maggie and Andrew came out of the side-door to the flat and hailed a cab. Then Richard and Jim came out of the main doors and went on down into the company car park. A few moments later Richard's Bentley Continental eased out on to Leadenhall and cruised off towards Fleet Street, at a speed dictated by the evening traffic of little more than walking pace.

'God,' said Robin. 'This is all a bit subtle, isn't it? I mean Nolan specifically warned Richard that he shouldn't be behaving like James Bond and here we are – pretending to be Plenty O'Toole and Pussy Galore.'

'Listen, girl,' said Frances. 'Don't fool yourself. In these overalls we look more like Rosa Klebb.'

'So,' said Robin with a chuckle. 'We work on the assumption that Nolan's men will watch our two cruising down Fleet Street while we sneak in from the back and raid your offices.'

'Probably being over-cautious,' agreed Frances. 'But you never know. Like Nolan said, we've broken so many rules already he'd have no difficulty getting a warrant out of a magistrate – and the boys down in Kingston looking into Smithers's death will want to be active too, remember. Once that happens, the discs and the tapes are all history as far as we're concerned. And I agree with Jim: it's only a matter of time before that happens. Better we have at least some copies they don't know exist. Then we can keep working in quiet, eh? It's the next step.'

'And oh my Lord,' said Robin quietly, almost mournfully, 'do we ever need a next step . . .'

The back entrance to Bacon, Constable's offices opened off Shoe Lane. The offices themselves were simply on the second floor of a large business premises, so the rear entrance was pretty well secured, Robin observed as Frances let them in. But, as with many such buildings, the security could really have done with some updating and a lot of strengthening. There was graffiti not only outside the doors but on some of the inner walls and passageways as well. One or two of the strip-lights were broken but the stairwells remained bright. 'We could do with CCTV cameras at the back as well as at the front,' said Frances, catching Robin's look. 'But the rent and maintenance charges are ruinous enough as it is.'

She put the key into the lock of her office's rear door and turned it. It stuck and she had to work it a little to make it turn. 'Looks like we'll need a new lock soon,' she said, frowning, as the pair of them entered.

The offices were not large but they were well designed. The rear door opened into a tiny kitchen with washing and coffee-making facilities and a microwave that stood on top of a little refrigerator. A side door opened through into a loo and a main door opened into the main office where the equipment they had come to check stood to the right of a large, solid desk – the tabular equivalent of Jim Constable in teak. Beyond that again there was a door through to a small waiting room and a main entrance through into the lobby, stairwell and lifts outside.

Without thinking, Robin closed the door behind her. The office was completely internal. There were no windows – their absence no doubt adding to the atmosphere of secretive exclusivity. Frances hit the light in the kitchen, then hurried through into the main office. The light from the kitchen door fell directly on to the recording equipment, and was sufficient for Frances at first. But then she hesitated, saying, 'Hey, that's not right . . .'

Robin joined her, and together the two women stood looking down at the recording equipment. The reel-to-reel and the cassette recorders were both broken, their spindles obviously empty.

'What the hell . . .' Frances crossed to the main light. As she did so, Robin pressed the button on the CD recorder and a minidisk slid out. 'Here . . .' she said, taking it and turning.

Frances pressed the light switch. No light. Instead, an immediate smell of burning filled the room. The light in the kitchen began to flicker. 'Get out!' shouted Frances. The pair of them ran back the way they had come, but almost as soon as she touched it, Robin realized that the faulty lock on the back door had given up the ghost. Her fingers simply slid round the patterned metal of the little knob. The bolt remained immovably in place.

'We can't get out this way,' she said.

'Through to the front,' ordered Frances. But as she spoke, there came a deceptively quiet 'Whumph' of sound. The kitchen light went out, but the office was lit by a sinister flickering brightness. It wasn't much, but it was enough to show the black cloud of smoke that came under the lintel and began to ooze across the kitchen ceiling.

Frances paused, then joined Robin. Both of them hurled themselves against the door but both knew that it was designed to open inwards and nothing they could do would budge it if the lock was broken. Side by side they turned and looked into the gathering brightness of the office, therefore. The clearer air below the billowing smoke was already thick enough to make them cough and gasp. They only had time for the briefest glance of calculation. The radio equipment was fiercely ablaze, spitting flame and sparks as though it contained an angry dragon. All that side of the room was burning from floor to ceiling. But on the other side, there seemed to be a passageway into the relative – temporary – safety of the waiting room. It wasn't much but it was all they had. Frances tensed to go at once, but Robin, trained for emergencies such as this on countless supertankers, took her by the shoulder. They invested thirty seconds at the wash-basin, soaking two washing-up towels and tying them safely round each other's faces.

Frances took the lead then, and they stumbled forward into the gathering inferno of the main office. The carpet looked like expensive wool but was all too flammable man-made fibre. The flames were flowing eagerly across it. The electrical systems in walls and ceiling were overheating, carrying the flames through conduits and spreading them more rapidly. There was a sprinkler system but in this section of the building it was malfunctioning.

Frances made it to the office's main door, though that meant she had to move out of the safe corridor towards the increasing inferno of the recording equipment. She turned the handle, but – as security dictated – it was locked. Choking, eyes streaming, on the very edge of panic, she began to sort through the keys that were still – providentially – in her hand. She felt Robin pressing tightly against her back, all too well aware of the speed with which the fire was surrounding them; with which the smoke and fumes were filling the room.

As Frances pushed the key into the lock, she felt Robin slide to her knees and gave a brief prayer that her employer was seeking clean air – not fainting dead away. Her own head was spinning and her hand was beginning to shake badly as great surges of adrenaline hit her system. Stubbornly, the key refused at first to slide home. Then, once it was settled correctly, it refused to turn. Frances started screaming at it, blissfully unaware that she was doing so.

On her knees behind the screaming detective, stooping to find some semblance of clean air, realizing that her shoes were beginning to melt – and the man-made fibres of her overalls were likely to prove as fire-friendly as the carpet – Robin dug the edge of the CD into the palm of her hand. She closed her fist around the recordable minidisk as tightly as she could, using the effort and the pain to steady herself. And, blessedly, she thought, there was a considerable draft of fresh air coming in under the door they were trying to open.

'Gottit,' shouted Frances and opened the door without further thought. Providentially, instinctively, she pulled the key out of the lock as she turned the handle and pushed.

Air from the outer room roared into the inferno and the fresh supply of oxygen fed the flames exponentially and instantly. The indraft sucked the women almost fatally back towards the flames – but the explosion blew them both out into the waiting room. Frances flew over a suddenly smouldering leatherette chair. Robin smashed a glass-topped table with her forehead. The magazines piled upon it soared up into the air and burst magically into flames as they flew. But both women, desperate in the knowledge that hesitation could only mean death, scrabbled through the smouldering wreckage.

Frances was on her knees when she reached the main door and it was only by a miracle that she still held the keys. She found the lock and the key that fitted it by touch and thrust it home.

The new-fed fire had attained a voice now; it rumbled and roared so powerfully that the outer room trembled in ready sympathy. The reeling Robin's teeth were chattering. The floor was shuddering like the back of a frightened horse. The door was rattling in its frame as though giants were beating against it from without. Frances forced the key inwards and felt the mechanism yielding almost as intimately as she felt the fibres across her shoulders melting and her hair beginning to crisp and smoulder. Burning paper was drifting down around her as though this were a snowstorm in Hell. She held her breath as she pushed again. She couldn't actually remember when she had last breathed.

The door remained wedged, the sucking of the fire forcing it into its frame with simple air-pressure, as it had done with the inner door. Weary unto death, Frances turned and pulled at Robin until her eyes focused beneath the mask of blood flowing down from her hairline into the blackened mess of the soaking towel over her mouth. *Little Red Riding Hood*, thought Frances drunkenly. She climbed to her feet, pulling Robin up with her. Side by side they leaned against the blistering paint of the door like a couple of little old ladies.

'Won't it happen again?' croaked Robin.

'Who cares?' screamed Frances. 'We open it or we fry. PUSH!' The last word was screamed with the last ounce of air from the pit of her lungs. She twisted the handle so hard she sprained her wrist and shoved so firmly she put her collarbone at risk. Robin heaved with equal, desperate determination, and the door swung open as explosively as the door into the waiting room had done.

Both women were blown out into the stairwell and headfirst down the stairs while the windows above them that overlooked Fleet Street simply exploded inwards to shower them with shards of broken glass.

'What in hell's name . . .' Jim Constable looked up incredulously as the windows along the front of his office building disappeared. The Bentley was easing at a snail's pace down towards Aldwych and had moved only its own length in the last minute, putting them exactly level with the building.

Jim pushed open the door of the Bentley and sprinted out in front of it, across the road and across the pavement to the doorway. Richard trod on the brake and stopped the car just before the swinging door hit a NO PARKING sign. Then he too was out, his outer door nearly unseating a motorcycle policeman who was weaving his way up the inner lane.

'BOMB!' shouted Richard. He gestured upward as a backwash of smoke and flame came out through the windows with the last of the glass and frames.

'Jesus,' said the policeman, and started shouting into the two-way mic. in his helmet.

He was still doing this when Richard and Jim came staggering back out of the main door. At Jim's side, Frances was weaving drunkenly, her arm across his broad shoulder. But Robin lay in Richard's arms like a corpse. As far as the policeman could see, her face was gone, leaving only a mask of congealing blood. Her hair was black and curled into a short afro style – but the clenched hands and dangling legs were white-skinned.

Richard pushed past him, slipping the faceless corpse into the passenger seat of his car. 'I think she's dead,' he said in a strange, dull voice. 'I have to get her to the nearest hospital.'

As he spoke, he turned a knob and slid the back of the seat down until it almost made a bed. 'Help me! She's my wife . . .' The woman's face rolled over, blood flowing past the black mess and the blisters down on to the battleship-grey leather. There were at least blood-filled pits which might be eyes. A kind of a hump for a nose. Then the blackness began again. It was difficult to tell how bad things were. The policeman was young and inexperienced but they looked pretty bad to him.

'All services alerted,' said the voice in the policeman's helmet. 'Fire Brigade and bomb disposal should be there in one . . .'

There was a wail in the near distance. Flashing lights.

'Right,' said the policeman. 'St Thomas' is your best bet, I'd say. Follow me. Is that thing as fast as it looks?' he added, nodding at the Bentley as he switched on his lights and siren. The traffic along the roadway in front of them parted like the Red Sea for Moses.

'You have no idea,' grated Richard, 'how fast this thing can go.'

24: Go

'Captain Richard Mariner is arraigned before you today, ladies and gentlemen of the jury, accused of Corporate Killing. A charge to which he has pleaded *not* guilty, but a crime of which we, the prosecution, will prove to you that he *is* guilty. Guilty, beyond a reasonable doubt.' Quentin Carver Carpenter QC straightened to his full height, and breathed in noisily and importantly, letting the words hang. Then he hunched forward slightly, grasped the edges of his robes and looked earnestly across the already humid air of Court One of the Central Criminal Court, the Old Bailey, fixing the jury with his gimlet eyes, like a winter wolf considering a flock of young spring lambs.

'The charge may be unfamiliar to you, because it has only recently been enacted. This is, in fact, the first time that the indictment has been tried in open court. A circumstance of which you can hardly be unaware, given the speculation which is rife already in almost every form of media in the country. Hence these august and historic surroundings in which we find ourselves today. Hence the world-wide public scrutiny of everything we do and say. Hence, again for the first time, the presence of news cameras within the very court itself.

'But let me assure you of the seriousness of this new but terrible crime. This is no mere media circus, ladies and gentlemen, like the divorce of some film actors or pop stars. Corporate Killing has been listed as a Class One Offence. This places it amongst the most terrible crimes a man may commit. It puts it on a level with atrocities such as genocide, treason, war-crimes and crimes against humanity; murder, torture and crimes under the Official Secrets Act. It is a crime, therefore, which our society views as even more terrible than manslaughter, infanticide, rape, mutiny, and piracy.

'And what is the general nature of the crime which finds itself in such horrific company? It is this: that the accused, as a senior officer in a public or private enterprise, through action or omission amounting to a gross negligence, shall cause the death of one or more persons to whom he might be supposed to owe a duty of care.

'Now, ladies and gentlemen, I can almost hear some of you asking yourselves, "But what do these fine sounding legal phrases actually mean in the real world of everyday life?" Allow me to explain . . .'

Richard sat between two uniformed officers, whose duty was to restrain him should he behave inappropriately or try some kind of escape, and looked across the court. His dull gaze swept past the vulpine prosecuting counsel, past the black-robed, white-wigged eagle of the judge, away into vacancy.

The air was thick and golden, full of bright motes that blazed like tiny stars and danced dizzyingly. He knew he should be paying the closest imaginable attention to the proceedings, but he was utterly exhausted; absolutely drained. He eased the breadth of his shoulders in the black worsted of his suit jacket and breathed deeply, inflating the snowy whiteness of his shirt-front beneath the sombre darkness of his tie. He rolled the weight of his head in a small circle, hearing his neck-joints crackle and pop. His mind cleared a little.

There was a clock on the far wall with a calendar beneath it that caught his attention incongruously. It was 10.15 on the morning of Tuesday, 2nd July. Richard knew the date and the time well enough. The case had started yesterday, on Monday 1st, just as His Lordship Justice Burgo-Blackstone had decreed with God-like accuracy several months earlier, and they had just finished empanelling the jury. Now, on Tuesday 2nd, the case itself was getting properly under way. Carver Carpenter was going to make his opening speech for the prosecution, outlining the nature of the charge and explaining how the prosecution were proposing to prove it to the jury's satisfaction beyond a reasonable doubt. Then he would begin to call the witnesses that he stated would do just that. The witnesses named in the lists Maggie DaSilva had read out all those weary weeks ago. In the order detailed there. Day after day; week after week if need be. And Maggie, as she had said she would, would cross-examine them, seeking to sow that vital seed of doubt even before she called her own witnesses in turn.

How many times had they discussed the routine? How often had they been through the procedure he must expect throughout the whole of the trial itself? It was as though he were trapped in some corner of Hell where he was doomed to go through the same thing over and over again.

'Now let us turn from the general to the particular, ladies and gentlemen,' continued Carver Carpenter. 'What is it that the accused, Captain Mariner, there, did or failed to do that led step by step through what we have called a *chain of causation*, to the deaths of Captain James Jones and the three officers he took with him on the terrible afternoon in question, desperately using the last lifeboat aboard the stricken and sinking *Goodman Richard* to seek for help and rescue? . . .'

Richard's mind drifted away, as it so often did, to that still more terrible, much more recent afternoon.

'GO! GO! GO!' called the motorcycle policeman over the sound of Richard's Bentley door closing, but Richard hesitated, investing an apparently wasted second in sliding the seatbelt across Robin's still breast and clipping it gently home. Moving in the dream-like slow motion of shock more terrible than anything he had ever known, Richard gunned the motor, looking along the street at the back of the rapidly moving rider. He flicked his headlights on to full beam, seeing them illumine even the early summer evening. He took one deep, tearing breath to steady himself. Then he floored the accelerator and felt the great car leap into motion.

It was as well the other cars in front had cleared the road as best they could, for Richard's foot remained flat on the floor as the Bentley slammed up through the gears, gathering itself into full-sprint. Within five seconds the Bentley was doing 70 and Fleet Street was opening into The Strand beyond the Temple Bar. He went past St Clement Danes at 100mph and Aldwych at 140.

Richard still didn't even ease off as he followed the motorcycle hard round left into Lancaster Place and began to thunder over the great span of Waterloo Bridge. Like a couple of fighter planes, they soared over the slow brown water of the Thames at its flood. Almost shoulder to shoulder the Bentley and the motorcycle soared over the Royal Festival Hall where it crouched beneath the great span on the South Bank, swinging right as they powered down the gradient on to York Road.

Here at last Richard had to ease off the speed as the two vehicles continued to part the traffic side by side, lights blazing, siren wailing, weaving from one side of the roadway to the other. They hurled past the rear of the old County Hall on to the southern end of Westminster Bridge itself.

Immediately on the far side of that, St Thomas' Hospital towered white and multi-windowed, and the motorcycle was able to guide the racing Bentley into the lanes marked for Emergency Vehicles Only, through the gates and up to the covered portal of Accident and Emergency itself. Six tyres left black lines smoking on the tarmac as the two vehicles pulled into the emergency bay.

The young officer had not been using all his concentration on riding. He had been yelling into his helmet mic. And to good effect. A crash team and a trolley came running out as Richard pulled to a stop. He was out of the vehicle at once, sucking his knuckles where he had skinned them on the release catch of her seatbelt. He pulled the passenger door open as the paramedic team arrived with a patter of footsteps and the scream of a wonky wheel.

Richard reached in for her, aware that he was in the way but unable to restrain himself. As he did so, her eyes flickered, parting the pools of congealing blood and fixing him with a steady grey stare. Lips parted, stirring the black cloth of her mask. 'Now that's what I call a *ride*,' she whispered, still alive after all. Still alive; just barely.

He went down on his knees then and the crash team had to pull him away in order to get to her. It was the motorcycle officer who eased him to his feet. 'We'll have to get the car round to the car park, sir. We can't leave it here in the way. Are you OK to drive it or shall I?'

'I can do it,' said Richard.

'Oh.' A little crestfallen. 'OK. I'll lead the way. A little more sedately, this time I think.'

'Ladies and gentlemen of the jury, this is the first crucial point of the prosecution's case. Was Captain Mariner, because of his well-publicized expertise in the fields of maritime working and ship maintenance, specifically given responsibility for health and safety matters aboard *Goodman Richard*? We will be showing you evidence that he was given such responsibility, in the minutes of the meetings of the charity board itself, paragraphs actually countersigned by the Chairman of the Board himself. That will be Exhibit One contained in the Jury Bundle, My Lord, which will be passed to the jury at the appropriate moment . . .'

'Thank you Mr Carver Carpenter, I see it. And, as you have broken the flow of your erudition precisely at the perfect moment, we will upon that point rise for the short adjournment. May I remind the jury that they should not discuss the case with anyone other than each other now or at any other stage of the proceeding, when they are outside the court-room itself. We resume at five minutes past two as usual. Officers, you may take the prisoner down. He has bail within the confines of the building.'

They had found a little waiting room. Frances Bacon had arranged a light lunch there and no sooner had Richard arrived than Maggie appeared as well, all white wig, black robes and Opium. Richard sat, dully, neither his eyes nor his interest nor his appetite tempted by the cold chicken or the salads spread before him. 'How do you think it's going?' asked Frances.

'Early days,' said Maggie, off-hand. 'We'll be shadow-boxing for some time yet. Any news from Jim?'

'Nothing yet.'

'Well, he'll be in contact soon I'm sure. Richard. Richard!'

'What? Oh, sorry. Miles away.'

'I know. You have been all morning. And if I've noticed you can bet the jury has. Look, Richard, Carver Carpenter may be as dull as ditch water, but it's your life he's trying to destroy. Try and look as if you give a toss!'

'Yes. Sorry, it's just that . . .'

'I know. Robin.'

'It's been hard.'

'I know it has, Richard. But things will just get harder and harder still unless you wake your ideas up. And soon!' As she spoke, she checked her watch and then she reached into her bag and pulled out a cellphone. She handed it to him and as if by magic it began to ring. He glanced up at the notice on the wall which said PLEASE TURN OFF YOUR PERSONAL PHONES. He keyed ANSWER and said, 'Hi, darling, how's things?'

Robin was in the operating theatre so long that her father and stepmother were able to assimilate the news, organize themselves, pack up and drive down from their great house Cold Fell, north of Carlisle, on the Scottish borders, to be with Richard before she came out into intensive care. She lingered in intensive care for three weeks while Richard spent his time almost exclusively in St Thomas'. The only lengthy periods he spent away from the sterile area outside her room were those he spent with the children and – once – with Frances and Jim. The weeks in intensive care were followed by a month in a private room while the physiotherapists worked on her in a range of areas.

Her facial muscles had been badly lacerated and required a lot of work to restore the vital immediacy of her usual expressions. And to do so – at her own insistence – without excessive scarring. Or, indeed, any visible scarring at all. This took more time still, but, she joked, with the grim, gritty humour that characterized her *in extremis*, that this was fortunate – it gave her hair a chance to return to the golden curls that had characterized it throughout her life so far. Luckily, the fire that had crisped her hair black had not damaged the scalp itself too badly.

Towards the end of this time she was happy to see the twins – though she still looked a little like a stroke patient who was also receiving chemotherapy – with her face strangely immobile in places and her head swathed in a head dress. But she saw them seated in a chair for the physiotherapists had a great deal of work to do beyond the reconstruction of her facial muscles.

Now, as she talked illegally to Richard – St Thomas' communicating via satellite with the Old Bailey hardly more than a mile distant – Robin was working on getting back on her feet. Rather like someone who has lost both legs, she was building up her ability to walk – and had set herself a deadline within the fortnight. She would be walking – running, perhaps skipping – when the twins finished their summer term in ten days' time. But in the meantime, the one place she could not be was in the court-room with Richard.

'How's it going, old thing?' she asked.

And Richard, suddenly alive and much like his old self – for the time being at least – answered with a laugh, 'D'you know, I really don't have the faintest idea . . .'

25: Whip Hand

'Now, Dr Walton, in conclusion, let us just clarify some important aspects of your testimony for the jury. Why did Charles Lee designate Captain Mariner as the board member responsible for health and safety?' Quentin Carver Carpenter assumed his habitual position, shoulders slightly hunched, hands grasping the edges of his gown. A really acute eye, like Maggie's, might just have seen the beads of sweat running down his temples from beneath the front edge of his wig. The temperature in the claustrophobic court-room was approaching the mid 30s Celsius.

'Well, sir, Mr Lee told me quite specifically, on more than one occasion, that he had concerns about the safety of *Goodman Richard*. But that he did not have the expertise to address such things himself. And that he had invited Captain Mariner to join us specifically to keep an eye on health and safety aboard.' The sweating doctor frowned as he gave his evidence, seeming to be fighting to remember it, word for word, like a schoolboy in an oral test.

'I see. And did Mr Lee tell you why he held such concerns?'

'They began with the most recent report that the marine surveyor prepared for the insurers.' The doctor relaxed a little – there had been hours of testimony so far – and tried to insert a personal aside: 'I read the report myself and could see nothing in it; but I am not an expert of course.' Carver Carpenter's gathering frown and gimlet eye returned the doctor to his prepared evidence, in some confusion. 'Mr Lee and Captain Jones both declared themselves less than satisfied however, and so Captain Mariner was invited on to the board. Mr Lee specifically told me yesterday—'

'*Dr Walton*, if I may interrupt you there and ask you to consider what you have just said . . .' snapped Carver Carpenter a little stridently, the beads of sweat running in gathering abundance.

'What?' The doctor seemed suddenly elderly, lost and confused. 'I beg your pardon?'

'May I request that the last piece of testimony be read back to the witness, My Lord? As I informed the court on Friday the doctor is recovering from an illness contracted on his return from a holiday in Rome and he is not yet strong. He has been giving evidence since early this morning and I believe that even a rest at lunchtime has not really relieved his tiredness.'

'Of course, Mr Carver Carpenter . . .' Burgo-Blackstone would have said more – but restrained himself in time.

'*Mr Lee specifically told me yesterday* . . .' droned the voice of the Court shorthand writer.

'Ah. Yes, I see. My apologies. My apologies, My Lord. What I should have said . . . What I had meant to say, was that Mr Lee specifically told me *at the time*, that he was fortunate to be able to call upon Captain Mariner. His presence on the board with those responsibilities would put his mind to rest. That is to say, the Captain's presence would put Mr Lee's mind to rest . . .' Dr Walton mopped his brow with a white handkerchief. As he did so, a ring gleamed on one of his fingers – a confection of gold and blue.

'And those were Mr Lee's specific words?' pursued Carver Carpenter. '"Put my mind at rest"?'

'Yes, they were.' The doctor put his handkerchief away.

'And did it? Did Captain Mariner's presence on the board put Mr Lee's mind at rest?'

'No, sir. Captain Mariner never seemed to take his responsibilities seriously. He rarely attended meetings. Mr Lee expressed reservations at several meetings when the Captain was not present. He did not allow the early reservations to be minuted – the Captain was his friend and employer, he said. But he initialled the paragraphs that expressed specific concerns in later minutes.'

'My Lord,' Maggie was on her feet. 'This is hearsay, My Lord.'

'It seems so to me too,' agreed Burgo-Blackstone. 'But I will let it stand because of its context. Are you finished with the witness, Mr Carver Carpenter?'

'I am, My Lord. Thank you, Dr Walton, that is all.' Carver Carpenter sat.

'But please stay where you are, Doctor,' persisted Burgo-Blackstone. 'I believe Mizz DaSilva wishes to ask a question or two.'

Maggie DaSilva remained on her feet and turned to the fray.

Robin Mariner leaned forward a little, all her considerable attention and acuity focused on the witness. A movement distracted her for an instant. It was Richard, also leaning forward, focused on the proceedings. *Good*, she thought.

It was Monday, 8th July, the first day Robin was able to attend, though she was only there for an hour or two of the afternoon session, then back to the hospital and into the physiotherapist's hands. But it seemed that Maggie had been correct when she said that – even for an hour; even in a wheelchair – Robin's presence would make all the difference to Richard.

The first few days had been taken up with Carver Carpenter's opening address, and then with the evidence given by the experts on wind, weather, and rescue in the Western Approaches. Under the conditions and upon the day when *Goodman Richard* was lost, and when – most pointedly – Captain James Jones and three senior officers had also been lost. Lost, presumed drowned at the recent inquest.

But, by all accounts, Robin had missed little – for the evidence had been as Maggie had predicted. *Yes, things were bad enough to catch a good few weekend sailors out and overstretch the services. But they weren't really bad enough to put at risk a properly crewed and well-maintained vessel. Even a four-masted square rigger. She had been badly sailed, therefore, badly maintained, improperly rigged and weakly masted.*

More than that they'd never know for she was far too deep to recover. Beneath the mountainous fangs of the Wolf Rock Reef . . .

Friday had begun Dr Walton's evidence, but the man had been plainly unwell, and so the court had risen early – just at lunch in fact – to give the witness, and the jury, some respite. But now they were coming to the meat of the prosecution's first main contention: that if the vessel was badly looked after, then that was Richard's fault. Something that Maggie was all set to question, whether the witness be hale and hearty – or as close to death's door as Robin herself had been.

'Dr Walton, I suggest to you that, rather than recollecting conversations with Mr Lee word for word, you are in fact inventing and interpreting. That you are reporting, in your own words, conversations that never actually took place verbatim but which you feel reflect something of Mr Lee's thoughts upon the matter. That you have constantly presented hearsay as fact.'

'No. That's not true. These were real conversations as I remember them, word for word.' The doctor looked around the court like a startled animal. After the sedate, gentlemen's club procedures of Carver Carpenter's examination in chief, Maggie's cross-examination clearly came as a surprise.

'I see. Remember, please, that these are conversations that took place over a two-year period which ended a year ago when Mr Lee actually vanished from the face of the earth.'

'Yes. That is correct.'

'And you haven't seen him or talked to him since?'

'Of course not!'

'Not yesterday? You did say *yesterday*, did you not?'

'No. That was a slip of the tongue. I . . .'

'Of course. I apologize if I sounded brusque. I was just clarifying matters for the jury. You see, my client has no recollection of Mr Lee ever discussing these matters with him. He had no idea that there was any specific area for which he was responsible. He believed that, like Miss Helen Levin, whose testimony we will hear later when she arrives from Hollywood, his place was merely to raise the profile of the charity and to raise what further funds he could through his business and professional contacts. Dr Walton, you and Mr Lee, in the face of the disaster that in fact overtook your bankrupt charity's only asset, have in fact concocted a farrago of fictional conversations and doctored records to try and shift responsibility away from yourselves.'

'That is not the case. Charles told me . . . Mr Lee and I had many conversations that were exactly, word for word, as I have reported them.'

'Word for word?'

'I have already said so!'

'You certainly seem to have a remarkable memory, Doctor.'

'There is a lot of memory-work in my profession. One needs to know one's patients, their illnesses and medications—'

'Quite. I understand. I wonder, Doctor, whether you could tell me the name of the hotel in Rome where you spent your most recent holiday?'

'Well, I don't quite see—'

'Indulge me, Doctor, please.' Maggie's tone became almost velvety.

'Really, My Lord –' Carver Carpenter half-rose fussily – 'I fail to see the relevance of this . . .'

Burgo-Blackstone nodded emphatically. 'I believe I agree, Mr Carver Carpenter. Mizz DaSilva—'

But Dr Walton answered, loudly and forcefully. 'The Hotel Milan. Yes. That's right. It was the Hotel Milan, near the Coliseum.'

'I'm afraid my information suggests that your amazing memory may have failed you, sir. In this regard at least. In actual fact it was the Hotel *Miami* where you stayed, Dr Walton.'

'Oh. If you say so. But I must observe that the location of my holiday in Rome was never a life-and-death matter. Unlike my talks with Mr Lee.'

'That is my point, Doctor. Those conversations that you remember so vividly were not as you put it life-and-death matters then either. Nor were they life-and-death matters a few months later when they, like the name of your hotel, might reasonably start slipping from your memory. They did not become life-and-death matters for more than a year. Where did you say your hotel was located?'

'Near the Coliseum . . .' Dr Walton looked hesitant, almost shifty.

Maggie shook her head, almost regretfully. 'Near the Trevi Fountain, I understand. And just across the road from a central Roman Masonic Hall.'

Dr Walton simply looked at Maggie, dumbfounded, his mouth working like that of a landed fish, his eyes bugging, his forehead streaming. The ring gleaming brightly on the knuckle that grasped the edge of the witness box.

Carver Carpenter rose. 'My Lord, my witness is not well. May I crave your indulgence upon his behalf?'

'Indeed, Mr Carver Carpenter . . .'

'My Lord, I must ask that I be allowed to continue. I have questions for this witness about his resignation from the board, about other conversations he had with Mr Lee regarding Lee's plans for the commercial broadening of the enterprise—'

'I am sorry, Mizz DaSilva. The man is not well and that is that. We will rise at once. You may question him further if and when he is strong enough. Now, as we did on Friday, we will rise a little early. Ladies and gentlemen of the jury, may I remind you not to discuss the proceedings of this court with anyone, in spite of the great and gathering international interest in what we are doing here. And the well-known prevalence of cheque-book journalism amongst our own media let alone the corps of the international press. At the first whiff of any untoward dealings, I will have the jury sent to a secure location and held there for the remainder of the trial. I trust I make myself clear, ladies and gentlemen . . .'

'I don't have to be back in physio. for another hour,' insisted Robin. 'Let's go through some of the stuff I missed when I was in hospital. What's our best hope?' Her presence among the defence team had galvanized them all, and had brought a surge of energy to her own battered body. She realized that at least a part of what had been so painfully wrong with her during the last weeks was the feeling that she had been isolated from the team, useless to the defence – and to Richard when he needed her the most. But in fact, as she soon learned, even lying bruised and broken in intensive care, she had been at the heart of what they had been doing; essential to their plans.

'Why is my wife's right hand bandaged?' asked Richard all those weary weeks earlier. 'Her hands weren't burned or cut as far as I can recall.'

'No,' answered the doctor. 'We're not sure what that was. Her palm is covered in ridges, almost as though her hand had been whipped. It's nothing dangerous medically, but it seemed to be troubling her. You've no idea at all, I suppose?'

Richard frowned, trying to think back. It had been more than a week since it happened; a week where the preparations for his case had simply been derailed by the police investigation into the fire-bombing of Bacon, Constable's offices. Arson was now attempted murder. Everything else was pushed aside by yet another police investigation – like a collision between a Mini and a lorry. Frances and Jim were with the police at the moment, though they had an appointment with him and Maggie later this afternoon.

But the doctor's quiet question pulled Richard back to the fatal moment yet again. The whole dreadful episode filled all of his mind waking or sleeping still, but only as a series of horrific, nightmare images from which he shied away. Grimly, he began to sort through them, looking through the glass into the little intensive care room at Robin's still figure lying at the midst of all that strange equipment, the heart of the machine.

Her fists had been clenched when he found her cocooned in glass on the smoke-filled stairwell. The image of them came quite suddenly. The sensory overload of the whole terrible memory. All the rest of her body had been loose, deathly slack. But her fists had been clenched, all the way down to the Bentley. And yet, when he knelt to release her from the car at the emergency reception outside the hospital here, her hands had been open. He had a clear vision of her hand lying like a lotus flower half open against the darkness of the battleship-grey leather.

Beyond cleaning the blood off the leather as soon as he got back to the H.M. car park, he had paid very little attention to the inside of the car. Robin had disapproved of it and so he had neglected it as part of his continuing care for her. Now he returned to it. And there, wedged in a tiny, leather and Wilton-walled valley between the side of the seat and the door-frame, edge-up, reflecting the colours of its environment like a chameleon, and therefore almost perfectly invisible, was the last remaining minidisk from the wrecked recorder in the office.

Richard pressed PLAY, eased the big silver plastic headphones over his ears and closed his eyes. They had all listened to the disk, discussed it – squabbled over what they thought they could hear on it. The only thing they had agreed on – agreed to accept, on Richard's say-so – was that the voice that answered belonged to James Jones, the dead Captain of the *Goodman Richard.* But, of course, after Inspector Nolan's comments and after everything else that had happened, Richard wasn't so certain now.

Or rather, he hadn't been until Frances Bacon made that vital link which pulled it all together in his mind: 'It must mean something, Richard, or the office wouldn't have been targeted. Bacon, Constable have been in the business for years. Nothing like this has ever happened before. Yet within a day of this phone call the office is attacked. Robin and I are damn nearly killed – though I think that could be as much to do with that faulty door-lock as with malice aforethought. But it happened. There has to be a link. Therefore this has to be vitally important.'

Then Jim had added, reasonably, 'Look. Richard, Maggie's voice expert Professor German has a copy now – but nothing to compare it with. You're the best man to help us. Put on the earphones, close your eyes, and make a mental list of the pictures and ideas the phone call actually calls into your mind. We know it's on or near a ship, on or near the sea. But there's a lot of ships and a lot of seashores in the world. If it's going to help us, we need you to fill in more detail. Any detail. No matter how small or irrelevant it seems.'

What he hadn't added was the most important thing – that set Richard's subconscious mind alight: it'll give you something to do that will take your mind off Robin for a while. Something that she got hurt preserving for us. Something that might make sense of what has happened to her – if you can explain it for us.

Richard pressed PLAY and eased the phones over his ears. He closed his eyes. His whole head filled with the whispers and crackles of connection, seeming to speak of vast distances and open spaces.

The *ring-tone*. Seemingly closer, apparently very close. Closeness dismissed as an illusion, like the distances had been. It was a satellite link. Of course there were distances. And it could be answered in Tooting or Timbuktu.

Five rings. The shock of the sound almost stopping his heart. So immediate, within the headphones, so intimate.

Connection.

Richard squeezed his eyes closed and allowed the sounds to speak directly to his imaginative memory, fleshing out each tinkle and whisper with the idea of what had made it, setting up a visual soundscape, as though listening to Beethoven's *Pastoral*, Dvorak's *New World* or Mussorgsky's *Pictures at an Exhibition* . . .

Clanking, *crashing*, a low powerful rumbling he hadn't noticed before, almost lost beneath the seagulls' cries and that strange flapping clapping. A crane or winch lifting. Grumbling and grating. Loading and unloading. Containers . . . ? The picture fell into place. A container ship in port, gulls hovering, cranes and winches working. Someone flapping and clapping. A grunting cry. Cut off at once.

'*YES?*' So loud it made his head ring. James Jones appeared in the phantom image, just as Richard remembered him, but clutching a cellphone, angry, worried; disturbed.

The sounds continued. Containers rose and fell behind him. Gulls wheeled behind them, white in bright sunlight and black against blue sky. And the clapping continued. Charles Lee appeared mockingly in the picture, clapping at the Captain's cunning in escaping wreck, inquiry, censure, perhaps criminal charge. Paul Ho and May Chung's evidence would speak of panic, when the masts went down, of recriminations and confrontations. But the prosecution would dismiss Paul as a babyminder, not a sail handler. And May as little more than a child in any case . . .

Distracted, Richard missed the rest of the moment, until Jones's next '*YES*?' half deafened him again and recalled him to the task in hand.

Jim's voice, '*CHARLES, IS THAT YOU*?' deafening – it was well he was prepared.

But after the echo, a surge in sound as though the equipment were trying to compensate. That flapping, croaking clapping sound. So alien. So familiar. Like the trace of a spice in the flavour of a curry.

'*WHAT*?' Simple confusion in Jones's tone. That this, of all questions, should have been asked of him now.

His own voice, '*JONES? CAPTAIN JAMES JONES?*'

Breathing. Breath sucked in with shock. Richard hadn't heard that before. That he had been found? That – like Richard on the far end of the line – he recognized the voice?

The rustle of movement as the call's recipient turned suddenly.

The clapping croaking flapping moving up, up and away . . .

CLICK.

The hiss of empty tape.

The picture conjured by the sounds still lingered in Richard's tight-closed eyes. James Jones, holding the cellphone, hesitated on the ghost of a container ship, with the crates being dropped and lifted behind him and the gulls and the sky behind that. And the outline of a dock area, white against the deep blue, sunwashed sky.

And a pelican flapping away down the wind clapping its beak open and closed as it went. An Australian pelican, like the ones in the advert Robin had found the phone number written on. Like the ones you found in Sydney, and a range of harbours up and down the eastern Australian coast.

Where the container vessel *Sanna Maru* was working currently, with Elroy Kim, her radio operator, waiting to be called to the Bailey, because he was the only man other than *Lionheart*'s Sparks to have talked to *Goodman Richard* that day. *Sanna Maru* : the one vessel that had come past *Lionheart* on the fatal day close enough for Richard to make out at least part of her name.

26: Trial

Richard watched Robin, thinking how infinitely desirable she looked. But utterly unavailable, unfortunately. And for the foreseeable future, too. He'd have to take up golf like William, his son, he thought. Golf and cold showers. Or go out sailing: that would be better – just as expensively distracting and the cold showers never stopped.

Robin was lying on her back in the physiotherapy pool wearing a black swimsuit. It was not designed to be anything other than the exercise garment that it was – as the movements she was performing were not designed to be anything other than simple, muscle-building exercises. But the swimsuit moulded itself to every curve and cranny of her like the pelt of a swimming otter, like the fur of a diving seal. And the exercise simply drove him to distraction.

They had discussed again the theory – which she shared with Frances Bacon – that the damage done to the investigator and herself by the arson attack had been almost accidental. That it had been caused as much by the faulty lock on the back door and their need to escape through the burning room as by the plans of the arsonists themselves. That already faulty lock had probably – as the police now believed – been finally, fatally damaged by whoever had broken in to plant the incendiary device. He could see how this all made her feel more secure – better to be an accidental victim than a target for assassination. But he had pointed out that it didn't make any difference at law – any more than if a punch in a brawl broke a neck instead of a nose. Certainly the attempted murder charge would be likely to stand if they ever caught anyone for the crime.

'That's not the point I'm making,' she had countered. 'I mean that, if the fire wasn't meant to kill us, then what was it supposed to do?'

'Scare us off. Destroy any evidence . . .'

'Or egg us on, perhaps. Like the magazine in *Argo*'s toilet. Point us in a certain direction. I mean, unlike everything else aboard, it was left there on purpose, wasn't it? Or do you think Smithers was planning to tidy up when he fell overboard with half a bottle of Scotch in him and got tangled in the anchor chain?'

'But why in God's name would anyone want to point us in any direction at all?'

'Why do they want to do any of it? Perhaps, like Jim said so long ago, it's all set up for something that has yet to happen. Perhaps Dr Walton did mean that he had spoken to Charles Lee yesterday. Perhaps it's all still working its way out and there's something important yet to happen.'

Richard shrugged. *Oxford v. Moss*, he thought. The secret test-paper read – the examination yet to be sat. They fell silent. Robin returned to her exercises.

As she went through the routine designed to strengthen the muscles of her damaged legs, she lazily did a kind of belly-up breaststroke from the waist down. With hypnotic regularity she gathered her heels into her groin as her thighs fell wide. Then she kicked out and stretched her thighs wider still – as wide as they would go – before drawing her ankles together, seemingly almost lazily, against the resistance of the water. From knees upwards, the muscles and tendons of the inner thigh gathered from rest to definition, from definition to rigidity as they pulled the splayed legs closed, toes pointed as though she were dancing water-ballet.

'Talking of being directed in certain directions, is there still no news from Australia?' she asked, more loudly than necessary and he jumped almost guiltily. She had seen the direction of his gaze and read his unmasked expression all too well.

But when he looked up at her face, the level grey of her eyes contained the warmth of an understanding smile. He grinned back almost shyly. 'Nothing,' he answered ruefully. 'After all our recent accidents and adventures, Jim was going to try the official route first, after he found where *Sanna Maru* is or is heading for – then go under cover only *in extremis*.'

'We'll need to hear from him soon if he's going to do any good.'

'I guess so,' he answered off-handedly. As though he had hardly thought the matter through. But she saw through his casual tone as clearly as he could see through the surface of the exercise pool. 'After all,' he added cheerfully, 'things only look bad now because the prosecution's been making their case. Things'll get better once Maggie gets under way.'

It was 14th July, the second Sunday of the trial. Last week had been spent with the prosecution using the glorious Helen Levin to drive the still ill Dr Walton from the jury's mind – though apart from glamour and publicity she had added little to the prosecution's case. Then, back to the meat of the matter, Carver Carpenter had produced the last and most junior of *Goodman Richard*'s officers, who had described the awesome rapidity with which destruction had overtaken the masts and rigging. The utter ruination their fall had brought to the deck and almost all the life-preserving equipment stored upon or beside it. He told of near panic amongst the youngsters and some of the officers – in the face of the calm control of Captain Jones and Second Officer Burke the sail-handler. He told of the way First Officer Ho had vanished below.

No, he admitted in cross examination, he had not seen the Captain order him down to look after the cadets, but would not have been surprised to hear it. He told of the rapid calculations made by desperate men in a tricky situation and the decision to go for help. A decision taken after contact with a larger vessel passing close by, he understood. It was a reasoned plan with a chance of success, he submitted. It was tragic that it had ended in disappearance and death rather than heroic rescue. These were good men and good messmates, he insisted

– even under cross examination. Good sailors all, betrayed by bad equipment.

Then there came a troupe of disgruntled cadets who backed his story from points of varyingly terrifying experience, thinly cloaked self-serving distress, and general ignorance. At the conclusion of each piece of evidence, Maggie whispered, 'Preparing to sue for damages . . .' time and time again. But each one digging a little deeper the hole the defence would have to climb out of if Richard was going to survive.

Then, more damagingly still, came an almost embarrassed group of crewmen and women from *Lionheart*. Their testimony bore out that of the officer and cadets from *Goodman Richard*, establishing in the jury's mind – reluctantly and therefore all the more forcefully – the awesome destruction that had been visited on the upper works and hull of the stricken ship. Any doubts cast in the jury's mind by the obviously self-serving cadets were soon expunged as even the descriptions of Richard's heroics that his crew – and employees – offered were twisted by Carver Carpenter into yet more proof of a ship destroyed by bad management. And the actions of a man driven by guilt and fear into putting himself and others at terrible risk simply in order to try and save his own sorry reputation.

Finally, as late as Justice Burgo-Blackstone ever let anything get on a Friday afternoon, Quentin Carver Carpenter had risen. 'My Lord,' he said. 'That does not conclude the case for the prosecution, but I must crave your indulgence with my final witnesses. Dr Walton as you know has developed pneumonia and is likely to remain in hospital for a while. Elroy Kim, radio officer of the vessel *Sanna Maru*, whose evidence should, ah, *sink the defence*, if you will forgive a little play on words, My Lord, is still at sea somewhere off the Antipodes. He cannot even be reached by videophone until he comes to shore. May I request that his evidence be held in abeyance, therefore, until later in the proceedings?'

'You may, Mr Carver Carpenter. And your timing, I observe, is, as ever, excellent. We will rise now. And if Mr Kim has not yet come ashore, we will proceed with the defence on Monday. Please prepare yourself accordingly, Mizz DaSilva.

'Ladies and gentlemen of the jury, need I say again what I

have said to you nine times now? You must not discuss this trial, or any aspects of it with anyone outside the courtroom . . .'

They needed one sort of news from Australia but they got another. There came a brisk rap at the door behind Richard, and Doc Weary breezed in before he could be invited. 'Brought you the Sunday papers,' he announced. Largely because I seem to be in most of them. Jesus, Robin, you look pretty hot for a cripple, girl . . .'

Doc was back for the Fastnet Ocean Race next month and had settled into one of the shipping yards Heritage Mariner had a part interest in near Southampton. Here he was fitting *Katapult* up and getting her ready for the qualifying races and such other sections of the Admiral's Cup he felt would hone her and her crew to the utmost. He was centred in Southampton and was avowedly sailing all the hours God sent – but he seemed to be up in London a couple of times a day. 'Aw come on,' he said when challenged, 'in Oz we drive further than that to get a decent breakfast in. Can I borrow the Bentley, Richard? I'm insured – fully comp – and I drive like your Great Aunt Jemima. You're not really using her at all . . .'

Doc chucked the papers down on to a table and started sorting through them for the sports sections and magazines that contained pictures of himself or his catamaran. Out of the pile slipped the money section of one of the big broadsheets. 'HERITAGE MARINER' said the front page headline ominously. 'HOW MUCH MORE CAN IT STAND?'

The first paragraph was in bold print and larger point than the rest. Richard could read it if he squinted a little.

> Every day H.M.'s charismatic CEO Richard Mariner stands in the dock of Court Number One of the Old Bailey drives down the price of his company's shares on the trading floors of stock exchanges world-wide. It does not matter that he is accused of something that has nothing to do with his own business. It does not matter that he loudly and repeatedly proclaims his innocence. It does not matter that he *is*, in fact, innocent until proven guilty under British law. Fighting the case is killing his company, little by little and day by day. And he knows it. 'We have

considered withdrawing the shares from trade on a temporary basis,' admits Harry Black, chief spokesman of H.M.'s accountants, BWG. 'But we have been advised that it would only further prejudice the case that Captain Mariner is currently fighting. It's a *Catch 22* situation . . .'

'We're pretty high up the favourites list,' Doc was exulting. 'Considering we don't have all that much recent Admiral's Cup form. Most of the ones fancied higher than us are well established – been at it for years. The only dark horse standing higher than we are with the bookies is this one *Tin Hau*. I don't know much about her. Old Royal Hong Kong Yacht Squadron by all accounts. I seem to remember a name like hers on the Sydney–Hobart a year or two back. But they've got everybody all a-buzz now. Hey, look at this. Robin. Look. If this doesn't heat up the old exercise pool, nothing will.'

This was a picture of Doc, all wild hair and bandanna, exclusive top-of-the-range Storm-brand *Seaspray* sunglasses in a black band across his eyes. Cheeks and nose zinc painted as though he were Sitting Bull on the way to Little Big Horn and grinning like a lunatic out of the asylum for the day. Standing framed like a nautical Titan against a royal-blue sky, at the great big hi-tech helm of *Katapult* herself. 'Not bad for an afternoon on the Solent if I do say so myself,' he said.

'Take it away,' said Robin lazily. 'Or something might boil over.'

'Not bad for a ship of her age,' said Patrick Cornwall, marine surveyor, soon after 10 a.m. a couple of days later. 'The deck needed a little work – I have noted here some half-dozen planks sprung and perhaps in need of caulking or sealing. That's deck planks of course. You are aware, I'm sure, that she was a steel-hulled vessel. And some of the rigging needed replacing, though I did not examine every inch of the suits of sails aboard. The footings of all the masts where they met the deck were beginning to perish – but that is not unusual. That junction – of deck and mast – is where most of the wear tends to come. It is not a danger unless it is left too long and it is easy enough to take care of. I can go into much more technical detail as to specific points if you wish. As to yards, halliards, coamings, carlings. Kedges knees and stanchions . . .' He hunched forward over his notes, alternately glancing up and down. He was past retirement age and growing a little hesitant perhaps, but teak-dark and good-looking. Maggie had great hopes for him – particularly with the six women on the jury.

'No, thank you, Mr Cornwall. Let us cut to the chase, as they say. Were you happy to award *Goodman Richard* her certificate of seaworthiness?'

'Subject to some work being done, yes, I was.'

'And did you see that the work had been done?'

'No, I did not. *Goodman Richard* left port before I had a chance to return but I accepted the assurance of Mr Lee that the work had been done and sent the certificate off with copies to the authorities and the Captain's copy to Brewer Street to be forwarded aboard.'

'Is this usual procedure?'

'It's been known. My concerns were small and by no means life-threatening as far as I was aware at the time. And there was an overlap in any case – her current certificate still had a week or so to run at that time. She was well able to sail and her handling would hardly have been affected even had the work not been done at that point. But of course, the work had been done. I had been so assured by Mr Lee. And I should say that this was not the fatal voyage. She sailed on safely for a year before she was lost.'

Maggie nodded, consulted her own notes, then asked, 'Were you surprised when you heard that she had been lost?'

'Yes. I must frankly confess I was. I am not myself anything more than a weekend sailor, you understand. And I was, coincidentally, out in the storm in question. But my little yacht *Grey Goose Two* survived and she's only a twenty footer; so I saw no immediate reason why *Goodman Richard* should not have done so too.'

'If it was not the ship herself, then perhaps it was the way she was handled? Can we have your expert assessment on that, sir?' demanded Maggie quietly, her voice low but forceful.

'Well, yes, but I must say it's little better than a guess. With all her sticks bare – or a storm rig up at the most – she should have ridden out worse weather than that. Bare sticks being masts with no sails and a storm rig being a few sails needed to keep some control of the ship.'

'That's what the coastguards and the coxswain of the St Mary's lifeboat told us, though they didn't explain the technical terms. Now, Mr Cornwall, please think: were you surprised to hear *how* she had been lost?'

'Again, yes, I was. There must have been a fair amount of canvas up to take two masts like that. Both at once, rigging and all.'

'*Canvas up*, Mr Cornwall. Not *masts weakened* by bad or improper maintenance? Not *rigging worn out* and in need of replacement?'

'It might be just possible, I suppose. If Mr Lee had been lying and nothing I ordered was done. If *Goodman Richard* had been battered about a good bit, in the hands of an inexperienced and careless crew. If health and safety had been ignored at every level. But the descriptions I have heard of the incident all convince me there must have been a fair amount of canvas up when the masts went down. And if that happened in the midst of the storm then that's seamanship not management. It's ship handling, not health and safety.'

'One final thing, Mr Cornwall. Square-rigged sailing ships like *Goodman Richard* have been common around our coasts for centuries, have they not?'

'Square-riggers have, yes. But not quite like *Goodman Richard*.'

'What do you mean?'

'She was modern. Steel-hulled, as I said. You couldn't get four masts rigged like that on any of the old sailing ships.'

'So she was quite modern, then, for a sailing ship?'

'That's right. Her keel was laid in, oh let me see . . . 1966 . . . Yes, 1966. She was launched in 1969.'

'So, although she looked quite timeless, she was actually less than forty years old.'

'Oh yes, that is quite correct.'

'Mr Cornwall, would you agree that many of the boats taking part in the Admiral's Cup this year are of greater age. That I myself have several friends – as do we all I am sure – who drive motor cars of greater age. And were you to holiday in some of the remoter regions of the world, you would undoubtedly fly in aeroplanes of greater age. I am certain that several of the so-called supertankers and container vessels which went past as she sank and were unable to come to her aid were of very much greater age. This was no ill-maintained ancient wreck just waiting to die. It was a well founded, *well maintained*, modern vessel.'

Maggie sat.

Carver Carpenter rose. 'Are you telling the jury, Mr Cornwall, that the only explanation for the loss of the *Goodman Richard* is ship-handling? That there is no other possible explanation?'

'No, sir. I don't think I said that and I certainly didn't mean to.'

'Very well. Then might I suggest to you, sir, that Mr Lee might actually have been a little, shall we say, *previous* when he said the repairs had been effected – for this was the time the first concern about health and safety was initialled in the minutes of the charity board. Please check the dates, ladies and gentlemen of the jury. They do tally, I assure you. He had, it seems, referred the matter to Captain Mariner even as he was talking to you, Mr Cornwall. And we are aware of what action the Captain took. None whatsoever. Health and safety might not have been ignored at every level – but it was ignored at one, crucial level. Then, indeed, as you say Mr Cornwall, the *Goodman Richard* was battered about. Across the North Sea – the notorious North Sea time and again on a regular basis. And down across Biscay – worse still – for month after month. And were her crew inexperienced and careless? Effectively, yes of course they were! They were cadets. They were boys and girls who came aboard to learn what they were supposed to do. Some half-dozen officers aboard were really capable of handling a ship such as this and the rest just glorified baby-minders. You have heard from the last of the ship-handlers aboard her – the only one left alive after the Captain's heroic attempt to get help. Did he say there were too many sails up? No, he did not. Did he say it all went by the board because of bad ship-handling? No he did not.

'Now, Mr Cornwall, let us forget about the age of the average Admiral's Cup competitor, of the occasional motor vehicle, the rare aeroplane and one tanker in twenty. This ship. The

Goodman Richard. Could she have been destroyed by the storm that did not touch your yacht *Grey Goose Two* because she was owned by people who did not bother to do the work they promised they would do – or any other work at all for the next twelve months at sea? Hard months in tough, stormy seas?'

'Well, yes. When you put it like that, of course sir. Of course it could have been gross neglect.'

Maggie half rose, aghast. Nowhere in any of their conversations in conference or even in his subsequent reports had he ever hinted at any such opinion. But before she could even call him back, Cornwall had turned and was on his way out of the witness box. And so she sat once again, stealing a sympathetic glance across towards Richard. He was white; stunned. Christ, she thought, thank goodness Robin was in physio. this afternoon. She didn't want both of the Mariners looking like that. But still and all, she said to herself, rising again to call the next name on her witness list, *With friends like that, who needs enemies?*

27: Error

During the succeeding days, Patrick Cornwall was followed into the witness box by the *Goodman Richard*'s Radio Officer, her First Officer, Paul Ho. Then by a series of cadets who were so different in aspect and attitude to the prosecution's cadet witnesses that they might have been on a different ship, undergoing a different adventure altogether. It was the defence's plan that these witnesses would be followed first by Doc Weary, then by Richard himself. And the prospect of this final ordeal added inexorably to the gathering tension Richard was experiencing as one hot, humid, oppressively tropical day followed another and Court Number One sweltered as though this were not London, but Calcutta.

The radio operator, overwhelmed, gave his evidence in a kind of whisper. His experience in the post was actually limited, he explained, and in fact the Third and Fourth Deck officers were more often at the radio than he was himself. On the fatal day, he had been terribly seasick and had only been at his post for part of the watch. He had not been in contact with any ship other than the *Lionheart* whose answer to his distress call had come blessedly soon after he made it. The Fourth Officer had been at his post before him. The Fourth Officer had contacted the coastguards and sent out the first distress, so he had been told. And then, yes, there had been the lightning strike. And he really remembered nothing more.

Maggie treated him almost maternally to get such information from him as she did. But he was meat and drink to Carver Carpenter who demolished him in no time flat.

Paul Ho described the onset of the storm, and his impressions of the deck work and the sail-handling that it brought about. He was able also to describe the sea-sickness which had spread to many more aboard than the unfortunate Radio Officer, the growing panic – and how he had been hard-put to contain it. The moment that the masts went.

'Were you on deck yourself at the critical moment?' asked Maggie.

'No, ma'am. I had been called below to a minor incident.'

'But the other officers were?'

'No. The Fourth Officer still held the radio watch but the Captain and his two main sail-handling officers were on deck of course with the cadets from Green Watch.'

'So, it was not a case of "All Hands On Deck".'

'No, ma'am. Nor, by the grace of God, were any of the cadets aloft when the masts went by the board.'

'Is that surprising?'

'I hadn't really thought of it in that light. I assume they were holding the Watch back, waiting to read the weather before sending them aloft in the storm.'

'But in any case, you were below when the masts went.'

'That is correct, ma'am . . .'

Ho described the sudden arrival of the shocked and soaking Green Watch, of the Fourth Officer's attempts to get help on the radio – only vaguely heard in the bustle and the growing panic which he and a team of senior cadets were working hard to contain. Of the arrival of the Captain himself and his terse explanation of the situation, the warnings about the deadly dangers of the storm-swept deck – and of the plan to get help. The replacement of the Fourth Officer by the Radio Officer and the sudden quiet after the last lifeboat had gone . . .

'Mr Ho,' said Carver Carpenter, rising to his examination, 'please allow me to clarify things for the jury. What precisely were your duties as First Officer?'

'Obviously I have been trained and am experienced in ship-handling, theory and practice, life-saving and distress, loading, unloading, damage control, first aid, navigation, watch keeping . . .'

'That's not what I asked. On *Goodman Richard*, what were your duties?'

'I held watches, practised first aid, oversaw lading, storage, galley routines. I set up and oversaw the watches for the cadets . . .'

'Ah. Now, can we be clear here for the jury? Were your responsibilities principally to do with sailing the ship or to do with the welfare of the cadets?'

'Cadet welfare, sir.' The answer almost grated out of Paul's throat. Clearly he did not like the fact and did not relish admitting to it.

'And did you yourself at any time oversee the disposition, changing or handling of the sails themselves?'

'No, sir.'

'Did you, at any time, actually go aloft?'

'Well, no, sir.'

'No head for heights, eh?'

'No, sir, not really.' He tried to make a joke of it; going down Dr Walton's dangerous road. 'I get dizzy stepping off of a high kerb.'

Carver Carpenter paused, letting the admission sink into the jury's consciousness. 'But you are familiar with the theory of sail-handling? Rope and canvas work?' His tone was patronizing – as befitted a sail-ship officer who was afraid of heights.

'Well, I'm a bit rusty on lays, bights and whippings. I was trained in powered sailing rather than canvas . . .' Paul's voice trailed off. He was aware that he was not making a good impression on the jury and yet seemed powerless to put things right.

'So your main function aboard was, as has been said earlier, *childminding*,' sneered Carver Carpenter. 'You were there as a kind of teacher – or more accurately a form-tutor. Perhaps even head prefect?'

'You could put it like that.'

'What you were not, and *are* not, is competent to pass any judgement on the sorry state of the *Goodman Richard*'s sails, masts and cordage. Nor upon the way Captain Jones and his sailing master were actually handling the ship when she so catastrophically let them down! Thank you, First Officer Ho.' He made the words 'First Officer' sound like an insult, and they echoed on the humid air as he gathered his robes about himself and sat.

Maggie re-examined, but never really undid the damage Carver Carpenter had done to Paul Ho's testimony. The cadets she called over the next day added to the First Officer's stature as a childminder – and as a steady man in a crisis. But it was not until Friday morning that there was any further comment on the crucial matter of sail-handling, and some further explanation of what was going on aloft when the fatal moment struck.

Cadet May Chung was by no means as large or prepossessing as some of the other witnesses. But there was something about her that claimed the court's attention at once. Sensing this, Maggie was willing to let her have her head. And May, forthright and unwilling to fancy up her evidence even with the simplest explanation, simply took no prisoners.

'You were the senior cadet in the Green Watch, I understand,' said Maggie.

'That's right. I was working with the Second Officer. He was teaching me sail-handling. I liked Mr Ho better, but Second Officer Burke liked me. Said I would make a good sail-handler. Pity there's no more ships like *Goodman Richard* left. I born too late, like grandmother Chung say . . .'

'I see. So you can tell us about *Goodman Richard*'s sails?'

'Yes, ma'am. *Goodman Richard* was a four-masted square-rigged sailing ship. She was ship rigged with five square sails per mast but she did not have spankers up. During time we worked her, we learned to rig and reef all jibs. Staysails on bowsprit and all masts. Sail, topsails, topgallant and royal on foremast, main mast, mizzen mast and jigger. We were up and down like monkeys when the weather was calm, but less so in bad weather. If the forecast was bad we usually took the sails off her and relied on the engine.'

'But not that day?'

'Engine stopped working. Water in fuel. Water every damn where that day.'

'So Captain Jones was relying on sailing out of trouble?'

'Seem like it. But even so . . .'

'You have doubts?'

'Maybe Captain and Second Officer they had a cunning plan, you know? Maaaaaaybe . . .' May drew out the last word sceptically.

'Can you explain?'

'Storm coming. They need storm sails up. Maybe reefed foresail. Maybe storm jib. That's what I think. Give her handling, hold her safe. Maybe that's what they plan but they just too slow, you know? Squall hit from South West, then back Easterly really fast. And they had all the wrong sails up. They have royals and topgallants on all masts. Full out, not reefed. No topsails or mainsails. You see? Royals right at the top of the mast. Topgallants next down but also high, high, high up mast. All wind's power hit right up at tip top of masts. Nothing down below to balance. Over she goes one way, bad roll. Big sea come up that side and threaten to swamp her altogether. Masts flex. Rigging strain. Hold together because the whole hull rolled right over with them. I thinking May, better blow up your lifejacket. But then back-wind. Great gust from the east – exactly the opposite way! You see? Ship's hull still under westerly seas. Hull not roll back to compensate. No big sails low down to hold her steady. All sails up top. Wind took them and ripped them right out. No flexing. No straining. Whole lot gone by the board. Sails, spars, rigging and masts. Wham! Bang! Gone! Just like that.'

Carver Carpenter rose a few minutes later after Maggie – having elicited a translation and clarified a few more points for the jury – sat.

'Miss Chung, may I ask what qualifications in ship-handling you hold?'

'I am not qualified. I not even get the certificate Second Officer promised.' May suddenly looked very young, like a child disappointed by Father Christmas.

'I see. And how many other sailing ships have you crewed?'

'None. *Goodman Richard* first. And, likely, last.'

'Very well, then may I ask how long you served on *Goodman Richard*?'

'Six months.'

'You certainly seem to have picked up a lot of knowledge in that time.'

'I'm a fast learner.'

'I don't doubt it. But still and all, Miss Chung, one must ask oneself, would even a fast learner learn to recognize a badly maintained rope, faulty rigging, weakened wood at the point where the masts went into the mast-holes in the deck?'

May opened her mouth to reply but Carver Carpenter proceeded ruthlessly. 'Because, you see, everything that you so vividly described – what of it I fully understood amongst the jargon – surely could have happened because the Captain expected the upper works to take the battering they received. A battering they received, it seems from your account, while he and the Sail Handler tried to assess the risks of sending your watch up to shorten the sail. Or perhaps even to rig the sails that you yourself suggested. But, fatally weakened through failures of maintenance, health and safety, they simply did not. They snapped and broke and went by the board, as you said, because they were old and rotten and weak.'

'No, sir,' said May clearly, freezing Carver Carpenter in a half sitting position. 'You ask if I recognize bad rope. Answer: Yes. I know all about ropes and lays and all the rest. So I tell you how *Goodman Richard* was rigged. Rigging was mostly three-stranded, forty-eight millimetre manila rope. Very good quality. Not perished or worn out. Breaking strain seventeen and one half tonnes. But where wear and strain was likely to be higher, she was rigged with forty-eight millimetre polypropylene, right-hand lay like the manila, breaking strain twenty-two and one half tonnes. The hardest working rigging was nylon and terylene right-hand lay, four tuck splice, breaking strain forty-two tonnes. Good rope. Yes. Also good rigging. The lay was important of course because if you use two ropes of opposing lay in one set of rigging you will find that they cause each other to unravel.'

One of Carver Carpenter's team came in at that moment and started whispering in the prosecuting counsel's ear.

But May was not about to be put off by such low tactics. 'We cadets were being trained to handle old-fashioned rigs of course. It was a sailing ship after all. So we mostly worked with the manila. Traditional. The other ropes and rigs were used for safety's sake. Therefore good rigging! Yes! Now, as to the state of the masts . . .'

'My Lord—' Carver Carpenter half-rose and hovered in the position, almost as though he were genuflecting to an emperor.

'Yes, Mr Carver Carpenter? Miss Chung, with the greatest apologies I must ask you to desist from giving evidence for a moment.'

'My Lord, I have just been informed that the *Sanna Maru* has just docked in Perth. Radio Officer Elroy Kim is ready to give his evidence if we can bring in the video link at once . . .'

'My Lord!' Maggie was on her feet. 'Surely we should not be interrupting the defence at such a crucial point . . .'

Mr Justice Burgo-Blackstone looked at the clock. 'Very well,' he decided. 'It is almost midday. We will rise for the short adjournment now. Ladies and gentlemen of the jury, I expect you back in court at five past one, not five past two. Please be very prompt indeed. Officers of the court will almost certainly be directing you to Court Number Six where we have available video-conferencing facilities.

'In the meantime, I hope that counsels for the prosecution and the defence have no plans to eat. We will be debating procedure in my chamber.'

Three-quarters of an hour later, Maggie, Richard and Robin were on their way to Court Six. 'I cannot believe he's going to allow it,' fumed Maggie.

'How can he?' demanded Robin. 'May Chung was the best witness we've put up so far and this is simply going to devalue her evidence.'

'I put everything I could think of to him, every precedent, every rule of procedure. All he'd say was *bring it up at appeal*.'

'Appeal?' Richard was horrified. Thunderstruck. 'Heritage

Mariner has been all but bankrupted by this affair so far. God knows what the shares have sunk to today. If this drags on into the appeal courts I might just as well sell up the whole company. If I can find anyone to buy it.'

'Don't get despondent, darling,' said Robin gently. 'I'm sure it's not as bad as all that.' She reached across and took his hand. 'The twins will be down from Cold Fell soon. That'll take your mind off things.'

'That's another thing,' he said a little desperately. 'Sending them off to your father and Helen for the first two weeks of their holidays because we can't fit them in down here, what with me in court and you in hospital . . .'

'Well, I'm coming out of hospital tomorrow and I'm sure you'll be out of court soon too.'

'Out of court and into prison by the look of things.'

'Don't be so gloomy, darling . . .'

'Yes, Richard, perk up,' said Maggie stoutly. 'You know that anything other than cheerful confidence will have a bad effect on the jury. Especially in the face of a set-back like this.'

'Ladies and gentlemen of the jury,' intoned Mr Justice Burgo-Blackstone at one minute past one on the afternoon of Friday 19th July, 'welcome to Court Six. Why are we here? You may well be asking yourselves. Well, what we have here is not a particularly unusual situation. I am proposing to depart from the procedure of a criminal trial, but this is hardly an uncommon occurrence – even though Mizz DaSilva has discussed the situation most vigorously. You will have been aware for a week that the prosecution did not quite finish its case. Mr Carver Carpenter has summoned one more witness. But this witness is a radio operator on a ship at sea who has not been available until now. And I understand that the availability of the witness is likely to be limited by the brevity of his ship's layover in port. I propose, therefore, to interrupt the defence's case – but very briefly I assure you – to accommodate the evidence of this last prosecution witness. I have, as I say, noted strong reservations on the behalf of the Counsel for the Defence, and can do no more than refer the matter to the wisdom of the Court of Appeal, should appeal be lodged against these proceedings, your verdict, ladies and gentlemen, or my judgement in the case.

'Now, to proceed. We have here all the facilities we need to video-conference with Australia and I am assured they are ready to proceed down there. Please cast your minds back to the prosecution's case as it stood after the evidence from the other, less forceful cadets we listened to last Friday. Ushers, please bring in the equipment. Mr Carver Carpenter, prepare to ask your questions.'

The combination of computer, Webcam microphone and TV screen looked identical to the system that had called Doc's testimony to the inquiry, thought Richard wearily, very near the end of his tether now, in spite of the airy lightness of this much more modern court-room. The screen itself was bigger, however. So were the speakers.

The usher pressed some buttons and fiddled with the handset. There was an abrupt hiss as audio contact was made, but the picture was slower to clear. When it did, there was not the one face in close-up that Richard – and everyone else – had expected. Instead, there were two men in clear head and shoulders mid-shot, with two more men slightly out of focus behind them. A fifth man stepped into close-up at last, but he looked nothing like the oriental radio operator the name Elroy Kim had conjured to mind.

'My name is Edward Grainger. I am Sergeant with the harbour police here in Perth. Am I speaking to Quentin Carver Carpenter QC, in the Old Bailey, London, England?'

'Yes, Sergeant Grainger, you are.' Carver Carpenter let the moment hang, savouring an overwhelming victory in prospect. 'May I speak with Elroy Kim, radio operator of the *Sanna Maru* container vessel, please?'

'No, sir, you may not. Radio Officer Kim has absconded, as have several officers of this vessel, which is currently under arrest here for Triad associated activities. I can, however, allow you to speak with the gentleman standing under police guard behind me.'

On that impenetrable note, Sergeant Grainger stepped aside and the broad face of Jim Constable came into sharp focus, frowning. At his shoulder stood a bearded and dishevelled man with long tousled hair and deep-set, hunted eyes. Jim gave him a none-too-gentle nudge and the bearded man said, loudly and clearly, 'My name is James Jones. I used to be Captain of the *Goodman Richard*. I have for the last year been stowed away in secret upon the vessel *Sanna Maru*. These men behind me are Second Officer Burke, Third Officer—'

Maggie rose into the pandemonium that broke out as the import of Captain Jones's words began to sink in. She looked from the gaping Carver Carpenter to the frowning, obviously thunderstruck Burgo-Blackstone. 'My Lord,' she said, just loudly enough to be heard. 'I imagine my learned friend may want to consider his position. I submit that my client no longer has a case to answer. I would ask your Lordship to direct the jury to return a verdict of Not Guilty at once and to discharge Captain Richard Mariner forthwith.'

28: Killing

Maggie and Andrew were all too willing to handle the press as soon as, under the eyes of the entire world, Richard was released from the court with no case to answer and without a stain upon his good character. Richard would have to deal with the excited reporters eventually but he was in no mood to do so now. The exhausted and drained Mariners willingly left their glowing legal representatives to it.

As soon as the formalities of securing his release were completed, Richard led Robin out through a private door and walked her over to the Bentley. Then he ran her back to hospital for her last session. Almost without thinking, he went back up Fleet Street to the great broad span of Waterloo Bridge, and sedately followed the route of his life-saving dash.

'You know,' she said quietly as they edged along towards the South Bank, high above the Royal Festival Hall, 'I could grow to love this car. You were right to choose her. I don't think even Daddy's Mulsanne could have got me to St Thomas' in time.'

'It wasn't the car,' he said. 'It was the poor bloody driver trying to keep up with that mad devil of a motorcycle cop. While someone who shall be nameless put blood all over his incredibly expensive leather upholstery.'

'That's what you say . . .'

He swung the great steely bullet slowly and safely down into York Road. And smiled. 'That's what I say.'

'Look, darling,' she continued in an all too familiar tone.

'Yes?' he answered, just a little guardedly.

'I'm coming out tomorrow . . .'

She sounded like the debutante she had been some years earlier, he thought indulgently. *Coming out.* 'Unh hunh . . .' he said.

'All hale and hearty and so forth . . .'

'In a pig's eye!'

'And you're quite miraculously off the hook . . .'

'"With one bound, Richard was free." Inspector Nolan said it wouldn't be like that at all. But, yes?'

'We really need to have a party, don't we? A good old-fashioned *The Mariners are Back in Town* party. Why don't we try Pont de Londres? I'd be surprised if Jean Philippe couldn't fit in a couple of world-wide media celebrities and a few of their friends. Even with almost no notice.'

'So we'll tell him it's for Maggie and Andrew, will we? Or shall I see if Helen Levin's still in town? She could bring Brad Pitt or George Clooney?'

'Don't be silly, darling,' she said after the tiniest hesitation. When she had clearly been thinking of taking his suggestion seriously.

Better be careful with the sarcastic suggestions, he thought, swinging past the back of County Hall. But he suddenly felt a surge of the old power; the old elation. The Mariners are back. Yes; it might be worth a party at that.

'When?' he asked.

'Tomorrow night. It has to be tomorrow night because Sundays are so dead. And the whole Cold Fell contingent will be descending on us on Monday. And don't worry. I'll do all the calling around. Not too many. Maggie and Andrew of course. As you said. Doc, Frances and partners if they want. Harry Black and his wife. Anyone else from H.M.? I mean it would have been Charles Lee in the old days, but . . . Well, there's Paul Ho, I guess. And wasn't that Chung girl a scream? Pity she's too young – I bet she'd be great company. There are a couple of people here at Thomas's who might be fun.' She concluded as Richard pulled into the hospital car park and she snapped off her seatbelt. 'Say twenty in all.'

Pont de Londres was packed the next evening; not a table – not a chair – unfilled. But, as Robin had suspected, the canny Jean Philippe had cleared a private room behind the main restaurant for them. Given the situation and the timing, their patronage was worth more than a double-page spread in *Gourmet* and *Good Living* magazines. And it would certainly mean a double page spread in *Hello* next week. *Hello* and *Tatler*, with any luck.

At 9.00 precisely, Richard handed the keys of the Bentley to the dazzled parking attendant and led Robin in through the main door. As ever, he moved quietly and modestly – never one to make a fuss. Robin, too, was moving a little more carefully than usual. Pacing herself, perhaps. But as Jean Philippe caught Richard's eye and came across to conduct the pair of them down the main path between the heaving tables, towards the door marked PRIVATE, the buzz of conversation around them swelled and died to utter silence. Richard for one was not surprised. Wherever he had turned today his face had stared back at him. It was like being trapped in a wilderness of mirrors. Front pages, news pages and gossip pages all full of the case. Financial pages – rather more welcome in their way – recording the meteoric rises in Heritage Mariner stock on all the world's exchanges as it powered back towards its old, pre-trial levels. All in all, stunned silence was just about what Richard had expected all along.

And then, sounding disturbingly to Richard like the sound of the pelican on the disk of the phone-call that had saved him in the end, someone began to clap. Then someone else called, 'Well done!' And the applause exploded right through the whole place. Applause, all too swiftly accompanied by cheering. Buoyant, uplifting. Overpowering.

Richard turned at the door, vaguely able to see a sea of smiling, cheering faces. He would have said something, but he could think of nothing adequate. And he could not have spoken in any case, for his throat was choked and his eyes were streaming. And they simply would not let him get a word out for they cheered and cheered and cheered.

The clapping and cheering went on long after Jean Philippe had closed the door behind them and handed them a napkin each – with one for himself – to mop their eyes. 'Strewth,' said Jean Philippe – who was neither as young nor as French as he seemed. 'I saw Elizabeth Taylor in *The Little Foxes* once. She got a five-minute standing ovation, just for walking on stage, before she even opened her mouth. But that's the first time I've seen it done in a restaurant!'

By 9.30 almost everyone was there, milling about cheerfully, congratulating Richard and Robin, clapping Andrew and Maggie on the back and asking Frances when she expected Jim back from Australia. The only people missing from the hastily assembled guest list were Harry Black and Paul Ho. But this was not a particularly formal party. Their absence did not hold the others back from grabbing a drink and digging into the buffet. And that was just as well, for when Paul Ho turned up at ten to ten, he had the redoubtable cadet May Chung with him after all. 'She wouldn't take no for an answer,' he told Robin almost sheepishly. 'She's hard to stand up to – like a Tai Fun.'

'Well, as long as her mother knows and doesn't mind. And we have Coke or Pepsi or something.'

'I am eighteen year of age,' said May. 'My mother, and more importantly, my grandmother, both know where I am. And I will have a Bacardi Breezer.'

Robin, also, found her as irresistible as a typhoon. But, when she saw the way the cadet looked with worshipful sheep's eyes at her saviour, Richard, she would happily have offered her Paul Ho – and a dozen more like him in exchange.

Doc was uncharacteristically restless and preoccupied. He hardly touched the lobster – even though it was a favourite of his; though he tried both the crisp duck-breast with blackcurrant dip and the charcoaled salmon steaks with warm potato, bacon and artichoke salad. He lingered over the spatchcocked chicken with roasted vegetable and harissa cous cous; and the butterflied lamb chops with green salad, rosemary and mint.

Jean Philippe, a yacht groupie and a fan of his big compatriot, had brought out a case of hard-to-get Swan special lager. The Doc, gratefully, sipped this and circulated nervously.

'What is it?' asked Richard at last. 'You're making the natives restless.'

'I want Harry Black!' said Doc. It was one of those phrases that seem to call almost magically for an embarrassing silence to echo through.

'Why do you want him?' asked Richard at once before anyone could think of a cutting come-back.

'I need him to crew *Katapult*.'

'What? Why? I thought you had your Fastnet crew all sorted and settled.'

'Well, I haven't. Things have been a bit weird down in Southampton, lately, you know? No. Not weird. Downright bloody queer!'

Providentially Harry entered right at that moment, breaking the second silence of the evening. He paused in the doorway, looking around the room. When he saw Richard he began to cross towards him at once.

Doc caught him by the butterfly lamb. 'Harry, how you fixed next month? Holidays and such?'

'What? Oh, I don't know . . . Last Minute Dot Com, I suppose.'

'Come crew for me? One of my blokes got caught in a hit-and-run last night. Right on a pelican crossing – green man flashing and all. Shattered his hip. Damndest thing.'

'We'll talk,' said Harry. And that phrase alone set Robin's antennae twitching even more than the way May Chung was looking at Richard after her third Bacardi Breezer. For she had heard the entire thing as she lingered by the lobster and she knew that only the greatest emergency would make Harry, who had dreamed of sailing the Fastnet while still in his cradle, so off-hand with such an offer.

She followed the worried accountant across to Richard's side, therefore, and stuck to them both like glue.

'Richard. Can we talk?'

'We're here to eat and drink, Harry.'

'And be merry,' said Robin, brightly. Then wished she hadn't for she was still superstitious after all the recent bad luck and was all too well aware of what came after *Eat, drink and be merry, for tomorrow . . .*

Harry simply paid no attention. 'You heard of a company called Whitesand-Sandarkan?' he asked.

'Big in shipping,' said Richard at once, frowning because he could not see the relevance. 'Hong Kong based. Fingers in every pie from Singapore to Sarawak. Charles Lee's territory. Or it used to be . . . Shipping and investment. Why?'

'They're moving their areas of expertise. They've set up a very active acquisitions arm recently. Within the last year in fact. Tiger Economy corporate raiders.'

'Sounds nasty! And?'

Harry pulled a flimsy out of his pocket. 'My office downloaded this half an hour ago and messengered it straight to me. The messenger thought they were mad. Stonking great motorbike roaring right across London – all for one sheet of paper. And on a Saturday. And in the middle of the night. Cost an absolute fortune. But I don't have a fax or a printer at home. I think they did the right thing, Richard. Look at it.'

Richard glanced down and Robin looked past his arm. The paper was an A4 colour print-out of a corporate news-page, the sort that every major company in the world displays – and a few who would just like to be major.

At the top, the company logo showed a tiger on a palm-fringed beach, simplified and stylized, but unmistakable nevertheless. 'WHITESAND-SANDARKAN' announced the title.

Beneath, came the headline: 'IMPORTANT ANNOUNCEMENT FROM WHITESAND-SANDARKAN'.

Beneath that, a sub-headline: 'Whitesand-Sandarkan Board Announces Acquisition of Western Shipping Legend'. And the story:

> At mid-day today Hong Kong time, the Chairman of Whitesand-Sandarkan announced that his company has acquired a controlling interest in the legendary London-based shipping company Heritage Mariner. During the last few weeks, the court case involving CEO Captain Richard Mariner, which has gripped the news media world-wide,

has driven Heritage Mariner shares down and down in price, the Chairman said. Whitesand-Sandarkan has been able to purchase all the shares available upon the open market and so has acquired control of the company itself.

There was more, but Richard jerked the paper down before Robin could read on. 'This simply isn't right,' he grated. 'The family hold a controlling interest. It's by no means common knowledge, but we have always held more than fifty per cent of the shares, specifically to stop something like this happening! Whitesand-Sandarkan – whoever they are – have got it wrong!'

He threw the paper angrily aside, and turned away.

But, seeing the expression on Harry's face, Robin pulled him back.

'That's not quite right, though, is it, Richard?' said Harry gently. 'It's not just the family, it's the family and the Board. You hold ten per cent, as do Robin and Sir William. The twins hold five per cent each. Five per cent – the late Lady Heritage's – is held in trust. Helen DuFour holds four per cent. Making up forty-nine per cent. The other member of the Full Board holds the controlling three per cent, taking it from forty-nine to fifty-two. And the other member of your board is Charles Lee, Richard. *Charles Lee*.'

'Do you see what you're saying?' asked Robin, breathlessly. 'Do you understand the implications?'

'Well,' said Harry, wrong-footed by the intensity with which she spat the question at him; feeling a little like a messenger he had once seen bringing bad news to Cleopatra in William Shakespeare's play. Expecting at any moment to have his hair pulled and his eyes clawed.

'It's all been a trap,' said Richard, straightening, his jaw squaring and his shoulders tensing as though for a wrestling match. 'The whole thing. A betrayal and a trap three years and more in the making. The invitation to join the charity board. The missed meetings, the doctored minutes, the loss of the *Goodman Richard*, the vanishing Captain Jones and the disappearing Charles Lee. The case. Almost certainly yesterday's acquittal, all designed to drive the share-price down until these Whitesand-Sandarkan people could afford to buy them. All except the family share. But if they hold the whole forty-eight per cent that is out there in the public domain, and if Charles Lee is with them – with his three per cent holding – then you're right. They're right. They've made a massive fortune overnight – repaid their investment ten times over if they bought at the lowest last week. We've been raided. Robbed. Ruined. Victims of the other kind of Corporate Killing!'

As Richard's blistering anger rang round the stricken silence of the room, it was the most unexpected voice of all that answered his anguish and his outrage.

'Charles Lee,' said May Chung dismissively. 'I know this Charles Lee. Maybe I better take you to see Grandmother Chung, Captain Mariner! And soon!'

29: Taking Stock

In the face of this new crisis, Richard and Robin went home. But it was a regrouping, not a retreat. A chance to take stock and plan the next step. Richard had been faced with ruin so absolutely for so long that this new challenge was not the straw that broke the camel's back for him. Like Robin's ill-fated party, it was a simple, enraging, energizing call to arms.

They arrived at Ashenden soon after lunchtime on Sunday and set about opening up the house. They had employed staff when they lived in Hong Kong, but apart from a gardener and occasional cleaners, they preferred to run the rambling old house themselves. Or, to be fair, Robin preferred to. But the cleaners had been in last week in preparation for the family's return and the gardener was still at work when the Bentley crunched up the drive and the pair of them climbed out of it.

Robin stretched extravagantly, amazed by how happy she was to be home, even under these circumstances. Especially under these circumstances, perhaps. Richard went round to get their cases from the boot. As he did so, Robin looked around, content to stand and think. In any case, it was Richard who had the front-door key. He soon popped up with the cases and walked towards the porch. They were travelling light. Everything they needed was here already, she thought, following – and what they needed for camping in London remained there. Robin herself hadn't needed all that much in the hospital and, with the preparations for the party, they hadn't even had the opportunity to replace the clothes she had been wearing when she was blown up. She had managed one hell of a posh frock for the party itself and some really wicked underthings beneath it, she thought with a tiny, almost guilty smile, which turned into a big smile and a moue of thanks as he held the door wide for her.

Richard hardly had anything in the bags he was carrying off upstairs, she thought, her mind still on domestic matters as she drifted across the hallway and into the big sitting room. He in any case was a bird of passage, preparing simply to greet his children, hold a conference with his father-in-law and return to Heritage House early next week. There was a lot to sort out – not least what May Chung's grandmother knew about Charles Lee that would help them. Robin would have liked him to stay, had planned on him doing so in fact. But Harry's news had put that plan away into the long grass.

Robin needed to remain. And, she thought, looking out through the French windows over the summer-still Channel at France, she was happy to do so. There had been enough adventures during the last few months to last a lifetime. In fact they had very nearly *out*lasted her own lifetime. She was still convalescent – there had been a lively debate on the drive down about the employment of a private nurse and/or house-keeper for the next couple of months, the resolution of which so far was, 'Well, we'll see.' And, to be fair, she was thinking seriously about it. Her near-death experience and long conva-lescence had made her ache to be with her babies – though the twins were in their teens now, and more than a handful than ever. She might indeed need some help if they were going to be difficult.

On the other hand, it had been the better part of a year since the family had been together properly, so they might be tractable, if she could come up with things for them to do that didn't cripple her physically or financially. Christmas had hardly been a success with Richard on bail and Easter had been little short of disastrous with the trial so imminent. Both were traditionally spent with parents – but, with the rigid restrictions to Richard's freedom of movement, it had hardly seemed worth the trouble. But everyone had found the changes to routine disturbing and unsettling. They had needed a holiday after each of the holidays – but of course, they hadn't had one.

As she thought, Robin wandered out of the sitting room into the other rooms downstairs and was happy to note in the last of them the pile of supplies Dottie Stephenson, their nearest neighbour and close friend, had dropped off in the kitchen. Robin herself would shop online sometime tonight and get a huge delivery tomorrow in time to feed her children's limitless appetites. Or that was the plan, unless Richard wanted to take the Range Rover into Eastbourne and buy Sainsbury's for her. Or the bulk of its stock, at least.

This thought was enough to get her upstairs, and she drifted into the other rooms, to the nice domestic sound of him unpacking in the master bedroom, humming quietly to himself. As always, he had been round and opened all the windows the moment he got up here. The air around Ashenden flooded in, simmering and scented, out of the still, summery afternoon. William's room smelt of roses from the big rambler growing up the side of the house, but Mary's looking over the garden was full of the straw-yellow scent of camomile from the lawn. It made both mother and daughter think irresistibly of horses – perhaps that was why they loved it.

The suite her father and stepmother would share opened to the back of the house and was full of wood smells from the hill behind and the sound of early evensong bells from the local church. The sound of the bells seeped through as far as the two spare bedrooms, Robin noticed as she prowled through them, though Richard hadn't bothered to open the windows in either of them. Full of aching contentment – and something more – she moved, catlike, back into the cool gloom of the corridor, walking on her tip-toes, tugging at warm cotton and fiddling with cool pearl buttons as she went.

Richard had emptied both the cases and put them neatly to one side. Ever precise and tidy – after all his years at sea –

he had piled the contents on their respective chests of drawers ready to put them properly away. As she arrived, he had just started on his own sock drawer, checking each pair was rolled just the way he liked it. He sensed her lingering in the doorway behind him and spoke without turning round.

'Evensong,' he said. 'I hear the bells. We could just make it if we hurry. Want to go?'

'What do you think?' she asked.

He glanced across at her, frowning. And found that she was leaning in the doorway dressed only in the sleekest black body – the one she had bought for her Welcome Back party. It was see-through and beneath its smoky darkness it was obvious that the physiotherapy had done more than simply repair the damage she had suffered. From neck to knees, her muscles were toned, defined. There was something powerful, almost animalistic about her; as though in the months they had been forced apart she had become an Olympic athlete. Under his suddenly burning gaze, she pirouetted like a ballerina until she faced him once again. She was panting now – and so was he. 'Hello, sailor,' she growled.

That was the last coherent thing either of them said for some time. And they missed evensong altogether.

The Cold Fell contingent arrived twenty-four hours later in two cars. They had driven down in convoy, Helen DuFour's big Citroën C5 Estate following Sir William's Mulsanne. And the reason for the unusual indulgence became obvious immediately. 'This is Eloise,' said Helen as she climbed out of her car. A tall, slim athletic-looking blonde shot Robin a shy smile, then followed as Helen took Robin's arm almost conspiratorially. William and Mary, Robin's teenage twins, followed behind her in their turn. 'I do hope you don't mind me bringing her. I could not run Cold Fell without her and I could not possibly do without her here for any length of time.

'Eloise is everything to me,' Helen confided, guiding Robin back inside as the men began to labour over the much more considerable baggage she had brought with her – though Helen was in fact 'travelling light' as well. 'I am not as – what you say? *Souple*? Supple? As *limber* as I was. Eloise is a trained physiotherapist. And when she is not making me like a prima ballerina, she is a first-rate housekeeper. She is Provençale, *naturellement*!

'I tell you I could not have handled the darling twins without her. She rides! You have stables nearby? She and Mary are constantly a-horse. And she golfs! On the rare occasions my darling Sir William cannot be persuaded to swing a club she will take care of your William. Which does he adore more? Golf or Eloise? Golf! Eh? But not for much longer, I think. Thank God for golf. It is like fishing – men spend hours doing it with almost no discernible result except that they leave us poor women alone!'

And so, through the practical Gallic wisdom of her stepmother, supported no doubt by the ready concern of her indulgently devious father, a nurse/housekeeper did in fact arrive to help them all with the twins. A nurse, a housekeeper and whatever the French was for Mary Poppins, thought Robin ruefully. Then she tore herself away from her stepmother and gathered her children to her for one big group hug.

'You get my fax, Bill?' asked Richard, heaving a case heavier than an anvil out of the Mulsanne's boot. He was able to start the conversation he was burning to have because the twins had gone in to greet their mother. But time would be limited because they would be back soon and he didn't want to talk in front of them.

'Yes,' answered Sir William. 'It came as quite a shock. Lucky Helen and the twins have been keeping the old ticker up to scratch. D'you think it's true? Could we have lost everything to these Whitesand-Sandarkan people?'

'There's a chance. What about Lee?'

'Still no trace. It's incredible. I mean – as you know – when he first went missing we turned London upside down. So did the police of course. Then Britain, then Europe. The authorities seemed to run out of steam after that but we kept on. Contacted Edgar Tan in Macau – remember him? Still the best P.I. in the area. And he went for it, covering all points East. Then we got people working in America and Russia into the bargain. As far as we could. I mean at that stage we still thought he could have been kidnapped, killed, God knows what. But nothing turned up. No ransom demand. No body. He's just bloody vanished and that's all there is to it.'

'Like Lord Lucan?'

'Yes. But there's no dead nursemaid. No dead anyone as far as we can discover. No question of any wrongdoing at all, in fact.'

'Not until Saturday, at any rate. And the *Sanna Maru* being Triad.'

They had to leave the discussion there as the twins brought Eloise back to help get the cases up to their respective rooms. And opportunity to continue it did not present itself until after dinner.

Alone in the study, the two men sat while Sir William sipped his favourite single malt and talked, while Richard checked his email. Like the snail mail, it was full of congratulations. But, unlike the post, it also contained the first messages of concern at the news that had broken in the financial sections of yesterday's newspapers.

'But, apart from Lee's latest starlet – who went off with a producer within the week – there was nobody else out there. We were his only friends really – apart from some yachting people. And they were more business associates. Like the charity folk. He'd no family; even those in Hong Kong are dead now I understand. No creditors. He left no huge bills. Maybe a tailor or two. He co-owned his yacht; his partner bought him out. He rented that flat in Mayfair and it went back to the landlord on the first of the next month. Finance company reclaimed his latest car. That was that. Quite amazing, really, when you look at it. Man must have been Teflon-coated.'

'Strange, though, how it all fits together.' Richard closed the email, signed off the internet and snapped off the computer.

'How d'you mean?'

'Lee's been gone for nearly a year now, right?'

Sir William nodded.

'But no one's declared him officially dead, have they?'

'Surely that's because he's probably still alive. Isn't it, Richard?'

'But, by the time the inquiry was sitting, a coroner's court had already declared Captain James Jones and his senior officers legally dead. And that was only a matter of months after *Goodman Richard* went down.'

'Yeeees . . .' Sir William clearly did not follow Richard's reasoning yet.

'Has there even been a coroner's inquest into Charles Lee?'

'Well, no. Should there have been?'

'That's just it. Under the circumstances, no; I don't think there should. I think that under English Common Law you have to be missing for something like five or seven years before you can legally be presumed dead. Unless, as in the case of Captain Jones and co., there is a very strong presumption that you are dead.'

'Such as having gone missing at sea . . .'

'Exactly. But you see what this means, don't you?'

'Enlighten me.'

'I could be charged with Corporate Killing because there was a presumption of death, a relatively quick inquest and a declaration of legal death. OK? But, Charles Lee is not likely to be declared dead for another six years or so, because he has vanished without any suspicion of foul play or fatal accident.'

'God, Richard, one can certainly tell where you've been during the last few weeks. You're starting to sound like Maggie DaSilva.'

'And it may in fact be crucial that Charles Lee is not declared dead – it's crucial if this is all some kind of plan at any rate – because the three per cent share holding he has are not his in perpetuity. He can take the profits, rights issues and returns from them. He can use them for surety, even. But he cannot sell them, give them away or leave them to his children in his will. They only belong to him during his lifetime. The minute he is legally dead, his shares are returned to Heritage Mariner. If Whitesand-Sandarkan are relying on possession of that three per cent, then they only have a controlling interest while Charles Lee is legally alive.'

'That's looking on the bright side, I suppose. But they are corporate raiders, asset strippers. They could do one hell of a lot of damage in six months – let alone six years.'

'I know,' said Richard, pouring Sir William another whisky. 'But it's worse than that, isn't it? Charles must be alive or Whitesand-Sandarkan wouldn't have access to his shares. I'd guess they've only used his disappearance and the trial as a smokescreen to distract us while they bought up the shares behind our backs. Maybe even set it all up in the first place, like I suspect. If they'd have tried it fair and square we'd have stopped them. And Charles could never have pulled this off within English jurisdiction in any case – he's blown the terms of his contract to Hell and gone.

'But Whitesand-Sandarkan did manage to buy them all. At a bargain basement price – with a huge profit achieved already. And in six years time, all Charles has to do is pop up again and prove that he's alive. Outside our jurisdiction, but alive. It could go on for years and years. That's why we have to fight now and fight hard. Our best weapon still is to find Charles and bring him home. Or, failing him, then his shares will do just fine.'

Richard sat, dumbfounded and looked at the share certificates. He knew every whirl and curlicue, the signatures and the names. And most especially he knew the numbers. They were Charles Lee's all right. What a pity they were just photocopies. He looked up at the skeletal old ivory face in front of him, gaping like a schoolboy. May's grandmother sucked on a cigarette through a green jade holder and speared him with a fathomless look from eyes that were almost as black as her chop-stabbed geisha wig. She spoke, rapidly, in Chinese that was so thick and slurred that Richard could not even work out whether it was Cantonese, Mandarin or one of the country dialects. But he didn't need to understand what Grandmother Chung was saying to him.

Even more at home in the office behind the heaving betting-shop than she had been in the private room in Pont de Londres, May swung one fashionably clad leg and observed her top-of-the-range trainers as she translated.

'This man Charles Lee is gambling man. Big gambling man. Gambling like opium to him, you understand? Since one year ago he has bet upon this race. Long odds. House offer very long odds. Very good odds. He wished to bet money or credit. He try to bet fast car. He say worth £100,000. Grandmother Chung say to him "No." If he bet £100,000 with her he must bet something she can hold and touch and keep against the wager.

'So he bet these. Grandmother Chung has valued them with discreet banker and holds them in secret. No one knows. If he wins then she will return them to him with his £100,000 at odds of twenty to one. That two million one hundred thousand pound in all. Big bet. Big race. But if Charles Lee lose this gamble, Grandmother Chung sell shares to you. Five times market value as big favour. Because you save life of favourite granddaughter.'

Excitement and hilarity warred hysterically in Richard's breast. Perhaps there was something more than nicotine in the fumes wafting through from the betting shop and the deeper, darker rooms beyond. This was simple madness, he thought. But it was all of a piece with the adventure so far. And he could well believe it of Charles Lee. To have planned the whole thing and put it into action with such painstaking care over so many months and years – and then to have risked the whole thing on a simple roll of some cosmic dice. It was Charles to the life.

It was Achilles, with his heel.

'What race has he bet on?' Richard asked, though his racing mind had made him suspect the answer already.

May didn't even need to consult Grandmother Chung. She knew the answer to that one herself. 'He has wagered on the Fastnet ocean yacht race. He has bet upon the vessel *Tin Hau* to come first, allowing for class and handicap.'

Grandmother Chung leaned forward and croaked through a cloud of foul-smelling smoke.

May listened, giggled, and translated. 'Grandmother Chung says now you know, what you do about it? You have too much Yang, she says, to allow Luck Dragon to achieve this thing for you. And also you not looking like Feng Shui man to her. She says, do you know how you can beat this Charles Lee, this yacht *Tin Hau*?'

Richard leaned forward, his face absolutely still and speared the old lady with the ice-blue of his most powerfully intense gaze. 'No, I don't,' he told her. 'But I know a man who can.'

THE ROCK

30: The Hard Place

The *Katapult VI* crewman crippled by the hit-and-run had been called Harry Hansen, Richard soon learned. So when Harry Black replaced him it was easy for the others. They just continued to bellow, 'Harry, get ready to gybe,' and so forth. But when Sam Wells got beaten to within an inch of his life by a gang of drunks outside the Jolly Roger a couple of days before the off, things got very much harder indeed.

They would have been made impossible for Doc and his crew, in fact, had Richard not been working effectively as extra crewman for the better part of the last fortnight. And had Cowes Week itself not been held back to the beginning of August that year because of the unusually heavy spring tides, allowing him the vital extra time to do so. Even so, as Doc said, when he called Richard on his cellphone from Sam's bedside in Southampton General Hospital, they were between a rock and a hard place.

During the last week in July, Richard went down to Southampton almost as often as Doc popped up to London. As he became caught up in the final preparations for the Fastnet Race, he took a room at The Star with the rest of them. But on those couple of vital nights after Sam was beaten up, they all started sleeping aboard *Katapult* herself, where she lay, moored off the green to the west of the Fairway and the Royal Yacht Squadron's H.Q.

That first day, however, they had met in Doc's room in The Star and sat on such pieces of furniture as the room afforded. Doc and the two girls, naturally, on the bed. Harry Black and Ben Caldwell leaning amenably, side by side against a chest of drawers. Sam Wells and Bob Collingwood in the two chairs, because they were the biggest. Richard paced as he explained to them what it was he needed them to do. 'Beat *Tin Hau*. Or, if that's going to be impossible, try your best to make sure someone else beats *Tin Hau*.'

'Be a damn sight easier to beat her ourselves,' observed big Bob Collingwood. 'Be black and white then. Cut and dried. Them or us.'

'That's the way we have to go in any case, isn't it?' mused deceptively mousy Joan Rouse. 'We have to beat them as soundly as we can, and hope there are no tricky handicaps or time penalties involved.'

'That's what we have to watch out for, isn't it?' demanded Amy Cook the navigator. 'I mean there are what, half a dozen well-fancied yachts in our class who do this thing every time. One or other of them seems to have won the Fastnet every race since the Millennium. A bit of a club, so to speak. *Tin Hau* and *Katapult* are the two best fancied outsiders so we were always going head-to-head, weren't we? But we simply don't know what handicaps and so forth the race organizers will put in place for all of us. Therefore if we get in among the leaders and stay there – which is what we planned in any case – we should keep *Tin Hau* well out of contention. But only if she hasn't got some kind of technical advantage we don't know about.'

'Or we aren't nobbled ourselves by some kind of penalty somewhere along the line. Other than that, it sounds simple,' said Ben from the chest of drawers. 'Get out in front, stay out in front, get back in front and keep our fingers crossed.'

'Well, it's a plan,' decided Doc. 'And like Brains here said . . .' he gave navigator Amy a hug, 'it was what our race plan was in any case. So let's go for it, eh kids?'

And that became – remained – the strategy. But like most apparently simple ideas, it required a great deal more in practice than it seemed to do in theory. But beating *Tin Hau* in particular gave them extra focus. A specific target for the race. So they went back to work with redoubled will.

And Richard rolled his sleeves up and went to work alongside them. He was simply amazed at how fast it all came back to him. It was a good number of years since he had crewed the first *Katapult* around the Arabian Gulf with Robin, Doc and Sam Hood. They had been basically pleasureboating then and this of course was very different. Crewing *Katapult VI* was like riding a thoroughbred after hacking around on a carthorse. Riding a thoroughbred 150% bigger than the original, needing seven instead of four to handle her. A thoroughbred which needed a good deal of extra tack, into the bargain.

The original *Katapult* had been entirely internally rigged. Her simple sails – mainsail and jib – had both been controlled by pulleys working within the super-strengthened hollow mast. The setting of sails and outriggers was controlled via a central computer designed to make pleasureboating almost as simple as riding a bicycle.

On *Katapult VI*, the basics were the same. The knobs and whistles were, however, different. They still had the almost unique suit of computer-controlled sails. But the overall square footage had risen exponentially. So, therefore, had the external rigging and the systems needed to winch, shorten and belay it all. This was a racing machine, moreover, not a pleasure boat; and so there was even more external cordage for when they wanted to vary the racing trim, set Genoas instead of jibs or deploy the big spinnaker.

There was change also in the way they could set the outriggers, much more variably hinged on almost impossibly strong joints that could lift the central hull out of the water to several different degrees, setting her up in various hydroplane modes. Outriggers extended with extra rudders of their own. Which of course made the steering even more complicated still.

But Richard worked alongside them and he learned it all. It was a huge release for him to feel, after nearly a year of powerlessness when his fate – and those of his family and company – had lain in the hands of prosecution and defence, that he had some control again. And some physical control, with a tangible outcome. That there was a problem here which could be solved through physical action. That – through working till his hands bled and his back was breaking, then working on until his legs were numb and he could no longer move his arms, and then working on some more – he was actually going to solve it all himself. Make up to Robin, William and Mary everything he had put them through during the last terrible year. The thought was energizing, motivating. A most potent release for all the helplessness and frustration he had been feeling for so long.

And it was as well he did so, for, like Harry Black, Richard was an outsider. This was a crew that had worked together on and off for years – long ago and far away; recently and near at hand. They had done the Sydney–Hobart together late last year. They had done the Morgan Cup late last month and the Cowes–St-Malo while Richard was still in court.

At Cowes Week itself, *Katapult* joined some of the Maxi races and Richard was able to get in a little race-toughening around the buoys in the Solent and away across Christchurch Bay. Watching as the big national teams racked up the points and outsailed most of the independents and learning yet more from what he observed; as yet unaware of how important the experience would be.

Many of the other Fastnet favourites were there, single hulled and multi; ultra-modern cutting-edge, or classic 1930s J Class restored. As well as national teams from all over the world, from Portland, America to Papua New Guinea. But *Tin Hau* remained aloof. Every now and then, between races, sailing out of the Solent round the Isle of Wight – exploring those early, vital tideways – someone from *Katapult* would see her tell-tale jade-green sails on the horizon and call to the others. But she appeared at none of the inshore races. Her crew came to none of the Yacht Club dances, receptions or parties that the others sometimes visited. She remained a slightly sinister mystery, therefore – even to those whose interest in her was merely to gossip and speculate over a flute of champagne and a canape.

The last time Richard saw Sam Wells was during the fireworks display on the Friday. Richard planned on watching just the very start of the magnificent show and then was driving back to Ashenden for the weekend, all too well aware that if he stayed much longer he would simply be in the way. But he was still in the car park setting the destination into the Bentley's GPS and working out his chances of getting the whole family down here for the off at midday on Sunday, when the hands-free phone began to buzz. And everything changed when he answered.

'Richard,' came Doc's flat, familiar tones. 'We're between a rock and a hard place, Sport . . .'

Katapult came thundering over the Royal Yacht Squadron line at full pelt, towards the front of the jostling pack of racers. Richard hung on to his allotted line and looked, simply awestruck. There were nearly three hundred in all – and every single one of them, it seemed, was as set as Doc and Richard on getting back from Ireland first. A stiff easterly whipped in over the wooded hills of the portside shore stirring the Solent up into a fair old chop. And the chop exploded into spray as the racing hulls tore through it. Within moments of the start of the race, Richard was soaking – and he knew he would stay that way for the next thirty-six hours at least until *Katapult* got back into Portsmouth.

Doc was at the big wheel of the helm, eyes narrow and hair flying as he eased *Katapult* round to starboard. He was seeking to settle her on to a course that would get her across the fairway and Cowes Roads into the channel between the Isle of Wight's eastern shore and Lymington Harbour. Richard had an instantaneous, mad, vision of all the busting sailboats wedging there in the narrows like shoppers wedged in the doorway at the start of the Harrods Sale.

But that of course could never happen. The narrows were not in fact particularly narrow at all – except on Amy's chart. And in any case, the fair cross-wind, easing round behind them as they began to swing westward themselves, soon began to sort them into line – ahead, like a squadron of Nelson's battleships. Genoas spread and spinnakers blossomed amongst the eager and they began to pull away. Doc preferred to lean on the outriggers at this stage and let the huge spread of *Katapult*'s normal canvas keep them in contention. 'We'll deploy the Number One Spinnaker when the wind dies down a bit,' he bellowed. 'Catch some of these eager fellows napping. Get ready for it, ladies and gentlemen . . .'

And, sure enough, as they came into the channel beside the Isle of Wight, the bulk of the island stole the wind. Out came the huge blue Number One Spinnaker, and *Katapult* settled to work. Beneath her, the tide was falling, and that favoured the big- and variable-keel boats which had large fins below to grab on to the outrush of the water. But Doc too had his outriggers, and the ability to dig them into the fleeing element.

The organizers might have held back Cowes Week to avoid the worst of the big spring tides, but there were still one or two massive movements of water up and down the Channel yet to come. The tide past Milford Point must have been ebbing at the better part of five knots. So, as they came out under the Needles and began to pick up that steady easterly again, all the tall ships there leaned into the broad reach; those eager souls with big sails up sending their crew out to lean out along the side or to hang on trapezes already. Not that Doc was above that sort of thing. 'Out on the port rigger,' he yelled as *Katapult* lifted and the aquadynamic blade of the starboard outrigger suddenly changed from white to green under the surface.

So Richard, Bill, Harry and Bob scrambled over the netting secured over the non-slip paint that covered the portside wing between the hull and the outrigger itself. Then Richard latched on to his trapeze point and missed the pretty sight of Christchurch slowly settling below the horizon altogether as he eased his aching back out from the port outrigger as the second hour of the race began. With the other big crewmen, he was using his weight to keep the hull more level with the water, the mast therefore more upright – and the sails, consequently, more purposefully in the wind while it was there and offering them so much help and power. 'Don't go to sleep out there,' Doc bellowed. 'I might just want to stow the jib and set the Genoa instead.'

Katapult, drifting southwards as Doc set her steadily across the steady blast of the easterly, was moving at thirty knots now. He wanted to be well out from St Anselm's Head on the southern coast of the Isle of Purbeck, which protected Poole Harbour, getting maximum benefit from the continuing tidal fall by the end of the second hour if possible, Richard knew. And he planned to be well off Portland Bill by the end of the third.

Like the rest of the crew Richard had slept aboard last night, conveniently able to go through the game plan yet again. Conveniently to hand in case the accidents to the two crewmembers so far had been something other than accidents after all. And they all knew the Channel well enough to put its vagaries into their plans. They all suspected that the wind would turn with the tide, or die away altogether. And they wanted to be well past Prawle Point and Start Point by then if possible. They could even be at the Eddystone Light, if they kept this speed up, thought Richard dreamily.

Then Bob Collingwood thumped him on the shoulder to get his attention and gestured. Richard twisted to angle his gaze in the direction of Bob's gesture. His shoulder dipped into the green crystal heave of a wave and he had to blink a faceful of spray away. He saw the foam of their passage spread out like white webs on the water as it rolled out of their wake. The wind seemed almost still, so perfectly were they harnessed to its rushing easterly power. The water of the Channel rose and fell away towards Le Havre.

And there, stunningly close, on the parallel tack and seemingly mere metres upwind of them, lay the sleek black hull and jade-green sails of *Tin Hau*. No, saw Richard at once. Not hull – *hulls*! Like *Katapult*, *Tin Hau* was a massive trimaran.

Her boom was high, and in any case it was swung well out towards *Katapult*, its end just kissing the tops of the biggest waves beneath her starboard side. Leaning back the way he was, with *Tin Hau* leaning over into the wind, Richard was able to see straight into her cockpit. And even, if he strained his neck a little, he could see beyond it to where the crew, like him, were standing up on their trapezes.

And there, exactly opposite Richard, hardly more than fifteen metres of wind-scrubbed, foam-flecked air away, red-clad, lifebelted and laughing, stood the unmistakable figure of Charles Lee.

31: The Light

The wind began to falter when Start Point was still a big black bulge on the starboard horizon, more than three hours later – nearly five hours into the race. That was when Doc called them all back in and set the outriggers to lift the central hull and cut the drag to a minimum. But by that time Richard had begun to see the light in earnest. Perhaps it was the realization that *Katapult* and *Tin Hau* could almost have been sister ships. Perhaps it was the revelation of seeing his erstwhile friend so close and in the flesh. Perhaps it was the timing – as the physical work and the effect of sailing *Katapult* up against *Tin Hau* in the hope of recovering the shares. Perhaps it was the realization that, unlike James Jones and the other missing men, Charles Lee was no hangdog, skulking fugitive. He had freedom of action. He had been able to come and go – discreetly perhaps, but freely and yet invisibly. He had abilities Richard had never realized. He had contacts outside the normal channels. He had power beyond the law. And in Richard's experience that meant only one thing – he had Triad contacts. He had gone through the ceremonies with the black hen and he lived under the godlike leadership of a Dragon Head.

All Richard's old Hong Kong hackles were up with a vengeance. He had made many friends in the old Crown Colony – and had always counted Charles Lee amongst them. But he had made many enemies also. Relentless, implacable enemies who had tried to destroy him before. Major amongst these was a Triad whose shipments of crack cocaine he had unwittingly – almost accidentally but very effectively – disrupted. And they had called themselves The White Powder Triad.

During the hours after he had first set eyes upon the laughing Charles Lee on the multihulled *Tin Hau* off Christchurch Harbour, Richard had much leisure to think. For he was stuck on the trapeze until Doc called him in. And, in spite of the gut-wrenching shock of recognition and the blistering rage that it had brought about, he had no intention of coming back inboard before he was ordered – even though he carried crucially important news. And it simply never occurred to him that he should pass it on to the police.

For Bob Collingwood had hit him on the shoulder to warn simply that *Tin Hau* was overtaking them. Bob could never have recognized Charles Lee; may not even have seen the crucial relevance of her design. And *Tin Hau* continued to ease past and began to slip clear. Any movement now would simply have let Charles and his vessel, his bet – and his Triad-financed grip upon Heritage Mariner itself – slip further into the winning position.

Richard hung in his trapeze, therefore, as *Katapult* thundered relentlessly down the Channel, lost in thought. Attaining, as he sometimes managed *in extremis*, that crystal clarity of reasoning which allowed him to see all the patterns of a situation. Triad involvement explained so much. Triad involvement had remained unsuspected because the Triads themselves were creatures of the Far East, not of the West End. But it was the Triads, after all, who moved so many Chinese into and out of England under the noses of the authorities. Cockle-pickers, prostitutes, waiters and waitresses. How easy it would be for them to make Charles Lee disappear, shipping one more nameless body out among so many brought so anonymously in. How easy it would be for them to keep him concealed in Hong Kong, Shanghai or even in China itself. Or, as with Captain Jones and the Triad ship *Sanna Maru*, to simply sail him to Australia.

How simple it must have been for a Triad like the White Powder Triad to suborn several officers into going aboard and stowing away upon a Far Eastern registered container vessel apparently passing their sinking ship by chance. An agreement confirmed with that one quick call from the Fourth Officer to Elroy Kim. If there was a good enough reason on both sides of the bargain; a sufficiently profitable deal. A big enough bribe. A sufficiently total revenge. And if nobody really cared about risking the lives of sixty teenage cadets. Of all the rest of it, that terrible arrogance was what came close to making Richard's heart burst with simple rage.

Even the name. Whitesand-Sandarkan. Was it close enough to White Powder? A Triad-owned Tiger Economy corporate raider seemed all too conceivable to Richard as he hung in his trapeze, the back of his head, super-sensitive, seeming to skim along the surface of the Channel – as his mind plumbed darker depths. For the end of the matter was clear now – the plan to steal his company and ruin him; ruin his whole family. And, once the final game was obvious, as Jim said, how clear did everything else become.

For it was Oxford v. Moss after all. Charles had given his Triad masters nothing physical at all. But at the same time, he had given them everything important. He had stolen nothing tangible. He had taken no money, only the shares that were his own. But he had given them the most vital intellectual properties that Heritage Mariner owned – fully the equivalent of that test paper read through early. And here was examination day at last. For he had taken east with him his knowledge of the *Katapult* series – their most vital, hitherto unrivalled, asset. And his knowledge of how the Chinese could reproduce her. And he had taken with him his intimate understanding of how Heritage Mariner's secretive corporate structure was organized. And he had placed it all in the hands of Richard's Triad enemies.

Charles had sailed in all six generations of *Katapult*. He knew them all almost as well as Doc. Perhaps over the years his plans had been beginning to form already as an insurance should ruin ever really threaten; as it had with the collapse of his scheme to duplicate *Goodman Richard* as a commercial pleasure craft. Perhaps from the very beginning he had been preparing himself in secret for this very race or some other just like it – for this very gamble.

He had known about *Lionheart*'s test run. He had been able to dictate *Goodman Richard*'s position just within her reach, the square-rigger's dismasting and the vanishing of the officers – hidden on *Sanna Maru* until presumed dead. And let the kids aboard take care of themselves. His own disappearance and the planned vanishing of the drowned Smithers. He had arranged clues, pressure, guidance – from the Australian advert in *Argo* with its crucial cellphone number to the arson that both Robin and Frances were sure had been yet more manipulation, not a serious murder attempt.

And that meant, as Richard had bitterly observed at Robin's Welcome Back party, that the inquiry and the Corporate Killing case had both simply been manipulated. Not in terms of bribing witnesses and slipping backhanders to police and lawyers, perhaps, but in stage-managing the 'facts' of his guilt. And, eventually, crucially, the facts of his innocence. All under such an inevitable glare of world-wide publicity. For it had all been about money and power. Not truth and justice at all. The wrong kind of Corporate Killing.

The men who had bought their Heritage Mariner shares

during the trial had seen the worth of their purchases rise by more than tenfold since its end. The White Powder Triad – Whitesand-Sandarkan – had made back many times over what Richard had cost them in lost cocaine all those years ago. And if *Tin Hau* won the Fastnet Race they would own Heritage Mariner into the bargain.

Richard had reached this stage in his reasoning when the Channel slapped him hard on the back of the head, Bob hit him on the shoulder again, and it was time to take his hot news back aboard.

Doc asked the obvious question first as they all stood in and around the cockpit, getting used to the new angle of the half-raised central hull – the new motion of their skimming vessel. 'You saw Charles Lee. Did he see you?'

Doc was at the wheel. Amy was down at the chart table and Joan a little deeper, in the galley – which was perhaps the size of a modest cupboard. Harry, Bob and Ben were clustered round the cockpit with Richard.

'He must have seen me,' said Richard thoughtfully. 'But I don't believe he recognized me. He certainly didn't give any sign.'

'OK.' The big Australian looked around. 'Now does this make any difference to our race plan?'

'Why should it?' demanded Amy. 'This Charles Lee can't control the wind and the tide, can he? Even if Richard is right about what else he and his Triad contacts can control. But I think we should alert the authorities at once.'

'I agree,' said Harry. 'The police have been looking for this man – as have we all – for a year. And now suddenly here he is. Why, they might even come and pull *Tin Hau* out of the race. That would suit your ends, wouldn't it, Richard? A disqualified boat can't win a race. The shares would be forfeit.'

'I don't think the police would do anything,' countered Richard. 'There's no case left for Charles to answer, is there? That's the real cunning of it, don't you see? My acquittal was the trigger for the endgame. That's when Whitesand-Sandarkan made their formal announcement. That's when Charles Lee reappeared. There's no case left at all. All that would happen if we went to the authorities now – if anyone in authority is actually going to want to speak to me of course – is that they'd likely check with *Tin Hau* and alert them that we know he's aboard. And that would make a difference, wouldn't it? It would make them much more alert and rob us of any advantage surprise might have given us.'

'OK,' temporized Amy. 'I can see that. No authorities then. Not until we get to Portsmouth at any rate. Then we can call them up and get them down while we wait for *Tin Hau* to arrive.' They all chuckled at that. But Amy frowned suddenly and continued, 'But just how far do you think these people are willing to go to win?' She paused. 'We're back to the first question, aren't we? Charles Lee can't control the wind and the tide, can he?'

'No,' answered Richard. 'But we now know the kind of person crewing *Tin Hau*, and perhaps who her secret sponsors are. We must ask – is there any way to cheat on the Fastnet?'

'Lots of ways,' said the ever practical Joan Rouse, her head popping up from the galley. 'He could have some kind of a motor hidden aboard. He could arrange some way to sail a shorter course. Or he could be trying to nobble the opposition.'

'That seems to be the preferred option. Having the opposition's crewmembers run down on pelican crossings and beaten up outside public houses,' said Richard. 'But that would be just the beginning of the campaign. Thank God we berthed her in a secure, well-guarded commercial yard. Thank God we've all been sleeping aboard. But now we'll have to look out for more of that thug-stuff under sail too.'

'OK,' allowed Joan. 'But I don't see how they could do all that much skulduggery without getting caught. Certainly out here. A motor would leave a tell-tale wake. All the major points are monitored and beyond them it's every man for himself anyway. Maybe they just reckon they have some kind of an edge over the rest of us. That they're going to be the best in any case. Given that they might try bully-boy tactics on the quiet. That'd be about it, though.'

'Unless,' said Richard thoughtfully – remembering whom they were dealing with in Triad terms. 'Unless they have some kind of drug they're trying out. Something that'll overcome exhaustion, firm up sharpness, let the whole crew stay daisy-fresh for thirty-six hours on the trot. That might make a crucial difference.'

'What!' scoffed Joan as she passed up six steaming, fragrant mugs. 'Something even better than my patented, magical, double-dark extra-black coffee? Be careful how you drink it. It's been known to break teeth.'

'Whatever,' decided Doc. 'Our best bet is still to keep up with him, watch him like hawks, and then outsail the bastard all the way home. Talking of which, I note the wind is dying down to the calm that Amy predicted. Come on people, coffee-break's over. Get rigged for light airs.'

Under Start Point they went, therefore, and eased into the gathering sunset as the wind died away to nothing while the tide beneath them slowed and stilled. They used the stillness to grab a quick bite – bacon, eggs and sausages in great thick doorstops of bread with more sweet black coffee. Bananas and chocolate followed. 'We've tried all sorts of rations,' confided Bob later. 'Special Forces stuff; custom-prepared – the lot. Dictated by weight and nutritional efficiency. Thank God we're back to sanity.'

Start Point had become a beacon of sunset brightness on the darkening horizon behind them when the west wind stirred with the returning flood of the tide nearly an hour later. 'Quick,' bellowed Doc, hitting the button to spread the outriggers again. 'Get the Genoa up. I want to go across this as fast as I can. Right, Amy? There's a tidal gate getting ready to catch a good few off Ushant and I want us well out of it.'

After the relative respite of light-airs sailing – which had actually involved a great deal of tacking and heaving – they were happy enough to break out the big sails again and start to beat across the wind. Amy and Doc remained on close lookout in the gathering darkness. First at the state of sea, then at their instruments and what they revealed when the sea was no longer visible. The tidal gate gathered in the relative narrows between the Brest Peninsula and the Scillies, where all the water flooding into the Channel out of the Bay of Biscay and the Atlantic beyond was constricted into a faster-flowing counter-current as the big spring tide began to gather towards the flood. Here the big boats with their deep keels could catch themselves at a serious disadvantage if they sailed too far south.

Doc worked them carefully westwards and only grudgingly

southwards therefore, keeping the bulk of the wind, but letting some of it pass them as he hugged the shore well away from the inward flood. But the shore itself forced him further and further south as eight hours ticked away towards nine and the Eddystone Light heaved past to starboard – so close they could almost touch it – then fell far away behind.

They made The Lizard at 10.30 p.m., beginning to drop behind schedule, with *Tin Hau* well out of sight. But the wind was freshening, they were out of the grip of the tide, and they felt a surge of grim confidence as they came about. By 11, they had the Lizard Light away high on the starboard side, Wolf Rock away on the port, intermittently bobbing up over the horizon and Tater Du on the starboard quarter with Longships behind it a mile or so off Land's End. And Pendeen on the road in towards St Ives, waiting to strike their eyes in another hour's time.

The wind was gathering gustily but *Katapult* was racing handily across it, close-hauled but lively enough. The night had thickened into darkness except for the great Trinity House lights, the occasional gleams from the coast – of lone car or isolated house – and those of other ships to seaward.

Richard, still on deck, and grateful that the blackness had stopped Doc's fussy search for better airs and slicker water, kept looking away to south-west, his eyes lingering on the spot where the Wolf Rock Light came and went almost mockingly, five or so miles away. That was where he was looking when the first rain spat in out of the wind, different from the spray only in that it was fresh-water, not salt. And that it signalled a change in the weather. 'OK, ladies and gentlemen,' shouted Doc as he too felt the sweet water on his lips, 'let's get the Genoa down and packed away. My navigator predicts a nasty blow coming. And so do my nose and my *water* as my Irish ancestors would have it.'

On the port tack, close hauled into the rapidly increasing wind and rain, *Katapult* chased *Tin Hau* away from Wolf Rock up into the Celtic Sea. And, with the last gleam of the place which had given him his reason for doing so still glittering in his slitted eyes, Richard chased Charles Lee. They hardly saw the Pendeen Light at midnight when it swung into the starboard quarter aft – like a reflection of Wolf Rock long gone from their port quarter aft. The weather had closed down in the meantime and the rain had become persistent, falling out of lowering clouds. But the wind continued to freshen as it swung round towards South South East. And while Doc held the course steady on 285 degrees according to the binnacle readout from the Fluxgate compass, the wind was coming equally steadily in from between 230 and 245. Their speed picked up to 20 knots and higher according to the complex digital display on the binnacle.

'Take it in a reef or two, then Richard and Bob go down for a couple of hours,' bellowed Doc. The watch and sleeping rota was something they had agreed last night – God! Was it only last night? thought Richard – when they had all of them slept aboard. But Doc was wise to remind them. Richard at least was semi-comatose, though alert enough to follow orders. By the time they were close hauled and ready for the long night run at 1.00 a.m., the Cornish coast was long gone behind them and the night was actually getting foul. There was nothing to see ahead or around. As the wind strengthened through the Beaufort scale towards Force 5, the seas were beginning to show white horses in the microseconds that he got to register the paleness before they reared over *Katapult*'s port outrigger – or the outrigger rode them down. The motion of the multihull was becoming lumpy and bellicose. The waters were beginning to batter her and she was fighting back.

Richard stepped down into the sole of the cockpit and saw at once that he would have to step mightily up over the weatherboard wedged in the door to the cabin below if he was going to get inside while keeping the ocean out. He found a handhold and moved down the stair like the Ancient Mariner. He staggered slightly and looked about, dazzled even by the dimness down here. Amy glanced up from her chart and pointed deliberately in three separate directions, one after the other. 'Toilet. Sleeping bag. Sleeping quarters,' she said distinctly, as though to a terminal drunk.

'I'll be able to pee if I'm careful. But I'll never be able to sleep,' said Richard. And, sure enough, his words were as slurred as if he'd just drunk half a bottle of Scotch. Better not get tangled in the anchor chain and pulled overboard like poor old Smithers, he thought as Amy gave a grunt of sceptical laughter and returned to the chart – on to which, Richard noted blearily, her sharp pencil was beginning to predict some really stormy conditions.

'Richard. RICHARD! *RICHARD!*'

Richard exploded awake. He sat up, smacked his head hard enough to see stars, looked around, waiting for his eyes and his head to clear. He had no idea where he was or what was happening. Then a torch beam illuminated an egg, bacon and sausage buttie and a steaming mug of magic coffee. 'You're on watch in ten,' said Joan. And, behind her words, a big sea thumped *Katapult*, making her stagger.

Ten minutes later, with the warm fullness of the meal still spreading from his stomach to the rest of his frame, Richard pulled himself into the cockpit. During the two hours of his sleep the wind had freshened through Force 5 to Force 7, just as Amy's notes had predicted. Doc had been replaced at the wheel by Ben Caldwell, and Ben looked battered, exhausted.

'You're up next,' he bellowed at Richard through the driving foam. 'It's easier than it looks and this is as easy as it's likely to be until we berth in Plymouth. All you have to do is hold her head at 285 degrees. It's there on the display right in front of you. You don't need to pay any attention to anything else much. You won't be able to do anything much about the speed. We'll be doing any sail-handling necessary and Doc'll be calling that when he gets up after Bob's watch.

'Don't worry about anything,' he continued as Richard squeezed in beside him and began to peer into the stormy darkness ahead. 'There's nothing out there but sea, and nothing in that direction except the Fastnet Rock, but that's four hours away. If we come up with any other boats you'll see their lights and if there's any problem call down and Amy'll give them a hail. Oh, and when you get used to it, you might want to try and vary the heading just a tiny bit . . .'

He suited the word with the action as he spoke and luffed up a couple of points to the wind. The result of this was that a particularly steep wave broke across *Katapult*'s three sharp bows instead of thumping straight into her side. 'See? Like that,' he called as the multihull fell off the wave into the trough and slid back to regain her original course under the pressure of the wind and the next smooth roller. 'She's all yours. And remember. You're not alone.'

But, as he leaned against the incredibly intense vibrancy of the helm, Richard felt very much alone. Alone except for the overpowering vitality of the vessel all around him. Through the big circle of the helm he could feel the humming, straining, exultant power of every strut, line and panel of her. It was like every fishing line he had ever held with every big fish hooked and fighting in it, all rolled into one breathtakingly thrilling ride. But the responsibility was almost as awesome as the experience.

It was all very well for him to know that Amy was just a call away at the chart table behind the running weatherboards. It was all very well to feel the others coming and going, sitting and waiting, coming and going again, round the edge of the cockpit behind him. To realize in fact that Doc was tucked none too snugly in the bunk beneath the rearmost seats, closed in as though encoffined. Because he knew that one wrong move from him and *Katapult* would spin, wallow, lose her way, her sails, perhaps her very mast, as *Goodman Richard* had done way back at the start of this. It was enough to keep even him from going over the details of the case again.

As the hours passed, the feeling also passed, however – though the wild exultation remained. And by the time Bob Collingwood came to relieve Richard, he had thought through no more clues, but *Katapult* was riding smoothly and fairly easily, her head swinging those vital points into and out of the wind as Richard luffed up to the wind, fell off the waves and regained the original trusty heading of 285 degrees according to the readout from the Fluxgate compass as digitally displayed on the binnacle readout before him.

After Bob's stint, Doc was back. And needfully so, for they were rapidly bearing down upon the Fastnet Rock, the halfway mark, and must prepare to come about. They had practised the manoeuvre and performed it countless times of course. But never in the pitch dark, without even the beam of the lighthouse to guide them, in weather that was rapidly deteriorating into a full gale. But almost magically, as Doc took the wheel, there was light. First, on the horizon away to starboard, a cluster of lights appeared on a steady headland and the scud of the clouds was high enough to let them linger, jewel bright, between the squalls. 'That's Baltimore,' called Amy, who didn't appear to have slept at all so far. 'Cape Clear behind it but there's no lights there.'

'There!' called Bob, echoing her word. Richard looked where the ghostly figure of his crewmate was pointing and in the darkness ahead there came a white diamond of light. There for an indisputable instant, then gone. Then back again. 'That's it. The Fastnet.'

Katapult seemed to leap forward on the call, and as she did so, there came a gleam of brightness all across the sky from almost perfectly aft of her. Richard looked back and there was the dawn, heaving dully into the wolf-grey overcast somewhere over Wales.

They came under the rock itself at seven on the dot – nineteen hours into the race. One hour behind their schedule. And, in spite of Richard's sense of isolation last night, they were not alone: dotted over the slate and spindrift waters at every possible point of the compass there were other boats. All of them heading for the cliff-faced, light-capped, shaggy little island that they all seemed to call The Rock.

Doc elected to take the inmost line possible. *Katapult* had very little draught, though her beam was nearly sixty feet, and she could skim safely over rocks less than a metre below the surface – if that surface were steady and calm. Rounding the Fastnet Rock in a westerly storm, of course, was something very different. But, as many of the others in the race were equally well aware, the closer you cut it, the faster you got round.

'Stand by to gybe,' called Doc as the great black cliffs heaved past, seemingly so close to the port outrigger that they would have taken Richard's head off if he had been out on his trapeze. Doc's voice echoed the booming of the wind and the screaming of the gulls that were being tossed about the sky like handfuls of crushed white tissue paper. They all tensed, all too well aware that if Doc called this right they would come about with one large manoeuvre and a few fine adjustments. If he called it wrong they could be fiddling about here for ages.

'Gybe-ho!' Richard flung himself to work, thankful that he was up here on the foresail – with the nets and the outrigger wing behind to catch him if wind or water tore him loose – and no big boom swinging over to behead him if he was unwary. Even under her severely shortened sails, *Katapult* slammed round with astonishing force and speed. The island – just large enough to contain the lighthouse – danced across the sea, simply seeming to leap from Richard's left vision to his right. The wind that had been numbing his left cheek all night and roaring spray – salt and sweet – into his left ear, now assaulted his newly sensitive right. His hair whipped almost painfully from one temple to the other. His left eye stopped streaming. His right eye started. What had been a view largely of sail became a view of distances and horizons. What had been the gloomy aspect of reluctantly departing darkness ahead, became the milky glimmer of stormy morning.

And, outlined against the sudden brightness, were the hulls of two other competitors, seemingly quite close in front. An outer vessel, powering past a slightly slighter, slower, inner. The impression – the action – was so swift and overwhelming, that Richard remained uncertain for the rest of his life exactly what it was that he had seen. For, as the outer vessel bore on, rigidly – intractably – along her new racing line, so the inner seemed to be forced harder and harder up against the forbidding rocks.

It was not a drawn-out process. It was instantaneous. An impression there and gone within the winking of an eye, so swift that Richard alone could see it, though he glanced around automatically, seeking a second witness. The inner vessel jumped high, half out of the water. She faltered, span. Her mast vanished. Her leaping hull settled back down in a terrible welter of foam, slid sideways and began to bob helplessly. And the other boat was gone, leaving the wreck behind. Long black multihulls riding low in the dark grey water. Nothing much of her visible at all, except a gleam of jade-green sails in the wan sunlight.

32: The Rock

During the next ten hours the wind continued to strengthen. During that time, the eye of the storm that had brought the foul weather in from the Atlantic swept in over Ireland, the Isle of Man and away up into Scotland. Amy traced it almost mile for mile across her charts. And she warned them about the conditions it was bringing down on them. But, with *Tin Hau* in their sights, they never thought of giving up. Or slackening pace. They hardly even thought of shortening sail as they chased her south-east again.

The storm winds Amy's depression brought with it blew across the Western Approaches, the Celtic Sea and Biscay at a steady 70 knots and gusted towards 100 in the squalls. They varied from south-westerly to southerly and back again. The seas the storm brought with it varied according to direction, depth, state of seabed and particularly state of tide. Sensible skippers in safety-conscious boats shortened sail, sat under bare poles, put out sea-anchors and hove to if they could not run for safe haven.

Tin Hau ran straight and true south-east, from the Fastnet Rock to the Bishop's Rock. She ran under all the green sail she dared to carry. And *Katapult* went after her, like a cheetah hunting a gazelle through the heart of a monsoon.

Richard had never worked so hard in all his life. The gathering force of the relentless wind made sail-handling enormously wearing – even though everything was shortening, shortening, shortening until they were forced to break the storm-sails out. They lost the number three jib altogether trying to get it down and replace it with the storm jib; an adventure that gave Richard bruised knuckles and a cut palm. And an enduring memory of several hundred square feet of reputedly indestructible material being flogged to shreds in an instant. They were able to free the lashing remnants before they broke the forestay only by a miracle.

But it was not the wind that really made the third leg so dreadful – it was the seas. All the way up from Land's End to the Fastnet Rock, *Katapult* had been heading into the westerly set of the sea, able to take the waves on her bow – even under Richard's relatively inexperienced hands. Even though, after Force 5, the waves had been breaking more and more powerfully into destructive walls of foam. For, as any swimmer, bodyboarder or surfer knows, even before he has set foot in a boat – it is the breaking waves that have the power. The simple crushing weight.

Coming back down on the south-easterly leg along *Tin Hau*'s wake, the waves were all tumbling in from the west behind them. Of course this affected the way the multihull rode the water. The easy, powerful swoops of motion were replaced by lumps and thumps as the waves beat against her square stern instead of her sleek bows. And having three square sterns made matters worse. Even though the outriggers each had rudders, the thin, strong sheets of metal in no way broke the force of waves coming crashing in behind them. Time and again a comber would break to one side or the other, smashing that outrigger forward, while the central hull sought to ride the smooth crest beside it. Wrenching the whole of *Katapult*'s frame almost painfully. And the frames of those within her.

Only a sailor of Doc's genius could have held the whole thing together. Now Richard saw the true importance of his apparently fussy search for steady airs and smooth waters. Seemingly by the force of his will, Doc held the vessel in the least destructive places between the winds and the waters, allowing the gale – even in the beam reach of the near southerly – to push *Katapult* on just a little faster than the seas.

Faster but not too fast. They wanted no great waves collapsing in on them from behind – and yet they could not fly too much more swiftly than the raging waters or they would find themselves leaping off the crest of a liquid cliff and pitch-poling down the rushing face, hurling head-over-heels to destruction. Just as Charles Lee had once done in his *Katapult IV*, and lucky to survive the destruction. Lucky for him; not for the rest of them.

But this perfect place between the howling winds and the raging waters was no certain, stable thing. Nor was it the work of just one man to keep *Katapult* within it. They needed to be constantly adjusting even the little storm sails, risking tacks this way and that as Doc sought the clear black way amongst the tumbling white teeth that would do the damage. Chilled and exhausted by noon, they debated the wisdom of a sea-anchor, screaming like drooling banshees in the wind and rain. But the mocking gleam of *Tin Hau*'s sails leaning across the near horizon ahead, drove them on to take one risk after another – as little by little and inch by inch they began to claw up towards her.

The Bishop's Rock Light heaved up out of the stormy sea, dead ahead at 5 p.m. precisely, twenty-nine hours exactly into the race. The two vessels came hurling down upon it neck and neck. 'Right,' bellowed Doc. 'I'm going on the inside of him as we go past. Then get ready to come round hard. The instant we're clear of the rocks we'll be coming on to new heading due east, straight past Wolf Rock and into Portsmouth before midnight, with this sorry green-sailed bastard bobbing in our wake!'

'You'll want to come round to 85 degrees,' called Amy, still wide awake and on top of things.

'It'll be time for a little something when we've settled on to our nice new course,' called up Joan.

Richard stood hunched at his place, watching *Tin Hau* racing along beside them. There were yellow-wrapped, full-hooded figures sitting up on the windward side, even in this – something that Doc had decided against, thank God. He looked slit-eyes amongst them for Charles's distinctive red.

But he wasn't there, so Richard turned his thoughts back aboard again. Doc had the variable outriggers to play with, he thought. *Tin Hau* didn't seem to. But what *had* she got? Other than a brutally ruthless crew. He glanced ahead. They were coming down upon the Bishop's Rock Light incredibly quickly. It was heaving the massive stone length of itself out of the raging seas like some gigantic dinosaur extending its neck above water in front of them. And no sooner had the image occurred to him than the dinosaur's black rock shoulders were there among the wilderness of foam as though it were about to rear out of the Western Approaches altogether like a prancing horse. 'Ready . . .' bellowed Doc.

Something popped into Richard's head then; something born of his experiences almost exactly a year ago when he had been sailing these exact waters in precisely these conditions in the SuperCat *Lionheart*. He could see the chart Tom had used to get them up to Wolf Rock as swiftly as possible. Standing out from the Bishop, according to that chart, there were reefs and islands stretching to the south-west almost like a wall lying just beneath the surface. He hoped most forcefully that Doc would remember it as well – or that Amy would remind him if he didn't. For as they came round the corner, turning 50 full degrees on to course 85 degrees, it would be standing there in front of them if they weren't very careful indeed.

And that thought made him remember what he had seen at the Fastnet Rock, just after they reversed their course. 'Watch it, Doc,' he said to himself – at the very instant that Doc yelled, 'Coming round fifty degrees . . . NOW!' and they came round.

Katapult's starboard outrigger lifted dangerously and Richard found himself looking down a considerable slope as he worked. The port outrigger disappeared deep beneath the foam-laced surface. There was no green there, he was surprised to see. Only storm-darkened grey and black.

The very instant he had secured his sheet, Richard looked back across at *Tin Hau*. She was coming on to the new course too and Richard, his seaman's eye alert, watched as she leaned even further across the wind. There wasn't much of a wake left in the wrack behind her but Richard was seawise enough to be able to carry the line of her original course in his head. And he watched her come round thirty, forty and fifty degrees – like *Katapult* had. Then sixty and seventy and more. '*DOC! LOOK OUT!*' he bellowed, unconsciously using his quarter-deck voice. '*Tin Hau*'s coming round on top of you!'

He looked ahead as Doc was doing, and saw the wall of the reef hurling up towards them, a simple standing ridge of white foam in the water under *Katapult*'s bows. 'LET GO ALL,' bellowed Doc. And put the wheel hard over. For a dizzying moment they were on a full collision course with *Tin Hau*, then the black boat readjusted its course and beat back to windward, coming on to the 85-degree course, due east past the Bishop's Rock, then on past Wolf Rock for Plymouth and home.

Katapult scraped past *Tin Hau*'s departing stern, the way coming off her, her sails flapping, tossing one way and then the other. She dug her port outrigger deep, and began to spin, turning her square back to the huge seas as she wallowed. A massive roller broke in over the stern at once and slammed into the cockpit like Niagara. The whole rear end of the central hull disappeared beneath the boiling water. A wall of white water more than knee high rolled forward and Richard found himself taking giant steps just to overcome it as he rushed back to help. 'Get her underway again,' he bellowed at the others. He had no idea of the correct sail drill or orders and prayed that they did.

The cockpit was a dreadful mess. Everything that could be washed out of it had been – seats, equipment, the lot. Mercifully, there had been no crew there for they had all been sail-handling. Or they too would have gone by the board. Doc was hanging crucified against the wheel, and there was no sign of life about him at all. As Richard stepped down into the sole, he saw that the weatherboards also were gone. Much of what had come in here had gone straight on down into the cabin. 'All right down below?' he bellowed. His words were answered by a string of foul female invective, which seemed positive at least. Except that it included the destruction of the radio with the inundation of almost everything else.

Mercifully most of the equipment on the binnacle was still working – including the readout from the Fluxgate compass – and so he pulled Doc away from the wheel and swung it round until the digital display read 85 degrees. Only then, holding the wheel and praying that *Katapult* would get some way upon her before the next big sea caught up with her, did he notice how strange the wheel felt. Where Doc had been thrown against it, the whole steel curve of the thing was bent well out of true. 'Joan,' he bellowed. 'First aid here.' He looked up along the length of the central hull, just in time to see the storm jib snap full. The sight of it made him duck automatically, so when the boom whipped over as the storm mainsail filled an instant later, it did not knock his head off after all.

'If you've finished with the sails,' he bellowed down the length of the deck, 'you'd better man the pumps. Who's best to help me sail this thing?' It was one of those moments that sorts out entire lives. There were others aboard trained for the emergency. There was an agreed pecking order; responsibilities awarded and accepted for an eventuality even as dreadful as this. But only Richard was quick-thinking enough, controlled enough and self-confident enough to take command in the instant. And the crew were individually and collectively so excellent that his unthinking – inexperienced – leadership was good enough for them.

As it happened, Bob Collingwood was slated to relieve Doc, but he was the strongest sail-handler. And, as her chart table had been washed away in any case, Amy came up and shared the helm with Richard. Joan called out that Doc was breathing, then she laid him on the composite skeleton of the after seat and began to check for specific injuries. Bill, Bob, and Harry took on the sails, and within ten minutes, *Katapult* was back in the race again. Richard was not a sailboat sailor, but Amy certainly was and together they came very close to replacing Doc. Their course was straightforward now – 85 degrees until they ran into Plymouth. And everything else relied as much upon experience and a weather eye as upon charts and instruments.

The first thing that he and Amy noticed was that the wind was moderating. The next was that the outrushing power of the last huge spring tide's massive ebb beneath them was confusing and steepening the waves. This was a very dangerous combination and Amy said quietly, 'We really need more speed if we're going to stay alive, let alone catch up with those bastards.'

More positively, it seemed to Richard that the unavoidable tidal ebb rushing westwards beneath the surface was beginning to slow even *Tin Hau*, gripping her in a way that it did not grip *Katapult*. Perhaps the stolen design of the Triad trimaran included some kind of centreboard after all, thought Richard. Some Chinese like to gamble. Some like to play things safe. Perhaps even with ship design. While, on the other hand, the water in the central hull was steadying *Katapult*, and allowing her the chance to carry more sail. He called, 'Bob! How much sail do we dare put on her?' At his call, the clouds in the west were briefly snatched away and the sun struck over the stormy sea, showing *Tin Hau* like a jade dagger, cutting through the sky half a mile ahead.

Bob looked around, literally sniffing the wind. 'Leave the storm mainsail up,' he said. 'We lost the smallest jib, so we'd have to go straight for the bigger ones . . .'

'She seems very stable to me,' insisted Richard. 'Dare we try the Genoa? That'd really put us back into the race.'

'Bloody hell,' said Bob. 'You're a bit of a madman on the quiet. Still like Amy says, wind's moderating. Sun's out. What've we got to lose? Other than the mast, of course . . .'

Joan left Doc and held the wheel with Amy. Richard went up and the four sail-handlers got the Genoa out and up in short order. Then, with Richard back at Amy's side, they hauled it as tightly as they dared and rushed on down towards Wolf Rock, hard on *Tin Hau*'s heels.

Richard knew these waters better perhaps than he knew any in the world. He kept *Katapult* inside the track he had followed all too often in the supertankers and container vessels coming and going to Europoort. He watched the distant Scillies swing along the horizon like a string of rough gold nuggets in the setting sun. He followed the course that *Lionheart* had followed a year and more ago, skimming like she did, over the thickening drag of the tidal gate. The course was the same, the conditions were the same. The vessel was different, but with the help of Amy, Bob and the rest, he was getting the best out of her he could. The best, in fact, that anyone could. And by the time the Wolf Rock Light was gleaming like a sunken emerald through the green hearts of the tall waves ahead, they were up with their quarry once again.

At once Amy whispered, 'Watch it!' and pushed the wheel against Richard's hands. 'He's driving us up toward the rocks again. Look.' And sure enough, the digital compass on the binnacle ahead of them was reading 83 degrees instead of 85. *Tin Hau* was forcing them over almost imperceptibly, degree after degree. 'Two can play that game,' said Richard, grimly. And he let the racing multihull's head fall off another point. 'Eighty two?' said Amy, her voice trembling. 'I'd say that was a very dangerous heading indeed.'

'It is,' said Richard grimly. 'It's what *Goodman Richard*

was drifting sideways along when she went up on to the rocks here last year. I had to bring my SuperCat *Lionheart* in on 262 to come aboard her.'

'Then why in God's name are we sailing along it now?'

'Because I learned something from that experience that I'll bet anything you like that no one aboard *Tin Hau* knows. Trust me?'

Amy looked up into the wind-ravaged, salt-grimed sleepless skeleton of his face, all white skin, black hair, black stubble and utterly mad blue eyes. 'Of course,' she said.

'Then let's do it!'

Richard eased back a point. Their course clicked round to 83. *Tin Hau* held steady. *Katapult*'s starboard outrigger seemed just about to graze her sleek black paintwork. Her green sails seemed to overlap *Katapult*'s long central bow. 'More speed,' yelled Richard, coming another point back round into the wind. And the sails indeed seemed to be overlapping, he thought. Certainly the straining bulge of the big Genoa – an insane sail choice or not – was stealing the air out of *Tin Hau*'s tight green storm sails. For the first time, it was the Triad-funded, Hong Kong dark horse that was beginning to falter. Now where was that red-clad bastard Lee? he wondered, as *Katapult* seemed to leap forward half of *Tin Hau*'s length.

If Richard was watching *Tin Hau*, seeking to distinguish the figure of his enemy – so at the least he could shout the promise of ruin and revenge – Amy was wise enough to be keeping her eyes fixed firmly ahead. 'Richard!' she screamed. 'We're running up on to the reef!'

She had to scream it twice, for Richard at last had found Charles Lee again. Bareheaded, laughing or shouting, hanging out on his trapeze in the midst of a team of four. The only one clad in poppy red amongst a bunch of daffodil yellow. Swinging out further and further, looking up at the mast from which he was hanging, and the full-bellied, bright-green sails.

'RICHARD!' screamed Amy again, recalling him to himself.

The instant Richard took his eyes off *Tin Hau* to look ahead again, the black multihull turned a point off the wind, coming near 83 degrees herself – crowding across his course again.

Trapping him between her port outrigger and the foaming rocks ahead – exactly as she had done at the Bishop's Rock. As he had seen her do to the poor little yacht at the Fastnet Rock itself. 'Steady, all!' Richard bellowed. 'We'll be coming round three degrees at any moment and things'll get pretty hairy.'

'They bloody will,' said Amy feelingly. 'Three degrees starboard and we'll ram him midships like the Roman galley in *Ben Hur*.'

'Three degrees to *port*,' said Richard. 'Coming round NOW!' He span the twisted wheel before Amy could stop him.

And round came *Katapult*. Three degrees off the wind hardly slowed the racing multihull at all. It loosened the strain on the big Genoa perhaps, but it wasn't anywhere enough to require a tack and the knotmeter didn't even flicker. 'HANG ON!' bellowed Richard. But he needn't have bothered. Everyone aboard was hanging on as tightly as they could – and most of them were praying.

Richard hit the button that deployed the outriggers as hydrofoils and they dug into the heaving water as the first white backwash from the Wolf Rock reef roared out towards them. *Katapult*'s central hull reared dangerously out of the water. The weight of water still down in her bilges was like ballast – as it had been in *Lionheart* under Robin's command at the beginning of this. But he had learned too, even from that. The weight of the water, untouched as yet by the pumps, made her stern dig deep, as *Lionheart*'s had done, but it held her steady as she sailed a straight course. Deeper it went. And deeper still, until the wake seemed to be closing behind them like the waves of the Red Sea on Pharaoh and his horsemen behind the fleeing Moses. Until only their tremendous speed was stopping it flooding aboard.

But the outriggers pulled in as well as pushing down. *Katapult*'s sixty-foot width shrank to fifty. Then to forty. And still she hurtled on, held steady in the rushing wind by the weight of the water in her central hull. And the cunning of Richard's plan was suddenly revealed to his marvelling crew. For there, immediately beneath the rearing bow of the rushing multihull, was the narrow, bottomless gap that had broken *Goodman Richard*'s back.

Foam-swollen rocks stood on either side of them like the

pillars of Hercules, cascading backwash by the ton. Spitting spray like thunderstorms. Beneath the weltering foam, the black rocks gleamed wickedly in the last of the setting sun. The sound, the sensation, the simple stench of death was almost overwhelming. But dead ahead there was that channel. A little more than forty feet wide, a couple of hundred feet long, straight as a die, and leading safely through the heart of the reef.

Richard flung *Katapult* into it unflinchingly, and she held her course unvaryingly even though the walls of rock and water seemed to top her mast on either side. 'She's gone!' screamed Amy. Then she had to batter on his shoulder and gesture. He glanced back to see *Tin Hau* explode against the outer reef. So intent had the Triad boat been on driving *Katapult* on to Wolf Rock that she had sailed too close herself. Leaning in just that little too far when Richard turned to port so unexpectedly. She must have been doing forty knots, he reckoned – *Katapult* certainly was – when she hit the immovable solidity of the reef. Richard had a horrific, instantaneous vision of her three black hulls flying up into a somersault, exploding to pieces as they did so. Of her rigging ripping away from her sides and whipping wildly free like the hair of a madwoman. Of her tall steel mast like a javelin hurled forward across the sunset sky and over the mountainous rocks, wrapped in the rags of jade green sails. Trailing behind it the broken marionettes of four bodies still strapped in their trapezes – three in bright butter yellow and one in bright blood red. And, like *Katapult*'s own, the steel javelin of *Tin Hau*'s mast, alone amongst the fittings of the boat, was never designed to float. It would strike into the bosom of the ocean, and pierce it to its deepest, darkest heart, hundreds of fathoms down, beside the wreck of *Goodman Richard* herself. Taking the dead men in their trapezes with it. Charles Lee, it seemed, would not survive his second pitch-poling after all.

In the blink of an eye there was nothing left to see.

Then Richard was facing forward again and fighting to control *Katapult* as she burst out of the narrow channel into the relative calm in the lee of the reef. He punched the outrigger control again and the great fins spread wide once more. 'Get that bloody Genoa off her,' he ordered. 'We'll be arse over tip like those poor beggars if we don't slow down!'

By the time they pulled out of the quiet water and into the darkening storm set again five minutes later, they were running under sensible storm sails and proceeding under more control.

'That was neat,' grated Harry Black, looming out of the thickening dark. 'Whether or not Grandma Chung gives the certificates back or not is immaterial now. They're worthless. We'll have to reissue Charles's three per cent and let it revert to the company as per contract. You've got your fifty-one per cent holding again. You've beaten Whitesand-Sandarkan after all. You've won!'

But before Richard could answer him, Doc sat up like a puppet whose strings have all been pulled at once. 'Hey guys, how're we doing?' he demanded, bright as a button, fresh as a daisy. Totally lost in shock.

'Do you know, I think we were winning,' answered Richard quietly, almost wearily. 'I really do think we were. Winning.'

Then he raised his voice and shouted, 'Prepare to come about. Joan, help Amy with the wheel while I help with the sailhandling. And then see if you can find the distress flares. If we haven't any radio we'll have to make do with them. We're going back to see if there are any survivors from *Tin Hau*. Sorry, Doc. Sorry, all of you. Maybe you'll win the next one.

'Wolf Rock, here we come!'

Acknowledgements

Wolf Rock is based upon legislation that has yet to be passed – though its likely content has been widely trailed over the years. Further, it concerns a race that has yet to be sailed. Research in preparation for it had to rely less on published authority – in book form or on the internet – than usual. It had to rely more than ever, therefore, on the help and speculation of friends, and it is to them that I owe the greatest debt.

Criminal barrister Richard Atchley was my legal sounding board right throughout, as he has cheerfully been on several occasions before. It was with Richard that I discussed the likely form of any legislation. It was he who supplied some of the legal authority for it and a great deal of what published speculation there is. He made sure I got the process and the timings as correct as the dictates of plot and practicality would allow. It was he who checked the typescript and ensured as far as he could that I did not get my bailiffs confused with my ushers or my examinations in chief mixed up with my cross-examinations. I have tried, within the dictates of an adventure-thriller plot, to follow the likely process from start to finish and I hope the pace does not flag. Where things are correct, Richard is most likely responsible – where they are not, then I have misunderstood or disregarded his patient advice.

The same is true for the sailing. Except for *The Fire Ship*, which introduced the *Katapult* series of multihulls into Heritage Mariner's fictional world, I have been hesitant to deal with small boat work. When I had to deal with the Fastnet, therefore, I turned to two active sailors without whose help I would have been all at sea with a vengeance. David McGregor kindly managed to fit into his busy summer's racing schedule a read-through of the first draft and was able to advise on the ways he would approach the race in the conditions described. And Peter Halsor also went through an early draft making sure I 'luffed up to the wind' and 'fell off' at the correct points; and followed the true course of my Fluxgate compass at all times. To both of these advisors I owe a great deal of thanks – though both have pointed out that anyone not taking a much safer course in the conditions described would be lucky indeed to survive.

Which brings me to my main written authorities for the opening and the climax of the story. Whenever I want to check on anything nautical, my first source is usually John Rousmaniere's *The Annapolis Book of Seamanship*. To this authority in this instance I added his definitive *Fastnet Force 10*, a blow by blow description of the tragic 1978 race which he himself had sailed. The conditions through which Richard Mariner sails *Lionheart* and, later, *Katapult VI*, are the conditions faced by the intrepid sailors in that race. The timings – which made both my sailors gasp – are based on the winning times of the most recent races, details of which are still available on the internet, and to which I refer anyone wishing to explore the real world of competitive sailing.

Finally, I must admit that, much against my family's wishes, I researched the Bentley Continental GT only on paper. My primary source was *Bentley A Legend Reborn* by Graham Robson in the Haynes Classic Makes series, published 2003. The specifications are accurate according to that publication, but I used my imagination with regard to settings, security and so forth. And, because I am very well aware of the astonishing breadth of general knowledge that my readers often display – certainly judging from the letters I receive – I should also add that Richard (for once) got it wrong. Peter Wimsey's motorcar 'Mrs Merdle' was not a Bentley but a Daimler (1927 12-cylinder 'double-six' four-seater, especially imported). Richard was right about James Bond's Bentleys, however.

Peter Tonkin, Isle of Man and Tunbridge Wells,
Summer 2004